Heart of Danger

Books by Lisa Marie Rice

Fiction
HEART OF DANGER
NIGHTFIRE
HOTTER THAN WILDFIRE
INTO THE CROSSFIRE
DANGEROUS PASSION
DANGEROUS SECRETS
DANGEROUS LOVER

E-Novellas
HOT SECRETS
FATAL HEAT
RECKLESS NIGHT

Heart of Danger

A Ghost Ops Novel

Lisa Marie Rice

An Imprint of HarperCollins*Publishers*

This book is fondly dedicated to the Brainstormers, my wonderful group of crazy writers, who helped me brainstorm this series. It wouldn't exist without you all.

And, as always, it is dedicated to my wonderful husband and son.

HarperCollins books may be purchased for educational, business, or sales promotional use. For information please write: Special Markets Department, HarperCollins Publishers, 10 East 53rd Street, New York, NY 10022.

FIRST EDITION

Designed by Diahann Sturge

Library of Congress Cataloging-in-Publication Data has been applied for.

ISBN 978-0-06-212179-0

12 13 14 15 16 OV/RRD 10 9 8 7 6 5 4 3 2 1

Acknowledgments

Another big thanks to my agent, Ethan Ellenberg, and my editor, May Chen, and the great team at Avon.

And thanks, too, to Adam Firestone, weapons consultant and combat consultant extraordinaire. All cool stuff is his. All mistakes are mine.

Chapter One

The New York Times—*January 6*
A *New York Times* exclusive

The New York Times *has learned that the fire on January 5 which destroyed a research laboratory in Cambridge, Mass., operated by Arka Pharmaceutical Laboratories, was not due to the explosion of a gas pipeline, as originally reported.*

The New York Times *has received exclusive information from a senior government official that the laboratory came under attack from a group of elite commandos under separate leadership in the U.S. military, known as "Ghost Ops."*

The U.S. military is forbidden to operate on United States soil under the Posse Comitatus Act.

The alleged leader of the top secret unit is the former commander of famed SEAL Team Six, the team that killed Osama bin Laden ten years ago, Captain Lucius Ward. Captain Ward's military records are sealed. The

New York Times *has been unable to access his records under the Freedom of Information Act.*

Forty-one people died in the conflagration at the laboratory, among them MacArthur Foundation fellowship winner Dr. Roger Bryson, a longtime candidate for the Nobel Prize for his work on the biochemistry of vaccines.

"We have reason to believe that the destruction of our Cambridge laboratory, which was close to a cancer vaccine, was the work of competitors hoping to stop our progress," declared Arka CEO Dr. William Storensen. "All efforts must be made to bring these criminals to justice."

This reporter has also learned that Captain Ward had several million dollars invested in a rival pharmaceutical company. Captain Ward's remains have not been identified.

The three surviving members of the attack commando team, whose names were redacted from the documents obtained by the New York Times, *disappeared en route to a court-martial in Washington, D.C. There is an outstanding warrant for their arrest.*

byline Jeffrey Kellerman

A year later
Mount Blue
Northern California

Her car died.

One moment her charming, lavender-colored little eCar, which infinitely preferred balmy climes, was bravely climbing the frozen, rutted road and the next it just stopped dead.

In the middle of a snowstorm. At night. On a deserted mountaintop.

There was nothing Catherine Young could do.

Oh God, she thought. *Not now.*

She pressed the ignition over and over again but the car was utterly dead. It was the latest generation eCar, and the salesman had assured her that if something happened to the main engine, there was an ancillary one with separate power guaranteed to take her at least another ten miles.

Every instrument was dark. Not even the inside lights turned on when she opened the driver's side door. She got a terrifying blast of snow and sleet like a fist to the face and shut the door immediately.

Her cell phone was dead, too. Utterly dead, screen blank. An iPhone 15, normally she could talk to the moon with it, but now it was an unresponsive, though still elegant, slice of metallic glass. Her tablet was dead, too, she found when she scrabbled in the backseat for her trusty iPad 8. For the first time in its life, it refused to switch on. It, too, was an inert piece of metallic glass.

GPS, dead. MP3 player, wristwatch, dead.

Everything dead.

It was impossible to see anything outside the car, to gauge how close she was to the edge of the road. The snow was too thick for that. She'd barely been able to see three yards ahead with the special halogen headlights on high. Now, with a dead car, no lights, no form of communication, she could have been on another planet.

A cold and hostile one.

She hadn't counted on being on the road after dark, and if she hadn't had a compulsion to find Tom "Mac" McEnroe so strong it was like the compulsion to breathe, she would have turned around hours and hours ago. But there had been no giving up, not even when she tried three dead ends and had had to painfully back out over frozen ruts and dead branches, trying to find a viable road, traveling all day, too driven by her compulsion to stop. She didn't—couldn't—stop, not even when light faded from the sky and the few flakes that had fallen turned into a tempest.

Finally, she knew it was the right road when she nearly plowed into a boulder, a hulking granite shadow darker than the night, right in the middle of the road.

She'd been told all of this, of course.

He'll kill your car, your cell phone, your computer, your GPS, your music player.

Not in words so much as in images. She'd seen herself sitting in a vehicle in the dark, no lights on. The images hadn't made any sense then but they did now.

She'd been told how to find him.

He will hole up somewhere on Mount Blue. Take the most deserted road. The road will be almost impassable. There will be an obstacle—a fallen tree, a boulder. Drive around the obstacle. He will know you are coming. He will find you.

This had been communicated in images as well, fuzzy and incomprehensible yet irresistible. She'd found herself on the dead-end road without having even thought about it during the course of the two-hundred-mile drive. She'd pressed the button to start the car and it was as if the car had driven itself here.

Only to die.

So here she was, clutching her useless steering wheel with two sweat-dampened hands, on a deserted mountain road, in a dead car, in the dead of night.

The wind howled.

The last human outpost had been forty miles back and that had been two stores and one of the last gas stations left in California. She'd glanced curiously at it as she drove by. She couldn't remember the last time she'd seen a gas station. This one had looked ramshackle and deserted, tattered, faded pennants flapping in the rising wind.

Heat was draining out fast. A vicious gust of wind rocked her car. She loved her car. It was sleek and stylish. However, though it was made out of a revolutionary lightweight tough resin that would tighten in a crash, it was no match for this gale-force icy mountain wind. What made it so good on the freeways made it a death trap in a freezing snowstorm.

Another gust rocked the vehicle, hard. The wheels on the left side lifted a little, then dropped the car back with a thump. Catherine's heart pumped hard as she fought panic. An image flashed in her mind. The car, buffeted wildly by the howling winds, slowly sliding off the road, tumbling down the mountainside.

It was a perfectly plausible scenario.

What a way to end her life—tumbling over the edge of a mountain cliff until her car smashed against an obstacle. A boulder, a tree. It wouldn't explode, of course. But if she lived, she'd be trapped in the wreck, bleeding out, with no hope of rescue. No one knew where she was. This was wilderness. It was perfectly possible they'd find her body only in the spring.

Another powerful gust. The car shifted, the wheels slipping an inch or two. She broke out in a sweat which instantly chilled her skin in the cold. A wild white sheet of snow lashed across the windshield, ice spicules chattering against the glass.

The steering wheel was frigid under her hands. She relinquished the wheel and tucked her hands under her arms. There were gloves in the baggage compartment but it was electrically operated and would never open now that the car was dead. The gloves might as well have been at the bottom of the ocean for all the good they could do her back there.

Catherine shivered again, a full-body shudder. She was a neurologist, but she was also an M.D. and understood very well what was happening. Her skin and lungs were shedding heat with every passing second and her body was trying to generate it by shivering.

Her core temperature would start dropping soon. The rest was utterly inevitable—confusion, amnesia, major organ failure.

Death.

This is insane, she thought. Yet it was the logical ending to the poisoned chalice at the heart of her life.

Her gift. Her curse.

All her life, she'd worshipped reason. Bound herself to rationality with iron clamps, studying math and biology and medicine and then neuroscience. Trying with all her might to banish her gift from her life.

This crazy quest for a man she's never met, this Tom McEnroe, was going to cost her her life. Like the appointment with death in Samarra, Catherine could evade her gift no longer.

The wind shook her car again, angrily, as if claiming it for its own. She shivered again. The cold was so intense it was painful. Pain was good. As long as she felt pain she was alive and the hypothermic damage could be undone.

Soon there would be no pain; she would be beyond rescuing. And then there would be no life at all.

Time stood still as she listened to her heartbeat in the darkness. At first she tried to count the beats to give herself a sense of time. After two hours she lost count. After another eternity, she felt the exact moment her heart started to slow. Her core temperature had dropped. She was beginning the slide into hypothermia. It felt as if she were already dead and buried deep underground.

Too exhausted for tears, Catherine leaned her head against the steering wheel, preparing to die. Hoping it would be quick.

A hard, loud rap startled her. She sat up, heart beating painfully, trying to figure out where the noise had come from.

The next instant her door was opened and an arm yanked her out into the snow. She stood there blinking. A big hand on her arm was all that was keeping her muscles from collapsing, dropping her to the snow-covered ground.

There was barely enough ambient light to see by. If the man

had been even a foot away from her she wouldn't have been able to see him.

He was incredibly close, though, close enough for her to feel his body heat, the first source of heat in what felt like forever.

He was huge, shoulders filling her field of vision, so tall she had to crane her neck back, though she couldn't see his features. He was dressed in black, head to toe, with a gun strapped to his thigh and a long knife in a sheath, face covered with a black ski mask with insectoid eyes, a sight so terrifying she'd have screamed if she had the breath.

A modern-day Grim Reaper, come to take her away.

"What do you want?" The voice was deep and low, carrying over the howling wind. Catherine was so shocked she couldn't catch her breath. One big hand shook her slightly, as if to shake her out of a trance, and the other moved to his face, lifted those insectoid eyes . . . up?

She was hallucinating. The cold was slowing her neurological processes down so much she was altering reality.

"What do you want?" The voice was a little more forceful now, a note of hostility in it. He shook her again.

Catherine took in a shuddering breath as reality realigned itself. This was no hallucination. It was a huge man, dressed for the snow, who'd been wearing night vision goggles.

"T-Tom," she stuttered. Her voice was hoarse, the first words she'd spoken in more than twelve hours, her mouth dry with terror. There was no way her scrambled mind could put together any kind of reasoning. The naked truth fell out. "Tom McEnroe. Th-they call him Mac."

She had no idea who Tom McEnroe was. For all she knew, this man had never heard of McEnroe. Or he was Tom McEnroe's worst enemy. He could either let her go or shoot her with that huge black gun strapped to his thigh. Or, considering the size of him, swat her right off the mountainside with one blow from that huge fist.

What he did was drop a hood over her head, slap plastic restraints on her wrists, lift her over his shoulder and stride away.

A woman's worst nightmare.

Catherine could barely breathe from the cold. Resistance was utterly beyond her. She couldn't see anything because of the hood, couldn't feel her hands or her feet, couldn't think straight.

And, lying over this man's broad shoulder, she knew there was no resistance possible to the kind of male power she could feel. He walked through the drifts of snow, in the howling wind, carrying an adult woman exactly as if he were walking unencumbered on a summer's day. There was no sense of strain or exertion on his part.

He was holding her legs down with one powerful arm. She tried an experimental kick but couldn't move her legs at all under the arm.

Wherever he was taking her, it wouldn't make any difference in a while. Her heart rate was slowing. She couldn't see herself but she knew she was turning white as the blood in her body rushed in to her core, the last part of her that would die. She barely had the energy to shiver anymore. All she could do was endure.

In the cold and darkness there was no way to tell time, but after what felt like hours the man stopped.

Wherever it was he was taking her, they had arrived.

Chapter Two

Goddamn!

Crazy bitch, driving up Mount Blue in a snowstorm in a little eCar and with no winter gear. He should have just left her in the snowdrift to die.

Tom McEnroe eased the woman onto the passenger side seat of his hovercraft, frowning.

He hated the thought of taking any outsider to the base, but this was a no-brainer. He had to know who the fuck this woman was because she knew his name.

She knew his fucking *name*.

Nobody knew his name.

It had been wiped from all public records when he joined Ghost Ops. Members of Ghost Ops had no relatives, no family, no friends. It was one of the conditions of joining. It made them better operatives. No distractions, no connections, no attachments.

But this woman knew his name. She was looking for *him*!

This was serious shit because every goddamned law enforcement agency was looking for him, too, not to mention the entire

U.S. military. And they weren't going to be tender with him and his men when they found him.

He got into the driver's seat and pressed the button for ignition. The baby started up with a purr. There was an airplane's engine in the hovercraft. It was powerful and silent and super classified.

Jon and Nick had liberated it from a top secret base a couple of months ago and it was worth its weight in gold. He turned the heat up to maximum, draped the woman with a thermal blanket and switched the seat heating up to high.

He ran back to her vehicle. Snow had nearly filled the footwell on the driver's side. He grabbed her purse and a small case she had on the passenger seat and ran back to his vehicle, leaving the door open. The car was trashed anyway. An EMP had taken out all the circuits and nothing short of a new engine would make it run. He'd send some men out after the snowstorm to bring it into their communal yard.

She was tugging at the restraints when he got back. "Stop that," he said, and she stilled, instantly.

Smart woman. He was dangerous when he was pissed, and she could probably read that in his voice.

"Where are you taking me?" she asked, working hard to keep the tremor out of her voice.

He had to give her marks for courage. She wasn't screaming and crying to be let go, flailing about, trying to hit him. He didn't have any chemical restraints with him and this weather strained even his driving skills. He'd have to knock her out if she interfered with his driving. He wouldn't like it but he'd do it.

"I'm taking you to somewhere warm, for starters, Dr. Young."

She quieted.

Mac looked down at the IDs he had in his hand, taken from her purse. California driver's license, two credit cards, company security pass, medical insurance hologram. All made out to Dr. Catherine Young.

She worked for a company called Millon Laboratories. He had no idea if she was a medical doctor or a scientist.

No matter. He'd find out soon enough. For the moment, they needed to get back fast.

Mac pressed the button that lifted the vehicle, moved the directional stick forward and glided off the road and in the direction that would take them back to HQ.

Catherine didn't realize they'd moved until she was pressed against the back of her seat. For a second her befogged brain thought the man in black was pushing her, but that wasn't right. He was next to her. She could hear him breathe, feel his heat.

They were in a vehicle that made no noise and, crazily, seemed to . . . to *glide*. The road she'd been on—track more than road—had been rutted, studded with stones, slippery with snow.

One of the many mysteries that would be cleared up, or not.

There was absolutely nothing Catherine could do so she did the only thing she could. Sit still and wait.

They traveled for a long time, though she had no way of knowing exactly how long. Maybe she was traveling toward Tom McEnroe, as she was compelled to do. Maybe she was traveling to her death. Maybe she was traveling to both.

However much she'd tried to avoid the bitter consequences of her gift, it had led her to this moment in which she was as powerless as a stick carried by a raging river down to the sea.

She was hooded and her hands were restrained but she wasn't uncomfortable and she wasn't cold. The strange vehicle was warm and the man had thrown a blanket over her. It was very thin, almost like a cotton sheet, but underneath it, she was incredibly warm.

It was a lucky thing she wasn't suffering from severe hypothermia. People died from rewarming collapse, a sudden drop in blood pressure that sends the system into deep shock, then death.

They rode in silence.

For one of the few times in her life, Catherine was tempted to just reach out and touch, touch the driver. Skin against skin. She never touched anyone if she could help it. Often the results were painful, sometimes dangerous.

Her hands were bare. Bringing her restrained hands over and touching him would at least tell her if he meant her harm. If she was being driven to her death.

If his mind was filled with hatred and violence, as many minds were, she'd fight to the death when they got out of the vehicle.

But there was nowhere she could be sure to touch his skin. He seemed to be covered all over in that light, tough material, including his hands.

Once again her gift was useless, dangerous. Driving her to danger, but giving her no way out of it.

She could do nothing but sit and try to keep her heartbeat calm and slow, try to empty her mind of all thought, try to just . . . be. If she was going to fight to the death at the end of this ride, she couldn't afford to waste energy on useless speculation.

She was on a mission to find this Tom McEnroe, propelled by forces beyond her control. And—God help her—propelled by overwhelming love for this McEnroe, for a man she'd never met.

Mac drove into the base of HQ, entering a vast cavern. Their security was tight—he'd designed it himself—but the remote sensors situated along the hidden route to the mouth of the cavern recognized the ID signals given off by the hovercraft. If they hadn't, an electromagnetic pulse would have shut the vehicle down well before it came within sight of the hidden entrance. The same EMP that had fried her car's circuits.

And if by some wild chance the vehicle didn't stop dead, whoever was manning the security monitors would give the order to one of their drones overhead and a tiny, powerful precision missile would be unleashed that would leave a smoking crater and some splashes of protoplasm and nothing else.

The hovercraft stopped, the cushions dropping them to the concrete floor.

Mac got out and opened the passenger side door. The woman, Dr. Catherine Young, sat still and unmoving. He would have thought her a statue if it weren't for the slight trembling of her hands. They were beautiful hands, he had to admit. And she was a beautiful woman, no doubt about that, either.

That made him uneasy. Beautiful women were trouble, always.

The woman he'd pulled out of the freezing car had been white-faced with cold, startled, then terrified, and with all that, so beautiful he'd taken her for a model. Some airhead, both stupid and crazy because otherwise what the fuck would she be doing on their deliberately crap, almost-impassable road at night in the middle of a snowstorm?

She wasn't an airhead, she was a doctor, so that left crazy. What the fuck did she think she was doing?

He'd been about ready to invent some story about being out hunting and being caught in the snowstorm and offering to drive her back to Regent, forty miles back down the mountain, when she'd dropped her bomb.

I'm looking for Tom McEnroe.

Mac didn't do surprise, but that—well, that was a real shocker.

After dropping the bomb, there was no question of driving the clueless, pretty civilian back down the mountain. She wasn't a civilian and she wasn't there by chance.

This was one dangerous woman.

A woman who knew where to look for him when the entire U.S. government didn't have a clue. She was possibly a spy, definitely a threat. And she wasn't leaving their compound until he knew who had sent her and why and how the hell she knew where to look in the first place.

And he wouldn't bet on her leaving the compound alive.

"Out," he said.

Mac trained hard men to do hard things. He trained men he knew perfectly well would be sent straight into lethal danger. They'd stay alive only if he trained them hard. Under fire, team cohesion was everything and he was team leader. He was used to being instantly obeyed because he *had* to be instantly obeyed. The alternative was death, and not a good one, either.

So his command voice was the voice of God, screamed straight into his men's ears.

Normally, he moderated his command voice for women. But right then he was mad and suspicious and he wasn't about to moderate his voice for someone who might be endangering his entire world.

No matter how pretty she was.

Her whole body shrank in on itself at that one barked word, which was the reaction of any small animal to a threat from a larger animal. Hunker down, become small. Then, to his astonishment, the woman straightened up, head high under the hood, shoulders back, visibly trying to give herself courage.

Well . . . *shit.*

Mac recognized that.

He knew all about trying to give yourself courage in bad situations. He'd been a prisoner of fundamentalist fucks in Yemen for two hellish months in which he'd been kept hooded and uncertain, knowing that at any moment he could have a blade to his throat or a muzzle to the back of his head. He knew precisely what she was feeling because he'd felt it himself.

If she was going to clock out, she wanted to go with her head high. Man, he knew what that was like. Knew it inside out.

For a second, just a fleeting moment, he identified with her, flashed on what this must be like for her. But then it passed.

Fuck that.

He couldn't afford to let himself feel anything for this woman. She'd come to him. Found him against all the odds. She'd cracked security designed by three men who were the world's greatest experts and he had no idea how she'd done it.

She was a menace—to him, to his men, and to this crazy community they'd gathered around themselves.

"Come," he said, injecting impatience in his voice.

He had to interrogate her as soon as possible. If this woman, however soft and pale and helpless she looked, turned out to be the tip of the spear of an invasion, he and his men had to scramble. The faster he found out what she wanted, and who was behind her, the better he could defend them.

She swung her legs out the open door, feeling for the ground with one booted foot. At least she'd had the sense to wear woolen pants and boots. Though her legs looked like they went up to her neck, she was only of medium height. Her foot tapped down tentatively, seeking firm ground. Finally, exasperated, Mac fit his hands around her small waist and bodily lifted her out and down to the ground. Like a dancer, she pointed one foot at the ground and seemed to land like some goddamned ballerina.

She felt good between his hands.

God-*damn*.

Shocked, Mac took a long step back. He had no business thinking that way. He was a soldier, now and forever. He hadn't left the military, the military had left him.

At heart he was *still* a soldier, protecting his own, and this woman represented danger. What the fuck did he care if she felt light and graceful under his hands, if she was beautiful, if she was brave? That made her doubly dangerous.

Bravery in an adversary was bad juju, he knew that.

Was sex messing with his head? It never had before. Sex was off the table when he was on a mission, and his entire life now was a mission, dawn to dusk. Of course sex had been easy to dismiss when he'd actually been getting laid, which was not the case right now and hadn't been for a year.

Man, if this woman could distract him, he needed to do something about that, ASAP. Get down off the mountain one night in one of their camouflaged vehicles, go to some dive in one of the nearby towns that didn't have vidcams and find himself a woman for the night. Or for however long it took to get this out of his system.

She was standing quietly, head high, the only sign of stress an accelerated rate of breathing and the trembling of her hands.

"Come with me," Mac said roughly, and took her elbow, setting off toward the huge elevator that would take them half a mile straight up.

She came obediently, which was smart of her. He didn't think he could hurt a woman, but he didn't want to put that to the test. He was the front line of defense not only for his men but for the Haven, and if he had to choose between this woman and those he protected, she'd lose.

He hoped it wouldn't come to that. Best-case scenario—keep her in isolation, extract what intel he could, particularly how she knew his name and in what general direction to find him, what she wanted, who sent her.

Jon had a drug he'd lifted from a pharmaceutical wholesaler that could wipe short-term memories. Couple the drug with a light anesthetic, have her wake up a hundred miles away with no memory of him or Mount Blue or Haven.

He tugged on her arm and she stopped obediently while he pressed the button to open the elevator doors. When they opened, he urged her forward with his hand pressed to her back.

The engineer who'd designed the elevator, Eric Dane, had had fun with the velocity. You'd never know it but the damned thing shot up more than two thousand feet in thirty seconds. It was a wonder nobody got the bends.

Dane was one of his strays. The engineer had gone underground when he'd blown the whistle on structural deficiencies he'd found on the Oakland Bay Bridge and had lost his job for his efforts. Two months after he'd filed a report with the authorities on the bridge's weaknesses, it had collapsed on the Oakland end after the mild '21 Halloween quake. Forty people died.

Dane's structural deficiencies report was wiped from the company files and he was blamed for the collapse. A multimillion-dollar suit was brought against him, but there was no one to sue. He'd disappeared.

One more in Mac's ragtag army of outlaws and runaways. Men and women who had come under his protection.

Dane had buffered the takeoff and slowdown at the top, so the woman would have no way of judging how far they'd come. For all she knew, they'd climbed a few stories in a building instead of shooting up a half a mile inside a mountain.

The doors opened silently. The hood baffled sounds so she wouldn't be able to tell that the elevator opened onto their huge atrium, which was their community's central square. There were four people in sight, working. One of them was Jon, who looked curiously at Mac holding on to the elbow of a hooded woman. Mac signaled with his head to the right. To their meeting room. He made the universal sign of a camera rolling and Jon nodded and took off.

Mac steered the woman through the benches and plants of their huge open space, knowing not much was penetrating the hood. Not sounds or light or smells.

As always, a huge spurt of pride blossomed in his chest when he came out into their outlaw community's central square.

It was beautiful. Mac got a real lift every time he crossed the square. It was filled with light day and night. During the day, the molecule-thick, totally impenetrable ceiling looked open to the sky and blazed with sunlight. Miniscule solar collectors around the rim flooded the square with light at night. The solar panels were also heaters at the touch of a button. The effect was startling. High overhead, sheets of snow fell from the sky and stopped, disappearing the instant they touched the screen.

There was greenery everywhere—lush, thriving plants that pleased the eye and gave off a fresh fragrance. Fruit trees, flower beds, glossy shrubs, small enclaves of grass.

The lush greenery was thanks to Manuel Rivera, the man with the golden hands. Jon met him when he went tomcatting in Cardan, a small town sixty miles away. They became friends.

Manuel was working eighteen hours a day trying to get his organic farm produce business off the ground. Jon found himself growing fond of the guy. On one trip into town, the owner of the bar Jon always stopped at told him Manuel had been attacked by "muggers," had refused to go to the local hospital and was in a room upstairs.

Jon ran upstairs, kicked open the door, took one look at Manuel, stopped the bleeding, lifted him over his shoulder, and brought him up the mountain, defying Mac and Nick.

By that time, though, Mac and Nick were resigned. Their ragtag community already counted Dane, a famous actress whose face had been slashed by a stalker, an ER nurse who'd had to turn away a pregnant woman with preeclampsia and no insurance, and about forty other refugees from modern life.

Manuel had sued a big agro business with test fields of genetically modified plants next to his, contaminating his organic produce. The day after the lawsuit was filed, two thugs had beaten him up, leaving torn-up pieces of the lawsuit fluttering down onto his blood on the ground.

The agro business was an offshoot of Arka Pharmaceuticals.

Manuel now filled their public spaces with plants and ran two huge fields of orchards and vegetables which provided them all with organic fresh fruit and vegetables.

In exile and hunted like animals, they ate like kings.

The lush greenery reminded Mac of what he was fighting for, and why he had to be wary with this woman. Everyone else at

Haven had found their way here by accident and by fate. This woman came specifically for *him*.

Mac opened the door of their meeting room and ushered her over the threshold. Jon would have already seeded the room with vidcams, tiny ones she wouldn't be able to detect. Jon and Nick would be watching from next door.

The woman stood quietly just inside the room. She didn't pester him to let her go, didn't ask where they were. He found that interesting. It showed self-discipline. Was she an operator?

Only one way to find out.

He pulled off his balaclava, tapped his wrist unit twice, unlocking her restraints, and whipped off her hood.

She blinked in the light, getting her bearings.

Mac watched her carefully. People see different things. Operators are always "on." They don't sign up by chance. They're born that way, hard-wired for trouble, then drift to where someone can train them and hone their gifts.

An operator would walk into a baby's nursery, check the exits and the kid's hands in his crib. Just in case.

So if she was here on an infiltration mission, she'd check his hands, check the door to see what kind of locking mechanism it had, check all the walls for windows and see what could possibly be used as a weapon. She'd do it fast, and in about a second and a half she could list in detail every single item in the room.

Mac could do it, Jon and Nick could do it. They'd been taught by the best, by Lucius Ward.

At the thought of his former commanding officer, Mac's heart gave a small pump of rage. He repressed the thought ruthlessly. Now wasn't the time. It wouldn't ever be the time. And anyway the fucker was living it up in Rio.

The woman didn't size up the room at all. She sized him up. Her gaze rested thoughtfully on his face, without even a flicker of attention to his hands. Even though his hands hovered over his Beretta 92 and the black carbon combat knife in its sheath. The knife was three hundred times stronger than steel. He could not just slit her throat but he could decapitate her without any effort at all.

An operator would have understood all that, instinctively. Would have upped the vigilance level, started dancing on the balls of her feet in anticipation of action.

Nothing like that. She simply stood before him, looking him in the eyes. Breathing regular, muscles relaxed, hands loose.

And Christ, she was beautiful. Right now, that was the only factor in favor of her being an operator. Services throughout the world were scrambling to recruit beautiful, athletic women, sometimes training them from high school on. "Honey pots" they were called—and they were spectacularly effective.

Ghost Ops had had two such women available, in training to make it up to the big leagues. Women so beautiful any straight man would let them get near because biology tripped them up. Conquest by hormones. The men the women preyed on never felt the knife that slipped between the ribs or the garotte around the neck or the microbullet between the eyes.

But Francesca and Melanie had had a look about them that was unmistakable. They could hide the fact that they were soldiers under fashionable clothes and makeup but they couldn't hide the fact that they were dangerous. If a man had eyes to see, they gave off danger vibes like beautiful rattlesnakes.

Nothing like the aura around this woman. She was too soft, too sad. This woman wasn't a predator. She looked vulnerable and tired.

Fuck this.

"Sit down," he rapped.

She looked around and took one of his easy chairs at the table they used for one-on-ones, ignoring the long table they used for meetings. He sat down across from her. If he shifted his knees, he'd be touching her.

He sank into the softness of his chair, making sure he didn't touch her. Wishing he didn't have to do this, wishing he didn't have to be here, interrogating this woman, knowing he'd have to make some hard choices if her story wasn't convincing.

Because he was the protector of his outlaw band and if he had to get rid of her to keep them all safe, he'd do it. He wouldn't like it but he'd do it.

By default, he'd been appointed king of his little kingdom. And though he'd rather be anywhere else, here he was, in his comfy easy chair. As a soldier, he'd never have allowed easy chairs in his office. Nothing easy about being a soldier; the harder the life, the faster you learned. He had a Ph.D. in hardship.

But here, goddamned if people didn't come to him with their problems. They were fucking civilians. Much as he'd like to, he couldn't order them to stand to attention and give a sitrep. The civilian world didn't work like that. So he'd learned to offer his people a comfortable chair and even a goddamned cup of coffee—he drew the line at tea—waiting for them to get to the point.

She sat there, not relaxed against the back of the chair but not tensely poised on the edge of her seat, either. She simply looked at him, as if waiting.

Okay, so he'd start the dance.

"Who the fuck are you and why are you looking for this guy—what the hell was his name?"

She never blinked. "Tom McEnroe. I'm looking for Tom McEnroe."

Mac had been trained to lie by the best. His eyes gave absolutely nothing away. "Never heard of him," he said. "And who are you? I'm not going to ask a third time, lady."

She drew in a deep breath and he kept his eyes on her face. Because for a slender woman, she had a really great rack. Which had nothing to do with anything, of course. Just an observation.

He was definitely going to head down the mountain next week and get laid, though.

"My name is Catherine Young," she said quietly. "Dr. Catherine Young. I am a neuroscientist and I work in a research lab, Millon Laboratories, about twenty miles north of Palo Alto. All of which you obviously read from documents in my purse. I am also an expert on dementia."

She stopped, as if giving him time to react.

Mac simply waited.

Dementia, huh? Maybe that was his problem. He was demented for not knocking her out and leaving her three hundred miles away from here. Yeah, he was losing it.

He couldn't see it, but he knew Jon was tapping away at his virtual keyboard. The woman had barely finished talking when Jon's voice came in over the invisible ear pod.

"She's telling the truth, boss. Catherine Anne Young, born August 8, 1995. Lives on University Road, Palo Alto." Low whistle. "Got more degrees than my dog has fleas. Cum laude, too. That is one smart lady. I'm looking at her driver's license, photo matches, and am now looking at . . . ah. At her company ID. Millon Labs. It all checks out."

Mac gave an almost imperceptible nod, which she wouldn't catch but Jon would.

Then Jon came back on. "Whoa, boss. Millon, the company she works for? It's owned by Futura Technology. And guess who the final owner of Futura is?" Jon sometimes got carried away with his own smarts. Mac could almost see him smacking himself on the forehead because of course Mac couldn't answer. "Sorry, boss. Arka Pharmaceuticals. That's who. Our luscious Dr. Young ultimately works for Arka."

Arka Pharmaceuticals. Their last mission. He and Jon and Nick had almost died on that mission and it had made them outlaws. The false intel that Arka Pharmaceuticals was working on a weaponized form of *Yersinia pestis*—the bubonic plague—had cost them everything.

Because there had been no plague, only some very bright scientists working on a cure for cancer. Because the mission had cost him his entire team. Only he, Jon and Nick had escaped. And because he and his entire team had been betrayed by their commander, a man they had all loved.

That was Arka Pharmaceuticals. And that was the company this woman ultimately worked for.

Mac didn't believe in coincidences. She might look soft, she might not be an operator in the technical sense and she might well be a doctor with degrees coming out her ears, but his first instinct was correct.

This woman was dangerous.

"Go on." She'd stopped and continued studying his face, as if it was giving something away. Good luck with that. His face didn't give anything away.

"I work mainly in the lab, but we have a ward of test subjects suffering from severe rapid-onset dementia. Men and women who are so far gone they can't remember their names, can't remember anything about their past. Some are barely sentient. We're working on a cure for dementia, a way to reestablish the synapses that have been lost. I'll spare you the technical details. Our protocols are highly experimental, very cutting-edge, but several offer a great deal of promise. Each test subject was informed of the risks at a time when two neurologists certified that they were of sound mind and each patient signed a release. Or, failing that, a family member with power of attorney signed. The patients were assigned numbers, which I would have objected to, but they were all well beyond recognizing their own names. There was one patient in the protocol group, however, known as Number Nine . . ."

Her voice trailed off and she looked down at her hands, trying to think of what to say next.

Mac let the silence go on for a while. Finally, he made an impatient gesture with his hand. "Number Nine? What was the matter with Patient Number Nine? Besides being nearly brain-dead."

Her eyes lifted. She had truly beautiful eyes. A light gray, rimmed with a circle of darker gray, surrounded by amazingly long, thick eyelashes. Possibly even her own, since she didn't seem to be wearing makeup.

Shit. What was the *matter* with him? Letting himself be distracted by pretty eyes during an interrogation that might have life-or-death consequences. Lack of sex wasn't an excuse. There wasn't any excuse. He forced himself to focus.

She just stared at him. Her face was soft, open, vulnerable. Much as Mac wanted to read operational awareness and craft in her expression, he simply wasn't seeing it. Everything he'd ever learned about interrogation techniques was signaling something impossible. Either she was very, very good—better than anyone he'd ever come across—or the woman wasn't lying. Was no threat to him.

Except . . . she'd come looking for him in a snowstorm. For him specifically.

Of course she was a fucking threat.

"Dr. Young?"

She started slightly, as if she'd gone into a trance. There were white brackets around her mouth and her nostrils were pinched. She'd driven up a mountain in a snowstorm and had nearly gone into hypothermia. She'd be exhausted. Now that he thought of it, he looked for signs of exhaustion and found them. She was swaying lightly in her chair as if sitting up straight took effort.

Mac had a thin membrane on his left forearm which was a keypad. He pulled up the sleeve of his sweater and typed under the table—*bring food and something hot to drink in 30 min*—and nearly smiled at the treat awaiting this woman, who didn't deserve it.

They had the best chef in the world here in Haven.

He lifted his hands up from under the table and gestured impatiently.

"What about this Number Nine? Who was he?"

"Number Nine was a large man, fifty-three years of age, according to his file, though he looked much older. Dementia patients often look ten, even twenty years older than they are. They are incapable of looking after themselves and age rapidly. Number Nine's files said he was a business executive who had worked for a succession of companies, the turnover being extremely rapid in the previous four years. This is consistent with a diagnosis of a dementing disorder. He'd be hired on the basis of his track record, then the company would discover he wasn't up to the job. And then soon, of course, the track record was one of failure. Divorced, no children. His medical plan didn't cover a shelter home. He enrolled himself in the program, while he was still capable of signing documents. Everything was normal, if anything about these patients can be considered normal."

Her eyes flicked to a pitcher and she cleared her throat. "May I have a glass of water?"

He poured her a glass and she drank, that long white throat bobbing. When Mac realized he was avidly watching her drink, he turned his gaze away.

Christ.

"Thank you." She put the glass down and smiled at him. He didn't smile back. It wasn't a smiling kind of situation. But as smiles went, hers was a thousand on a scale of one to ten. Slightly shy, warm. Creating a tiny dimple on her left cheek.

Oh, fuck me. *Get back on track.*

"So something about this guy—this Number Nine—didn't add up?"

"There was something about him, yes, that was unusual. We have developed a semiportable functional MRI and we use it to track changes in the patients' brain scans. Seeing what stimulates various parts of the brain, particularly under the drug protocol.

"Dementia has many origins. Sometimes it is a series of mini strokes that choke off oxygen to sections of the brain, making them essentially dead tissue. Alzheimer's is the result of plaque that tangles the synpases, exactly as if the brain gums up. All of these have distinct fMRI signatures. Number Nine had something else altogether. The brain scan of this patient made no sense to me. His brain was damaged in a completely new way. The clinical symptoms were consistent with dementia but the scans weren't. Dementia patients have a general overall degradation of function due either to apoxia or plaque, in the case of Alzheimer's. Mainly centered around the hippocampus. Here I was seeing degradation of the striatum, unusually so. The patterns were strange. If I hadn't seen the patient myself, I would have said that his brain had been . . . destroyed by an outside force. A little like a cloak thrown over the higher functions. But underneath, the scan showed a great deal of activity, like a banked fire. He tried to communicate verbally, but it wasn't working. He became exhausted. Dementia patients forget words. It didn't seem like this patient forgot words so much as was unable to physically get them out."

Though Mac still didn't see the connection, the fact that this was a company controlled by Arka Pharmaceuticals made it definitely his business.

"So . . . what? You read his mind?"

His sarcasm got more of a reaction than he thought it would. She jerked slightly, eyes rounded.

"No." She drew in a deep breath. "No, I didn't read his mind. They don't teach that at med school. I found the key by sheer chance. I was typing my notes onto my iPad when his head jerked. His eyes went from my pad to me and then back to the tablet. I turned my tablet around and was astonished when he started keying in letters."

"Okay," Mac said. "I'll bite."

"He wrote that I should say nothing and turn off the vidcams. I have a security code that allows me to do that. However, so it wouldn't alert the guards watching the monitors or any bots that might have been established, I simply created a loop of him sleeping."

Smart thinking. Even if she wasn't an operator, she had some good moves in her. But then, Mac reflected, you don't get several Ph.D.s by being dumb.

"From then on, we communicated laboriously, by fits and starts, over the course of two days. The first thing he told me is that his name wasn't the name we had in our files, Edward Domino, which immediately made me suspicious. Dementia can merge into psychosis easily, and dementing patients are often paranoid. I've had patients who insisted they were John Kennedy, George Washington, Marco Polo, Albert Einstein. So I was prepared to hear something preposterous, but he gave me another name which meant nothing to me. I have a feeling, however, that it might mean something to you."

She stopped, looking at him. Mac turned his face to stone.

She sighed. "Lucius Ward."

"Holy. Shit," Jon's voice said in his ear. Mac could hear Nick swearing in the background.

"The name means nothing to me," Mac said, raising his eyebrows slightly. He felt as if he'd been sucker-punched but nothing showed on his face. "Why should it?"

"I have no idea. All I know is the fierce determination of this man—whether he was Edward Domino or Lucius Ward makes no difference to me. He communicated with great difficulty, he sweated and he shook, but he wouldn't give up. He repeated his name and said I absolutely had to find Tom McEnroe. That's a direct quote. He spent an hour, white-faced with fatigue, telling me this. He also gave me something." She dug in a pants pocket and brought something out in a small fist. She tossed it onto the table, where it rolled a few times, then stopped a few inches from Mac's hand. He stared at it, barely able to breathe.

"Jesus Christ." This time it was Nick's voice coming in over his earbud. "The Captain's Hawk."

It looked like nothing. A tiny, almost invisible pin made of black metal. Only under a microscope could you see that it was beautifully detailed. The pin was a hawk in flight, perfectly crafted down to individual feathers, a tiny gold stripe running down its back. It was made from the barrel of the gun that had killed bin Laden.

It was the badge of a Ghost. Ghosts were banned from having flashes or insignia of any sort. They were even banned from wearing U.S. military uniforms. They were only allowed that one tiny badge, smaller than a shirt button. There had been only seven of them in the world, and only one with a thin stripe of gold. The one that belonged to the Ghosts' commanding officer, Captain Lucius Ward.

One thing Mac knew—traitor or no traitor, Lucius would have relinquished his Hawk pin only on death or in the direst emergency. Even if he'd betrayed his men, even if he'd sold them out, even if absolutely everything Mac thought he knew about Lucius was wrong, this one thing wasn't wrong. It would take a cataclysm or death to pry Lucius's Hawk from his fingers.

"Do you know what that is?" she asked.

He searched her eyes for irony but found nothing. She was genuinely puzzled. Well, considering the fact that the existence of Ghost Ops was SCI—secret compartmented information—and that only a handful of people in the world knew about them, and even fewer knew of their secret badge, it was entirely possible she had no idea what the Hawk was.

"No." He leaned back in his chair and crossed his arms over his chest. "Should I?"

"I have no idea." She closed her hand over the Hawk and held it casually. Not knowing that the little metal pin represented blood, sweat and tears on a vast scale and was the symbol of a man Mac, Jon and Nick had loved like a father. A man who'd betrayed them. Who'd led them into a trap of fire, sacrificed them as casually as you'd swat at flies. For money.

She sighed. "He was trembling when he gave it to me, as if it were something that meant a great deal to him. But he was trembling before then anyway. The more we communicated, the more motor control he lost." She raised her eyes to his. "Even more important than the badge, though, it seems, was to find this Tom McEnroe and give him a message."

"And what message would that be?" Mac asked, his voice casual, though his heart had begun a low, deep thumping inside his chest. This was way beyond what he had bargained for.

The three of them had simply assumed Lucius had disappeared with his money to some Caribbean island or some enclave in Southeast Asia. If there was one man in the world who knew how to disappear, it was Lucius Ward. He was a master of the art.

They'd often bitterly speculated how he would be in some tropical paradise, a rich man, while they lived as outlaws.

And then it turned out he was in some lab only two hundred miles from here? Hurt and sick? For a moment, Mac battled with himself. The idea of the boss hurt and sick and alone was impossible to bear. He could hardly sit in the same place with the thought and his hands literally itched to get going, to go get the Captain who was . . .

The man who had betrayed them. Mac had to keep reminding himself of that. The Captain had betrayed them, led them into a trap, left them to die.

She opened her hand and studied the small badge thoughtfully, as if answers could be found in it.

"He said—he said I had to find this—this Mac." She lifted her head and Mac saw pain and sorrow in those huge gray eyes. "He said when I found him to tell him *Code Delta*. I don't know what that means."

But Mac did.

Danger.

* * *

The huge man leaned back in his chair, fist beating lightly on the desktop. Catherine's heart rate jumped even though he wasn't giving off danger vibes. Or rather, though he looked dangerous, very dangerous, he didn't seem out of control, and he hadn't threatened her directly.

Most violent men had their temper on a short leash. It took very little to set them off, and anything could do it. A wrong word, a wrong look.

Catherine had dated a man once. They'd met in a bookshop, reaching for the same book. They'd had coffee in the in-shop Starbucks and he asked her out to dinner the next night. Catherine was wary of men, but he'd seemed so nice—soft-spoken, funny and smart. They hadn't touched but she'd liked him. They'd had a great meal. Back in his car, she'd decided to let him kiss her and that she'd accept another dinner invitation. And maybe on the weekend she'd invite him over for lunch.

Nice and slow. The way she liked it.

And he'd leaned over, fisted his hand in her hair and kissed her hard, aggressively, opening her jaw with his other hand and thrusting with his tongue. He took her completely by surprise and she resisted.

He liked that. Oh yeah he liked that. A lot.

And what he was inside, under that nice, bland exterior, rushed like ice over her skin. Swirls of violence filled her head, red-tinted and hot. Sickness pulsed through her in nauseating waves, nearly overwhelming her. It had been there all along, and she hadn't seen it because she hadn't touched him. She recognized at his kiss that violence filled him, as if his skin was a sack full to the brim with it. All it took was the slightest abrasion and the skin broke and aggression and violence came geysering out.

She'd pushed at him and run to her small house, slamming the door behind her, panting. Listening until, finally, she heard his car tires squeal as he took off fast.

That night had been like a watershed, the lowest point of her life. After slamming the door shut, she'd slid down the wall, huddling in on herself and trembling for hours.

It had occurred to her for the first time that maybe this was it. It was never going to get better, ever. She'd misjudged the man because she kept herself so isolated. And she kept herself isolated because her gift poisoned the well whenever she wanted to get close to someone.

The episode scared her so much she hadn't touched a man since, for fear she'd chance upon someone else just brimming with violence.

That wasn't the impression she was getting here, though granted, she wasn't touching him. What she got was impenetrable granite. Massive self-control. What was under it was invisible to her. It might be violence, it might not, but whatever it was, it wasn't going to come geysering out. It wasn't going to come out at all.

She met his eyes. Women tended to look people in the eye, but some men interpreted that as aggression, as lack of respect, and responded accordingly. She didn't get the sense in any way that this man was out of control. On the contrary. Every single line of his big body remained still, clearly leashed to his will.

Even though he was armed to the teeth.

There was a big black gun strapped to his right thigh and a big black knife in a sheath on his other thigh. He didn't need them. His entire body was a weapon. There was power in every long line of him. Leashed, potent, unmistakable.

His winter wear was some kind of high-tech stuff—thin black non-reflective material—and it showcased his body, one of the strongest bodies she'd ever seen. Extra wide shoulders tapering down to a lean waist, long, powerful thighs, long arms and massive hands at the ends of them.

This was truly a formidable man and he'd glowered at her during the entire interrogation. Fierce, dark eyes fixed on hers, as if waiting to catch her out in a lie. Well, she was too steeped in neurolinguistics to make any mistakes in eye displacement even if she *were* lying. She knew precisely the body language necessary to convey truthfulness. If she wanted to lie, only an fMRI would show it because she couldn't force her brain to light up specific areas.

She wasn't lying so it wasn't an issue, but the quality of the man's attention was such that she was certain he'd unmask untruths coming from anyone he cared to unmask.

His entire body language was still but wary. He didn't trust her, not an inch. Had she made any kind of aggressive or even evasive move, there was no doubt he'd have snake-fast reflexes. So she stayed still, too.

But now she'd fulfilled the mission a sick man had sent her on, one she'd been helpless to refuse. It was done, for better or worse. The tension was seeping out of her and she had to force herself to stay upright in the chair and not slump with fatigue. Unfortunately, she was sitting on an amazingly comfortable chair, so maybe he didn't do interrogations on a regular basis in this room.

Most interrogations took place in uncomfortable environments.

She didn't look around but she'd observed enough to know that it was a comfortable room, pleasant even. Interrogation rooms weren't supposed to be pleasant, they were supposed to be austere and forbidding. Sort of like a jail cell, which is where you went if you lied.

What time was it? It must be close to midnight. She'd slept badly the past night, unnerved by Patient Nine.

Patient Nine—Lucius—had been so desperately insistent, the force of his will had simply washed over her, prickling her skin. The images coming from him had been so very strong, the strongest she'd ever had. As if the barriers between them had dissolved and she was in his damaged head. There were images there, true, not words, except for that one name, murmured brokenly over and over again. Tom McEnroe. Mac. Mac. Mac.

The images were clear. The mountain. Lonely, broken roads. Obstacles. A dead car.

And, horrifyingly, his own death. Cold stillness, his body on a steel gurney with runnels. A body laid out for an autopsy.

Lucius Ward was ill but not at death's door. His EEG was pathological but his heart and lungs functioned well. But the image was insistent. He expected to die soon.

He had been agitated yesterday, trying desperately to talk, clinging to her arm with an emaciated hand that still held surprising strength. His throat clicked, over and over, words that weren't coming out, only a thin trickle of air escaping from his mouth, with a short hum. His eyes bulged, the cords in his thin neck stretched. His mouth opened and closed with a clatter of teeth.

His efforts to speak were so heartbreaking, she couldn't stand it. Bending down to him, fixed in his wild, desperate gaze, she bent her ear to his mouth.

He managed one word.

"*Run*," he whispered, and she'd broken out in goose bumps.

Troubled, Catherine had gone home. She couldn't eat and couldn't sleep, and finally the next morning she decided to follow the pictures in her head. Something about the wild fear he had instilled kept her from calling in sick. She simply left.

The man in black stood up suddenly and looked down at her. "Stay here," he commanded, and walked out.

Stay here. Well, where would she go? The door opened for him and closed behind him before she could even think of making a break for it.

She looked down at the tabletop. The grain of the wood was unusually fine and she fixated on it until her head drooped. She jerked upright. She'd nearly fallen asleep in the chair.

Were they going to keep her here all night? There were only two chairs. Maybe she could use the other chair for her legs and try to catch a few hours of uncomfortable sleep.

She shifted uneasily, stiff and sore, exhaustion seeping into her bones. Hunger and thirst were added to the discomfort of exhaustion. She turned her head to eye the door. There was no doorknob. It had somehow swished open for the man in black and swished closed again with no visible command having been given. There was no keypad, and even if there were, she didn't have the code.

The door whooshed open again unexpectedly and she turned in her chair, heart pounding, muscles tensed for danger.

But it wasn't danger, it was only a teenage boy holding a big tray. She was so surprised that by the time she thought to react, to engage the boy in a conversation, to try to pry some information out of him, he was gone, the door whooshing open and closed for him as if invisible genies inhabited the place.

A cornucopia lay before her. Her stomach rumbled loudly, the wonderful smells sparking some kind of intense endocrine reaction.

Her hand trembled as she picked up the first thing close to her hand. A taco. But not just any taco, oh no. Maybe it was extreme hunger, but the tastes were incredible. Stone-ground cornmeal shell, fresh tomatoes, perfectly cooked spicy meat . . . even the lettuce was delicious. The best homemade guacamole she'd ever tasted. A baked potato with fresh clotted cream and freshly chopped chives. A salad of tasty red tomatoes drizzled with extra virgin olive oil. A huge slice of the best peach pie she'd ever tasted, so good she nearly laughed aloud as she brought the fork to her mouth.

A pitcher of absolutely fresh juice. She could taste apples and carrots and a touch of lemon. It went down her parched throat like a dream and it was like being in a garden on a summer's day.

Oh man, if they were going to kill her at least they were serving her the best last meal ever.

Chapter Three

Arka Pharmaceuticals Headquarters
San Francisco

His private cell buzzed. Dr. Charles Lee, head of research, frowned. It was late and he was expecting the results of the Africa trial. Nobody should be calling at this late hour. He checked the number, set the phone in its dock and pressed the icon for hologram. The shaved bullet head of his chief of security at the Millon lab, Cal Baring, appeared in 3D. Baring was scowling ferociously, but then he usually did.

"Yes, Baring?" Lee continued scrolling through research data. Though one's instinct was to address a hologram because it was so lifelike, it wasn't necessary. "What is it?"

"It's about Dr. Young, sir."

That caught Lee's attention. He looked up from the screen, frowning. "What about her?"

Dr. Catherine Young was crucial to the Warrior program. She was a brilliant researcher. If she were in Germany she'd be Frau Doktor Doktor—a double Ph.D. in biology and neuroscience, and an M.D.

Though incredibly smart in terms of scientific research, she also seemed to be clueless in terms of the broader picture, focusing narrowly on the dementing patients they sent to her, not questioning how they got that way, which was perfect.

Unlike Roger Bryson in the Cambridge lab. His questions had become irritating, then dangerous. He deserved to die in the fire, he had become much too curious and insistent.

The ironic thing was that he really had come up with a cancer vaccine, the formula for which was now safely in a vault in the Ministry of Science in Beijing. A canister of the active vaccine had been removed from the Cambridge lab just before the Ghost Ops strike and taken to Beijing by diplomatic pouch. All the members of the Politburo had been vaccinated.

Later, when the world was theirs for the taking, the vaccine would be offered to all ethnic Chinese.

Lee had been born Cheng Li thirty-eight years ago on the outskirts of Beijing. His father was a doctor but he wanted to secure a future for his only son so they immigrated to San Francisco with his paternal grandfather when Lee was seven. His father's medical degree wasn't recognized so he drove a taxi.

Stupid man. His father had died old before his time having done menial labor for thirty years, for what? So Lee could become an American.

He became an American, all right. In a city like San Francisco with its fusion population, he fit right in. He learned perfect English, played basketball in high school, liked jazz, went to Stanford on a scholarship. His parents were ecstatic. But his *yéyé*, his grandfather, a noted scholar who had unwillingly followed his son to America, made sure Lee kept his Mandarin up, made sure his calligraphy was perfect, filled his head with tales of the once-powerful Middle Kingdom.

Lee's father was too busy, too tired to notice or even to care that his son was faking loving the American dream. Because he was. By the time he was seventeen, already a sophomore neurobiology student at Stanford, he realized the enormous mistake his father had made. Because America was the past and China was the future.

His sophomore year, the OECD officially announced that the Chinese economy was bigger than the American economy. And growing, as the American economy was not.

It was clear all around him—Americans were *poor* and getting poorer. It had lost its faith in itself and was hunkered down, hoping the new winds blowing over the world would pass soon. But that was not the nature of the winds of change.

Lee had kept in touch with old school friends back in China, many of whom were now in positions of power. One in particular, Chao Yu, was now right-hand man to the Minister of Defense.

Lee and Yu had been working on the plan for four years now, ever since Lee realized the potential of the Warrior project. Yu was his conduit to the Ministry of Defense via encrypted, very long-wave propagation channels. The NSA was too good for them to be able to entrust the plan to satellite transmission. They communicated through the earth itself as they built the Warrior project from the ground up.

Lee had thought it might take a hundred years for China to rule the world. Which would have been fine. China had always taken the long view. America operated on a quarterly basis. Three months was a ridiculous time horizon. China operated on a century basis.

But with Warrior, China could take over the world in one short year. And Lee would return triumphantly to the homeland he had never forgotten, a hero and a powerful man. The man who had been the ultimate weapon in China's hands.

He, Charles Lee, was going to make history.

Super soldiers. The dream of every military force since time began. Smarter, faster, tougher. The Americans had a comic-book hero for this—Captain America. But Lee and Yu were going to create one for real—Captain China.

So far everything was on track.

With the exception of the Cambridge lab—and General Clancy Flynn had taken care of that—things were going well, though some technical problems remained. But all in all, the plan was coming to fruition along the scheduled timeline.

The Cambridge lab fiasco had yielded some advantages, however. Three gifted soldiers—true warriors—to experiment on. Three men he could do anything to, study as he wished.

It was perfect terrain for testing their protocols. Artificially dement them, bring them back, then harvest their brains and analyze the neurological tissue. Testing on warriors would have proved impossible if they were of sound mind and body, but they'd been reduced to physical and mental shells and were harmless.

He focused again on what Baring had said. "What about Dr. Young?"

"Dr. Young didn't show up for work, sir. We were only informed an hour ago."

"Did she call in sick?" Lee asked Baring.

"No, sir. And she's not home. We checked."

Lee felt the faintest prickle of unease. Dr. Young was right in the middle of the analyses of the beta doses. She was a dedicated researcher. Not showing up for work was so unusual as to warrant an alarm.

She had no idea what she was really working on, but if she ever got the big picture, as Dr. Bryson had, she would be very dangerous. But Bryson had been skeptical by nature, which Young was not. "She might not be answering the doorbell."

"When I say 'not home,' sir, I mean just that. We scanned the house. There was no one inside."

The chill grew stronger. This was very unlike Dr. Young. "Did you track her cell?"

Baring's voice grew cold. His words were staccato. "Yes. Sir. Not transmitting."

This had been a bone of contention. Baring wanted to inject micro tracers into every single researcher on the Millon campus, but Lee had turned the request down. There was massive IQ on-site. All it would take was for one researcher to figure it out and the news would spread and there would be hell to pay.

Lee made sure the scientists working at the Millon facility saw the project only through straws, but they were very bright men and women and were perfectly capable of putting two and two together. That was why the average stay at Millon was six months. An exception had been made for Catherine Young because Lee felt her work shouldn't be interrupted and it would take another scientist six months just to get caught up to speed.

Young was tasked with making an fMRI map of the altered minds, creating a baseline for further research. Her work had to remain confidential, which is why Lee had planned on having Baring terminate her once the map was complete, instead of transferring her.

Young knew a lot. More than enough to create trouble.

He kept her under surveillance. Baring's surveillance had been very tight in the beginning, but nothing had shown up and they'd decided they could take it down a notch or two.

And now she'd slipped through their net.

"What about her car?"

"Not transmitting. Transponder dead." Baring's lips clamped closed in disapproval.

Baring had petitioned to put trackers in staff cars, too. But most of the staff had electric cars, which would soon become mandatory in California anyway. All cars were run by microchips which were hackable with just a little effort. There Lee definitely ruled against Baring. An external tracker on a car would be a dead giveaway that something was wrong, particularly when any car could be hacked as long as it was running.

All eCars had transponders which allowed them to send out an emergency signal.

So Catherine Young's car was somewhere out there, but not running and the transponder was dead.

Lee drummed his fingers on the console, once. It was all he allowed himself. No one knew better than he the importance of keeping body language serene.

"Did you check the cameras in the lab?"

"Yessir." Even in the hologram, Lee could see Baring's color change, face becoming ruddy. "Of course."

"Anything untoward happen yesterday?"

"It didn't seem so. Sir." Baring's jaw muscles tightened, as if he'd been questioned.

Then again, what would Baring know? He wasn't a scientist. He couldn't follow any of the researchers' work.

"Did she seem . . . agitated in any way? Did she do anything different?"

Lee watched Baring's disembodied head. Even just a few years ago there was half a second's delay in holographic telephony, sometimes making conversations surreal. But Arka had state-of-the-art technology and Baring reacted in real time. "No, sir."

"Who was she working on yesterday?"

"Number Nine, sir," Baring replied.

Lee felt that prickle of coldness once more.

Baring had no idea who Nine was. It was a good thing that Captain Ward had always worked in the shadows. Only a handful of people were familiar with his spectacular military career. Baring was ex-military but he came from infantry. What Ward did had always been above Baring's pay grade.

This was nothing. And yet . . . Catherine Young disappearing after working on Ward was not good.

Ward was the key, Lee was sure of it. They were so close, so very close. SL-57 hadn't worked, but each successive iteration brought them closer to their goal. A virus-borne cocktail of hormones and chemical stimulants to neurotransmitters and muscle enhancers was being fine-tuned. Currently, the protocol to enhance intelligence and speed of reflexes caused fulminating dementia in most patients, but they were closer to understanding the cause and reversing the effect. SL-58 was being tested. Right now, in fact.

It had been a top secret government project known by the harmless name of Strategic Leadership that Lee had run under the orders of General Clancy Flynn, the money coming from a black fund Flynn controlled. Flynn was retired now, CEO of a private security company. Lee knew that Flynn wanted to create an unstoppable private army via SL.

Flynn was funneling private money into Arka's research at the Millon Labs. He was pumping close to ten million dollars a year into Lee's project. Flynn's projections were of one billion dollars profit the first year, and double that within three years once the project was viable.

But Lee had no intention of letting Flynn get his hands on SL once it was perfected. Millions of vials of the first effective doses were going straight to the People's Republic of China to be manufactured on an industrial scale and administered systematically to the seven million troops and the forty million reserve troops of the PLA. It would become literally unstoppable. China would be unstoppable.

When the secret program began seven years before, it had been given the anodyne and generic name of SL for Strategic Leadership. But Lee knew that SL stood for Shen Li.

Warrior.

He'd hoped, for symmetry's sake, that the brain of a warrior would give him and his country the means to conquer the world. It would be fitting. Captain Lucius Ward was one of the best warriors America had ever produced.

But perhaps it was not to be. Pity.

He would wait for another day or two for Dr. Young to show up. If she didn't, he would terminate the Captain and autopsy his brain and move on. The formula was close.

China's time was almost here.

In a few hours he'd be watching test results of a beta version that just might be the right formula. If it worked, he was months away from his goal, a triumphant China.

Mount Blue

"Well, what the fuck do we know about her, besides the fact that she's smart and enjoys really good tacos?" Nick Ross asked. His dark, hard face was as expressionless as Mac's own.

They were in Mac's study, watching Catherine Young on his 3D monitors.

"Well, we know she's a babe," Jon said cheerfully. "What?" He opened up his hands when Mac and Nick turned to him. "She *is* a babe. That hair, those eyes, those boobs . . ."

"Jon . . ." Nick let out a long breath, an attempt at restraint.

No one would believe that Jon Ryan could be anything but Surfer Dude. Sun-streaked blond hair, laid-back 'tude, a weakness for truly garish Hawaiian shirts and women, he was as lethal as Mac or Nick, but it didn't show.

Men instinctively moved out of Mac's way and out of Nick's way, but they always underestimated Jon and were always really really sorry afterwards. If they lived long enough to be sorry.

"She says she's treating the Captain," Mac reminded them quietly, and it was like a large, dark stone dropping into a pond. "He's alive and he's close, according to her. He's not sipping tropical drinks in Bali and he's not living upriver in the Mekong and he's not in Tajikistan." Some of their favorite speculations because Lucius was intimately familiar with those places. Like he was intimately familiar with Colombia, Sierra Leone and the more remote islands of Indonesia. If it was tough and remote, Lucius knew it. Their speculations that he might be in Bali with a couple of women and a mansion had been tinged with bitterness because that new deluxe life would have been bought with their lives.

"Hot or not, we're going to have to get more intel from her. She's lying about the Captain but she knows something and we're going to have to find out what." Nick's voice was low. He looked each of them in the eye. "By whatever means possible. Though I wouldn't advise trying to fuck it out of her. No time for it, not even for you, Jon."

Jon breathed out a sigh of regret. None of them was capable of hurting a woman, but Jon had seduced his share of intel out of women.

Not Mac. Women didn't fall for Mac. Women didn't even like looking at him. One look at his face and they either ran screaming or decided he was good for one thing and one thing only—a fuck. After which they were gone.

Fine by him. He'd been born ugly with big, irregular features. An opponent who'd had a boot knife and slashed his face open with it had scarred one side of his face, and then the Arka fire that had burned the other side of his face had taken care of the rest. Most people flinched when they saw him the first time. They avoided looking at him as if looking at him could cause them harm like that Greek lady with the snakes for hair who turned anyone who looked at her to stone.

He'd had a hard life and it was reflected in his face. Mac didn't give a shit. In the military, he did what he had to do and he did it well, and what he looked like didn't make any difference at all to the outcome. The only time he thought about it was when he was undercover, because he was memorable. Not in a good way.

"Mac might have better chances than I would," Jon said, waggling his eyebrows. "With that handsome mug of his."

"Cut it out," Mac growled. They didn't have time for this.

"No, dude. I mean it." Jon suddenly turned serious, the expression odd on his good-looking face. Mac had watched him hosing opponents with his charm, wielding that bright and merry smile while slipping in the knife. His face wasn't made for seriousness. Seeing him so sober and serious was strange. "The chick likes you."

Mac didn't surprise easily but he felt his jaw unhinge slightly, then snapped it closed. "What the fuck are you talking about?"

"The chick?" Jon insisted. "The lady doctor? The one you just spent an hour interrogating? 'Member her? The one we're watching now?"

"Can it, Jon." Nick's voice was low with menace.

"She digs you," Jon continued as if Nick hadn't spoken. "Man, she looked at you like you were smokin' hot."

Mac made a sound of exasperation. Jon liked to razz on him but now wasn't the time. On the monitor, the woman had finished the juice drink and was polishing off the last of the peach pie. Man, she must have an amazing metabolism to eat like that and stay so slender. Either that or she'd been starving.

At the thought, a slight worm of unease went through him. He was hard, yeah, but he wasn't cruel. It wasn't a happy thought that she might have been hungry while he was interrogating her. Starving a woman . . . well that officially made him a prick.

He was a badass but not a prick.

"Shit, look at that chick eat," Jon said. "Nice manners, but she's packing the stuff away."

"She was hungry," Mac said curtly.

"Yeah." Jon nodded. "For you."

"Fuck off, Jon." Nick gave Jon's shoulder a sharp blow. "We don't have time for this. The fuck's wrong with you?"

"Hey, man, I'm serious. Wait, wait! Let me show you what I mean." Jon reached over and touched the screen, dragging his index finger from right to left, rewinding. "Where . . . there it is! The moment Mac takes her hood off."

All three men turned to the monitor, though Mac didn't know

what the hell he was looking for. He'd been there and hadn't noticed anything. All three watched as Mac held open the door and ushered a hooded Catherine in with a hand to the small of her back.

Now *that* he remembered. Vividly. Sleek muscles, narrow waist, some really nice smell as she walked past him. He rarely touched women except for sex. It had felt nice and he'd squashed the thought immediately. Until she convinced him otherwise, this woman was the enemy.

"There!" Jon shouted, and tapped the screen to freeze it.

"What?" Nick asked, baffled. Mac frowned and leaned closer to the monitor, trying to figure out what Jon saw. He looked at the tableau, his frozen self with the hood in his hand, holding it high, having whipped it off the woman's head, her hair gently raised from the friction with the hood forming a halo around her head. She was looking straight at him and the screen save caught that second in which she first had a glimpse of his face.

Dispassionately, Mac had to recognize that the woman was truly beautiful. One of the most beautiful women he'd ever seen. Gorgeous light gray eyes, high cheekbones, full mouth. It was a bone-deep beauty, the kind that could never fade. She'd be a gorgeous centenarian. Whatever makeup she might have started the day with was long gone, though it wasn't a face that needed enhancement. It could have done with some color, though. She was white as ice.

Other than that . . . what wasn't he seeing?

"What?" Mac echoed.

"Her face, goddammit!" Jon tapped the screen, his finger making a little thud on the glass right over the image of her face. "Look at it!"

Mac and Nick stared at the screen, then at each other. What the fuck?

Jon gave a snort of disgust. "Jesus, observation skills zero, both of you. You know what I'm seeing? Nothing! That's what I'm seeing."

Mac and Nick glanced at each other again. Mac shrugged. "Hell if I know what he's talking about."

"She's not afraid, you asshole!" Jon shouted. "I defy any human being, let alone a woman who is by all accounts a geek and is certainly not an operator, to be kidnapped, taken somewhere unknown, have the hood whipped off unexpectedly and see your face and not shit herself with fright. Come on, you know what you look like. God knows you use it often enough to intimidate. It's not working with her. *Look, goddammit!*"

Mac looked. The screen shot showed Mac with his war face on while Catherine Young looked straight up at him. Her face showed exhaustion, vulnerability, tiredness. But not fear. No fear at all.

"Dude." Jon turned to Mac. "You're terrifying. I know you and know you're one of the good guys. But shit—sometimes you scare *me*! Think about it. She's not scared. She's not taken by surprise by your ugly scarred mug. So—either she already knows what you look like or she falls into instant love. And I opt for Door Number One."

"He's got a point, Mac," Nick said slowly, eyes riveted to the screen. "No offense, but how can she see you suddenly and not run screaming? Particularly since basically she's your prisoner? Can she—does she know you?"

That one Mac could answer. "Never seen her before in my life."

"Then—there's something there we're not seeing, not understanding."

The three men were silent.

"She saw a photo of you somewhere," Nick said slowly. "That's the only thing I can think of. That's why she was prepared."

"Negative," Mac shot back sharply. "We're fucking *ghosts*."

No way. Lucius had ruthlessly destroyed all documentary evidence of their existence in and out of the military. And when the Captain did something, he did it thoroughly.

"Unless . . ." Jon began, a frown of concentration between his blond eyebrows.

"Unless?"

"Well, crazy as it sounds, she's saying the Captain sent her." He held up a hand. "Wait. I'm not saying she *was* sent by Lucius, I'm just saying *she's* saying Lucius sent her. And, well, just about the only explanation I can come up with for her reaction when she sees you for the first time is, ahm . . ."

"Lucius described me to her." Mac kept his voice flat. "She knew what I looked like because Lucius told her what I look like. Which would mean that she's right. Lucius is in Palo Alto. And in trouble." He gritted his jaw muscles, looked at his teammates. "Code Delta."

The meal was so good it might even be worth getting offed afterwards.

Catherine would have sworn her stomach was so knotted up she would barely be able to choke down a few bites, but at the mere smell of the food, her stomach simply opened up like a door.

Maybe it was the animal in her, she thought, that wanted to live. The lizard part of her brain waking up, pushing for survival.

She'd spent her childhood and teen years suppressing the lizard brain, believing her gift came from the unconscious. She never let herself be swayed by emotion, by need, ever.

And yet the scientist in her knew that was nonsense. Whatever it was that allowed her to read emotions, it wasn't a *thing* that could be exorcised from her life. It could be suppressed for a while, sure. She should know because she was the Queen of Suppression.

But when it came roaring back, it was so strong it was uncontrollable.

Maybe that was why she had reacted so very strongly to Nine. To Edward Domino, alias Lucius Ward. He'd come into her life after a long period of repression. She'd immersed herself in her studies, cut herself off from most human relations—certainly from anyone who could evoke an emotional or sexual reaction—and thought she'd rid herself of her dragon.

But the dragon had come swooping back in on black-and-gold wings, breathing fire.

Her gift hadn't become weaker through suppression, it had become stronger.

The clearest reading she had ever had in her life from another human being had been from Patient Number Nine. Lucius Ward. Crystal-clear, so specific it was as if she'd been handed written instructions for use.

All her other readings had been mostly vague and cloudy. She could pick up on the major emotions—fear, hatred, hidden love, shame, ambition—like picking up on the loud bits of a symphony. Other emotions underneath had been harder to catch or to interpret.

This was something far from the reassuring pilasters of science holding up her world. This was—something else. The fact that she was here—had been *propelled* here by forces beyond her control—was a function of pure instinct.

Instinct told her to eat and drink and she did.

The instant she drained the last of that amazing juice, feeling a billion vitamins coursing through her system, the door whooshed open again and she turned to watch the big man in black enter the room.

He walked over to the other chair and sat down.

For the first time, Catherine noticed how he moved. He was huge, but moved with enormous grace, like an athlete. He obviously was an athlete, among other things. He had the body of an outsized linebacker, bulging muscles evident even under the clothes. He'd shed the tough impenetrable outerwear like an exoskeleton and was now dressed in a black sweatshirt, black jeans, black combat boots. He'd pulled up the sleeves of his sweatshirt, showing strong, muscled forearms with highly raised veins. His body had increased the veins to pump more oxygen into the muscles. An automatic bodily response that couldn't be faked and that spoke of hours and hours of working out.

Or fighting. Because he was a warrior, not an athlete. The weapons at his hips showed her that.

He sat down in front of her and looked at her, dark eyes unblinking.

There was a slight abatement of the heavy waves of suspicion that had enveloped him like smoke. Though he was far from welcoming or even trusting, there wasn't overt hostility.

"Thank you for the food," she said politely.

He dipped his head. "You're welcome." The deep, low voice reverberated in the room.

"I was hungrier than I thought."

Maybe she could trick him, and he'd answer *I noticed*. She was absolutely positive there was a camera in the room, though it was invisible. Nowadays vidcams were in patches slapped on walls and doorknobs and windowsills. They'd have watched her every move; certainly she was being watched right now.

But she underestimated him. He didn't so much as flicker an eyelash.

Okay. Try another tack. "I'm surprised you fed me."

His eyes narrowed. "I don't want to starve you to death. All I want is for you to be gone."

"I understand that." Catherine leaned forward on her forearms. "I also understand that I'm eventually going to end up several hundred miles from here with a headache and no memory whatsoever of the past twenty-four hours or maybe even forty-eight hours, depending on the dose of Lethe. My company invented it. In-house we call it MIB. For Men in Black. Only it's not a light that shines in your eyes, it's drops in a glass. So I'd like to thank you for not MIB'ing the carrot and apple juice because I have some more things to say before you do."

Aha! Anyone less adept than she was at reading body language would have missed it because he didn't move a muscle except for an involuntary twitch of the sternocleidomastoid muscle in his right jaw. Not all the training in the world could stop fast twitch muscles taken by surprise. Still, he was very very good.

She was better.

"Patient Nine didn't say so in so many words—" Actually he hadn't said it in *any* words, just vague images of shadowy men. "But I think that there are several of you here. Two, maybe three others. Like you. Somehow friends of his?"

Again, he didn't move a muscle, but a coldness crept over his features.

"Not friends of his?"

Silence.

"Look." She bit her lips. "Before you knock me out, I want to know that somehow I got this message across. In the way it was given to me. I—" She hesitated. Stilled her trembling hands under the table. Tried to calm her fast-beating heart. "I came here at some personal risk. Because a patient of mine, a man who is deathly ill, could find no rest until I promised him I would make every effort to find—" *You*, she thought. Find *you*. "To find this man, this Tom McEnroe. Mac. To give him that object I gave you, the tiny metal hawk, and to tell him Code Delta. You can believe me or not believe me. But I am telling the truth. And I think your friend—at least he considers himself your friend—is in danger. I have no idea if any of this means anything to you, Mr. McEnroe. Because that's who you are. I hope all of this makes sense, because otherwise I have just made a huge mistake."

Calmer now, having done all she could do, she placed her hands on the table, as if laying cards down. And she had. She'd laid it all out for him, for this tall, deadly-looking man. She'd done her best and possibly risked her life.

The rest was up to him.

"Tell her the truth, Mac," Jon's voice said in his ear. "I think the time for games is over."

"Yeah," Nick echoed, ever laconic.

Mac sat, eyes narrowed, looking at the woman carefully. She

sat completely still under his gaze. He got no read off her, none at all. She could be telling the truth, she could have been sent by their traitorous former commander, Lucius Ward, to trap him. She could have been sent by goddamned Martians for all he could tell.

Shit. He'd been trained in interrogation techniques. They all had. He didn't like torture, not for intel. If he had to off someone, he just did it without drawing it out. Pain wasn't always useful if you wanted the truth. Most everyone would say anything, anything at all, certainly what the interrogator wanted to hear, just to make pain stop, go away. But he'd interrogated his share of shitheads and had made them talk and pain had been involved.

Men like Mac or Jon or Nick wouldn't talk at all, under any conditions. They'd been trained to resist torture, but beyond the resistance training, they were unbreakable. They'd been selected and tested for that trait, then hardened, like hardening steel. And most of the time they had a discreet suicide method on them.

Just check out. Try pumping a corpse for intel, asshole.

So he knew all about breaking people down and—

Shit.

He couldn't do it with this woman. Just couldn't.

What the fuck was the matter with him? She'd *found* him. Nobody could find him.

"Take it from the top," he said. "Beginning to end. And make me believe you or I'll MIB your medical degree out of you."

She sighed. "Okay. My name is Catherine Young. Someone on your team"—she looked around the room, but the vidcams were invisible—"maybe several someones, the ones who are listening to us right now, has Googled me, I'm sure. So you know I am who I say I am, because you've already seen the documents I have on me—my driver's license, my company ID. You probably have my high school picture."

"Roger that," Jon said quietly. "She's good."

She was. It wasn't anything that argued in her favor.

"Go on," he said.

She watched his face carefully. "I have always been interested in the brain. My Ph.D. thesis was on dementing pathologies. Dementia is a very interesting pathology, the brain winding down. Understand it and you understand how the brain works, only in reverse. I worked at a research lab at the University of Chicago and published some papers on dementia. Millon Laboratories recruited me on a one-year contract to examine some test subjects who were undergoing an experimental protocol. Some of the patients showed almost complete recovery of function. Millon will be looking at billions of dollars in profits if it comes up with a cure for dementia. There are more than ten million patients suffering from dementia worldwide. That number is set to double in twenty years. So you can understand this is a huge priority for the lab."

"But there was a problem," Mac said. The basic interrogation technique was repetition. Have the subject repeat the story over and over again, and if there's something that's a lie, it will come out.

"Yes, there was. Functional and behavioral. Some of the patients . . . made no sense. Scientifically speaking. And I discovered that I was being followed."

"Whoa," Jon murmured in his ear.

"Followed?" Millon's security system must suck if a civilian—a nerd to boot—busted them. "How so?"

She sighed. "I'm a scientist, which basically means I'm a trained observer. People forget that about us. I kept seeing a couple of men, rotating. They thought that glasses or hats made a difference, but they didn't to me. And my computer was hacked several times on the days I was studying the special patients. I keep a little trapdoor open, just in case. It's called Red Hat and it is absolutely reliable."

"She knows her computers," Jon said in his ear. "Red Hat's a really good sniffer. Not many people know about it."

"And I set little traps." She shook her head, long, shiny hair rustling on her shoulders. "I can't believe they fell for it but they did. I'd leave a stack of printouts on my desk, then leave for half an hour. And sure enough—they'd have been moved. Not by much, once by only a tenth of an inch, but like I say, I'm observant. There was nothing in the printouts of any use to anybody. All my observations went into a highly encrypted thumb drive. They were really stupid and really easy to fool."

Her voice was sarcastic. Whatever had happened between her and Millon's security, she had only contempt for them.

"Okay." Mac nodded. "Let's get back to Patient Nine."

"Yes," she agreed, "let's."

"Do you have a description?"

"I do, of course I do. But I fear that the man I describe wouldn't be recognizable to anyone who might have known him in his previous life. I'd say he's lost about forty percent of his body weight and he has had numerous surgeries." Her lovely features tightened, a cloud passing over the sun. "The surgeries weren't in his clinical file, which is unacceptable. I asked the administrative department and got nothing but crap runaround." Those full lips pursed, her displeasure clear. "The records were lost, then at another office, then hadn't been digitized, which is nonsense . . . it was always something. He'd undergone an extensive set of surgeries, at least five that I could count. It was right there on his body, plain as day."

"Where?" Mac asked.

"What?" Her head whipped up, more shiny hair shifting on her shoulders. It was an amazing color, all natural. He'd been wrong to think it was just brown. It wasn't. There wasn't a chemical product on earth that could color hair about twenty different colors, from ash blonde to chestnut to black, going through the whole gamut of red. The ceiling light was right overhead and her hair was so shiny he looked away not to be blinded.

"What?" he said instinctively.

"Boss," Nick murmured in his ear. "Not a good time to go mentally AWOL."

Mac clenched his jaw, ashamed that Nick had to call him to order. What the fuck was this—getting distracted by a woman's *hair*? Lucius would be ashamed of him.

At the thought, another pang of pain shot through his chest. He shouldn't be thinking that Lucius wouldn't approve of something when Lucius had fucking *sold them out*. For *money*. Lucius had forfeited his right to tell him and Jon and Nick anything, even inside Mac's own head.

He reran the tape in his head.

"I said, where were the surgeries? His body? Bones reset? What?"

"No, no. All over his head and a cluster at the base of his spine. All neurological surgeries. He was messed with, heavily. And by experts. At one point it looked to me like he'd had two probes inserted in his brain, but they were removed."

Mac had to repress the wince. He hated doctors and hospitals. "What were the operations for?"

"Well," she said, looking down at her hands as if for inspiration, "that's the thing. I don't know. Millon doesn't have us working in teams, for some reason, so I was the only one trying to figure this out. Particularly since Patient Nine's clinical charts weren't available. I ruled out cancerous tumors or even benign tumors. He didn't have epilepsy. And Patient Nine had extreme difficulty forming words or making signs so he wasn't any help. There were other anomalies, too."

He'd caught her out. Now he *knew* she'd been sent by an enemy. He jerked his head back.

"Yeah," Nick said grimly in his ear. "We caught it, too."

She continued. "Nothing about the patient's functional MRI made any sense. His dementia, which was clinically speaking quite severe, didn't correspond in any way with known neurological patterns of dementia. I was so puzzled by the man that I took his fMRIs and EEGs home with me to study. And then—"

"And then?" Mac drummed his fingers on the table. Yeah she was pretty and yeah she was smart, but he was going to get the truth out of her if he had to inject a triple dose of Trooth in her.

She leaned forward, looking him in the eyes. So this was where the big-time lying was going to start.

"After he gave me the message to find Tom McEnroe he was so drugged the next few days he was barely conscious. Then yesterday—the day before yesterday now—I came in and he was in a terrible state, thrashing wildly against the restraints around his wrists and ankles. When he saw me he stilled, motioned with his head for me to come closer, signaled for use of my keyboard. He asked for me to cut the vidcams and I did, and then he wrote they were going to kill him soon. He was . . . very convincing."

"Though he was sick," Mac noted.

"Yes, though he was sick. And of course paranoia is actually a symptom of dementia. I tried to calm him down because he was bleeding at the restraints. He said once more I had to find this man called Thomas McEnroe. Mac."

"I don't believe you," he said harshly.

Her smile was sad and tired. "No?"

"No. You said he couldn't form words, could hardly think straight, and yet here he was telling you all of that. How does that work?"

She watched him for a full minute, breathing quietly. She gently tipped her hand to the side, letting the Hawk she'd been holding roll onto the table. Her hand trembled but her gaze was steady.

They watched as the Hawk rolled once, twice, making a tiny rattling sound in the quiet room. Mac knew Jon and Nick were watching, listening.

And then his world turned upside down.

She reached farther, her hand covering his, grasping it.

At first he thought it was a sex move, otherwise why the fuck would she be touching him? And, God, their two hands together were so damned erotic. His hand was dark and powerful, nicked and scarred and rough. A workingman's hand. Hers was slender, long-fingered, elegant. Pale creamy skin over delicate bones. A pianist's hand.

The contrast was arousing, female over male.

So that's the way she wants to play it, he thought, and then he was swept away by a blast of painless incandescent heat that moved from his hand up his arm and across his chest. It was as if his body had been taken over by an alien entity. An entity that was warm and enveloping and sweet beyond description. For a second he wondered if he'd been drugged. If her hand somehow contained a micro-syringe and she had injected a dose of . . . something in him. He had no idea what. He'd never heard of a drug that could do this.

Any further thought was impossible, he was in the grip of something powerful, more powerful than he was. He stared at her face as her features tightened, almost as if she were in pain. Her eyes glowed, as if some kind of light bomb had gone off behind them. As if they were a source of light themselves.

That incredible heat now flowed through his entire body, suffusing it with a golden glow. He was completely blocked, as if in a cube of amber. He couldn't move a muscle, each element of his body locked into place.

"Boss?" Jon asked softly in his ear. "You okay?"

"Should we come in?" Nick growled.

Only it turned out he wasn't frozen, he wasn't locked. It's just that his body didn't want to dissipate that heat. He could move, and he did. A short, emphatic shake of his head. *No.*

"Okay." Jon let out a long breath. "Standing down. We don't like it but we're standing down."

He jerked his head. *Yes, stand down.*

"You are grieving," she said softly, that luminescent, hypnotic gaze never leaving his eyes. "Grieving badly. There is such sorrow in you, it swirls around like black smoke. You were betrayed by a man you loved like a father. A man you trusted wholeheartedly. Everything you knew about this man led you to believe he would die rather than betray those who trusted him, and yet—he betrayed you. For *money*. It hurts your heart even to think of it."

His hand had jerked slightly under hers and she exerted a slight downward pressure.

It was ridiculous. She was a small woman. Slender, even fragile. Her hand was almost half the size of his. The idea that she could force him to keep still was ludicrous. And yet here he was, utterly incapable of moving even an inch away from that glowing light gray stare, her small hand tethering his.

"You're hurting," she whispered. "So much. And you can't show it because . . ." She tilted her head, as if listening to something, though her eyes never left his. "Because people count on you. And you'd rather die than betray them the way you were betrayed."

He couldn't move. Nothing moved except his lungs. He felt as if she were flaying him alive, but painlessly. And at the same time, for the first time in his life, he knew someone else could see inside him.

He'd worked a lifetime to keep his inner thoughts secret. As a child in violent foster homes, most thoughts or desires led to beatings. Later, in the military, nobody gave a fuck what he thought or felt about things as long as he did his duty, and he liked it that way just fine.

Except Lucius. Lucius had seen into him. The pain rose helplessly, like black tidal waters, choking him. It never stopped. A year and it could still ambush him.

"So sad," she whispered. "You're so sad. And yet under the smoke burns love, and duty. You're determined to protect your people. A life where you can't protect the innocent doesn't make sense to you. You'd die to keep them safe."

Her words were a distant flutter, the sound hummingbird wings might make if amplified. They barely registered. What registered was this hot, melting sensation inside him. For the very first time in his life he felt a connection to someone that was blood- and bone-deep. It was nothing like the loyalty he felt to his men or had felt to Lucius. That had a different flavor, was something else entirely. However strong his ties might be, there was a definite place where they ended, and that was his skin.

Here there were no boundaries, none. He could feel his heartbeat—slow, steady—and hers—light, hammering, almost frantic. He was inside his own skin and inside hers.

It was crazy. Was he drugged after all? He hadn't felt the prick of a needle, but maybe there'd been some kind of contact patch . . .

Her soft voice continued, her eyes a light hypnotic silver. "You're worried that I'm a danger to you. That somehow your enemies have found you and that I am their representative. I don't know how to convince you that who sent me was no enemy of yours. And that I don't represent any danger to you or . . ." She tilted her head slightly, watching him. "Or to your men." Suddenly, she whipped her head around, hair whirling out from her head, then falling back onto her shoulders. "They're watching us. Listening. Ready to come in to save you if I put you in danger. And yet"—she lifted her hand—"the danger doesn't come from me."

It all stopped. Dead. And it was like being dead. Where before there had been emotions swirling, bright and warm, heat and light, almost like a carnival going on inside him, now inside it was still and silent. Like a light switch being thrown. A switch that turned him off.

She was still watching him steadily, sadness and knowledge in her silvery gaze.

"I'm not anything you should fear, Mr. McEnroe. Or should I call you Mac?"

Chapter Four

Arka Pharmaceuticals Headquarters
San Francisco

The room was dark, the computer monitor bright. It was 9 A.M. Zulu time and Sierra Leone time. Though it was a chilly January evening in Northern California, in Sierra Leone it was a hot day.

Lee looked down like God at images Flynn's company, Orion Enterprises, piggybacked off Keyhole 18. Flynn himself was in the fancy company headquarters building in Alexandria, Virginia. Today, SL-58 was being field-tested. Orion had administered 50 cc's of SL-58 to each operative, the dose calibrated to last at least forty-eight hours. Well over the time it should take them to make their way from the diamond mine in the hinterland of hell to hell's own port, Freetown.

The mine was very rich, the path to market incredibly dangerous. There were not one but two rebel armies camped out in the jungle, marauders living off terrified villagers and hijacked convoys. So far, one convoy in three made it intact to Freetown. A 66 percent loss was unacceptable, even for the richest diamond mine in the world.

The Amsterdam-based diamond consortium had hired Orion to provide security for the diamonds and Flynn had promised the moon to the consortium in exchange for a million dollars a trip. Considering the haul on each trip was worth roughly five hundred million dollars once the diamonds were cut and set, the consortium had agreed. But Orion had one chance. If this convoy went the way of the others, it could kiss the contract goodbye.

Lee wasn't interested in diamonds or even the money, though he would get a substantial bonus if this convoy and successive convoys were successful. The bonus would help him speed up his plans.

This was a trial run in another sense, too. A state-controlled Chinese mining company had found a huge deposit of iridium, the largest in the world, in Burundi. No one else knew of the deposit.

With access to plentiful iridium, China was guaranteed to be the world leader in microchips for the next two decades. The mine was even deeper in the hinterland, in the no-man's-land where artificial lines on maps meant nothing.

If SL-58 turned out to be successful for Orion, it could be administered early to the Chinese troops who would set up a convoy to take the mined iridium east to the Indian Ocean, then by ship to China.

Lee's main monitor had shown the Orion convoy starting out at first light. Two Unimogs in front and two more at the rear guarding the central security truck carrying a titanium vault with 5 kilograms of uncut diamonds.

Since the nuking of the Orapa diamond mine in Botswana the year before, diamonds were the most valuable commodity on earth.

Three vehicles including the armored truck carrying the diamonds. All heavily armed, each vehicle with a mini gun firing .50 caliber bullets at the rate of a thousand a minute. Flynn had said they were carrying more than fifty thousand rounds of ammunition.

In Nanjing, fifty members of the elite "Flying Dragon" squadron were waiting, pending the outcome of today's trial. If it was successful, SL-58 would be administered and in a month they would start accompanying trucks of iridium to the waiting ships.

For now, it was Flynn's men who were being tested. Some ex–U.S. military and several South Africans familiar with the African bush. Each soldier had received an injection of SL-58 the previous evening. Orion's men had been told it was a benign, long-lasting amphetamine that would let them stay awake and alert for the twenty-hour journey.

Lee was sending everything to Beijing via long burst encryption.

It was an important trial. It was an important day. The first field test of the drug. So far, so good. The field doctor's report had been mundane, even boring, which Lee approved of. Boring was predictable. Boring was good.

Lee had watched the recording of the convoy starting out at 5 A.M. local time, the trucks heading out precisely, well-timed and well-organized.

The speed and precision of the soldiers at departure were visible, almost tangible. Lee wasn't a logistics expert but he had some idea of what it took to get a convoy of twenty-five men going. They did everything at top speed, quick and efficient. While the men were loading the trucks, Lee had to check the monitor dashboard to make sure the recording wasn't somehow fast-forwarding. But it wasn't on fast-forward. Everything was in real time. The men were walking as fast as most men could run, loading movements a blur.

Flynn was watching in Virginia, observing the tactical situation. Lee watched with a scientist's eye, delighted with what he was seeing.

It was as if the soldiers' movements were choreographed. Worked out beforehand and rehearsed a thousand times. It could have been on Broadway. However good Flynn's men were, they couldn't be that good. He was seeing the effects of SL-58.

They moved fast and precisely and were bristling with weaponry. But trouble was brewing.

Lee switched every five minutes to IR and noted human-sized bodies in the jungle, starting about a hundred meters from the staging area.

Flynn had noted, too, and reported. The men were perfectly aware they were under observation.

At first the red dots could have been any large mammals, but their stillness over time as the convoy was marshaled and then set off could mean only one thing—rebel soldiers, observing.

Doubtless the rebels were in radio contact with other soldiers along the route—the only road to Freetown. It was a well-known technique—attack convoys away from home base.

Well, if they attacked the enhanced convoy they were in for a nasty surprise.

The orders were to barrel ahead. An ordinary convoy would take three or four days to get to Freetown, traveling between 15 and 20 miles an hour during the day over the badly rutted road, laagering at night. This was to be a straight run, with no rest stops, pissing in bottles, shitting in cans, eating MREs. These soldiers wouldn't need rest stops. All they needed after the injection was a minimum of 8,000 calories a day and they could drive and fight nonstop for forty-eight hours. Twenty hours was nothing.

A twenty-hour convoy run would guarantee an increase in profits of 300 percent for the diamond corporation and would represent a cash cow for Orion. But more important, it would be the first successful battlefield test run of SL-58. If it was successful, Flynn would be allowed to play with it for a year, during which time the Chinese would be producing it in industrial batches and injecting its soldiers. After a year of field trials through Orion, Lee would destroy the lab producing it, destroy the formula and the few scientists who knew of it, and would be exfiltrated from America, bound for Beijing before the first bomb detonated in Millon's labs.

Lee had read up on his African history. African battles were often won by sheer numbers. After the Battle of Isandlwana, Western forces knew they had to be overwhelmingly better-armed to prevail. This was going to change the face of battle in Africa.

Flynn had briefed him on the convoy.

The Unimogs had FLIR to detect hostiles, Ground Penetrating Radar for mine detection, with armored chassis. Each vehicle had side- and top-mounted .50 cals, and below them, microwave blasters calculated to cook the hostiles the bullets didn't get.

Lee wasn't a soldier but even he was taken aback by the appearance of the convoy. You'd have to be insane to attack it. Of course, the Lord's Army was almost by definition made up of insane soldiers, drugged up, recruited as children and impervious to fear.

The convoy took off, fast and smooth. From the satellite images it almost looked like a living organism. Lee knew that the vehicles were in constant contact, with monitors showing displays of braking and acceleration of each vehicle, allowing the distance between the trucks to be minimal.

As they took off at dawn, the recorded IR images surrounding the camp scattered. A few red spots tried to run alongside in parallel but soon gave up—the convoy was moving too fast. Forty miles west, a conglomeration of red spots broke up like an ant colony that had had a stick poked in it. They'd received word on the radio that the convoy was arriving. But they were thinking in old terms and were still setting up traps by the time the convoy shot past, in tight and deadly formation.

The next trap was set a hundred miles farther west, where the road led through a steep valley, a classic ambush point. Lee smiled at the ant-like movements at the narrowest point. He didn't have to be a soldier to understand that short of unleashing an Armageddon of bombs, they didn't stand a chance. The convoy would speed by them with nary a scratch on the armored sides of the Unimogs.

This was going to work.

He pressed a button. "Looking good," he said to Flynn.

"Yeah. Real good" was the reply.

Flynn would watch every second but Lee had work to do. He minimized the screen, reviewed some autopsy reports, then went for coffee. The canteen had just purchased a shipment of Blue Mountain Arabica and it was delicious. He'd bring a box of the stuff with him when he left for China. Which might be sooner than he thought.

Back in his office he gave a glance at the monitor, then frowned. A side monitor showed progress as a blue line on a detailed map of the terrain. They should have been a third of the way to their destination but it looked more like halfway there. He punched in a query and stared at the answer in astonishment.

The convoy was traveling at 60 mph, an insane speed for heavy vehicles over rutted roads. Lee opened the screen but couldn't follow the individual vehicles behind the lead. The satellite image showed only a thick plume of dust rising high.

All the contractors' enhanced intelligence and strength, all their state-of-the-art gear wouldn't help if one of the heavy vehicles toppled over. It would be like a wounded elephant, and the other trucks would have to establish a perimeter of defense while trying to winch the fallen truck upright. Word would spread fast and soon they'd have a thousand Red Rebels or Lord's Army crazies shooting at them.

Insane.

He glanced at a side monitor showing data and blinked. The vehicles were *speeding up*. The speed was now 67 mph.

Flynn's cowboys were endangering the entire mission. He moved to link with the former general when he heard Flynn's booming voice with a deep southern accent fill the room from the speaker. His red face scowled from a small square on the bottom right-hand corner.

"What the fuck is going on, Lee? I'm clocking these bastards at 70 mph. The *fuck* are they doing?"

He was right. They were traveling at 70 . . . no 72 mph.

"Mr. Flynn," he replied coldly, deliberately omitting his usual deferential title of general. "I have no idea what your men are doing but they are running the risk of crashing the trucks at this speed. I see rebel activity ten miles ahead. The road's in real bad shape there. If they crash there they will be in major trouble."

His IR monitor showed a mass of red lights under the tree canopy ten miles ahead, invisible in the normal satellite images.

"They know that," Flynn growled. "They're seeing what we're seeing."

"Then this recklessness is doubly inexcusable," Lee said coolly.

Flynn didn't answer. The former general's breathing was loud in the room. He was a man who liked his pleasures at the table and in bed, and every time Lee had seen him over the course of the past two years, he'd been ten pounds heavier and ever shorter of breath. Right now his face was red and swollen on the monitor, a heart attack in waiting.

Greedy Americans, Lee thought with disgust. Always more, more, more. Like monstrous ticks engorging themselves until they burst. You couldn't find a fat general in the entire People's Liberation Army.

"Jesus," Flynn rasped. "What are they doing?"

Lee focused on the main monitor, unable to believe what he was seeing. Was something wrong with the satellite camera? No. The camera was showing events in real time and what he and Flynn were seeing was the convoy slowing down. At the choke point of the valley road.

50 mph
35 mph
20 mph

Lee watched, unbelieving, as the convoy rolled to a stop in perfect synchronization.

Flynn was shouting. "Hardy! Rollins! Come in! What the fuck are you doing? You're surrounded by hostiles! Do you have mechanical malfunction? Why are you stopping?"

A deep voice came over Lee's speakers. Not speaking to Lee but to Flynn. "No, sir, no malfunction. We're just taking the fight to the enemy." The voice sounded super excited, panting.

Lee remembered listening in on the radio reports at the beginning of the convoy's journey. The voices had been laconic and emotionless. Fighter pilot voices, relating facts like automatons.

"Negative, negative!" Flynn was screaming. "Do not engage! Repeat! Do not engage! Just take that goddamned convoy to Freetown!"

A click. No answer. Excited voices in the background, the sounds of men piling out. Lee didn't need the audio feed, what was happening was perfectly clear. The monitor showed the overhead feed, men spilling out of the front and back trucks.

Lee knew nothing about military strategy but even he knew that a stranded convoy surrounded by hostiles should be setting up a perimeter, hunkering down, guarding the shipment. Instead, the men poured out of their trucks and ran straight into the jungle, rifles to shoulders. One by one, the red points, like ants milling around an anthill, stopped. Whatever else they were, Orion's soldiers were excellent shots. Four of the men had powerful lethal tasers and were taking down rebel army members five at a time, mowing them down.

But however crazy brave, however well-armed, however excellent shots they were, the Orion contractors were outnumbered several hundred to one.

The Orion contractors were easy to follow even under the canopy. Their heat signature was significantly lower due to the body armor they wore. The first contractor fell two minutes into the battle. Another a minute later.

It was a massacre. The men fought hard, but for every rebel army crazy they killed, fifty, a hundred took his place. They were so outnumbered the rebels could have been armed with clubs and Flynn's men would have eventually succumbed.

Soon, all the Orion contractor IR signatures were still. Each contractor had a swarm of rebels around him and Lee realized with a sick lurch to his stomach that they were being ripped apart.

It had all happened so quickly, so unexpectedly, that there was silence at Orion headquarters. Then—"What the fuck happened there?" Clancy's rough voice screamed. "What did they do? Why didn't they just ride on through as quickly as possible? Did your drug rob them of intelligence? What the hell did you give them?"

Lee had an idea what had happened.

On the monitor, rebel army members were filing out from under the canopy onto the open road. Lee suppressed the urge to vomit. Several were prancing in the road, severed heads impaled onto their bayonets. They swarmed around the two trucks. The armored truck was impenetrable, but even if they could break into the back, the payload was in a titanium vault. It was safe from the marauders. But the diamonds were stuck on a road in the middle of the jungle, surrounded by heavily armed lunatics. They might as well have been on the back side of the moon.

The drug was too strong. The soldiers' enhanced aggression overwhelmed their desire to complete the mission. Which meant that SL-58 was unusable.

Flynn was breathing heavily and Lee wondered whether he was working his way up to a heart attack. They were looking down at a huge fortune in diamonds that was completely inaccessible.

"What was that?" Flynn rasped. "SL-58?"

"Yes," Lee said.

"You get me SL-59. Damn quick."

Chapter Five

Mount Blue

He sat back, narrow-eyed. Still and unmoving. The man known as Mac. Huge, unsmiling, grim. Scarred. Armed and lethal.

She'd realized who he was from the moment he'd whipped off her hood. Patient Number Nine's image of Mac had been that of a strong man with scars, but no details. That hadn't mattered at all. What Mac looked like made no difference. It was just externals. What mattered was *him*. The essence of him, and in that, Nine had been incredibly clear. Strong, hard, unyielding. Fiercely loyal, honest, just. A hard man, a tough enemy. No better friend.

She'd been almost certain before, but after touching him, all doubt evaporated. Everything Nine had communicated about Mac had been clear in the man she touched. She'd recognized it all instantly, like hearing the exact same chord of music heard the previous day. If he'd been a color, it would have been the exact same hue.

There was violence in him, too, though, and again she questioned her sanity in tracking this man down. She'd been compelled, that was true. But maybe she could have stopped herself somehow. Locked herself in her house and thrown the key out the window. Gone to the airport and taken the first flight out of the country, one way. Got herself arrested.

No. Her shoulders slumped just a little, then she straightened them. There was no force on earth that could have stopped her in her quest. She'd almost died in the car and maybe she'd die here, in this quiet room somewhere, wherever it was. But nothing could have kept her away. Even now the echoes of the compulsion she felt stirred in her blood.

The man's huge hands uncurled, the movement you'd make before reaching for something. Possibly that big black gun strapped to his right thigh.

The violence in the man sitting across from her was very real. She knew that loyalty burned bright in him but it wasn't loyalty to *her*. She watched him carefully but she knew that if he decided to move against her she could never be fast enough, strong enough to prevail. He could crush her head with one blow of those enormous hands.

"It's pointless insisting you're not Mac," she said quietly.

"Ah!" The noise came from deep in his chest, his huge hand lifted and swept the air. She recognized it as a gesture of frustration one second too late.

She flinched, bringing her arm up to shield her head. It was irresistible, unstoppable. Her heart had pumped out the blood in one liquid flash as her body flooded with panic. By the time she recognized that he'd punched nothing but air, she was hunkered down in the chair, instinctively trying to present as small a target as possible.

He growled. There was no other word for it. A low sound of disgust deep in that barrel chest.

She straightened slowly, trying to find enough air to say *sorry*, heart still pounding from the aftermath of blinding terror.

"I'm not going to hit you. I don't hurt women." He said each word clearly and they fell like rocks from his mouth, as if each one hurt.

And in a flash, Catherine understood. She had no idea whether the understanding came from some deep-seated emotion in him she'd felt on touching him and hadn't had time to analyze or whether it came from old-fashioned insight, but she'd touched some hidden nerve in him. Crossed an invisible but very real line.

Still . . . he looked so incredibly frightening. His size alone was enough to make you shrink back. Coupled with his scarred face and the smashed nose, he looked like someone you'd be terrified to meet in a dark alley.

Most people would instinctively react to him in fear, drawing back without knowing anything about him. Though there'd been the violence she'd sensed in him—dark swirls of it—and he'd killed, the violence was controlled by iron clamps. He wasn't a man to lose control. He wasn't a man to hurt the weak.

"I know that," she said gently, straightening up. She felt more than saw him relax a tiny bit. "I'm sorry I flinched. It was an instinctive reaction. I should have known better. You haven't hurt me up to now and . . ." She looked down at the tabletop, wondering if she could say it. She looked up, into hard, dark eyes. "When I touched you, I felt it, that you don't hurt women or children. Felt it very strongly. So I really don't have an excuse." She blew out a breath, opened her hand, the hand that had touched him. "None at all."

When she'd touched him, he'd been so easy to read. Unlike most people, he didn't have layer upon layer of self-serving nonsense, of hypocrisy, of self-indulgence and a total and utter lack of self-knowledge. He knew himself, inside out. His emotions had been clean, clear, even pure, even the dark ones. Nothing sick or psychotic at all.

She hoped. Catherine was flying on nothing but a wing and a

prayer here. The gift she'd fought all her life and that had reared up and bit her in the backside with Patient Nine was still a mystery to her.

Could she trust it?

Because the truth was, she was locked up here, with no idea at all of where "here" was. She was this man's prisoner. There were other people here, she was sure. If there were, they were his people. No one was going to rescue her. No one even knew where she was. *She* didn't know where she was. Even if she had a working cell phone, which she didn't, and she had someone to call for help, which she didn't, she didn't know where she was.

She was his prisoner and she had to take it on faith, faith in her despised gift, that he wasn't going to hurt her. Wasn't going to kill her.

He nodded once, dark eyes on her, and stood up abruptly.

"Come," he said, and walked toward the door.

Startled, Catherine rose and followed him. Just when she thought he'd smash his already smashed nose against the door, it whooshed open, and she walked out of the room, following those broad shoulders.

And stared.

The change in the air crossing the threshold had been like crossing from night into day. The air became cooler, fresher, with the slight tang of oxygen and the scent of a forest. They were on a corridor a couple of stories high overlooking a huge atrium. She grabbed hold of the top rung of the balcony and leaned forward.

It was such an extraordinary sight she had trouble processing what she was seeing. A huge vault with twinkling lights like stars. It took her a second or two to realize the lights were evenly spaced and artificial. The vault was transparent, like glass, only no glass she knew of could cover such a space and still keep the cold out.

Down below, two stories down, was a richness of glossy green plants crisscrossed by pathways, small lights threaded through the branches of trees and squat cylinders with glowing tops at five-foot intervals providing light.

It looked like a fairyland.

A couple of people were walking the paths, otherwise the area—as large as a mall parking lot—was deserted. But then again, it must have been well past midnight.

One guy two stories down was pushing a hand truck with boxes on it. He happened to look up, gave a two-fingered salute off his forehead, then disappeared into the greenery.

"It—it's beautiful," she breathed, then looked sharply up at Mac.

It was beautiful, but it was also hidden, as he wanted to remain hidden. It was a town, only a town turned inward, not outward. Tucked away, mysterious, remote.

Man, he was so going to zap her memories. This secret community was going to be MIB'ed away forever and she was sorry for that, because it was the most interesting place she'd ever seen.

A huge domed space with a lush park along the bottom, plants twining around the balconies ringing the area. Doors opened off the balconies. She had no idea if the rooms behind the doors were occupied or not. So far she'd seen exactly three people here. But what she saw was well-designed, well-tended, pristine.

Someone had to do that.

Two more people walked along a path, a man and a woman. The man looked up, did a little double-take at seeing her, then waved to Mac. He gravely dipped his head. They walked off, heads together, discussing something earnestly.

This was a community. People lived here, worked here. It was gorgeous and hidden and unlike anything she'd ever seen before. The huge black arching dome with the twinkling lights, the intense greenery, the curving balconies looking a little like the New York Guggenheim.

"So beautiful," she repeated in a whisper.

To her surprise, he answered her.

"Yeah." His big hands clutched the railing so hard the knuckles turned white, then lifted. "We want to keep it that way." He turned his head to her, look penetrating and hostile.

"Where are we? And what is this place?" She lifted her hands, palms out. The universal sign of surrender. No threat. No weapons. "You're going to MIB me anyway. Why not let me know where I am? There are obviously other people around. It's so well-cared-for, so well-planned. Down there it looks like a park. And all these doors . . . people live here. Work here. Cook here. That meal was, hands down, one of the best I've ever had. If that's the way you feed your prisoners, I'd love to know how you treat your citizens."

"You'd be surprised who the cook is."

Her eyes widened. It was the first thing he'd said to her that wasn't a question or a threat. For a second, she thought she saw astonishment on his face, too. That he'd talked to her openly.

But then she wouldn't remember any of this. She was going to have her brain zapped, poof, gone. She wouldn't miss the memory of sitting in her freezing car, waiting for death. And being scared nearly out of her wits at the huge man with the black ski mask rapping on her window. But the interrogation . . . she could admit to herself now how much Mac fascinated her. And this huge, gorgeous space under the dome, unlike anything she'd ever seen before. She was sorry that would have to go.

It had all been such a surprise. The name of the talented cook would be nothing in comparison. "Try me."

"You might have heard of her. Stella Cummings."

Catherine's jaw dropped. "Oh my gosh! Stella Cummings, the actress?"

He'd taken her utterly by surprise. Stella Cummings had been a child actor who'd won an Oscar at fifteen and another one at thirty. She'd been attacked by a stalker and had disappeared from view, completely. It was as if the earth had opened up and swallowed her whole. Online tabloids had an entire *Where is Stella Cummings?* industry going.

"I don't suppose—" This was so stupid. For all she knew she was going to be killed soon. And yet here she was, morphing into fangrrrl. "I loved her in *Dangerous Tides*. If she's around, could I meet her? If she doesn't want to talk about acting I can compliment her on her taco. It was great."

"Let's go." He took her elbow and started walking. Startled, she had to trot to keep up with his huge strides.

"Where are we going? Am I going to get to meet Stella Cummings?"

"No." His jaws clenched. "Maybe. Maybe tomorrow. Right now I'm taking you to your room."

He shut up after that and she couldn't pry another word out of him. Questions were useless and after a few minutes it took all her breath to keep up with him.

They circled the huge space until they were on the opposite side from the interrogation room and went down a story. He stopped in front of a door and touched a part of the wall that had no distinguishing characteristics. No buttons, no panel, nothing. But when he tapped a specific spot the door whooshed open.

He gestured with his hand and she moved toward the threshold gingerly, heart pounding. For just a second back there, she'd had the impression that he was . . . well, not softening toward her, but at least not hugely hostile. And she'd thought maybe they could sit down and talk things over now that she'd read him.

But no. He was ushering her into a dark prison cell. Four walls, no windows. Only blackness.

She walked in slowly, giving a quick glance back at the door. No internal handle. No way out.

A prison. A check of his dark eyes confirmed that.

Nobody on earth knew where she was and her lonely life was such that no one would think of looking for her. Maybe she was going to be left in this room to die. It wouldn't take much. Just leave her here until she rotted. No one to know, no one to care.

Just one woman, in a closed room, forgotten. Time passing. Dying locked up, alone, weaker and weaker until the darkness closed in.

Her throat tightened. Her chest wouldn't—couldn't—move.

He stepped behind her, that huge body almost pressing against hers. A huge force, pushing air ahead, forcing her to stumble another step inside. Farther from the door, farther from the light of the corridor.

She gasped in a breath, another. *I can't do this,* she thought. All her resources were gone. She was exhausted and terrified, a drumbeat of terror in her head. A dark tide of it, lapping higher and higher. Soon she would drown in it.

She stumbled another step forward, then turned, craning her head a little to look Mac in the face. She could barely make out his features in the backwash of light from the doorway.

She had to know, had to. Was she going to be closed up here and left to die?

"May I—may I touch you?" she gasped.

There was barely enough light to see his frown, his head jerking back in astonishment. Without waiting for an answer, she reached for his hand, clasping it in hers.

Heat. That was the first thing she perceived. His huge hand was hot, as if he were a radiator himself. Her own hands were chilled and the heat of his simply sank into her through the skin, sank deep into muscle.

And then—"Ah!"

She let his hand drop, missing the connection, the heat immediately.

No use clinging to him, to a man who distrusted her, who considered her a threat.

But who wasn't going to kill her. That had come through loud and strong. This wasn't going to be a permanent prison. However long she was going to be locked up, it wasn't going to be forever.

Or so she hoped.

Without a word, he stepped back beyond the threshold. The door whooshed closed and the room lit up. There was no specific source of light, no lamps and no fixtures. Just light.

The room was comfortably furnished, large and spacious. It had seemed sinister in the darkness but now that it was lit it was just an ordinary room, larger than most hotel rooms, with a queen-sized bed, a sitting area with two armchairs, a desk doubling as a table. A quick glance into the room beyond a door showed a very nice bathroom. Stocked, she could see, with a tall stack of blindingly white towels, a bar of soap and a brand-new ultrasound toothbrush.

Okay. A Hilton-level prison. She could do that.

To her surprise, she found the small bag she'd packed, just in case her quest required an overnight stay. She had her small cosmetics case, a nightgown, slippers.

A shower made her feel better, more human. She'd been on the road and on the run for almost twenty-four hours. She crawled into bed and stared at the ceiling,

Everything ached, everywhere, inside and out. Her body and her head and her heart. A wave of loneliness washed over her. Touching Mac had reassured her that he wasn't dangerous to her, not in the sense that she feared.

But . . . what did she know? Could she be sure? Her gift was so unreliable. Maybe she should have cultivated it instead of pushing it away with both hands, forcing it back into the deepest corners of her mind like a nasty, broken, misshapen twin of herself.

The gift had never been wrong, though it had so often been incomplete. Discerning top notes, the emotions of the moment, utterly missing crucial underlying emotions, because she didn't want to explore, couldn't stand delving into the truth of people. So she often got people wrong because she hadn't been able to discern tones and shadows underneath the strongest emotions.

Mac might not be planning her death, but he had no particular incentive to keep her safe, either. And yet . . . yet there'd been . . . *something.* Something there, something elusive. Some faintest feather tickling her mind, like a gentle finger touching her.

It felt like safety.

Was it real?

Probably not.

Why should this man care in any way for her? Anyone she'd ever dated considered her a freak. And sex . . . well, that never worked out well.

She was tired. Tired beyond today's stressful events. Tired of being who she was, tired of being pushed and pulled by things inside her she had no control over, tired of knowing things she shouldn't.

Tired . . .

The lights went suddenly out and she fell into a deep, dreamless sleep.

January 7

"Maybe I should just keep her locked up until she starves to death," Mac said sourly the next morning.

Nick and Jon didn't pay him any attention at all. They were riveted to the Hawk emblem, Jon studying it carefully, then passing it on to Nick.

Jon looked up briefly, white teeth flashing. "Nah. I'll bet you've already sent Stella to bring her breakfast."

Mac's teeth ground together. Busted.

Right now his prisoner was being tortured, lashed with the whip of the best breakfast ever cooked in the history of breakfasts.

Nick didn't look up from the Hawk. "Wouldn't be efficient. To kill her. Until we figure this thing out."

"Shit." Jon cocked his head as he stared at Nick. "More than ten words from Nick. All at once. I think that's a record, isn't it, Mac?"

Mac met Jon's eyes for a second. Nick had only been a team member for a week before the shit came down. He'd been introduced by Lucius—and goddamn, there it was again, that blow to the heart—as the sixth man after Randy Higgins had been lost in a HALO jump. Parachute malfunction two miles up was unforgiving.

Nick had quietly joined the team, doing exactly what he was told, efficiently and well, without speaking more than a word or two at a time. None of the Ghost Ops teammates had a life he could or would talk about, but clues would come out. Mike Pelton's southern accent. Jon's California Surfer Dude drawl. Rolf Lundquist's love for skiing and intimate knowledge of the Rockies.

Not Nick. He could have been hatched in a lab for all the clues he gave to his past.

"Fuck off, Jon," Nick said unexpectedly, and it was so unusual for him to react that Jon blinked and shut up.

Nick had been scrutinizing every molecule of the Hawk. He finally placed it carefully down on the table and looked up, meeting Jon's eyes, then Mac's.

"It's real. And it's his."

Mac nodded. He'd come to the same conclusion himself.

"Yeah? And so?" Jon finally broke the silence. Surfer Dude didn't do too well with silence when they were off an op.

Nick frowned. Expressions on his dark face were even rarer than words.

Jon turned the emblem over in his hand. "I mean—if this is real, then—then Lucius what? Gave it to the woman? Instead of lazing about in his villa on Capo Verde or Bali he's in a lab in Palo Alto with his ass hanging out? Does that sound real? Is that even possible?"

"I didn't know him like you two did. Never really had a chance to. So I don't know, but . . ." Man, Nick was on a roll. Several sentences. "Could it be we're wrong about him?"

"You mean about what went down?" Mac asked harshly.

Nick nodded.

Mac and Jon exchanged glances. Jon had been as devastated as Mac. Like Mac, he'd considered Lucius a surrogate father and had taken the betrayal hard. Nick had simply gone into stoic mode, the betrayal one more shitty thing in a shitty world. It had brought Mac and Jon nearly to their knees.

"Mac?" Jon asked. "You think—"

Mac shook his head sharply. He didn't know. The betrayal had been bad enough. The idea that Lucius might have been betrayed himself, might be in serious danger . . .

"It depends on the woman." Nick seemed to be the only one who could think clearly about this. He turned to Mac. "Looker like that, I think you should interrogate her more fully." And then, to Mac's astonishment, Nick grinned. It lasted just a second and then Nick's features rearranged themselves into his usual stony façade, but it had been there.

Jon picked up on it. "Yeah, man. Interrogate her. Get to the bottom of this. The front, too." He waggled his eyebrows. "Hands-on interrogation, if you get my drift."

"Idiots," Mac growled. But he'd had a punch to the chest at the thought of putting his hands on her, dammit. That mass of shiny hair, the silver gray eyes and vulnerable expression blossomed in his head and something stirred throughout his body. Stirred south of the border, too. Shit. He started getting a chubby and had to will it down.

That shocked him. He was a focused man, all business, all the time. Sex had its place, a narrow enclosed space, usually bar to bed, couple of hours max. Then back to business.

The woman was fucking with his head. He'd thought of her all night, dammit, and not in a strategic way. Nope. Not focusing on her story, pulling it this way and that looking for holes, which is what he would have done with anyone else.

All night he'd stared at the ceiling, wide-eyed, remembering that burst of heat rushing through his veins at her touch. He'd never taken drugs. His entire childhood had been spent around people who retreated into drugs to wipe out their reality. He was thirty-four and he was sure that most of the people he'd known as a child were either dead or wished they were. So no, drugs had held no appeal. He didn't want to die, he wanted to live, fiercely. He always had.

But one kid had explained to him the rush of heroin as it hit the system. The kid rented his ass out on a nightly basis to get it and hated himself 23/7. That one hour of heroin was worth it—worth the pain and degradation. Worth being treated like butcher's meat. Worth being beaten and abused every night. He'd said that when the drug entered him, all the bad things went away and it was like being in heaven, if heaven existed.

Well, fuck it if that wasn't a pretty good explanation of what had happened when Dr. Catherine Young touched him. A rush. A rush like nothing he'd ever felt before. Like having his heart stroked by gentle hands. Like having his mind invaded by an angel.

He wanted to snort. Angels. There were no angels in this world and there was no other world. Angels didn't exist, and no one had stroked his heart. Not that he had one anyway.

Damned if he understood what had happened, though. *Something* had. Something huge and scary.

She'd pulled this stuff on him out of thin air. How had she done it? Maybe it was like those magicians onstage who pulled up a member of the audience and asked them to think of a number and write it down. He'd always suspected those acts to be pure bluffs and the members of the audience part of the act.

But what Catherine Young had said had been, terrifyingly, the pure truth. She'd read him. Nailed him, like a butterfly to the board.

Mac wasn't used to being seen, understood. He was used to

being obeyed. The men under him in Ghost Ops knew damn all about him and that was the way he liked it. The only person to have a slight insight into him had been Lucius and already that had made him uncomfortable.

Even now, even in exile, Nick and Jon and the rest of the small community they seemed to be building knew him as a tough, strong leader with no chinks in his armor, nothing there to hang on to but a big, hard, shiny surface.

So being understood like that—it was scary. Even scarier was that he'd liked it, for that short burst of time in which she'd touched him. Before his head could catch up to what she was doing.

It had been like a shot of heroin to his system, and like any addict, now he craved it. He'd spent the night thinking of it—thinking of *her.* Remembering that soft touch, the rush of warmth spreading in an instant from her hand to his entire body, zinging through his veins.

She'd . . . glowed, while touching him. Like some unearthly creature. As if there were a thousand-watt lamp inside her beaming light and warmth. In that instant, she'd been impossibly beautiful, the most beautiful woman in the world. Some enchantress from another planet, too delicate and beautiful for this one.

That hadn't lasted. When she'd broken the connection it was as if something had broken inside her. That pale skin no longer glowing but ashen. Shadows under those beautiful eyes. Nostrils pinched and pale.

That had kept him awake, too, because the glowing fairy princess from Planet Zog had been fascinating but the vulnerable, fragile woman who'd sprinkled fairy dust over him and paid a price for it nearly broke his heart.

He'd had to fist his hands to keep from putting his arms around her. He, Mac McEnroe, balls-to-the-wall tough guy who could and had watched enemies die by his hand without blinking, had been about to put his arms around a potential enemy. A completely unknown entity, who had somehow found them in their hideout. Someone who could put his community in jeopardy.

"Okay," he said, putting on his war face, making his voice cool. "I'm going to see what else I can get out of her."

Nick gave a curt nod, turned away and picked up the Hawk again.

Jon grinned and made kissy noises.

Mac flipped him the bird and walked out.

Chapter Six

Arka Pharmaceuticals Headquarters
San Francisco

The next morning, a vein in Lee's temple started throbbing. He looked at the attendance sheet for work at the Millon facility. Dr. Catherine Young had not clocked in for the second day in a row.

He'd sent the Africa footage to the three research scientists at the Palo Alto Millon lab who were part of the complete protocol. Even so, they didn't have the full picture, of course. All they knew was that they were engaged in secret military research beyond their normal duties. And that they were earning $100K a year more than the regular research scientists. They had no clue that Lee had another agenda entirely, which was, of course, perfect.

The day Lee defected back to the mainland with a complete program to turn the Red Army into history's greatest military machine, he'd leave behind a charred corpse in his car at the bottom of a ravine and clues that would implicate the three scientists in treason.

He was so damned close and yet so far! The Orion Africa debacle was going to set him back by months. His new life was dancing out of his grasp.

He tapped a holographic image of a lock and key on the monitor to his right. It immediately dissolved into Baring's bullet head.

"Sir?"

"Dr. Catherine Young hasn't come in to work this morning, either. Check hospitals within a hundred-mile radius and check police reports. Break into her home and see what you can find and make sure she knows we looked. Report back in an hour."

"Sir."

Lee drummed his fingers on the shiny teak desktop, jaws clenched as he thought.

What had happened to Young? Had she been mugged, had she had a car accident, was her lifeless body at the morgue? That would be very unfortunate, as she seemed to have an almost uncanny ability to understand the workings of all the iterations of SL on the human mind and was able to make an fMRI sing. If anyone could tweak the molecule, give them another iteration, it was Dr. Young.

She was the very best imaging analyst he'd ever come across. At times it seemed to him that she could look at an fMRI and figure out what the patient ate for breakfast. In her hands, each image yielded so much data they were creating the fullest map of the human brain in existence.

Why wasn't she at work? The woman who was all work and no play?

She had no friends among her coworkers, and the baseline vetting his security staff had done on her hadn't turned up a large number of friends. Any friends at all, actually.

She seemed to be wedded to her work, arriving early, leaving late. She showed no signs of political awareness or even unusual interest in the company she worked for.

No, Lee decided. She wasn't spilling her guts to the FBI right now. Something must have happened to her. Had she spent the night with someone and was still there? Somehow Lee doubted that. She seemed as sexless as she was friendless.

It had been a real selling point with him.

He regretted bitterly his decision not to place tracers in the cars of his top research staff.

The instant Young showed up, a company transponder was going into her car, one that wouldn't turn off when the car was turned off. Or better yet, Baring would slip into her bedroom, anesthetize her, and inject minute traces of a radioactive isotope with a specific signature into her. She'd never know, and they'd know her whereabouts at all times.

And when SL-59 was complete, tested and flawless, when it had been delivered to the People's Liberation Army, Young would be slated for destruction. Together with Clancy Flynn, she would be the only one who could recognize what had happened to the soldiers of the PLA. They both had to be silenced. The loss of one blowhard former general and one mere woman was nothing in comparison to the plan.

Catherine leaned forward on her elbows, fascinated. "Come on, Stella. Tell me the truth. Is Gary Hopkins a good kisser?"

God, *that scene*. The world's most famous kiss, an iconic image, on the poster of *The Hunter.* Stella and Gary being pulled apart by enemies, their only point of contact lips locked in a kiss.

Catherine put down her perfect cup of coffee next to the plates which had once held a perfect stack of blueberry pancakes and a perfect whites-only cheese omelette, and the bowl which had once held perfect homemade yogurt with a dollop of perfect homemade strawberry jam.

It was more food than she'd been able to consume in one meal for as long as she could remember. She'd eaten every delicious bite and had scraped the bowl of yogurt, making an embarrassing sound.

It was, hands down, the best breakfast she'd ever eaten, and that included in France. But now that she was replete, fascination with the woman sitting across from her held her in its grip.

Stella Cummings, once the most famous actress in the world, who'd commanded $20 million a picture, whose face had graced a thousand gossip magazines, who'd been a celebrity almost as long as she'd been alive until she'd disappeared from the public eye.

That woman had been a fashion plate, waif-thin and blindingly beautiful. Remote, untouchable. Perennially unsmiling and gorgeous in the pictures of her on the red carpet or in the tabloid snapshots. A twenty-first-century Greta Garbo, only thinner.

The Stella that sat across from Catherine was a healthy-looking woman who was no longer beautiful and laughed constantly.

Her face had been savagely slashed then carefully put together again by a master plastic surgeon, but nothing would ever make her beautiful again. Catherine forgot the scars ten seconds after Stella had knocked on her door bearing a tray of delicious-smelling food.

Stella gave a lopsided smile and rolled her eyes. "Gay, honey."

Catherine's eyes bugged. "Gary Hopkins is *gay*?"

"As a plaid suitcase. Like Lawrence Rome. The two actually dated."

"Man." Catherine sat back. Gary Hopkins and to a lesser extent Lawrence Rome were the epitome of macho. Ripped and brooding. Gary had personally saved Planet Earth by his courage and ability with humongous weaponry in *Deadly Evil*. "Makes a girl think, doesn't it? Though I suppose he was too good-looking to be straight."

They both turned as the door to Catherine's room whooshed open.

"Speaking of good-looking men," Stella said as Mac walked in.

He gave her the hairy eyeball, but she responded with a sunny smile.

Catherine could barely move. The instant Mac filled the doorway, her muscles were paralyzed, the breath left her body, her palms started sweating. Though her muscles were in lockdown, inside she was a riot of boiling emotions she could barely understand and couldn't control.

He fascinated her.

That über-male thing made up of long, lean muscles, shoulders out to here, huge, capable hands that looked like they could snap a man's neck in two and then repair a tank. He made Gary Hopkins look like a cocker spaniel.

Then there was the fear thing. She'd touched him and had felt that he didn't plan on killing her. Today. But her gift was uneven, unreliable, incomplete, and she knew he had violence in him. Violence he could wield like a surgeon, but still.

She could very well be wrong. The expression on that flat, ugly yet compelling face was stony. There was danger in every single line of his big body and she had no guarantees that the danger wasn't to herself.

And then there was the attraction thing. Last night she'd been exhausted, frightened out of her mind, in the iron grip of her compulsion. But now, rested and refreshed, the sudden appearance of Mac made her heart leap in her chest. Part of it was the fear and part was the fascination, but a goodly portion of it was sheer old-fashioned sex.

He turned her on.

It happened to her so seldom she barely recognized it as something belonging to her. The whole sex thing was so incredibly fraught with problems, whole thorny forests of problems, she'd more or less given up on it.

Her body hadn't. It was as if her body had been quietly lying in wait to jump for something it wanted and it turned out what her body wanted was Mac. She shuddered. This wasn't just inappropriate, like getting a crush on your married dentist or your banker. This was dangerous. Because the man who walked in, swept the room with a fierce scowl and stood there like an immovable force of nature, was terrifying.

She had no idea of his background but he looked like a soldier, and not the ceremonial kind who stood around in a fancy uniform with a long, shiny sword and who knew how to snap out a salute. No, he looked like Special Forces. The kind of guys who came in under cover of darkness, snapped necks rather than salutes, then left quietly before you even knew they were there.

He distrusted her. That had been made very clear. He distrusted her, didn't believe her story, half suspected she'd been sent to spy on him.

What a terrible trick biology had played on her that this man—huge, dangerous, a man who didn't trust her—was the one man she had a violent sexual reaction to.

It was explicit, too, which terrified her. It wasn't a generic attraction, the kind you'd feel for some good-looking man who crossed your path, even though Mac was the furthest thing possible from good-looking.

This man, this particular man with the muscles and the scowl and the scarred face, he was the one she reacted to as if her body had been waiting all its life for him and him alone.

Her brain telling her body *forget it* didn't work.

Her heart was pounding so hard she thought she'd crack a rib. She didn't dare move, didn't dare speak, because then he'd know she'd started trembling the instant he appeared at the door.

Oh God.

Heat blossomed between her thighs and she was shocked to feel her vagina clench once, very hard, just as it did in her infrequent orgasms. Her chest was tight, yes, but her breasts felt swollen, heavy. Most shocking of all was a weak, trembly feeling, as if all he had to do was hold out one big hand and she'd run straight to him.

That was the scariest thing of all. She couldn't throw herself at him because he wouldn't catch her.

He might end up shooting her, actually.

Mac looked around at the ruins of breakfast, then pinned her and Stella with a hard look. He addressed Stella. "You about done here?"

"Yes, I'm fine, thank you, Mac. Thank you for asking." Stella tilted her head and studied him. "Always a pleasure to be around a man who minds his manners."

His jaw muscles worked so hard his temples moved. Catherine would bet that anything that made the temperomandibular joints work so hard had to hurt the teeth.

That stony face showed no expression at all. Catherine wondered at Stella, who seemed to be totally indifferent to his mood.

"Stella," Mac growled.

"Mac . . ." she answered, in an exaggerated imitation of his growl. To Catherine it seemed like baiting a bear, but Stella just looked exasperated, not frightened.

There was a stalemate of some kind. Catherine could practically see the lines of male and female will crossing. Amazingly, Stella won.

She pointed to the coffeepot. "Coffee? I still have enough for a cup."

He hesitated, but Stella went ahead and got a cup from a cabinet. To Catherine's surprise, there was a full complement of teas, a small sink and a microwave inside the cabinet. If she'd known, she'd have made herself a cup of tea last night.

Stella poured Mac a cup and handed it to him. "There you go, black no sugar. Just like your heart."

Mac put the cup down on the table hard enough for a couple of drops of coffee to slosh over the edge. "Goddammit, Stella—"

"No, you listen to me, Mac. Do you realize that this woman—" She made a graceful move indicating Catherine, reminding her all over again that Stella had once been one of the greatest actresses in the world. "Do you know she thought she was a *prisoner* last night?"

Catherine made a sound, choked off before it could make its way from her throat to her mouth. She tried to hunker, to become invisible. Stella turned to her. "Didn't you?" she demanded hotly.

Mac was looking at her narrow-eyed, face of stone. Oh God. She nodded, throat too tight to talk. It hadn't even occurred to her that she wasn't a prisoner.

"Well, you weren't," Stella said. "I can't believe he'd make you think that for *one second*. This community doesn't do prisons."

Her eyes were the same eyes that had burned from the screen. Wide, pale blue, almost transparent, still beautiful and expressive, notwithstanding the scar that slashed from the right eyebrow to the edge of a sharp cheekbone, barely missing the eyeball. Those eyes had been magnificent on the screen but were even more powerful in real life. "She wasn't a prisoner. Was she, Mac? You tell her she wasn't locked up like an animal. And if you did lock that door you can forget about eating. Like, forever. You can cook your own damned meals from now on."

That grim face winced, as if in pain. Catherine understood completely. Now that she'd tasted Stella's cooking, banishment from her meals was indeed something to be feared.

"You weren't locked in." The words sounded forced. Painful to say.

Catherine shuddered. *She hadn't been locked in last night.* Those miserable hours huddled in on herself, wondering if she would ever be let out of the room—that hadn't been real?

She stared at Mac. He stared back.

"Oh Christ," Stella said, and uncurled her long legs from around the chair legs and stood up. She marched over to the door and slapped a spot to the right of the door, halfway up. "There's a slight indentation. Press it and the door opens. Press it twice and it locks. Come try it."

Keeping a wary eye on Mac, Catherine walked to the door. Stella took her hand and pressed her fingers to the wall. It wasn't visible to the eye but it was clear under her fingers. A slight round indentation. She pressed it and the door whooshed open and that fresh plant smell filled the room.

"See? Not a prisoner." Stella was much taller than Catherine and looked over her head to Mac. "Not only is she not a prisoner, but I think she's found her way to us. I think she is one of us."

Catherine had no idea what Stella meant but Mac did. He winced again and shook his head. Stella sighed. "Christ, Mac, you're hopeless. Go on. Show our guest around."

"All right." If his jaw got any tighter, the skin over his cheeks would crack.

Stella turned to Catherine. "See you for lunch. I'm making radicchio risotto and pear tart. I make a mean risotto if I do say so myself. You'll like it."

"I bet I will. And for the record, I love risotto," Catherine said fervently. "I'm looking forward to it." She watched with a touch of unease as Stella left. As long as she was in the room, there was an air of . . . normality. Three people, talking.

With Stella gone, Catherine was left with this mountain of a grim-faced man who seemed to dislike her and yet who turned her on so much she couldn't think straight.

God, what a miserable combination. The worst.

She was in this strange building at his complete mercy. The door might or might not have been locked last night, but the fact was she wouldn't have dared to leave the room to wander around even if she hadn't been locked in. Even supposing she'd found a way out, they were still in the mountains, far from any town. If she'd tried to escape, she'd have frozen to death.

So she was a prisoner in fact, though one who was being exceedingly well-fed.

He was staring at her, no clue whatsoever as to what might be going through his mind, though it didn't look like anything good.

"I'm supposed to show you around," he said, his voice a low rumble. "So let's go." He stepped back and opened a huge hand.

O-kay.

Might as well fall down that rabbit hole. Catherine stepped out, crossing the big corridor outside the door and leaning against the railing.

Wow. What a rabbit hole, leading straight into Wonderland. Gripping the railing hard, she stared.

Last night she'd been too exhausted and too terrified to really take it all in, but now in the full light of day she saw . . . a city. Some kind of underground city, hidden from the world, stretched out before her. Buildings amid lush greenery, people walking with purpose on the brick and stone pathways. Someone sweeping away leaves, someone else opening doors, putting out two tables . . . a café! Sure enough, a man and a woman sat down and a waiter came out and took an order.

More people started crisscrossing the area below, some following the paths, some cutting across, as people did. Everyone who looked up saw Mac and waved. A couple of men gave a sort of ironic salute.

She glanced up at Mac, saw his nods and realized that she was indeed inside a community and Mac was their king. Or at least their leader.

And no matter how forbidding he looked, no one cowered. The salutes and waves were cheery and informal.

More and more people were pouring into the commons area below. Some had specific tasks—sweeping the paths, taking something from here to there.

The sky above was bright blue. If she hadn't seen it last night, she wouldn't have imagined that overhead was a huge glass dome. She'd have thought the city open to the elements. And yet what she knew was a dome was completely transparent.

"Where are we? What is this? If it's a city, it's one I haven't heard about. A city carved out of a mountaintop. Or rather in a mountaintop."

The look he gave her was sharp. She shrugged. "We traveled uphill. That's the only thing I know about where we are. I'm surprised I haven't heard about this place."

"Don't be surprised. We designed it to be off the map and off the grid."

Catherine blinked. "Off the *grid*? You mean nobody knows you're here? But—" Her mind whirred. "I mean modern towns need infrastructure, connection to the electricity grid, water mains, the internet . . ."

"We are completely self-sufficient." Mac's face gave nothing away, but she could detect a note of pride. "We have our own electricity." He looked up and, startled, Catherine looked up, too. "That dome? It looks transparent but it's not. It's graphene, one of the strongest materials on earth, one molecule thick. There are tiny solar panels embedded in the dome. We have plenty of energy. And water. We have our own internet infrastructure and our own food supply."

"The entire community must want fiercely to be off the grid. Who are they?"

He stood staring down into the huge atrium, muscles working in his jaw. It looked like he was literally chewing on his words. Three people crossing a grassy area looked up and waved. He nodded curtly.

"Mac?" Catherine hesitated, then put her hand gently on his forearm. It was covered by his fleece sweatshirt. The only thing she felt was hard, warm muscle. And a shiver running through her system.

He jerked and she pulled her hand away as if she'd touched a hot stove. Regretting her instinctive move the instant she'd made it. Nobody liked to be "read" by her. Why could she never remember that?

"Sorry," she whispered.

He shrugged. Clutched the railing with white knuckles and looked out over his domain.

She had no idea where this compulsion came from but she had to know about this place. A place she'd never heard of and could barely even imagine existed, though she was looking right down at it. A place out of space and time.

"Why do you want or need to stay off the grid?" Her voice was low because her throat was tight. It almost hurt to get the words out and if she hadn't burned with the need to know she wouldn't have asked the question.

He looked down for several minutes. Another person looked up and waved. The pathways below were busy with people bustling to and fro. Very few couples. No children at all.

He wasn't talking, though judging from the bulging jaw muscles, the words were right there in his mouth.

She swallowed. "Remember, Mac, you're going to MIB me. Whatever you tell me will be lost to me, forever. I'm a neuroscientist and I can tell you that memories after administration of Lethe are physically lost, together with a few million neurons. So there's no way I could talk, ever."

She eyed him hungrily, happy he wasn't looking at her. The memory of Mac McEnroe would be lost to her, too. She'd never had a physical reaction like this to any man in her life before and it was possible she never would again. Even the memory of her body heating up, of the shivers of recognition and danger and desire would be lost forever.

"Mac?" She tried again. "It seemed as if Stella wanted you to talk to me. She said something about me joining the community. I guess she meant the community here?"

He closed his eyes as if in pain and took in a deep breath. Wow. She'd touched a nerve, a painful one.

Well, of course.

Catherine Young didn't do communities. She was always rejected like foreign tissue. In her family, in the small town in Massachusetts she grew up in, in college and graduate school, at her first job in Chicago. By the time she got her current job she didn't even try to fit in. She just went in to work, did her job, went home. Any attempts at joining groups inevitably failed.

Different, different. She was *different*.

Never mind. She'd formulated the words in her head but they hadn't left her mouth when he turned fully to her, eyes pinned to hers. And to her vast shame, having him look at her so intensely made her knees weaken. She had to consciously stiffen them to stay upright.

This was terrible. Her own body was rebelling against her, turning her weak when she should be strong. Mac waved a big hand at the scene below. An elderly gentleman saw, thought Mac was waving at him and waved happily back.

"This was originally a silver mine. It was panned out and abandoned way back in the 1950s. I knew about it because I grew up in a series of foster homes down in the valley. They weren't the kind of foster homes that kept a close eye on their kids. All they kept their eye on were the bank accounts, to make sure the state paid on time. When I was fourteen, I found a motorcycle abandoned in the junkyard. I'm good with my hands. I scrounged parts, built it up. Spent the next four years until I joined the military exploring. Found this place. When we needed a hideout, I brought us here."

He needed a hideout? Catherine didn't go there. Of course he needed a hideout. This *was* a hideout, like the famous Hole-in-the-Wall in the Wild West. A place where, if you could find it, if you could make your way there, you'd be safe.

She looked around, then back at the man who was watching her so steadily. "You did some work." That was an understatement. What she was seeing wasn't an abandoned mine. It had been turned into a high-tech town.

"Yeah." One side of his hard mouth turned up and it took her a second to recognize it as a smile. A smile seemed like the furthest possible thing his face could do, something completely alien to it. And yet—and yet it was a nice smile, small though it was. "We had to."

He stopped, head cocked, and tapped his ear.

"Yeah," he said suddenly. "Roger that. Coming right now." And he grabbed her elbow and started walking, grim-faced once more.

Smiling time was over, evidently. And whatever had happened, it involved her. She looked up at him, searching for clues. His face was so hard, so remote. Nothing at all could be read there.

Catherine trotted to keep up with him, wondering whether she was moving to her doom. If she was, she was moving toward it fast.

They walked along the corridor until they came to the glass-enclosed elevator. It whooshed down so quickly and silently it was almost like flying, opening onto the floor of the atrium.

Mac took one of the pathways and Catherine followed. It was like plunging into a forest. The greenery was even denser than it appeared from above, a thick green canopy that wouldn't be out of place in Amazonia. The air here felt cooler, smelled incredibly fresh, as if it were the outdoors instead of in some kind of high-tech cavern.

It wasn't just a city park, a pretty break in a wall of buildings like most city parks were. It felt primal, not decorative. Utilitarian, all that beauty a side effect. Every now and again she saw signs of small-scale cultivated crops. A pumpkin patch with plump orange pumpkins the size of boulders. Another small patch of artichokes. They passed a grove of oranges that smelled divine, rushing past it so fast she barely had time to smell it.

Again, everyone they met waved hello to Mac and looked curiously at Catherine being tugged along. The looks weren't hostile in any way. Just curious. One man dressed in work clothes with a tool kit belt tried to stop Mac, who rotated his index finger—*later*—and whizzed past.

They pulled up in a side corridor where Mac ran full tilt toward a white door. Catherine was about to shout at him to stop when the door slid open at the last second. She rushed through it behind him and it slid closed behind her the moment she crossed the threshold.

Chapter Seven

Arka Pharmaceuticals Headquarters
San Francisco

"Still gone, boss." Baring was reporting from outside Catherine Young's home, a very modest bungalow not far from University Drive.

"Video," Lee replied, and a holo appeared in front of him. The outside was unassuming. Real estate prices were extremely high in the area and young professionals couldn't afford much more than what Catherine had rented. "Get inside."

Baring picked her lock and entered.

Interesting.

The outside was bland, but Young had turned the inside of her home into a jewel.

Very interesting.

Lee had always considered Young an excellent researcher with nothing else to her. He had his security team check everyone's finances as a matter of course, with a bot checking for unusual income or expenditures. Young's finances had never triggered a trip wire, ever. Her only income was her salary, and she saved 10 percent of it regularly, the rest going to normal expenditures and the maximum allowed in the company 401(k) plan.

Young was the most talented and least interesting of his employees. No boyfriends, few social contacts, no vices.

Maybe the inside of her house could be considered a vice. It was decorated to within an inch of its life. Lee was impressed and a little uneasy. A hidden artistic streak was out of character for Young. He'd have felt better if the house had been as bland as she was. As she appeared to be.

The inside of her house was such a jewel he wondered uneasily what else Catherine Young might have hidden from him.

"Got something, boss." Baring and his two colleagues had cleared each room, finding nothing. Now they were in her bedroom. Baring stood at her bed. The tiny but powerful video camera mounted on his shoulder showed Lee exactly what Baring was seeing.

Young had a big down-filled emerald green comforter on her bed. Next to the edge was a square indent, the size and shape of a small carry-on suitcase. Some neatly folded clothes lay on the comforter as well. Clothes that had been discarded.

Young had packed a bag for a trip.

Scenarios raced through Lee's mind. He was almost certain no information had been stolen from the lab because they had stringent security measures in place. No researcher was allowed to take data home with them. That didn't mean she hadn't figured out a way to smuggle data out. He was now faced with a very tedious security inventory that would interrupt work flow and slow his schedule down. Not to mention the fact that their best scientist was now gone, perhaps selling secrets to third parties or the U.S. government or the Iranians.

She was, of course, a dead woman walking, but first they needed to find her.

"I want you to go through her house inch by inch and I want some information on where she's gone by the time you're done. Is that clear?"

Baring nodded. "Yeah. How careful do we have to be?"

Lee thought of all the trouble Young was causing him at a very delicate moment in the project. "Take the place apart if you have to," he said.

"Yeah, boss." Baring turned away.

Morrison was checking her laptop, and Lee could hear breakage in what he supposed was the kitchen and he watched for a moment as Baring began methodically slashing all soft surfaces in her bedroom. Cushions, pillows, comforter, mattress. Then he began taking apart a dresser drawer.

It had beautiful lines, what the Americans called Shaker furniture. Lee was a man who appreciated simplicity, beauty. Pity. Still, if there was anything hidden in it, Baring would find it.

He listened and watched for a moment more. "Don't come back here until you can tell me where she is," he told Baring, and pressed a button.

The hologram winked off.

Chapter Eight

Mount Blue

"Sitrep," Mac barked, asking for a status update, coming to a halt. Catherine skidded to a stop behind him, panting, resisting the urge to plant her hands on her thighs and lean over, gasping for breath. *He* wasn't winded. His deep, low voice contained a note of menace. "What the fuck is so urgent I had to come running and bring her?" He shot a thumb in her direction.

There were two men in the room, some kind of high-tech paradise. There were monitors everywhere, most the fancy, very expensive hologram type. There must have been fifty of them. Her company lavished money on its equipment and even she didn't have this kind of computing and screen power. She saw other equipment, some she recognized, some she didn't. There must have been a million dollars' worth of gear in the room.

There were two men in the room, sitting on transparent Ergonos, the most expensive office chairs on earth. She'd asked for one but it had been denied in the last budget round. She'd even contemplated buying one for herself but they cost more than her car.

Though invisible, they were made of some kind of material that molded itself to each body that sat in it, programmed to provide exactly the right kind of support precisely where it was needed.

The two men in the room looked as if they were sitting on air but there was nothing delicate about them. One dark, one blond. Both looked tough, no-nonsense. The blond one was manipulating images so quickly she could barely grasp what was showing on them, flicking them away with movements of his fingers, like a keyboard artist playing some arcane tune.

Though there was one image . . . then it was gone.

They both turned to look at her and here, too, she saw stone faces. Completely without expression.

The dark one stood, moved away from the Ergono. He gestured with his hand. "Have a seat, Dr. Young."

She looked up, startled. He wasn't quite as tall as Mac but he was still much taller than she was. "I'm afraid you have me at a disadvantage, Mr. . . ."

"Nick." His voice was low. Abrupt. "Please sit. We've got something to show you."

Show her? She sat and nearly moaned at the absolute comfort of the chair. It was important not to look down because she'd see herself ostensibly sitting on thin air. Some got so dizzy they couldn't use Ergonos.

"We're here," Mac said. "*She's* here. So what is it that couldn't wait?"

"I set up a bot, boss," the blond one said. He looked like a surfer who killed. Sun-streaked hair, colorful Hawaiian shirt with golden parrots and acid green palm trees, and a shoulder holster. "On principle. Just a little program set to notify me if anything of interest happened at 27 Sunset Lane in Palo Alto. Set it up last night."

Catherine gasped. "That's my address!"

"Yes, it is." Mac nodded at the surfer. "So?"

"Yeah, well Dr. Young here doesn't believe in security apparently." The surfer shot her a disapproving look, blue-green eyes narrowed in disapproval. "Not one vidcam, not one. And your lock is crap."

She was being criticized! Catherine drew in an outraged breath. "First of all, the house isn't mine, it's a rental, so elaborate security systems would be a waste of money. And that lock isn't crap! I had it changed when I moved in! And I'll have you know it's top of the line."

The surfer looked at Mac. "A Stor lock."

Mac made a disgusted sound in his throat.

Surfer Dude continued. "So though the good doctor here lives in trust of her fellow man, it's a good thing her neighbors don't. There are vidcams both in the house across the street and the house across the backyard. I hacked them and fiddled with the settings so we had front and back views and set up another bot to send a signal if there was movement at number 27, and sure enough, here's what I recorded ten minutes ago." He flicked two fingers and a hologram appeared in front of her.

Her sharp intake of breath sounded loud in the room. The images were silent but eloquent.

A bald man, not tall but broad-shouldered, dressed in black, leading two other men up the small walkway to her front door. They buzzed once, twice. Waited.

"You know them?" Mac asked quietly behind her.

"The man ringing my doorbell is Cal Baring. He's head of security for Millon. I've seen the other two around, but I don't know their names."

Baring made the researchers' lives almost impossible with his constant demands for security. All in-house phone conversations were recorded, which made communication dull and stilted. The protocol for entering and leaving the research labs was so tedious no one left the premises during work hours, ever.

Catherine had worked in Boston, which had a miserable climate compared to Palo Alto, but researchers often stepped out into the company park for a breath of fresh air and a break. Not at Millon. At times she felt like a prisoner.

Baring himself was a humorless thug.

He moved his head a few inches left and right, his hands worked at waist level, and . . . her front door opened. To anyone not paying attention, it would look exactly as if he'd opened it up with a key.

Baring and his goons walked in, bold as you please.

"Hey!" Catherine reached forward, her hand passing through the hologram. It was so clear and perfect she'd forgotten for a second she was watching something far away.

She had no idea how far away because she had no idea where she was.

"So much for top-of-the-line locks," Nick said, and the blond man clucked his tongue and shook his head. Clearly at her insanity.

"That was ten minutes ago," the blond said. "Now I'd really like to know what they're doing in there."

"So would I," Catherine said heatedly. "But unfortunately, if I didn't surround myself with paranoid security outside, I sure don't have a surveillance system inside my own home."

Surfer Dude cocked his head. "Hmm, I don't know about that. What's your email?"

She looked at the blond. "What?"

"Your email," he repeated patiently. "Because I have a little trick up my sleeve. But it has to be your personal email, not the company one."

"Cee-dot-young-at-gmail-dot-com."

"Do you use a desktop or a laptop at home?"

"Both, actually. A desktop in the guest bedroom which is my study and a laptop in the bedroom. We're not allowed to take our work laptops home. For security reasons." She steamed at the thought of Baring enforcing that rule while waltzing into her own home.

"Great." The blond was typing furiously. "Because I think we're gonna have to know what they're doing all through the house. So I will just work my magic, switch them on and . . . voilà!" he ended on a note of triumph.

It *was* magic, because there were two holograms, side by side. Like a 3D movie. One showing her bedroom, from the point of view of the table where her laptop sat, and the other in the study, looking out from the monitor of her desktop. Crystal-clear images of the three men, crossing back and forth.

Surfer Dude had somehow remotely switched on her computer webcams without activating the screens. That was seriously good hacking.

No sound, though. The men went about their business in complete silence.

No, wait. "Clear!" a voice shouted offscreen.

"Clear! Clear!" two other voices echoed.

The man in her bedroom was looking at her comforter, fingers tracing something.

"What's he doing?" she whispered.

"Something made a dent. He's tracing the edges," Mac said quietly behind her.

She swiveled her head and looked up at him blankly. This was so far outside her area of expertise, it felt like she really had fallen down that rabbit hole.

Baring fingered some clothes she'd left on the bed while packing and knowledge came to her in a sick rush. "He"—she swallowed heavily—"he knows I packed a bag."

"Bingo."

Baring cocked his head, eyes unfocused. She couldn't figure out what he was doing, then realized he was listening to an earbud. "Yeah, boss," he said, and pulled out a big black knife she hadn't even noticed.

"Boss?" Nick turned to her. "Who's his boss? Who does he mean?"

What was he doing with that knife?

"Huh? Oh. Well, technically, the CEO of our company, James Longman, is his boss. But he's away at a conference in Hong Kong. So I don't know who he's reporting to."

Baring held the knife by its haft, blade down. He lifted the knife over his head, bent slightly, and slashed a pillow on her bed. It was so outlandish a move that Catherine could only watch, blinking.

"Whoever he's reporting to is a real fuckhead," the blond said, anger in his voice. "Baring's been given orders to trash your house."

He *had*. Under Catherine's horrified gaze, Baring and his two men set about systematically vandalizing her home. They were very fast and very thorough. She watched as that black knife slashed every soft surface in her bedroom. There was nothing much in the study except a worktable and chair, so they hadn't gotten to it yet, but the sounds of broken crockery and splintered wood could be heard from the kitchen.

And soon enough, the sound of splintered wood came from the bedroom itself. Baring went through her Shaker chest of drawers, thoroughly, systematically, throwing everything on the floor, then pulled out all the drawers and tipped it over.

She gasped. The knife rose and fell and soon her lovely chest of drawers was shattered. He hunkered down on his haunches and went swiftly through the contents.

He rose and went to her closet. The door shielded him from view but there were ripping sounds and pieces of material floated in the air.

Catherine didn't have that much. She was a saver and had simple tastes. In the space of a quarter of an hour, as she watched, shaking, every single item she owned was sliced or shattered or crushed.

"Why on earth are they doing this?" she said finally, when she could form words around the dryness in her mouth.

"Looking for something," Nick said.

She swiveled to look at him. "Looking for something? Looking for what? What could I possibly have that would interest them? There's nothing valuable there at all. Certainly nothing that would warrant a scorched-earth search like that."

"They're looking for intel," Mac said behind her.

Nick and the blond man nodded grimly.

Intel—the military term for information. It confirmed a secret conviction she had that Patient Nine and these men were ex-military.

"On what?" Her mouth was numb. It was hard to articulate words. "There's nothing in my house to find."

"That's not what they think." The blond shot her an assessing look. "They clearly think there's something there. Something they want. Something they need. But . . . looks like they didn't find what they were looking for after all."

The frenzy of destruction was nearly over. No, she thought. It hadn't been a frenzy. That would imply emotion. It had been utterly cold and calculated.

It had been a declaration of war.

Baring and his two men stopped, conferring in the wasteland of her bedroom. They were speaking in low tones, heads together. Her computer microphone couldn't pick up what they were saying, but their body language was eloquent. Whatever it is they wanted from her, they hadn't got it.

Baring closed her laptop and they lost sight of him. There was a close-up of a goon fiddling near her desktop and the picture disappeared there, too. Her desktop had a mini quantum hard disk that was easy to detach.

They trooped out together from her bedroom into the living room and out the front door.

Surfer Dude flicked two fingers and a few seconds later the vidcam over the lintel of the Fredericksons' showed the three men walking quickly to a big black Compass and driving away. Baring was carrying her laptop and she had no doubt he also had her hard drive.

Good luck with that. She cleaned her hard drive every evening, storing everything in the cloud, access to the cloud only by an encrypted code she'd designed herself.

Mac spun her around in her chair and for a second she was dizzy, spinning on air. A complete metaphor for her life. Nothing underneath her, nothing holding her up.

"What's your take on this, Doctor?"

She thought, hard.

Everything had changed, on a dime. Like a supersaturated solution crystallizing in an instant.

These three tough men in the room with her had just become her friends and allies. She hoped. She had to stay here if Baring was after her. There was nowhere else for her to go, because if they were looking for her, no question, they'd find her. She didn't even remotely know which steps to take to disappear.

That cold, merciless destruction of her pretty little house, put together lovingly piece by piece, had been infinitely more frightening than if crazed methheads had entered her home with a pickax.

And—it suddenly occurred to her—Baring was backed up by one of the most powerful corporations in existence. Millon was partially owned by one of the largest companies in the world, Arka Pharmaceuticals. The head of research at Arka, Dr. Charles Lee, often showed showed up at Millon.

Baring would never pay for what he did. She knew enough to know how it worked. Millon and Arka both kept whole flocks of lawyers on call for just such things as this. Hard-pressed and money-starved local law enforcement officers would be no match.

"What's my take on this?" Her shoulders lifted and fell. She did it more to move her muscles than anything else, because she felt paralyzed by fear. Like some creature caught in headlights, knowing the oncoming truck was coming too fast to escape. Her muscles felt stiff and uncooperative, and she had to fight to keep from curling in on herself, just folding in, forgetting the whole outside world. "I have no idea. None. I have no idea what they were looking for, except that they didn't find it. Which means—"

"Which means they'll look again. Harder, this time. And if they can, they'll press *you* for answers. And press hard. Those aren't the good guys." Mac's voice was implacable.

She shivered, remembering Baring's stony, cruel face. "Yes, they will. And no, they're not."

"*We're* the good guys," Blondie said, pointing a thumb at his chest, then Nick. "Even big guy over here, no matter how scary he looks."

Mac looked over, just moving his eyes. Yes, he did look scary. She had to hope she'd read him correctly. She had no idea whatsoever what the other two men were like. All she had to go on were her animal senses, the instinctive low-level early warning system all reasonably attractive women developed in urban areas, and that system wasn't pinging.

"And a good thing, too," Blondie continued. "Because it looks like what that book said. You can't go home again."

The dark, quiet man—Nick—was even more explicit. "If you want your life back anytime soon, we'd better figure out what they want."

"You're safe here," Mac said quietly. "I'm still not too sure how you got here, but we're really hard to find. And as you know, we kill any vehicle getting within five miles of this place and kill their commo system, too."

She was having a delayed reaction. Her hands started shaking so hard she had to put them between her knees because though there were no crazy vibes coming from any of the three men, danger vibes were. Whether they were dangerous to her or not, they were clearly hard men, like soldiers or cops, only with something more. Tougher, less friendly.

Talk about being between a hard place and a rock. They had to believe she was harmless. Otherwise they'd MIB her and let her loose like a house-trained pet released into the jungle. She'd wake up somewhere with no knowledge of the past two or three days and no clue that Cal Baring and his goons were trying to track her down.

If she asked them not to take her memory away, that would raise suspicion like nothing else. Oh God. The thought of waking up in some hotel room with no memory, no way to defend herself . . .

A chilly wave rose up in her and she shivered, huddling in on herself. It was almost impossible to breathe; her chest would only do this jerky, raspy, panting thing. Spots danced before her eyes.

A huge, hard hand landed on her neck, pressed down until her head nearly met her knees.

"Breathe," a deep voice commanded from way above her. It sounded like it came from the ceiling. She gasped. The hand tightened slightly. "Breathe," the voice commanded again.

She did. First one deep breath, then another. Something lightened inside her chest, her heart went from trying to pound its way out of her rib cage to a dull but fast rhythmic beat.

"You okay?" Mac asked.

"Never been better," she gasped, immediately ashamed of herself. A lifetime of hiding her emotions from others and now these three men were watching her naked panic, her humiliating fear, and there was nothing she could do about it. Control—the iron control she'd spent a lifetime honing—eluded her, had simply disappeared.

The big, heavy hand on her neck squeezed slightly, not painfully. Then the hand lifted and, crazily, she missed it. Only when the hand was gone did she realize that she could have read Mac while his hand was on her neck, but she hadn't. She hadn't read him at all. Had no clue what his emotions were. All she knew was the effect he had on her.

The door whooshed open and a man rushed in—pale, thin, balding. He was wild-eyed. "Mac! I can't find Pat or Salvatore. We need help in the infirmary, quick! Where are they, do you know?"

The three men rose. Mac frowned. "Down in Silver Springs."

The pale man held up a wafer-thin piece of plastic. "Pat's not answering and neither is Salvatore. How can they not be answering?"

"Shit," Blondie said, running a hand through his sun-streaked hair. "Pat told me she was negotiating for a new imaging machine that hasn't hit the market yet. She was—" A sidelong glance at Catherine and his jaws clamped shut. Whatever it was he was going to say, he wasn't going to say it in front of her.

A thin sheen of sweat covered the pale man's face. "They're not supposed to be gone at the same time. And why aren't they answering their phone?"

Mac rose. He was so close to her, Catherine had to crane her neck to watch his face. He flicked a glance at her and answered without Blondie's hesitation. Maybe he trusted her more. Then again, maybe her memory was going to be wiped and she wouldn't remember a word of this.

"Pat and Salvatore told me the new equipment is held in a shielded shed because some of the medical equipment the company sells has radioactive isotopes. So they won't be reachable." He looked at a huge black wristwatch and frowned. Even in the bright overhead light nothing in the wristwatch reflected light. "They should have been back by now."

"Fuck." The pale man's lips folded in. Sweat now ran down his face in rivulets though it was chilly in the room. "What the fuck we gonna do?"

Mac looked at the pale man with a frown. "I've had training as a medic, Sam. You know that. What's wrong?"

"You might be trained as a medic, Mac," Sam answered, "but I don't think your training will cover this. It's Bridget and she's about ready to pop her kid. Any minute now. So you know what to do?"

There was absolutely nothing even remotely funny about Catherine's situation. She was trapped among possibly hostile men, another band of definitely hostile men had trashed her apartment and were looking for her.

But for one fleeting second she nearly laughed out loud at the expression on Mac's face.

He had trained for bullets and broken bones but childbirth had him panicked.

Childbirth?

Shit, shit, shit.

Bridget was the wife of Bobby "Red" Gibson, the community fixit guy. Red could repair a rocket ship on its way to the moon. He kept their community running and Bridget helped Stella with the cooking.

Bridget had been lured to the States from Ireland on the promise of a contract as a nanny for a very wealthy West Coast family and had ended up being little more than an indentured servant. One, moreover, that the husband of the household had his eye on.

She'd fallen in love with the estate handyman, Red. When Red heard her screams as she resisted rape, he rushed in to rescue her and punched the industrialist in the mouth. The industrialist had ties to the mob. Red and Bridget fled with the clothes on their backs.

They made their way to Haven the way everyone else did—seemingly by some kind of dog whistle sent out to only those capable of hearing it. Both of them were mainstays in their little community and everyone was looking forward to the birth of Bridget's baby, the first in Haven.

It was like *everyone* was expecting that fucking baby, not just Bridget.

They were all, to one degree or another, outlaws and outcasts. Exiles in their own land. They'd made a sort of a country of their own here and now the first citizen was about to be born. The idea made even Nick smile. Occasionally.

Now this baby everyone was looking forward to, who was supposed to be born in a month, was coming early, right when the two nurses who ran the infirmary were both away.

Sam, Nick and Jon were looking at him. He was their fucking leader, wasn't he? So why shouldn't they look to him? Except . . . fuck.

Childbirth.

Mac knew how to deal with most situations. His medic training had been thorough. He was good with injuries, had dealt with a lot of them in the field. Pack a bleeding wound, start up a field IV, splint a broken bone, fine. But a *premature birth*? Not so much.

For the first time in living memory he was paralyzed by indecision. With any other situation he'd have said to hold it until Pat got back but even he knew babies waited on no one. They arrived on their own goddamned schedule. And a month early—what the hell did that mean? Would they be needing an incubator? Because they sure as hell didn't have one.

So what the fuck was he supposed to do? He had no clue and he did not want to fuck this up. He was looking forward to this birth as much as anyone. He was goddamned if he was going to lose the baby or the mother.

"I can help." Everyone turned at the soft words. Catherine twisted her hands. "I don't practice medicine, I'm a researcher, but I am an M.D. And I rotated through OB-GYN for three months. I want to help."

"Absolutely not." Jesus. They had no idea who this woman was. How she'd found them. He couldn't send her to the infirmary, expose even more of their secrets.

And then there was the question of the weird effect she had on him. She was way too beautiful for her own good. Certainly for his own good. Everything about her made him edgy, restless. No *way* was she—

"Fantastic," Sam blurted out. He grabbed her hand and started running.

Chapter Nine

email from Special Projects Section
Ministry of Science and Technology, Beijing

Operation Warrior

Dr. Lee—We have followed with great disappointment the latest experiment. The People's Republic is negotiating with the Burundian government for access to their iridium deposits. The rebel Army is active in the area of maximum concentration of the iridium deposits. We were hoping to implement Operation Warrior very soon. The failure of SL-58 means a delay of another six months at least.

In the meantime, Dr. Huang Wu of the ministry has requested funding for large-scale weaponry which includes sonic waves that have been shown to disable humans in experiments conducted on prisoners in Haerbin. Funding has been granted. It has been decided at the highest levels of government that the Red

Army will either pursue your protocol of enhanced abilities or a protocol of enhanced weaponry. The decision will be taken in six months' time, after which no matter what your results, you will not find an infrastructure in place in the military to achieve your project.

Do not disappoint me and the ministry. The People's Republic is moving inexorably toward its destiny.

Minister Zhang Wei

email from Chao Yu

The Minister is truly angry. Do something fast.

Lee stared at the screen long after the information had been understood. Understood but not absorbed. From childhood he had trained himself to control his emotions but something stirred deep inside him, something that could not be instantly repressed as unproductive.

Rage.

Rage was not productive but it was what he felt behind the barriers he'd erected between himself and the world.

Sonic waves.

He sat, staring ahead, feeling hot surges of shame and anger pulse through him. Sonic waves were *toys*. Weapons out of science fiction comics from the thirties. Mechanical, uninteresting. Once the weapons were used once or twice, the enemy could easily find a way to block the sounds and the vibrations and the People's Army would be just as exposed as before.

It was unthinkable that the Minister did not understand that. A child could understand it. No, the only possible way to leverage the power of the PLA was to make each soldier as effective as ten.

Hardware wouldn't do it. Neither would software. But meatware would.

He sat, frozen, for over an hour, steeping in the unfairness.

He was risking everything—his career, even his life—to develop the ultimate weapon for his homeland. And they treated him like a lackey. He was going to make China the world's dominant leader for the next thousand years and this was how he was treated?

The Minister would rue this day. Lee would see to it personally.

In the meantime, he had another protocol to use on the Captain and the others. Then the Captain would be harvested, his brain studied in molecular detail. Much information would come from that.

That eased the tightness in his chest a little. The Captain had proved the most retractable of the test subjects, by a factor of ten, yet experiments on him were yielding extraordinary data, notwithstanding the man's resistance.

Lee considered it a sign of his superior scientific detachment that he hadn't had the man put to death yet. He was a scientist, not a mortal who exacted revenge at the cost of scientific progress.

But—soon the harvested brain cells of Captain Ward would be more useful than his beating heart.

And Lee looked forward to that day.

Mount Blue

"Push. Push now. We're almost there." Catherine kept her voice low and calm but a rush of excitement prickled her veins. The baby was coming! After four very intense, at times frightening hours, the baby was coming.

Arriving at the infirmary, she'd seen two terrified future parents, lost and scared and excited, in equal measure.

There had been some hemorrhaging but she had stopped it. So far, it had been a healthy, easy birth. The parents had been scared because the nurses they trusted to deliver the baby weren't here. The only person here was a stranger their leader didn't trust.

Mac's body language had been clear on that. He rarely took his eyes off her and was always within a hand's span of her. However, for someone so large, he managed to never be in the way. He was simply . . . there. Like a huge guard dog.

He didn't interfere but he didn't stand around like a lump of protoplasm as most men would have, either. She had to give him that. Actually, he'd helped, handing her instruments whose name he knew, keeping close to her without in any way impeding her movements.

The woman—Bridget—had been in labor for two hours before they called Catherine in but was barely dilated. Effacement was almost complete and contractions had been coming every twenty minutes when Catherine entered the room. They soon started coming harder and faster. It took Bridget three hours to dilate to 7 centimeters, huffing and puffing and clinging to her husband's hand.

Catherine moved carefully, making sure her movements were calm and reassuring. It wasn't hard. From somewhere deep inside came a vast assurance, an ease she'd never felt during medical school or her internship. Medical school had been training scenarios and the internship had been mostly observation. This wasn't a training scenario or observation, this was the real thing.

Bridget *needed* her.

When she'd walked into the infirmary, the first thing Catherine had done was take Bridget's hand and tell her she was here to help. A tidal wave of emotion had washed through her, and for the first time in her life, it hadn't hurt. Bridget was scared and excited, in love with her child and with its father, who was holding her other hand.

No dark swirls, no hidden hatred or aggression waiting like chunks of barbed wire to hook and hurt Catherine. There was nothing there that hurt at all, nothing to recoil from, just the bright colors of Bridget's love and fear, the echo of her husband's love for her and their unborn child, and at the very heart of it all, a bright, shining light that was the baby, working hard to be born.

"We're close, Bridget," Catherine murmured, and the woman blew locks of sweat-soaked hair out of her eyes. Catherine shot a glance at Mac. A moment later, a sponge soaked in cold water was pressed into Red's hand and he started wiping the sweat away from Bridget's face and neck. "Very close."

It was time now. Bridget was almost fully dilated. Beneath her hands, Catherine could feel a vast strength gathering, something bigger than Bridget, something that connected to the earth and transited through one small woman and one tiny, powerful source of light inside her belly.

The power swirled and pulsed.

The fetal heart monitor showed the tiny heart beating perfectly, and when Catherine switched on the speakers, there it was—a healthy 140 beats a minute. As if the baby's heart were beating fast with excitement at entering the world.

Bridget's husband, Red, never let her hand go, not once, not even when she was insulting him, screaming at him, promising no sex for the rest of their lives. Ever. He hadn't even blinked, just held her hand tightly and breathed with her.

Touching Bridget—*oh man.*

Catherine was nearly overwhelmed by the emotions of the woman. Joy. Pain. Love. Excitement. Fear. But above all, love. Love for the child being born and for the man whose hand she was holding as if it were a lifeline and whom she was insulting with every word that popped out of her mouth.

And behind all that—the faintest echo of something else. Another set of emotions. Almost—another soul. Like an angel hovering, like a sun spreading light and warmth. Steady and sure.

Suddenly, Bridget's belly rippled and she groaned through clenched teeth. She clutched Red's hand so strongly her knuckles were white.

Between Bridget's legs, Catherine saw a tuft of dark red hair. *The baby!* Every single thought fled her mind as she concentrated on bringing a new life into the world. She knew what she was doing. The instructors in OB-GYN had been thorough and strict. But more than the scientific knowledge of how babies were born, she was imbued with some magical substance that led her through the process as if she'd been born to it. Something that steadied her hands and heart and voice. As if she were plugging into some arcane knowledge base connected with the very earth.

Her hands moved of their own accord, quick and sure. Bridget was panting now, the ripples coming faster and faster, one closely following another. Her face was ferociously scrunched up in concentration. Red's eyes never left her face. Bridget's entire body worked hard, seized by some outside force working its way through her.

"You're doing fine, Bridget. That's right, the baby's crowning, another few pushes and we're done and you'll have yourself a beautiful new baby to love, just a few more, that's good, concentrate on your breathing, excellent, you're being very brave, that's right . . ." Catherine was barely conscious of what she was saying, she just knew that as she spoke, as she touched Bridget's thighs and belly, Bridget's fear diminished, as if each word Catherine said whisked some of the fear and pain away.

She could feel the effect of her words, the effect of her presence, feel how reassured Bridget was because she was there. A force was being handed back and forth, power surging between them.

The infirmary was superbly well-equipped. Someone who knew what they were doing, someone with a lot of money to spend, had bought just about everything that could be necessary. If you needed open-heart surgery or brain surgery you should probably go elsewhere, but otherwise, the infirmary had what you needed, including episiotomy scissors.

She made a tiny, controlled cut to help Bridget. They had Derma-Glue, which eliminated stitches that often carried infections, for after the baby was born. It was a miracle that was saving lives in the few hospitals where it was available. This small outlaw infirmary seemed to have an unlimited supply.

Bridget was red-faced, trying to control her panting, face contorted as her belly rippled again. "How. Much. Longer." She puffed between contractions.

Catherine smiled at her. "Not long now. Do you know what you're expecting?"

Red answered. "No. We wanted the surprise."

Another huge contraction. Catherine could hear Bridget's teeth grinding. Another inch of dilation. A little more and the baby would come out.

The room was cold, as infirmaries should be, but Catherine was sweating. She tried to wipe the sweat from her brow on her sleeve but it was awkward. A handkerchief appeared and wiped her face.

Startled, she looked up at Mac. His face was grim, as always. But the gesture had been kind.

"Thanks," she whispered. He nodded, stepped back slightly. There, without being too close.

Bridget gave a controlled scream and Catherine concentrated on the new life coming out of the woman. In a few minutes of blood, sweat and tears, a miracle happened, and a little baby girl with bright red fuzz covering her head slid into her waiting arms and started wailing.

And the world stopped. Simply stopped.

Catherine looked down into the small red face, eyes scrunched closed, mouth open, and felt her entire being suffused with light. Pure golden light, spearing through her. This little girl was hope and joy and innocence. Was light in darkness, joy in sorrow, hope in despair.

There was no precedent in her life for what Catherine was feeling, holding the tiny baby girl in her arms.

She was connected to the earth, to the sun, to every human being who had ever walked the earth. All their hopes and dreams—everything a human could be—was contained in this tiny little creature.

"Hello," Catherine whispered, dazzled beyond bearing. Her cheeks were wet and her vision was blurred, but she didn't realize she was crying until that handkerchief appeared again.

There was no thought in her of the origin of that handkerchief, of who wiped her face. Of the fact that she was in a hidden location. She might have days—hours—to live. The man behind her was powerful in every way there was. Physically and mentally. He was armed and dangerous and that didn't even cross her mind until later because right now she was holding everything good and true about the world in her arms.

Red bent forward and kissed Bridget and that small act broke her out of her reverie.

"What is it?" Bridget asked, eyes half-closed. She must have been exhausted, but she had a dreamy smile on her face.

"A girl. A beautiful, healthy little red-haired girl. Ten on the Apgar Scale. Probably fifteen, actually, on the scale of one to ten." Catherine laughed from the sheer joy of it. "What are you going to call her?"

"Mac," Bridget and Red said together, and the big man behind her made a low sound in his throat.

"Mac." Catherine cleared her throat discreetly. "That's, um, an original name. For a girl."

Bridget met Red's eyes and spoke. "She would have been Mac if she'd been a three-headed Martian. We owe Mac our lives. There's never been any question of what to call our baby." Darkness crossed her tired features. "Not that her birth will ever be officially registered."

Oh. If the little girl's birth wasn't going to be registered, that meant—that meant they were on the run. One more secret of this secretive place to tuck away. But secrets didn't matter right now. What mattered was the tiny creature in her arms.

Catherine walked over to the basin, carefully washed the baby. Mac. It was really hard to think of her by the name of the huge dark warrior in the room. She wrapped Mac up in another clean blanket and walked over to Bridget, who was sitting up, Red's hand supporting her back, and placed Mac in her arms.

She didn't need to touch anyone to understand the emotions between the two. You could almost see the waves of love washing back and forth between mother and child.

Quietly, Catherine disposed of the placenta and cleaned up the birthing area.

"Try putting her—Mac—to the breast," she suggested softly. The baby could wait, but Bridget couldn't. Catherine didn't understand what was going on, but it looked like though this baby was clearly wanted, they were having a child in difficult, perhaps dangerous circumstances. Nursing her child would reassure Bridget that the sacrifice was worth it. Skin-to-skin contact—there was nothing like it. "Babies should nurse as soon as possible after birth."

Catherine reached out and gently guided Mac's little head to Bridget's breast. In her stint in OB-GYN she'd heard a nurse describe how a newborn crawled up her mother's abdomen to her breast and latched on all by herself, finding the nipple with a little sigh of relief.

Mac opened her little rosebud of a mouth and latched onto her mother's nipple. She suckled contentedly, tiny hands kneading her mother's breast like a kitten's paw, her father's hand cupped over the back of her head.

Everything Mac needed to know she knew already.

She was loved.

It was there in her mother's eyes and her father's gentle touch. Catherine watched the small family fold in on itself, secure in their love for each other. Every touch had confirmed that the love was genuine, the kind that lasted a lifetime. And the little girl—pure magic.

Whatever dangers this family faced, they'd face them together.

Feeling all of that even secondhand dazzled her. She'd never encountered that connection between two people, as if they were one. And now a third person—tiny but so powerful Catherine could still feel the effects of her luminescence—had joined the circle.

Powerful emotions rushed through her.

It was too much.

She was exhausted, a deep physical and emotional exhaustion.

She'd spent a lifetime shielding herself from others. This little trio on the bed—father, mother and child—had cracked her open, overwhelmed her with their feelings beating against her like a hot wind scouring her. She had no defenses left.

Their voices dimmed. Her eyes blurred, the room blurred. And a strong hand gripped her arm. Behind her Mac stepped up close, so close she could feel his body heat, so close she'd touch him if she took a deep breath. He was like a wall behind her, holding her up.

A sharp knock and Stella walked in, pushing a serving cart.

"Whoa, party time! We've got something to celebrate here!"

Behind her, Surfer Dude, and the dark man, Nick. Behind them, ten, no, fifteen, no twenty people, laughing and chattering, filling the infirmary. Noise and colors and voices.

Sharp pops and Surfer Dude was pouring champagne into flutes which had been lined up along the cart. There seemed to be endless bottles of the stuff. He poured by simply walking along the flutes with a tilted bottle. As fast as he could pour, they were lifted away, to be replaced by other glasses.

He lifted the empty bottle, grabbed another one, nodded with satisfaction at the label and popped the cork. "Good stuff," he noted.

He thrust a flute in her hand, smiling at her. "Forgot to introduce myself back there. Name's Jon." Something soft and cylindrical was thrust in her other hand. "Have a cigar." He beamed. Then he turned to give Mac a glass.

Catherine put the cigar down and sipped the champagne. Good stuff, indeed.

Bridget, still nursing, held a flute and so did Red.

"Okay, guys, settle down." The noise level dropped a little. Stella lifted her glass, the harsh overhead lights illuminating every single scar and the beauty beneath it. "I propose a toast, to the newest member of our community. The newest but . . . not the last."

Her eyebrows waggled as she looked across the room.

A pretty brunette choked on her champagne, blushing bright red. She looked up in indignation at a tall, thin man. She narrowed her eyes at him. "You talked!"

His head reared back in surprise. "No I didn't, honey! Promise!"

"Never underestimate feminine intuition," Stella said smoothly. "So. The toast." Something changed in her voice and a sudden quiet descended on the room. Catherine could feel Stella's power, her charisma. She attracted attention like filings to a magnet.

"To the newest member of our community. To the *other* Mac. May she grow strong and loved. May she be blessed with health and community. To Mac!"

"To Mac!" Everyone in the room echoed the name, the overhead light reflecting brightly off the crystal flutes raised in salute.

A quick glance up at Mac's face and Catherine froze. He wasn't looking at Stella, he was looking at *her*. He didn't look away when she caught him staring, either. His gaze wasn't seductive but it wasn't hostile. It was . . . it was something and she had no idea what. The temptation to reach out to touch him, to understand what was going on in that head of his was so strong she had to curl her hands into fists to stop herself.

And . . . well. The temptation to touch him just to feel those muscles was strong, too. Nearly irresistible. He was made of a substance harder than human skin. Like steel, only warm. And steady strength underneath it.

Catherine often felt the frailty of people under their skins.

Their hopes and dreams, sure. But also their fears and insecurities. What made them shrink in terror, what baffled them, what weakened them. Love slipping through their fingers, the small acts of cowardice that peppered their lives, lies and swindles and vices—all there under her fingertips.

There had been nothing like that touching Mac. He was a force of nature, a man of granite self-control, with no chinks in that muscled armor and no weaknesses. There was anger there and a strong sense of betrayal, but something rocklike, too. She'd never been near anyone like him and the urge to touch him, one last time, was almost overpowering.

A tall, thin, pale woman and a short, stocky, dark-haired man slipped into the room.

"You guys missed all the fun!" Jon called out. Voices vied to fill them in on what they'd missed. Pat and Salvatore, the nurses. When they were briefed on what had happened, they both lifted a glass to her and she lifted hers in return.

"Catherine."

She swiveled her head in surprise. Stella had her flute still up and was looking straight at her.

"Listen up, everyone. I've got another toast, an important one. To Catherine, who helped bring the latest addition to our community into the world, even though"—and here she narrowed her eyes at Mac, Nick and Jon, each in turn—"even though she hasn't been treated too well by us." Stella stopped and slowly looked at every person in the room. "There is an us. We've come to this place by ones and twos. Found our way here because . . . because the outside world became too dangerous for us. Here we've found refuge and protection. Mac and Nick and Jon—well, who could ask for better protectors? We've found each other. So tonight we have two new members of our little community. Mac, a tiny baby girl, and Catherine, who found her way to us the way we all did. By the strength of her heart. So . . . to Catherine!"

"To Catherine!" The room echoed with the roar. Several clapped loudly, others joining in with enthusiasm. The noise level was incredible.

Glancing over at the bed, Catherine saw that baby Mac slept blissfully through it all. Maybe babies had some kind of radar that let them know which loud noises were dangerous to them and which were not. This roar was definitely benign. The roar of happy people, raising their glasses in a toast.

A toast to *her*!

It was dizzying. She'd never been toasted before. She'd never been at the center of so many beaming faces before. Faces beaming at *her*!

Someone spilled some champagne on her and laughed. "Drink up!" someone shouted, and they all did. Catherine, too. The champagne was delicious, heady. It tasted like bottled moonlight, crisp and clean and probably 90 proof since it went immediately to her head.

Jon was now a supercharged sommelier, walking around with a bottle in his hand, pouring constantly. When one finished, there'd be a pop and another would appear.

The noise and laughter rose.

An arm jostled her and she stumbled, felt herself start to fall. Mac caught her, held her upright. He simply wrapped his big hand around her upper arm and straightened her. The other huge hand was on the small of her back, pulling her to him. She was—she was in his embrace.

Looking up, all she saw was hard, square jaw, slight five o'clock shadow and shuttered eyes. From this angle the burn scar stood out, rippled skin casting small furrowed shadows. The knife scar on the other side of his face was a keloid slash, like a tribal scar.

Their eyes met. The raucous sounds in the room faded away to nothing. His eyes were deep brown with lines of lighter brown in them. Dark and compelling and impenetrable.

Did he dislike holding her? It was impossible to tell. It was impossible to tell what he felt about her. All she really got from him was strength and power.

One thing she knew, though. He wasn't letting go of her. He held her tightly against him, so tightly she could feel the cut muscles of his chest through the black sweatshirt he wore, down to the individual muscles. Such amazing power. What must it be like to be so powerful?

"Great job!" A laughing elderly gentlemen threw his arms around her from behind, pushing her even more tightly against Mac. "Welcome to Haven!"

Someone on her left hugged her. She couldn't tell if it was a man or a woman. Someone else hugged her to her right. A woman this time, soft and smelling of lavender.

Someone tried a group hug and tripped, champagne spilling onto the floor. A laughing man and woman squeezed her shoulders. Behind them, others pressed forward until there was a tangled mass of happy people clustered around her like barnacles.

Her head swam. She was slightly claustrophobic but that wasn't it, even though she was so tightly squeezed between a wall of flesh and the hard wall of Mac's chest. Claustrophobia always came with a tinge of fear.

There was no fear here, none at all. Nothing to be afraid of, nothing threatening her. Just very happy people celebrating a happy event.

But . . . they were all touching her, as if it were a competition to see who could grab the biggest piece of her. However friendly the gestures, their emotions pulsed and swam around her.

Catherine had rarely had two people touching her at the same time. Now there were twenty, more, maybe, pushing and shoving and trying to hug her and kiss her cheek, laughing. A few wiped tears from their eyes.

There'd been suffering here, there was worry, there was sadness. There was great joy and a sense of companionship.

Someone touched her neck—a runaway. He'd escaped with his life from somewhere, he was still scared. Someone else—determined to find a niece who was in the hands of a gang. Sorrow and anxiety, a burst of great affection for someone, for . . . Mac! For the larger Mac, not the baby.

The emotions fed on each other. Each person had a history, a highly emotional past, not always pleasant. They were happy to be here in this specific time and place but there was an outside world pressing in, threatening . . .

The threat felt like ropes around her chest, dark and burning. There was love here but no safety except the safety provided by the three men in command. Catherine perceived the underlying fear and the threats, and yet in Mac's embrace, the part of her touching him was free of fear, while the part of her being touched by others was absorbing it, she was a sponge soaking up the dark tides rising, rising . . .

And her knees buckled.

Fuck.

Catherine crumpled in his arms. Mac tightened his hold on her and turned to everyone who'd been crowding her. He knew his community was celebrating, and not just the birth of the little girl.

Named Mac. Jeez. What the fuck was that about? You couldn't call a little baby girl Mac. He'd have to talk to Bridget and Red about that.

"Okay, gang, listen up!"

Mac had a deep voice and he knew how to put command in it. In two seconds there was utter quiet in the room. Everyone had stepped back and were now recognizing that Catherine was unsteady on her feet.

"I know you're all happy about the birth of Mac." He had a straight line of sight to Bridget cradling the baby, Red by her side. "And you two—you're gonna have to rethink that name." He put a hard, stern note in his voice but Bridget just smiled at him sleepily. "And I know you are all grateful to Catherine for her help. But I think we're overwhelming her."

Yeah. Nearly freezing to death in a snowstorm, interrogated by professional soldiers who'd been subjected to SERE training, watching her home being trashed by thugs, delivering a baby . . . yeah, that would try anyone, let alone someone as fragile-looking as Catherine Young.

She stirred. "No, really." She smiled weakly. "I'm fine, I—"

"Shut up," Mac growled. He'd felt her buckle, felt now the weakness, could even feel the effort she was making to stand up straight. She was trembling.

The hell with this. He scooped her up in his arms.

He turned with Catherine in his arms and stopped when Stella put a hand on his shoulder. She was frowning with concern, accentuating the scars left by the knife slashes. "Take her to your quarters, she'll be more comfortable. I'll send some tea in."

He nodded and walked out.

"I can walk," Catherine protested.

Yeah, she probably could. But shit, she felt really good in his arms.

He had spacious quarters—a large apartment really—two floors down. He stood for a second outside his door. The lock was biomorphological, set to recognize his body shape, together with the shapes of Nick and Jon. It didn't recognize his shape with Catherine in his arms so he had to enter in a code in the alphanumeric keypad hidden in the wall.

Mac had to suppress the shocking thought that he'd better reset the biomorphological lock because it wouldn't be the last time he'd have Catherine Young in his arms.

Where did that thought come from?

Mac walked into his quarters and moved into his bedroom. Bending, he pulled back the covers and laid her down.

He missed that warm, slight weight in his arms immediately. For minutes, he hovered over her, still touching her, unwilling to let her go completely.

New terrain.

Mac's body did what he told it to do, no more, no less. The idea that he'd hover over a woman because his arms simply didn't want to obey him shocked him as much as the boner in his pants.

Christ.

Get a grip.

It took every ounce of self-discipline he had to straighten up and let her go and that scared him.

Her eyes were half-open when he unzipped her boots and removed them.

"What are you doing?" she whispered. Her eyes were such a brilliant gray he was almost glad they were half-closed. They were mesmerizing. It was hard to look away from her.

"Making you comfortable. You're dead tired. You delivered a baby." She looked so lost in his huge bed, he picked up her hand. "Rest now," he said, keeping his voice low. "You're safe now. Don't worry about anything. I'm here."

Man, how could he expect her to feel safe when last night he was interrogating her, fully armed, suspecting her of being a government spy? What a fucking stupid thing to say to her.

But to his surprise, her lips turned up a little as her eyes closed. "Safe," she murmured. Her hand curled trustingly around his, then she turned her head and went out like a light.

Mac pulled up the covers, smoothing them over her shoulder with his free hand. He wanted to sit down at her bedside. He stretched with his foot for the chair because, well, he didn't want to let go of her hand.

Sitting, he wrapped her hand in both of his and watched her face, trying to figure out the enigma that was Catherine Young.

She looked so very fragile, lying there. She was pale, nostrils pinched with stress, frowning even in sleep. The rest of her was fragile, too—slender, fine-boned.

Catherine Young seemed so heartbreakingly delicate, almost frail. Like she'd break if you touched her too roughly, though he'd treated her roughly and she hadn't broken, not at all.

Whatever her motives, it took balls the size of refrigerators to set off on a quest to find him with just a few clues from a madman.

The idea that the madman might be the Captain was shunted aside. It hurt to think about it. He'd deal with that later, with Nick and Jon.

Whoever sent her on that chase had given her crumbs to go on, and by God, she'd done it. She'd tracked him down when no one else had. She hadn't crumbled under interrogation, either. She'd stuck to her story and had been meek but not intimidated.

And watching her help Bridget give birth. Man. She'd been gentle, reassuring, utterly competent. He shuddered to think that he might have had to do that. Mac knew all about stopping bleeding, broken bones, bullet holes. But helping a child be born took a whole set of skills he didn't have, never would have, either. Though she said she wasn't a practicing physician, Catherine had stepped right up to the plate and delivered a healthy baby into the world.

Into *their* world. Their first new citizen, delivered by the latest addition to their community.

Because Catherine was now one of them, there was no hiding it, no running away from it. It was a simple fact.

His people had come to him one by one, sometimes in twos and threes. They recognized him and they recognized each other and they now had recognized Catherine.

So what the fuck was he supposed to do with her?

He watched her, holding her hand in his. She'd turned in bed and now her face was in profile, only her head and hand outside the covers. She was so fucking beautiful. He'd tried so hard not to notice, but his body laughed at him and reacted the way a healthy male body reacted to a spectacularly beautiful woman.

Usually, that wasn't a problem, he had himself under control. He could control his heart rate, his reflexes, his thoughts, his cock. They'd been taught that in BUD/S but he'd already known how. You didn't survive his childhood without massive self-control.

And he'd learned early on that it was useless getting a hard-on for beautiful women. He'd been born ugly, grew up ugly, and the fucker with the knife and the massive firestorm at Arka that had melted part of his face had just made things worse. He rarely looked beautiful women in the eyes because it could come across as aggression. He'd learned long ago to tuck his dick between his legs when he desired one because it just wasn't going to happen.

He'd been aroused in the interrogation room, but had been able to dial his dick right back down because she'd been so scared. Mac was scary-looking and if you were his enemy duck and hide, but the thought of intimidating a woman for sex made him physically ill. And besides, Nick and Jon had been watching, so the hard-on just had to go.

And it went.

It was harder to rein himself in now. By some magical alchemy, Catherine Young was inside his perimeter in every way there was. She'd been accepted by his ragtag town and he accepted that her safety was now his responsibility. He didn't like it, but there it was. She was in.

She wasn't awake to see him look at her with heat in his eyes, so he could, well, fantasize.

Mac shifted in his chair, his hard-on like some heavy, uncomfortable *thing* hanging onto the front of his body. He hadn't had a woman in a long long time. While he was a SEAL, it hadn't been much of a problem. Ugly as he was, there were plenty of women who got off on nailing SEALs. It gave them bragging rights if nothing else.

He still remembered the SEAL groupie in Coronado who'd asked if she could make a plaster cast of his cock. But first she wanted him to depilate.

She already had twelve trophies, lined up on a bookshelf. With names, dates and number of times they'd fucked.

Jesus.

In Ghost Ops, everyone's dicks were lashed down, including Jon's, who used to go through women like good ole boys went through free beer.

Ghost Ops was all about being invisible, untraceable, hidden. They became non-people with no credit history, no leases or mortgages or utility bills or cell phones linked to ordinary providers, no car registrations, no driver's licenses—nothing. That went with no sex life because you had to tell a woman *something.* Women were curious and if they liked the sex they were likely to want to stick around, and inevitably they'd find out that Joe Smith didn't really exist.

So Ghost Ops was mainly a no-sex zone, not to mention the fact that since the day they were established, the six-man team had been almost constantly on ops. And their downtime wasn't at home—because they didn't have homes anymore—but quarters on some scrubland a hundred miles from the nearest town or road, a place they'd dubbed Fort Dump, a place no woman would put up with on pain of death, let alone for sex.

And after the Arka disaster—well, being on the run for your life and hiding out didn't really bring out the warm and sexy.

So Mac sat, watching Catherine's face, holding her hand, vainly trying to will away the blue steeler in his pants and trying to remember the last time he had sex.

He couldn't.

It wasn't just that it was probably lost in the mists of time, or not just that. It was that he had problems remembering anything about other women while looking at Catherine. It seemed impossible to him that he could ever have wanted another woman because the most desirable woman in the world was right in front of him, sleeping in his bed, her hand in his.

Every other woman in the world just slid right out of his head, never to return.

Catherine's eyes moved under her lids, back and forth, as if she were reading something. Her hand gripped his and she opened her eyes.

He moved his hand so that his thumb rested on the inside of her wrist.

"Hi," he said softly. "You've been asleep. You were exhausted. I brought you here so you could rest."

Her eyebrows pulled together as she slowly looked around the room then brought her gaze back to his face. "I'm in your room?"

Quarters was more like it, but he nodded. "Yeah." He held up the hand that wasn't gripping hers. "But don't worry. You're in no danger from me. I'm not going to hurt you." His mouth quirked. "Even if I wanted to, which I don't, every single person in this community would rush in and beat me up if I touched a hair on your head."

She listened to him carefully, hand gripping his. It was strange, how she wouldn't let go of him, just hung on tight. Where her hand met his, his skin was warm, and it was almost as if there were some kind of glow.

Shit, he really needed to get laid if holding a woman's hand was making him hot.

She took her time answering, searching for something in his face.

It made him almost—but not quite—uncomfortable. Women's eyes didn't linger on his face. Certainly not beautiful women's eyes. People looked at him briefly, then usually focused on a point past his shoulder. Only his men and the people of Haven looked him straight in the face.

And Catherine Young.

After looking at him for a long time, she finally spoke in a soft voice. "No, I'm not afraid you're going to hurt me. Not at all." She stopped, bit her lip.

"You have something else to say? Spit it out."

Her hand moved in his, warm and soft and spreading . . . something where skin touched skin.

"You're not going to like it," she warned.

Hell, there were a lot of things he didn't like. That didn't mean he couldn't face them. In the field, you faced what came at you, dodging whatever was incoming if you could, dealing with it head-on if you couldn't.

"I'm a big boy," Mac answered.

She smiled, her first smile since waking up. Gentle and sad. There was no happiness there, only pain.

"I know you are, Mac. I know *you*. I know you inside out, whether you want to believe me or not. I know you are a dangerous warrior on the battlefield and that you couldn't hurt an innocent. Simply couldn't."

His hand had jerked but she just tightened her grip. It was ridiculous. His hand was almost twice the size of hers. His grip, like that of all SpecOps soldiers, had been tested on a dynamometer and had clocked in at two hundred pounds. Over, in fact, the scale. And yet he couldn't pull his hand from hers.

Her eyes searched his. "We have a connection, Mac. Whether you like it or not. And I think you can feel it, too."

He shook his head even as he knew he was lying to himself. He felt it. Some kind of electric thing, a prickling warmth spreading from his hand up his arm . . .

"Did you somehow drug me?" he blurted out.

Catherine gave a startled laugh. "No, of course not."

It was the only thing that made sense. What else could explain this feeling, something warm coursing through his system? And Catherine—she was glowing from within; whereas before she'd been pale and pinched now she was slightly flushed and radiant, as if there were a lightbulb inside her.

What was this shit?

His cell gave a soft two-note beep. Incoming text. A white beam shot out, moving until it found a dark surface to project on.

Outside the door. Stella

Grateful for the distraction, Mac pulled his hand away and stood up. Goddammit, his fucking knees felt weak. What had she done to him?

"What is it?" Catherine sat up, the bedsheets falling to her waist.

Mac was acutely aware of absolutely everything. The sound of the sheets sliding down, the brush of her hair against the pillows she stacked behind her, the soft sigh of regret when he pulled his hand away.

And, crazily, he felt . . . bereft. As if he'd been snatched from somewhere warm and welcoming and plunged into an icy cold reality. His hand felt cold. Everything felt cold and alien, including himself.

"Stella," he said, holding himself utterly still, because the temptation was to crawl in with her, looking so mussed and delectable in his bed. Her smile had faded at his reaction, though. She hugged herself and shivered though it wasn't cold in the room.

It was never cold and never hot in Haven. It was always a steady 73 degrees.

"What does she want?"

"To feed us, is my guess." Mac turned and walked to the door. And damned if it wasn't hard. What was this shit? It was like walking through mud, each step away from her harder than the step before until he was straining to get at the door. It took his hand two seconds to reach the command on the wall, and when he went to touch it, he saw his fingers were trembling.

Fucking trembling.

His hands never shook. He'd killed at a mile out. He'd defused bombs. He'd stuck his hand in a scorpion's nest. It never shook. *Never.*

But it was shaking now.

The door slid open and a cart was standing right outside. He pushed it into the room and back to the bed, fast, as if a rubber band had been overstretched and was now flinging him back where he belonged.

Catherine watched him, silver gray eyes huge, full lips slightly pinched, biting back words.

She scooted over to the cart filled with food, leaned over and took a sniff. She unpursed her lips and offered, "Wow. This looks better than Fortnum and Mason, in London."

London had been a fleeting impression of old and new buildings, on his way to Heresford for cross-training with SAS.

"Are you hungry?"

"Starving."

Yeah. She would be. She'd missed lunch because she was helping one of his little tribe into the world.

Haven wasn't a place where people went hungry. There was

plenty of that in the world outside. Mac had been so rattled by this woman that he hadn't looked after her at all.

So, yeah, he needed to feed her.

He hadn't thought of it, Stella had, bless her. She had tons of help in their communal kitchens but she would have prepared this stuff herself. She liked Catherine.

"Okay, let's see. We have hot sandwiches . . ." He pulled the crusty top off one. "Looks like pulled pork. You aren't a vegetarian, are you?"

"God, no." She shook her head sharply, smiling.

He handed her a sandwich wrapped in cloth, his fingers brushing hers and goddamned if his hand didn't heat up. *Must be the sandwich*, he thought, but he really didn't believe it.

"We've got several types of sandwiches: tuna on whole wheat, roast beef on white roll—"

"Baguette," she interrupted.

"What?"

"It's a baguette. French bread."

"Oh." He held the bread up. Looked like a roll to him. "All right Olives, mushrooms, cheese, roast potatoes with rosemary. And, let's see—we also have a couple of wraps. Stella's big on wraps. She wants us all to cut down on carbs. These sandwiches are an exception, just for you. We have some kind of salad with goat cheese on top, eggplant Parmesan." He opened another container hoping to see something with some grease and carbs and was disappointed. "Orange and fennel salad. And here, hmmm, apple, carrot and pine nut salad. Jesus, Stell . . . you're overdoing it. But we also have an omelette—Stell's great with omelettes even though this one might have dicey stuff like arugula or radicchio—she's big on radicchio." He lifted another container lid. "Green stuff." He closed the lid back.

"Let me see." Catherine lifted the lid and sniffed. "Braised escarole with balsamic vinegar."

Mac had no interest in that. He continued rummaging. "Dessert's got to be here somewhere. Oh, yes, thank you, God. Cookies. And ice cream." He looked up to find her watching him with a slight smile on her face. "So, what do you want?"

The smile widened. "Everything. I'm so hungry I could eat a raw horse. Knowing it's Stella's cooking, I'm about to rip those things right out of your hands."

He didn't particularly want to smile but found his lips curling upward. It was impossible not to smile at that face. "Wouldn't want that. So I guess I'll just give you some of everything. There's enough for seconds and thirds."

He stacked her plate high with Stella's food, liking everything about this. The beautiful woman who now had a full smile on her face. In his bed, in his quarters.

For most of his life, his bed had been empty, his life survival and leadership. The last year he'd spent constantly on the lookout because they had powerful enemies. They had the fucking U.S. government looking for them and he was under no illusions what would happen if the government found them. Whatever the powers that be had been told about Ghost Ops, the men hunting them had been given specific orders. Shoot on sight.

They'd escaped once on their way to a court-martial. The government wasn't going to make the same mistake twice.

Everything that could be done to keep him, his men and their people safe, he'd done. But any soldier was familiar with the ways of that fuck Murphy so Mac was constantly on the lookout for trouble. Paranoia was the hallmark of a good soldier. He had every right to be paranoid, and he was.

Not to mention the fact that somehow—he had no idea how—he'd been elected something between mayor and king of Haven. People now started coming to him with technical problems and organizational problems and lately—Jesus!—emotional problems.

So besides keeping his people safe he now had to keep them happy and spiritually fulfilled.

Mac wasn't a priest. Though, come to think of it, lately he'd had the sex life of one.

So, yeah, sitting relaxed on his bed with this gorgeous, smart woman, eating delicious food—that made for a nice break with his reality.

She'd settled with her back to his headboard, a big plate on her lap, some green-and-orange concoction in a tall glass on his nightstand. He lifted his own glass. "What the fu—what the hell is this?"

She laughed, head tilted back, long white neck exposed. Man, she had a pretty neck. He scratched his own, which wasn't pretty, and studied hers. Necks like that were made to be touched, but this woman was too beautiful to touch. Off-limits.

"You don't have to censor yourself with me, Mac. I'm a big girl. To answer your question, I think it's carrot juice and mint." She lifted the glass and took a long drink. Mac followed the movements of her neck as she swallowed and his dick swelled even larger.

Thank *God* he had on tight jeans and a long sweatshirt—his usual uniform in Haven. This moment was too good to ruin with a hard-on that couldn't go anywhere. Because, really, what would a woman like her be doing with a man like him?

They were like Beauty and the Beast, not to mention the fact that there was probably a million-dollar reward on his head. His face, Nick's face and Jon's face were no doubt on some playing cards in a Most Wanted deck. The operator who smoked him would get one big honking promotion.

So, no. Sex wasn't going to happen. However horny he was, she wasn't. He knew what aroused women looked like and acted like, and this wasn't it. She wasn't sneaking looks at him, checking out his package, casually putting a hand high up on his thigh. Standard fare for the bar chicks he picked up. Used to pick up when he used to have a sex life.

She just looked . . . happy. As happy as anyone can look whose home was trashed.

"What?"

She'd said something.

"I said, how do you like the juice?" There was patience in her voice, like someone dealing with the demented.

He took a long swig. "Frankly, I'd rather have a beer. Don't know why she didn't include one."

She smiled. "I'm sure if you call Stella she'd have a beer or two sent up."

He was tempted for about two seconds. Then—"Nah. It's okay." He took another swig of the stuff, not because he liked it but because he didn't want to interrupt this. Whatever this was.

Catherine bit into one of the roast beef sandwiches, chewed, sighed and swallowed. "Man this stuff is good. She's amazing. Does she cook like this all the time?"

She was smiling right at him and it was really natural to smile back, though Mac wasn't much of a smiler. Good thing there were no vidcams in the room because Nick and Jon would have a heart attack if they saw him now. Lifting his mouth, showing his teeth. Not scowling. Talking.

"Pretty much. We're all addicted now. Any other food tastes funny."

"I bet." She took another bite, then put the sandwich down. "So . . . what's her story? How'd she end up here?"

Mac hesitated. Stella's story belonged to the community, not to outsiders.

Then again, Catherine was one of them and she needed to know the story. If it turned out she wasn't one of them, she'd be injected with a really big dose of Lethe, enough to cover three days, and set loose in the valley.

Mac's spirits dimmed a little at the thought, but it was what it was. "You know she had a stalker, right?"

She nodded. "It was in all the blogs and gossip sites."

"Well, the blogs forgot to mention the fact that the fuck had been stalking her for *years*. Sending razor blades in roses, live scorpions in jewelry boxes, once a diamond ring on the leg of a giant tarantula. All that good stuff. And her fucking entourage hid all that from her. They vetted everything that was sent to her and vetted her calls. Assholes never let on that she was under threat, because it would upset her and upset their meal ticket." Mac's fists balled. The thought of it still drove him crazy. "She had no idea a crazy fuck was after her." He breathed in deeply, let it out in a heavy gust. "Sorry."

"I saw her face, Mac," Catherine said quietly. "Crazy fuck is the least of it."

"Her agent hired a bodyguard. She thought he was her personal assistant. The bodyguard intercepted about three attempts on her life but was under strict instructions not to let her know. She was filming *High in the Sky* and people were starting to talk Oscars and nobody wanted her off her game."

Her small fist clenched and she bounced it off her knee. "That's unforgiveable," she said quietly.

It was a good thing the bodyguard was already dead. Otherwise Mac would have been tempted to have a word or two with him, of the physical variety.

"Yeah. Anyway, one night, right after the party when they finished filming—Stella told me it's called a wrap party—she gave her housekeeper and driver the night off and went to bed around two. The coroner says that the bodyguard was killed around three A.M. His throat was slit. At the autopsy it turned out that the bodyguard had a point-three blood alcohol level. He was essentially in a coma. Easy prey."

"God," she breathed.

"Yeah." His jaw muscles flexed. "So the fucker had total access. Really went to town. She had almost fifty cuts. Several sliced right through her cheek. Lost a third of the blood in her body. It was only by some miracle that she kicked at him, he slipped in her blood and fell on his knife. She called 911 and they did their job. Unlike the bodyguard."

"She disappeared after that, didn't she?"

"Took six surgeries and a year for her to start to heal. In the meantime, the guy was jailed, then released on bail because he had money. That's when Stella took serious steps to find a place to hide—and then at trial the fuck was judged insane and remanded to a psychiatric prison."

"And escaped," she added quietly. "I remember now."

"She'd always loved cooking and she ended up as a short-order cook at a greasy spoon in Montrose. Sixty miles from here. Jon loved the food there, had made friends with her."

"Jon?" She tilted her head, a little frown between her eyebrows. "Oh. Yeah, right." Her face cleared. "Surfer Dude."

"Surfer Dude, yep." Mac nodded his head. It was great hearing her say that. Jon was used to being underestimated.

"Jon was with her when the news came on and the anchor said that her attacker had escaped from the psychiatric institute. She started shaking so badly she couldn't hold anything. Her scars were barely healed. She couldn't speak, couldn't think. Jon invited her up here and she came and we can't do without her now."

Catherine gave a sigh. "Well, she's clearly at home here."

Yep. Stella was one of them. No question.

"What did you guys do for food . . . before?"

"Before?"

"Before Stella. Did someone cook?"

He winced just thinking about it. "There weren't too many of us then. We've . . . grown." Mac watched her carefully but she didn't take him up on the opening he'd given her. A spy would have used this moment to gently probe, find out more about Haven. And even if she wasn't a spy, most outsiders would be curious about them. Who they were. What they were.

Not Catherine. She just sat quietly and listened.

"So you all cooked?" she asked.

"Nope. Nick and I did." His mouth turned down. "We nearly had a mutiny once. Then Stella came and everyone was happy. She saved our bacon."

He blinked.

He'd made a goddamned *pun*! Since when did he make puns?

It startled a laugh out of her, jostling the plate she was holding on her knees. "Oh!"

They both grabbed for it. Mac was faster and she ended up holding his wrist, fingers curled around him.

Everything stopped. It felt like his heart stopped, too.

No sound, no movement. No laughter now.

There was a sudden, immense hush in the room. Catherine's smile faded and God knew he didn't feel like smiling. Couldn't. Something huge was happening, something completely new, some outside force taking over his body.

Where she touched him, heat rose, painless fire, searing him inside out. Light glowed from him, from her. For a second he wondered whether they'd been irradiated, it was that intense. Her hands melted into his wrists, or at least that was what it felt like. As if they were fused, as if they would never be separated again. Tendrils from her hands sank into his, invisible tendrils tethering him to her. He couldn't move his hands, not an inch. The mere thought of separation from her was too painful to even think about.

He felt his blood pulse into her body, he felt parts of her inside him. He could hear her heartbeat. He could freaking *feel* her heartbeat—not through his hands but through his own heart, because it was as if her heart were beating inside his chest.

Light and heat filled him up and his head buzzed, became light, threatened to float away. He swayed as if in a wind, but there was no wind here, only her hands on him, in him, reaching deep inside him.

An explosion behind his eyes, lighting up everything in the room with a surreal light, like a flashbang only without the noise. Everything brilliantly illuminated as if on a stage.

Emotions. Intense and sharp. Fear and loneliness and desire. Intense desire, but it didn't have the taste of his own desire. Someone else's desire. Someone else's emotions. Somehow he was in someone else's head and he was feeling desire, hot lust for someone . . .

He saw himself from the outside, as if looking out through someone else's eyes. Through *her* eyes. Catherine's eyes . . .

. . . so very attractive. . .

The vagrant thought, as clear as if someone had whispered directly into his ear, wafted across his consciousness. It galvanized him, broke the spell.

Holy shit, that thought was about *him*! He jerked away from her touch as if from an electric prod, his movement so abrupt her plate toppled and fell to the floor.

He didn't pay it any attention, he barely noticed over the sudden thudding of his heart, the adrenaline of danger pumping way too late through his system. Whatever the fuck had happened to him, he hadn't been fast enough to stop it. No warning signs at all, just that one lightning-fast fatal blow.

"Shit!" His fists clenched. He couldn't hit a woman, didn't have it in him, but by God . . . He bent and put his face next to hers, making sure he didn't touch her anywhere.

She'd gone dead white, gray eyes huge in a shocked face, pupils dilated. She shrank back, face pinched, nostrils white with tension.

"Did you just drug me?" he barked.

She had to swallow first. Even her lips had gone white. "No," she whispered in a shocked voice. "No, of course not. I keep telling you that."

Mac picked up the sheet and grabbed her hands using the sheet as a barrier. It would have been better to have latex gloves but he didn't have a pair with him. The sheet would have to do. And even if it didn't protect him, it provided at least a psychological barrier because he knew, the certainty like a deep, dull ache inside him, that touching her was bad for him.

Or good for him.

Or . . . something. Something overwhelming.

He scrutinized the palms of her hands, checking carefully, inch by inch. There had to be something there . . . maybe microneedles embedded in the skin, some capsule she could break and that worked on contact. Something.

He was rough but she didn't protest. Just let him study her hands. They were beautiful. Slender, long-fingered, soft. And however hard he looked, devoid of any drug-delivery systems he could see.

He looked up from her hands, which trembled in his. "Do you have some way to hypnotize me?"

Her voice was stronger now. "No."

"Then tell me what the fuck just happened here!" He threw her hands down, took a step back, furious. "I fucking touch you and it's like my lights went out. What the fuck was that?"

She straightened up, pulling up the bedclothes, bunching them around her neck as if a few yards of material could provide a barrier if he chose to attack her.

If he had been capable of laughter just then, he'd have laughed because a blanket wasn't going to do it. He wasn't going to hurt her, but he was goddamned going to find out what had happened. How the fuck she'd caused him to lose control of his senses just then.

And how the hell she'd managed to convince him that a woman who looked like her could feel desire for him. That was a crazy trick.

Hypnosis made sense. He'd had an out-of-body experience for just a second, as if seeing himself outside himself. And he'd hypnotized himself into feeling she wanted him. What he'd felt was his own freaking desire, not hers. Those whispered words, there and gone, not a voice really but the faintest breath of a thought . . . *so very attractive.*

It had seemed to come from her. Somehow she'd planted lies in his head, hallucinations, because no way was Catherine Young going to find *him* attractive.

He was a man of iron self-control but he was hanging on to it by a thread. He wanted to smash something, hurl something across the room, break something. *She'd been in his freaking head!*

She'd come here, found him against all the odds. Come with this harebrained story of Patient Number Nine, which he and Nick and Jon had half believed, so maybe the brainwashing had started right away. Then she insinuated herself into their community—what was that if not the work of an infiltrated agent? She worked for their enemy anyway—Arka.

Arka dealt with some nasty shit. It was altogether possible she carried a canister of something—some new psychotropic drug that altered reality.

He loomed over her. He often used his size to intimidate the enemy. He'd never done it with a woman but there was always a first time for everything. He leaned in close, resting the knuckles of his left hand on the side of the bed, staring her right in the eyes.

In the light of the lamp her eyes were pure silver, reflecting light rather than absorbing it. She stared into his eyes, then looked away, silver darts that gleamed. Even without makeup her eyes were gorgeous—huge, with thick, dark lashes. That silver sheen so bright . . .

Mac shook himself. Man, whatever she'd used on him, it was potent stuff. He'd never gone into a little fugue about the eye color of a suspect he was interrogating.

"What did you just do to me?" His voice was low and deadly. He didn't have to project that; he felt deadly in every cell of his body.

He leaned over farther and rested the knuckles of his right hand on the other side of her hips, careful not to touch her anywhere. She was caged in by him now. He knew he filled her line of vision. She wouldn't be seeing anything now but 240 pounds of strong, angry male bearing in on her.

Her back was pressed tightly against the headboard and her heartbeat fluttered in the artery of her neck. She was breathing shallowly.

She was scared. Good. Because she had access to a kind of weaponry he had no defense against. A weapon that could fell him as surely as a stun gun or a .50 cal.

And she was bearing a deadly message—to go rescue Lucius. He, Nick and Jon were the protectors of their community. If they got killed because they walked into a trap, who would defend Stella, Bridget, Red, little Mac? All the rest of them?

"Okay. You're going to get one chance at this, because if I get the feeling at any time that you're lying, I'm going to handcuff you, take you down to the infirmary and shoot you up with so much Lethe you'll wake up in a week. And if you piss me off too much, you won't wake up in a motel room. You'll wake up in the snow, three miles from the nearest road. Nod if you understand me."

Her head jerked down, then up.

"Nod if you believe me."

Her head jerked again.

"Good." She'd better believe him because he was speaking God's honest truth. Mac was good at interrogation, at intimidation.

But this was something entirely new. He wasn't used to interrogating when he felt his entire existence was under threat.

It wasn't his life that was in jeopardy. He was used to life-threatening situations and was fully prepared to die in the line of duty. But this—this was something he didn't understand and it scared the shit out of him. This was an annihilation of his entire being, everything that he was, yet leaving his body intact. "Now let's start from the top because you've been lying to us since I grabbed your sorry ass out of that snowstorm."

"No," she whispered. "I haven't."

Shit. How could she look so beautiful, even now? Pale and scared of him.

Mac was used to attractive women looking scared of him. He had scary looks, he always had. He'd had *don't fuck with me* vibes all his life.

Women saw what they wanted to see and in him they saw threat, and not in an attractive package. He could have worked around that if he'd been rich because the accoutrements of wealth were as powerful a draw as good looks. Fancy clothes, fancy cars, that groomed spa look . . . women responded to that powerfully.

But even if he had the money, which he didn't, he had spartan tastes. So what women saw was what they got. And what they saw was a guy who could keep it up for a good long while. If they closed their eyes they wouldn't have to look at him.

That's what they got and that's what they did.

And fuck him if this woman wasn't looking at him in an entirely new way.

The fear was gone. He had no idea how that happened. But it was unmistakable. No fear. No dread. No disgust.

Her eyes had turned soft. There was even some color back in her face.

Fuck this.

"Go over it again." His jaw clenched so hard it was a miracle he wasn't cracking teeth. And they didn't have a dentist at Haven yet, though it didn't matter. With all the money Jon was scamming, they could afford to send the residents down to the most expensive dentists in California. "Tell me again how you happened to be on the road up to us. It's a disused road and there was a roadblock. It was snowing. You were crazy to try to make your way up there in the snow, in the dark. You knew something."

Her eyes widened. "I told you. Patient Nine was desperate to contact you. He told me I'd find you somewhere on that road up on Mount Blue. But I went up the wrong road, several wrong roads, had to backtrack and got caught in bad weather. Then my car died and you know the rest."

Shit. Lucius knew he'd spent his teens exploring the mine on Mount Blue. On one of the rare occasions when Mac got drunk, he told Lucius he was going to buy the abandoned mine when he retired and live there in isolation.

He narrowed his eyes and put his face closer. This woman could be a world-class liar. But even the best liars in the world had tells. Tiny ones, but he was an observant man. He wasn't going to let the slightest sign escape him.

"You're a doctor. You have a top-level job at a big research lab. And you want me to believe that you would drop everything and go on a wild-goose chase on the say-so of a man you yourself diagnosed as demented?"

Her eyes searched his, making little silver darts like small bolts of lightning. "It's the truth," she whispered. "I told you the truth."

His jaw set. "No, you haven't."

"Yes." She drew up in a deep breath and looked like she was steeling herself for something. Finally. Maybe she was going to tell the truth. "Except for one thing. I lied about one thing."

All right. This was going somewhere. She was going to confess. He leaned down until his nose nearly touched hers. "Spit it out."

She didn't flinch. "Patient Nine didn't tap things out on a keyboard. And Patient Nine can't talk. Not a single word."

Chapter Ten

Orion Security Headquarters
Alexandria, Virginia

Clancy Flynn thumbed through the job offers, the fruit of his subtle campaign testing the market waters. He'd wanted to see what the market was like once a stable SL was available, and holy shit, the market was booming.

He was going to make a fucking fortune.

He leafed through the offers for bids. He'd discreetly let his primary clients know that there was a possibility he could do security jobs in half the time using a third of the personnel. Security was a crowded market, getting more crowded by the day. The world was a dangerous place, but it was filling up fast with former soldiers. Plenty of manpower, highly trained, well-armed, tough. A lot of companies were springing up, vying for work.

Security cost money, though, and Flynn knew his corporations. Security was something corporations spent money on grudgingly. Shareholders didn't like that item in the budgets because there was no return. By definition, security wasn't an investment. Shareholders couldn't get it into their greedy heads that security was the *condition* for investments. The thing that let them sit back, do no work, and rake in the money.

Flynn had let word get out that he had a new technology that would allow him to bid for work cheaply. He chose the companies he contacted carefully. They wouldn't be curious about the technology, all they cared about was the bottom line. Most of the work would be done far from the view of the suits in the boardrooms of corporate headquarters.

They bit.

He stared at the spreadsheet, which represented more money than he ever thought he'd see in his lifetime. They were listed there, like low-hanging fruit.

A one-year contract for security for gas pipeline construction from the Tengiz Field in Kazakhstan to Baku in Azerbaijan, seven million dollars. A one-year contract for security for new Brazilian-owned oil wells in Iraq, ten million dollars. A one-year contract for timber operations on an Indonesian island known for Muslim terrorism, five million dollars.

If SL had worked, he could have used teams of ten men on each job, tops: $100K per operator, three million dollars. It would have left him with a profit of nineteen million dollars. In one year. He would double that the year after, once it had proven its worth on the market.

Lee had told him that he was sure they had the right formula. He had found something in Lucius Ward's head that had been the key to the correct dosage. It would have been the very first time something in Lucius Ward's head would have been useful to Flynn.

Sanctimonious bastard.

Ward had been tripping Flynn up his entire military career. Flynn had always outranked him because he knew how to play the Pentagon game, but Ward had been a slippery bastard, always outshining him. Fucking hero. And then setting up Ghost Ops. Fucker had placed himself completely outside the military command structure and had become untouchable.

The Ghost Ops team had been damned effective and Ward had grown in power and prestige. And since Ward was such a canny son of a bitch, he'd picked up on what Flynn and Lee had been working on. Flynn had sent the orders under the secret code that was the only thing that could send Ghost Ops on a mission. A code emanating from the White House—from the Commander in Chief herself. Ward believed he had gone on a sanctioned op.

It had been dangerous. If Ward had in any way questioned the op, he would have found out it didn't come from his command structure and he would have tracked it back to Flynn. And if there was one thing Flynn knew, it was that Ward was a vindictive son of a bitch.

Flynn could have kissed his life and his pension goodbye and would never have had a chance to enjoy his newfound wealth as an entrepreneur. If Ward had found out the orders came from him, Flynn would either be tits up in a grave or scrounging money for margaritas in a village in Costa Rica, constantly looking over his shoulder.

But Ward had been about to blow the whistle and the op had been put together on the fly. They'd gained a year, a year in which SL should have come online and started making them rich.

Fucking Lee. So fucking slow.

Flynn was leaking money by the day. And the Africa fiasco had set them back for who knew how long?

He went on the encrypted line not even God could hack and sent an email to Lee. It used a domain name guaranteed anonymous.

To: One@noname.com
From: Two@noname.com

Speed things up. I've got clients waiting. You've burned through ten million dollars so far and I have nothing to show for it. Either I see progress soon or I'm pulling the money and going to Nova. I heard they're working on neural enhancers. They might have more luck than you.

Two

He sat back, a grim smile on his face. That should stir Lee up. Put a fire under his skinny ass. Lee couldn't get anything done with just the Arka research budget. Flynn's money was key.

Make the fucker squirm.

Flynn sat back in his ten-thousand-dollar designer ergonomic chair and clipped the tip of a hundred-dollar Arturo Fuente using a five-hundred-dollar cigar clipper. He lit it with his antique Dunhill solid gold lighter he'd picked up in London for twenty thousand dollars. It had belonged to a former king, the Duke of Windsor, and it had made Clancy feel . . . powerful. He would hold it in his hand and know he could indulge himself with no problems whatsoever. These days, there were few appetites Flynn had to deny himself, all of them impossible on his military pension.

So Lee was going to have to goddamn get going or Flynn was cutting off the teat Lee'd been sucking on.

Mount Blue

His eyes widened in surprise. Catherine understood very well Mac wasn't often caught by surprise. She'd felt his vigilant nature under her hands, but even if she hadn't, his body language was clear.

He scowled at her. "He didn't type? He can't fucking talk at all? He told you how to find me, didn't he? Or is all that a lie, too?"

She searched his eyes. Deep brown except for those lighter striations of yellow.

She closed her eyes but it didn't help. His striking face seemed tattooed on the inside of her eyelids. Strong features, weather-beaten skin, a nose that had been broken several times, a firm mouth that never smiled. The scar rippling over the left-hand side of his face that looked as if it were a river of flesh flowing down him. The other scar like a memento in skin of pain.

She saw his features but she saw so much more, not only through the projections of Patient Nine, who loved him like a son, but now through her own fingertips, her own skin speaking to her.

There was violence there, yes. But also such goodness and loyalty. He had the fearlessness of a man unafraid to die. He wasn't suicidal, by any means, but his head and his heart believed there were many things worse than death. Betrayal, treason, cruelty. They were worse than death for him and he'd die rather than be guilty of them.

He was towering over her, trying to intimidate her, and if she hadn't been what she was, if she hadn't felt the core of him under her hands, she would definitely have been terrified. This man emanated danger and violence. He looked like he could snap her in half without breaking a sweat. He looked like he'd enjoy doing it.

But that wasn't what he was about and she knew it. Knew it deep in her bones, deep in her very cells.

The intense ferocity he was directing at her was the color of fear. Not fear for himself but fear for the people he held dear, the people he clearly led and protected. Bridget's feelings for this man had been so sharp and intense. He'd saved her from something. There had been bright gratitude, the jewel tones of admiration, threads of affection running through it. Almost love, though nothing like the love that had been in her for Red and for their little girl.

Mac was their leader and he stood for them, was their bulwark against a world that had not been kind to them.

It was fear for his people that had him narrowing his eyes, making his deep voice so rough and dark, had him leaning in so close.

And because she knew him, knew the essence of him, Catherine narrowed her own eyes and snapped, "Back off."

His eyes flared, a deep frown between his black eyebrows. The frown was almost permanently etched into his face, which meant he frowned a lot.

"What did you say?"

"Back. Off." Catherine waved him back.

It was bad enough keeping her wits about her when she was exhausted and stressed. With this man right in her face, it was almost impossible.

Not to mention the fact that there was that annoying *tug* toward him. Almost a tropism, like a sunflower to the sun.

Patient Nine's love for him had rubbed off on her. And now that she'd seen him, been close enough to feel his heat, smell the clean smell of him, touch him . . . she was one step away from the precipice of falling for him herself. Firsthand, not secondhand. Mentally, she windmilled her arms because falling for this man, right now, would be a disaster of epic proportions.

Still . . .

He's so attractive . . .

The thought wafted through her mind once again, as it had before. Since when was she susceptible to beefcake? Beefcake was definitely not her style. Definitely a brains-over-brawn woman. The few men she'd dated had been the weedy type, made for lab coats hanging off narrow shoulders.

This warrior who looked like something out of the mists of the dawn of time, this man somehow had a hold on her.

. . . so attractive. . .

Get a grip, she told herself sternly. And she *did* have a mission.

He'd backed off. But lying in bed meant a huge disadvantage. She stood up facing him, gingerly testing the ground, remembering the moment when everyone's emotions had overwhelmed her, remembering the moment her knees had weakened. She swallowed as she surreptitiously tried to find her balance.

A large hand steadied her.

God, he towered over her, watching her out of narrowed eyes, dark pupils reflecting a pinpoint of light from the bedside lamp.

He let go of her arm, ran a frustrated hand through his hair. "You've got a lot of explaining to do, lady. And you're not leaving here until I understand what the hell is going on."

"Let's sit down," she murmured. Her legs felt weak but she managed to make her way to the table without betraying any physical weakness. She made it just in time before she would have collapsed.

The weakness was devastating and a whiplash contrast to the powerful strength that coursed through her while touching this man. He infused her with . . . something. Extraordinary. In all her life, no one had ever given *her* something via her curse, her gift. It had all been one way, their emotions crowding into her, swirling inside her, overwhelming her. Never had she received something that could be considered a gift.

It had been incredible, feeling all that steely energy, but now that she wasn't touching him it was gone, just when she needed it.

They sat, facing each other, like adversaries. Which, of course, they were.

Remember that, Catherine. However much she liked him—and she liked him against her will—he wasn't her friend.

She clasped her hands in front of her, to still them.

He mirrored her gesture, but unlike her, it definitely wasn't to still them. "Okay," he growled. "This has gone on long enough. I'm grateful—we're all grateful—for your help with Bridget and . . . the baby." His mouth quirked, unable to say the baby's name. Mac. "But that doesn't change anything. The fact is we've got some vulnerable people here, people I want to protect. People you might hurt. I have no idea how dangerous you are to us, and that bothers me. No one should be able to find us here, but you did and I want to know exactly how you did that. And if I don't hear something that convinces me, please believe me when I say I will blast your mind back to last week. After which I will make damn sure you never find your way to us again."

"Oh, I believe you," she said softly. And she did.

He stared at her unblinkingly, then leaned back a little. "I'm listening. And I particularly want to understand how the hell this Patient Nine of yours gave you all that information on me. He couldn't talk. He couldn't type. What the fuck could he do?"

Something terrible was happening. Catherine needed all her wits about her. She needed to explain something that was inexplicable, outside the bounds of anyone's experience. She needed to convince this tough man she wasn't a threat. She needed to convince him to help Patient Nine.

All of this while she couldn't think straight.

She thought straight for a *living.* Clarity of mind, an ability to focus—that's what she was about. She was a scientist and her mind was her weapon. Right now it was misfiring badly.

Just seeing him across the table from her messed with her head. Possibly messed with her neurons.

Was there a scientific explanation for this? She'd gone into neurology with a hope of understanding who and what she was, but so far science hadn't helped her.

One thing she had known up until now as a bedrock fact was that without touching, her connection didn't work. The instant she lifted her hand, the person she'd been touching turned back into an enigma and she moved straight back into her own skin, totally unable to read the person who a second before had been open to her.

The connection was lost in an instant.

And yet . . . *She still felt him.*

She was still attuned to Mac in some unfathomable way. Oh God, was this permanent? *She was still connected!*

She looked at him, disconcerted. It was like being in two heads at once, like having double vision, only worse.

She closed her eyes, tried to distance herself. Pictured herself turning her back on him and walking away.

It helped. When she was a tiny dot on the horizon she opened her eyes and felt whole again. Alone again.

"Okay. I need to backtrack a little. Tell you—tell you a little about myself."

He didn't answer, merely bent his head. *Go ahead*.

"Yes, um." Catherine licked her lips and he stared at her mouth. She stopped immediately because—God!—a bolt of heat shot through her. Heat and a thick feeling, pooling in her groin. *Desire*. Hers? *His?* Her eyes locked with his. "I need to tell this all my own way."

He dipped his head again, dark eyes never leaving hers.

O-kay. Time to do this. Catherine had never laid it out for anyone. All there, on the table. Everything she was. The freakishness of it. The weirdness of it. Being completely different from every other person on the planet. Everyone she knew had run shrieking without ever even understanding the whole of it. How could he be an exception?

But—and it always came back to this—this was her mission. A desperate man had pinned all his hopes on her and she had to do this.

Showtime.

"I'm, um . . . I'm different. I'm not like other people."

"Go on." His voice was low and steady.

Here goes. "You know that I can—I can feel people's emotions when I touch them," she said carefully.

"I got something of that yesterday." He was watching her cautiously.

She bit her lips and nodded. It was impossible to read his face except that he did not look happy.

"It's—it's sort of a gift. But it feels like a curse most of the time and it comes and it goes. I was twelve before I realized that this didn't happen to everyone. Luckily I had very cold parents who hardly ever touched me. So it wasn't until adolescence that I discovered what I could do. *Really* discover it, I mean." Her parents had loathed each other, and every time as a little girl Catherine touched either her mother or father all she got was an arctic blast of hatred. Instinctively, as kids do, she avoided the source of discomfort.

"After several instances of people looking differently at me when I said something I shouldn't have known, I finally got it that what was normal knowledge for me wasn't for other people."

Looking differently at me. The words sounded so normal, everyday fare. Everyone got askance looks, didn't they?

Catherine had had iced drinks thrown in her face, like in that ancient TV show *Glee,* only less fun. Her first car had been a ten-year-old Economo she'd bought her senior year with money working in a supermarket weekends and one afternoon she'd come out from school to find the tires slashed.

Kids avoided her in the hallways. Nobody wanted the locker next to hers.

In high school more or less everyone's emotions were raw and scorching just under the surface. The most popular girl in the school—at home, her father was abusing her. Surrounding her was a bright mirror-like surface of happiness and beneath was darkness shot through with a burning desire to die. The linebacker who couldn't see a female without wanting to fuck her, a dark and painful compulsion. The science nerd who hated everyone with a viciousness that shocked her. It had all been too much. The only solution—don't talk to anyone, and above all, whatever you do, don't touch anyone.

High school had been her own solitary private hell.

"What do you know? What do you pick up on?" The questions sounded reluctant, as if asking them meant he bought into the whole thing, was diving into the madness headfirst. "What kind of intel—info—do you get?"

She thought carefully. "I can't read minds, if that's what you think." Until Patient Nine at least. "It's not like a radio station that broadcasts the thoughts in your head as if they were the evening news." He relaxed slightly. He was hiding something. That was cool. Everyone had secrets. God knew she had her own. "I don't know what's on your grocery list or what's in your bank account or who you're meeting for a date. I don't know specifics. But . . . I'd know if you were worried or happy or sad." Or suicidal or homicidal or schizophrenic. She suppressed a shudder.

He sat still, processing this. She let him work his way through it because it was a lot to swallow. Blinking as if just coming out of a cave into the sunlight, he leaned forward a little. "Let's fast-forward to Patient Nine."

"Okay. You believe me then?" She looked at him hopefully.

"Let's say I'm suspending disbelief." He drummed long fingers on the table. She stared at his hand, so big and powerful. The skin was rough, not a pampered manicured hand at all. A long white scar covered the back, flanked by tiny white lines, like a ladder. A wound, stitched up. "It's a lot to take in."

She nodded. It was.

"So . . . Patient Nine. At Millon Laboratories." His face was impassive. No expression at all, except grimness and intense focus. "How long have you worked there?"

A sudden bust of impatience seized her. "*Come on!* Stop that! I saw the computing power you've got here, Mac. Don't forget that. A clever man—and you all strike me as clever men—can find out just about anything with that kind of crunching power. You probably already know my grade point average in high school, the classes I took in college, you most certainly know how long I've been working at Millon."

She didn't even try to keep the sharpness out of her voice. What the hell. She was baring her soul here and he was playing games with her.

He wasn't taken aback by her outburst. He just dipped his head. *Point taken.* "So let's cut to the chase. Tell me what you do there. Your duties."

"Running a dementia project. I told you."

He cocked his head slightly to one side. "What did you read off the dementia patients?"

"I wear latex gloves. We all do."

He said nothing, just watched her.

"Okay," Catherine sighed. "Sometimes I touched them."

"And you read—?"

"Darkness," she said softly. "Despair. Sometimes—nothing."

He flinched slightly.

"Yes. It is a terrible disease. I wanted to have a hand in helping to do something about it."

"So you have the patients for how long?"

"Six months. We test various drug protocols. We were very excited about a new drug. It has gone through several iterations. It sometimes re-creates new neuronal connections that bypass the damaged areas of the brain and is definitely in line with the latest hypotheses of the brain as a connectome. Management believed we might be on to a miracle drug. We'd tested it on chimpanzees and their problem-solving abilities shot up." She stopped, remembering the chimpanzee massacre with a shudder. "Unfortunately, one iteration was a major fail. We were drawing up protocols for human trials when it emerged that after about a month of treatment, one of the iterations of the prototype drug drove the chimpanzees insane. There was an uprising. An entire generation of chimps had to be put down. They were highly aggressive, out of control. It was a disaster."

"Move on." His jaw muscles clenched. "Patient Nine."

Yeah. Happy to move on, very happy.

The massacre of the chimps had been a dark cloud hovering over the lab for months.

"Of course. Patients are switched out on June 30 and December 31. So on December 31 we had a new intake, twenty patients. I started work in the new year on January 2 and took the original anamneses. Patients One through Twenty, suffering from severe dementia. I assessed them all, going over their medical records. Everything had to be impeccable because if the new drug with the new molecule worked, we had to have a baseline. So though the patients' medical records were complete, we started again from scratch. They were too advanced to do the usual mini mental exams but we did everything else. Fundoscopy to measure intracranial pressure, EMGs to measure fasciculation, the Barré test for pronator drift . . . the lot. Then each patient had a complete blood workup and a functional MRI."

He hadn't looked lost and his eyes hadn't glazed over. He'd had medic training. Clearly he was familiar with medical terminology.

"Immediately I saw that there was something . . . different about Patient Nine."

"Different how?"

She shrugged. "I couldn't put my finger on it until the fMRI came back. Functional MRIs in dementia patients show completely different patterns than in normal patients. And they show inactive areas. Did you ever see those maps of internet connections in North Korea before the Uprising and the founding of the Korean Republic?"

He nodded.

"It's like that in dementia patients. Entirely blank areas, in human brains that have more connections than there are stars in the Milky Way. Patient Nine's scan was completely different. Clinically, he showed signs of very advanced dementia. But his scan—it was, well, it was one of the most unusual scans I'd ever seen. It was as if—as if his mental faculties had been artificially suppressed, but underneath there was cognitive function. Highly unusual."

"What did he look like?" His eyes had sharpened, narrowed. He seemed to be listening to her with his ears, but also with his eyes and his skin, attention completely focused on her.

"Tall," she answered. "Even bedridden. His charts put him at one meter ninety-five, weight sixty-five kilograms, down from probably one-ten. He was emaciated. He'd once been a muscular man, but now his skin hung off his bones. That is usual in advanced dementia cases. Patients lose their appetite, sometimes they even forget what food is for, or they mistake objects for food. Everything is haywire. He was, to use a layman's term, a mess."

"Did you have background information?"

"No." She shook her head. "I told you, they were referred to by numbers. Everything except their medical background was redacted from the file so our observations would be unbiased. But—I think he was in the military."

"If you have no info on him and he was bedridden, how could you assess that?"

"I touched him."

"Touch . . . *touch*?"

"Yes. I don't use my ability"—*curse*—"for research purposes. There's no way I can corroborate what I learn. It's untested, unscientific. Misleading, even. I never know when I can trust it."

"Have you ever made a mistake?" His voice was quiet.

"Mistake?"

"Yeah. You ever get a bad reading? Think someone was real happy but turns out was suicidal? Think someone was in love and he stabbed the girl instead? Get it really really wrong?"

"No." She shook her head. "Not that I know of."

He digested that while she just looked at him. She was finding it hard to concentrate because he was this huge . . . distraction, sitting right across from her. Filling her field of vision, sucking all the oxygen out of the room, taking up all of her head space.

He was fascinating to look at, a magnet for the eyes. Her eyes, at least.

She'd spent almost her entire life in school. Three years ago she'd left the confines of graduate school only to move directly into a research lab which was virtually indistinguishable from her university lab, except the equipment was better and more expensive.

And every step of the way, the men were clones of each other.

The only variables were height, otherwise the men she'd spent all her grad student and working life with were virtually the same. Thin, because science nerds don't have time to eat. With glasses, old-fashioned as that was. Surgically enhanced eyes still had trouble coping with the close work required of someone staring into the small screens of electron microscopes all day, and since nerds weren't vain, it was just easier to wear glasses. In a world where no one wore glasses anymore, it was like a sign, right there on their faces. *I am a nerd.*

They had no muscles, none. Building up muscles required time and desire and the men she worked with had neither. They lived entirely in their heads. Their bodies were an afterthought.

And they had no hormones, or at least none that she could detect, not that she was any kind of an expert.

They were the exact opposite of the man sitting across from her, who was huge, heavily muscled, fairly oozing testosterone and pheromones.

Everything about him was so fascinating. He was like some chimera, some wild mythical beast of the forest suddenly come to life. She could observe him for days, a little wary, as you should be with mythical creatures. He could disappear, he could leap on her . . . you had no idea what he could do.

The men she was used to had vague gazes, inward-directed, trying to puzzle out the secrets of nature. This man seemed to know them already. His gaze was direct, knowing, hard. A man who lived in the real world. And that body. Wow. A body like that should be illegal. Or at least he should have the good taste to keep it away from susceptible women.

He leaned back slightly, big hands on the tabletop. They were incredibly fascinating, too. Rough-skinned, nicked, callused. With that long white ladder-like scar across the back of the right one.

He kept perfectly still. She'd never seen anyone, man or woman, who could keep as still as he could. As he listened to her, he moved only his eyes. It was like sitting across from some huge jungle cat crouching, stealthily awaiting its prey.

Her.

"Patient Nine." It wasn't a request.

She looked down at the table, as if there were some fact there, though of course there was nothing but a wooden surface. But she didn't need a memo. Patient Nine was etched in her memory with acid.

"I first saw him, as I said, on January 3." She remembered it so well. She'd spent New Year's Eve and New Year's Day on her own. Going in to work had been a relief because at least she'd hear human voices. "Patient Nine was physically in a bad way. As I said, he'd had numerous surgeries, and though the wounds had all closed without infection, sometimes you could tell that he'd had surgery on top of surgeries." She shuddered at the memory. There had been something . . . unsettling about seeing a man who'd been worked over so much. "He was restrained. His eyes were closed when I came into the room. I'd dedicated the morning to going through all the patient files, checking their paperwork and giving them a physical examination. Just getting a baseline, like I said. Then I went into each room to get a feel for them. Just a preliminary check. Patient Nine was unresponsive, as were most of them. I was taking his BP when all of a sudden his eyes opened wide and he grabbed my wrist, above the latex glove. It was . . . it was a shock."

Open, aware eyes, deep and pained but fully human, fully alive. It had shocked her, she'd been so used to the dull, dazed eyes of the other patients, once human, now so lost.

This man wasn't lost, not at all. He was tethered by the IV lines and he couldn't speak but he was aware. Terribly aware.

"He spoke to me," she whispered, remembering that electric moment. "He told me he was trapped. Some terrible wrong had been done. People he cared about had suffered. He needed . . . he needed something very badly. He wanted something to be done but I couldn't understand . . ."

Catherine looked Mac straight in the eyes. His dark eyes were watching her intently, unblinking. "It was minutes before I understood he wasn't actually speaking. Not with his vocal cords. His mouth wasn't moving. This was all done . . . mentally." Her hands lifted, spread, dropped helplessly back on the table. "Or telepathically, psychically. Or *something*. I have no idea how he was talking to me. It had never happened to me before."

He didn't question any of this. "Was he using words? In . . . your mind?"

She shook her head sharply. "Some words. It was hard to tell, a lot of it was a jumble. But I got the heart of his message. Images, mostly. A building, in the snow. Voices shouting. Men pouring out of hidden recesses, armed, attacking other men. Funny-looking guns. Shots being fired. An explosion and a fire so hot the snow melted almost instantly. Men with some kind of luminous stripe on their helmets, going down."

Mac's eyes grew even darker. She could feel his attention sharpen to a point.

"You have to understand that this had never happened to me—I'd never seen so clearly before. Usually all I get are feelings. This time I saw the images and felt the emotions at the same time. Danger, like a knife cutting through me. Some deep sense of betrayal, something dark, something that cut off my oxygen. Over it all . . ." Her voice dropped to a whisper. "Over it all was your face."

He didn't move, didn't betray any emotion, but Catherine felt his surprise like a whip. "*My* face? You sure?"

She nodded and swallowed heavily. In the vision given her by Patient Nine, the entire right side of Mac's face had been black with burns, raw red skin showing underneath the charred skin. Horrible burns, out of a nightmare, now just scars. "Yours. And the emotions connected to it were pain and sorrow. His. Patient Nine's." She searched his eyes. "This is making sense to you, right? The burning building, the firefight and the massive fire afterward? Betrayal?"

He nodded slowly. "That's all you got?"

"That day, yes. That, and an overwhelming sense that no one should know. It felt . . . imperative that we keep this a secret." She remembered staggering back, nearly faint from the intensity of what had been blasted at her. Feeling naked and bare, as if her skin had been flayed. Wondering if she'd had a psychotic episode, or maybe even some type of seizure. "The next day I wasn't taken by surprise. I was also very aware that the sessions are recorded. The sense that this was a secret—that people would die if it weren't kept a secret—was very strong, almost crippling. It was one step short of full-blown paranoia, and I tolerated it because it felt so very real. Back in my office, I ran the tape of our session to confirm that from the outside, no one could tell anything had happened. A patient had grasped my arm, that was all. Advanced dementia patients have lost all fine motor skills. Unless they are sedated, some flail wildly. There was nothing on that tape that could have raised eyebrows."

Mac was so still he could have been a statue. "And the next day?"

The next day she broke with protocol and started the process that led step by dangerous step to this hidden place and to this moment. "The next day I turned my back to the camera and took my right glove off and held Patient Nine's hand," she said softly.

He understood, pursed his lips and blew out a silent whistle. "I take it both those things were no-nos."

"Absolute no-nos," she agreed. "Being-kicked-out-and-blackballed-forever no-nos." She closed her eyes for a moment. Even in retrospect what happened next was overpowering.

"Lose-your-job, security-called, your-things-packed-in-a-box no-no?" he persisted.

"Yeah. All that good stuff."

"It was brave of you to do that, then."

Catherine looked at him, startled. Was he making fun of her? But looking at the grim lines of his face, she decided no. He wasn't making fun of her. That face looked as if fun was not in its vocabulary.

"Yes, well, um . . ." That face was so absolutely fascinating. It had been in her head for days now, had been her obsession. She'd risked everything to find the person it belonged to and she had. Mission accomplished.

But that face was even more of an obsession now that she'd found him. *Concentrate, Catherine.*

"This time, it was more forceful than the day before. Almost as if new neural pathways had opened up in me or in him." She shrugged. "I couldn't tell. It was the same as before, very clear but somehow . . . weaker, too. With a sense of huge struggle to get to me. I checked his chart and he'd been sedated with a stronger than usual dose. His eyes—" She closed her own, remembering.

"His eyes?" Mac prodded.

"Tragic and lost," she whispered. Patient Nine's eyes still haunted her. A look so desolate it alone had been enough to propel her into possible danger. "Trying so hard to communicate with me. He was struggling desperately with the effects of the drug. It should have knocked him out yet there he was, weakened terribly, but still awake and aware. I had the sense of . . . of an iron will underneath it all. The sense of a man who simply would not—could not quit. Didn't know how to quit."

He nodded abruptly. "Yeah."

"But the cameras showed him as awake, when he shouldn't have been. So I squeezed his arm, closed my eyes. He got the message and pretended to sleep. Then I—" She closed her own eyes as she remembered taking that big step straight into sedition. "I changed the nurse's orders, canceled the next day's dose. The next morning, from my computer, I established a long loop of Patient Nine sleeping, overrode his video monitor and pasted the loop in before I went back to him."

"Yeah, you said." For the first time a ghost of a smile crossed his lips. "Sounds like you're as good as Jon at hacking. That's scary. So what happened?"

The memory of what happened next was so intense it almost hurt. "We did this Vulcan mind-meld thing."

His eyes widened. "Mind meld?"

"Yes. It's the only way I can describe it and believe me when I say that has never happened to me before. Not that I ever tried." She shuddered. "I never wanted to crawl inside anyone's head, ever, but I did then. Right inside, like falling down a rabbit hole into a completely new reality. I almost forgot I was me."

"What did you see? Inside . . . inside his head."

"You, mainly," she said baldly. "I'd seen the scenes the day before but now they were clearer. You were front and center, wearing black like you are now, only a thicker jacket that looked funny and thick black glasses. Goggles, really. At times with a helmet with a bright point of light on it. Slumped against a steel wall with half your face nearly burned off. Then rising again, bleeding. I saw other men but they weren't as clear to me as you were. Throughout it all, watching this battle, watching you, Nine was blasting me with a compelling desire to find you, no matter what. Like I'd die if I didn't find you."

Desire wasn't the right word, it had been more than that. A compulsion—a dark one. A craving. A deep drive to find Mac—a man she'd never heard of, never seen before, a man she had no reason to believe even existed in real life as opposed to existing only in the smoky ruins of Nine's head—had been as strong as the drive to breathe. Vitally, crucially important.

"Though you don't know me." His voice sounded thoughtful.

"That's right. I had no idea who you were." She didn't want to but she leaned forward, for no other reason than simply to be closer. Shades of the compulsion she'd been infected with, but also sheer . . . attraction. This man was like a lodestone, like some huge planet exerting gravity to her satellite moon. "I don't know how to describe what went on. He wasn't speaking to me except in images and the images weren't in any order. But what blasted through me was your face, a name—Mac—and Mount Blue."

His face tightened and his eyes narrowed.

She sighed, preparing herself to navigate the shoals of suspicion. If she weren't in her own head, if she were Mac, she'd be suspicious, too.

"I understand you, um, didn't—don't—want to be found. That was in the mix, too, the fact that finding you would be hard, dangerous. The emotions, the visions were clear about that. Nine wasn't tricking me into thinking it would be easy. He knew it would be tough-going. But then he also gave me a way to get to you. He was sure you'd be somewhere on the mountain. What was in my head was a trail, a dirt road. Then a roadblock, something that would stop me. I was supposed to go around it or over it, somehow get past it and continue. And then I saw myself stopped in my car. I could *see* it. Me, in a stalled car, unable to go any farther. I should just sit and wait and you would find me. And when you found me, I was supposed to give you that small pin. I have no idea if he knew what season it is because the images in my head were of summer, not winter. The road was a dirt track but clear. Maybe he didn't realize we're in the dead of winter. Dementia patients lose all sense of time and of the seasons and I think he'd been drugged for a long time on top of that, though his charts showed nothing. Still, yes, it was incredibly stupid of me to set out on a quest to find you when the forecast was for snow. All I can say is that it was either try to find you or have a heart attack or have my head blow up, the drive to find you was that compelling."

She let out a deep breath. There. It had all been said.

"Show me," he said suddenly, fire in his eyes.

Show me. Her breath caught.

All of a sudden, an image bloomed in her head of her stripping for him. Standing up, pulling her sweater up and over her head, shimmying out of her pants and panties, unhooking her bra. All while he watched with those dark dark eyes which had turned blazing hot.

Show me. The vision came unbidden but she couldn't pretend it came out of nowhere. It came from somewhere deep inside her, some place that had iron filings all of a sudden aligned with the magnet that was Mac.

A man who was in hiding, a man who distrusted her. A man who might at any moment blast her mind into next week, as he so charmingly put it.

And right now, every move of his made the muscles deep in her belly pull and clench.

"What?"

A big hand unfurled, palm up. He moved his hand to the center of the table.

"Show me." Impatience in his voice. Calling the crazy lady's bluff. "Read me. Do that thing again, only not my feelings. My thoughts."

Suddenly, that hand seemed so enticing and inviting. Huge and hard and there, waiting for hers. An invitation that had never been extended to her, ever. Everyone ran away screaming the instant they got a whiff of her talent—her *curse*—never to return. But not this man. He wanted a demonstration. He wanted to touch her.

Had she ever held hands with a man before? She'd been to bed with a couple of men after a few kisses and some dates, but holding hands? Like walking home after a date, hand in hand? Hmmm.

No.

Her last date ended after dinner, without the movie, the balding banker leaving her at her doorstep, burning rubber in his desire to get away from her just as fast as his BMW could carry him because somehow she'd brushed against him as he radiated lust for the hot, hunky male waiter and without thinking she let on that she'd tuned in to his attraction.

She'd had to switch banks.

There was no touching anyone she didn't trust and she trusted no one. Maybe that explained this wild desire—this driving compulsion—to lay her hand in his. It had nothing to do with reading him and everything to do with touching him.

"Read me." Again that impatience in his deep, rough voice. Eyes blazing with challenge. "Tell me what I'm thinking."

It doesn't work that way, Catherine wanted to say, except—who knew how it worked? It just did, completely independently of her will or even desire.

There was absolutely no disobeying this man, though, not when he was sitting like a force of nature across a small table, hand outstretched, emanating huge vibes of attraction. He was a natural leader, the true alpha male humans had been programmed to follow by thousands of years of dangerous history.

Her hand moved of its own accord.

Without thinking about it, without willing it at all, Catherine reached out and put her hand in his. His large hand immediately curled up around hers until her hand was surrounded by warm, hard male flesh.

Oh my.

It felt so very good. *He* felt so very good. Her hand tingled, warmth prickled all the way up her arm. It was like being encased by hot steel.

“Well?” he asked impatiently. “What am I thinking?”

She was completely overwhelmed by the physical sensations buzzing through her, rattling around in her head as she looked at her hand which had disappeared in his. His grip was strong, unbreakable, yet painless.

“What?” He tightened his grip for a second, breaking the spell.

Castle gates clanging down, defending the citadel. Iron control like a wall, dark and impenetrable.

“I don’t know what—” she began in a whisper when all of a sudden she did. She did know what he was thinking. Feeling, rather. And . . . oh my.

The dark, impenetrable wall fell, crumbled. Behind it was a white-hot blast of desire, like walking in front of an open furnace. Blinding heat that reached right past her skin into her body.

He scowled, shook himself as if rejecting something, but didn’t let go of her hand. “What are you getting?” he asked impatiently.

A lifetime of training, years and years of suppressing the truth when it was unpalatable and unwanted crumbled, too, and the truth simply plopped out of her mouth.

“Desire,” she breathed. “You feel desire. For me.”

Waves of it, lapping up against her like a hot sea.

Utter silence. Neither of them breathed. He finally broke the silence, his deep voice low, quiet in the quiet room. “And what do you feel?”

The truth. It came out of her like water upwelling from a spring. Unstoppable, real. “Desire,” she whispered. “Back.”

He stood up so suddenly the chair toppled over, skittering to the wall unnoticed as he rounded the small table without letting go of her hand. He used her hand in his to pull her up and out and straight into his arms and his mouth came down on hers and the world spun around her and she was lost.

Chapter Eleven

Desire.

Christ, she called it desire but it was more than that. Whole worlds and universes more. Something bigger, something unfathomably greater. Something completely outside his ken.

Mac had felt lust plenty of times, he knew exactly what it was and what happened to him when it struck. There was this matrix, this pattern, and he was intimately familiar with it, followed it, every time. It had never occurred to him that there was something else.

It was something learned by rote, followed instinctively, like a playbook. ABC.

See a woman who wasn't a dog, didn't smell, had all her teeth, sniff her out and, if she was up for it, tell his dick to rise and stay up. And it did, of course. It always did. He never had to think about it. Never had to feel about it.

Fucking was fun, good sweaty exercise. The aftermath . . . not so much. It was true that Mac had perfected all the get-out-of-Dodge-fast moves and wasn't often caught in bed in a post-coital glow. He wasn't looking for love and neither were the women, just some fun and release in bed and that's what they got. No more, no less.

That was sex.

This? This was something else. Something infinitely more powerful, overwhelming, something that hadn't even crossed his horizon in thirty-four years of living.

He looked down for one second at Catherine's beautiful face. He had a soldier's ability to grab impressions in a second and in that split second before he kissed her he marveled at just how fucking beautiful she was.

Huge light gray eyes with that dark blue rim around them, reflecting all the light in the room in silvery flashes, pale perfect skin, high cheekbones rounding down to a firm little chin and right there the world's most delectable mouth, soft and puffy and quivering.

Shit.

Her whole body was quivering, shaking, he could feel it in his hands, against his chest. She was what? Scared? Of him?

No. She wanted him.

He fisted his hand in her soft, shiny dark hair and plunged into her, like a high diver going off the deep end. A very very deep end. Like he was falling endlessly down to the bottom of the world with nothing to stop him.

Oh, right. There was something stopping him.

Clothes. His, hers.

Shit, they had to be gone, right now, because anything standing between his skin and hers had to go. Now.

He'd undressed plenty of women in his time, but this stumped him because he had no idea how he could undress her when his mouth refused to leave hers and his hands were filled with warm woman and had no desire to lift them away, none.

Her mouth—oh God. Soft and warm, tasting like wild honey. He held her tightly against him so he could feel her all along his front and it was like electricity buzzing against one side of him while the other side of him was in coldest outer space.

For a second he wondered how he could get to a place where he was being touched by her all over, front and back, head to toe, but the laws of physics were a bitch and wouldn't let him. But by Christ he wanted it.

They broke for a second, two microns of distance between their mouths. Mac pulled in a deep breath, pulled her back to him and latched onto her mouth like a dying man. If he were dying, her mouth would revive him, no question, her tongue alone gave him jolts like those patches reviving dead men. The hand holding the back of her head slid down and his fingers touched petal-soft skin. He ran a finger along her neck while he bit her lower lip and felt her vibrate, felt her tongue flutter.

Fuck, fuck. Not only her tongue. Felt her cunt flutter! Felt her muscles pull hard from her stomach to her groin and felt his cock lengthen at the same time in answer.

He was *in* her, in her head, could barely distinguish between his arousal and hers, and knew he had to be in her body, too, right now, or die.

"We have to get our clothes off," he whispered against her mouth.

"I know," she whispered back, and licked his lips.

His dick swelled even further against her belly, one strong, almost painful pulse and it was either be in her or go crazy.

He was used to moving fast.

In the field you were fast or you were dead, one or the other. He was fast. And he was fast now, movements precise and quick as if he were field-stripping his gun, something he'd done a thousand times until his hands knew the movements better than he did.

This was something like that, only he'd never stripped a woman like this, fast and rough. Someone who looked like him had to have a little finesse but—whoa—there was no finesse in him at all, just a sort of fiery desperation.

Fast, fast, fast.

Her sweater and bra, his sweatshirt, tee. He was kissing her again before they hit the floor. Everything else could be done while kissing her, without leaving her mouth because that was how he was breathing, living—through her mouth.

He was trembling. Mac didn't tremble, not anytime, not under any circumstances, but here he was, shaking, wanting to jump out of his own skin. Or hers, because at odd moments, like a flash across his consciousness, it was as if he were in her skin, not his.

What she wanted could be read in her skin, in areas of heat he could read through some brand-new sense that had suddenly blossomed into life. She was hot, glowing all over, with her breasts and the area between her thighs emitting an extra bright golden heat. She wanted him to touch her, right there. Touch her skin with his.

But—they still had some clothes on.

With shaking hands, he unzipped his jeans and they dropped to his boots but then decided getting her naked took precedence. He simply couldn't stand not being able to touch her all over for even a second more.

He reached for the button of her slacks and missed, amazed at himself. He could defuse bombs with rock-steady hands but here he was—fumbling at a button, taking a full minute to slip a little round of plastic through a hole, trying and failing to catch the zipper's pull. What the fuck? His fingers felt big and clumsy, like robot fingers, barely in his control.

Mac was in control, always. Particularly with women. Most women agreed to fuck him on an implied understanding that he knew what he was doing, because sure as hell he had never landed a woman in his bed on the basis of his looks or his charm or his money. So he had taught himself control and smoothness. There hadn't ever been a woman who could break that control.

Ah, but this wasn't any woman. She was pure hot magic, probably a witch who'd cast a spell on him because this was way outside any experience of sex. Way outside any experience of anything, actually, with all this crazy shit about flitting in and out of her head, her body . . .

Ah! Pants undone, falling to her ankles together with panties, bunching around her boots. She glowed in the low light, there was no other word for it. Long, slender, strong legs, pale and smooth. An image of them tightly clasped around his waist nearly buckled his knees. He closed his eyes because looking at them made him harder than he had any right to be.

She gave a little sigh and he opened his eyes a fraction of an inch. She watched him out of those bright silver eyes and he wondered if she could feel the lust coming off him like steam. Sure she could. Even a normal woman would. He was holding her tightly against him, so tightly his stiff dick rubbed against her belly. She didn't need to be a psychic to figure out what he wanted.

She looked down at herself. "I feel a little foolish standing here with my pants around my ankles. Maybe I should, um . . . you should—"

"How do I get your pants off without letting you go?" he whispered. He could barely get the words out given the heat steaming in his head. His hands wouldn't open.

"You can't." Her push took him by surprise. In ordinary times, he'd barely register a push from a woman who weighed half what he did, but he was off balance anyway and he staggered just a little. Just enough to open his hands and let her go.

Catherine bent gracefully and in seconds slipped out of pants and panties and socks, and oh dear sweet God, there she was, standing before him naked.

She was blindingly beautiful. He wanted to close his eyes because she was just too much but then he didn't want to miss anything so he kept them open. Didn't want to miss one inch of that creamy skin, the tender dips and hollows, slender but shapely curves. Long, swanlike neck, delicate collarbone. Narrow waist, smooth little belly, a soft cloud of dark hair between her thighs, the pale, puffy lips of her sex peeking through. Her breasts—Jesus. Perfect. Milky white, soft, with pale pink nipples.

Her left breast shook slightly with the beating of her heart. He stared and saw her nipples become rosier and harden, just by him looking at her. She blushed suddenly, a rosy color reaching down to her pretty breasts and he felt it, felt a wave of heat move over him, too.

He was frozen, eyes greedily taking in every smoothly perfect inch of her, his dick trying to reach out to her, when she made a small noise in her throat and waved a hand at him.

He looked down and besides his ridiculously swollen dick, pulsing with every heartbeat, he was hobbled by his jeans rumpled around the tops of his black combat boots.

He looked like a dork, but when he lifted his eyes and saw the heat in hers, he didn't give a fuck. In seconds, boots, socks, jeans were off and kicked to the side, Catherine was in his arms again and he was groaning with delight as every inch of the front part of his body touching her lit up like klieg lights.

Kissing her and kissing her and kissing her, he ran his hand down her back, blown away by the softness of her skin, by the feel of her sleek, smooth muscles, then down over her ass, down down . . .

He cupped her, waggled his hand. She obediently opened her legs and he slid a finger around, inside her. She was wet. She was small but wet and yes, he could do this. Because with all that his brain was blasted and he was burning up with the need to enter her, he didn't want to hurt her. Not even a tiny bit.

Some women liked it rough, and man, that was fine by him. Hot, sweaty sex, pounding into the woman, yeah that had always worked for him.

But he was touching most of Catherine and he knew—not because she told him in words but because every cell in her body spoke to him—that she didn't like rough sex. That she was relatively inexperienced. That she was turned on but that he had to be careful.

All that was in him, a part of him now, like his hands and his legs.

Later, though. He'd treat her real gently later because right now, he couldn't breathe from wanting to be inside her, and though he tried hard not to be rough, he wasn't gentle, either.

One hand under her ass and he lifted her. Naturally, like breathing, her legs opened, clasped him around the waist, and just like that, he was in her, and holy shit, it was like plugging his dick into an electrical socket.

Every hair on his body stood up. He stopped breathing, all his senses turned inward, concentrated on his dick tightly wedged inside Catherine Young and he shook with the intensity, his legs weak, ready to buckle, his dick swelling, swelling . . .

He exploded. He didn't even know it was going to happen until he was flying apart, his entire backbone liquefying and pouring into her, taking his brains and what felt like most of his internal organs with it.

It went on and on, every muscle in his lower body pulled tight, straining, grinding into her while he held her so close to him he could feel her heart beat fast and wild against him as his hips tensed with every pulse of his dick. It took forever, so mind-blowing he lost the sense of himself as something separate from her, his entire being concentrated on where he touched her and particularly where he was buried deeply inside her.

At the last pulse, his head dropped down to her shoulder and he watched a bead of sweat, two, drip onto the smooth, pale skin of her back.

He was strong.

He could travel fifty miles in a day carrying a 120-pound rucksack. He could bench press 400 pounds.

Right now he was incapable of carrying his own weight, let alone hers, too. He was about to collapse to the floor when a warning bell sounded in his hollow head. Collapsing to the floor with Catherine in his arms could hurt her. He wouldn't collapse in a controlled fall like they practiced in training, rolling and curling to absorb the shock. No, he'd simply drop where he stood, falling straight on top of the slight, soft woman in his arms.

He'd hurt her.

He shuddered at the thought. He'd rather be shot in the face at point-blank range.

Mac took one step toward his bed—two steps would have been beyond him—and followed her down, still inside her, still kissing her.

It was so intense he had to lift his mouth from hers so that huge electric buzzing could stop for a second. Then he missed it and buried his face in the cloud of hair around her head and simply breathed her in.

Even when he stopped coming inside her the intensity of the climax was still there. His cock felt raw, surrounded by tight heat, the pleasure so intense it bordered on pain. He was lying on her slender, smooth body, probably crushing her but there was no energy to lift himself up to take some of his weight on his elbows. And abandoning the feel of her along his chest—nope. Not going to happen.

He lay like that, gasping for breath, buried deep inside her, her long, slender legs wrapped around his thighs for a century or two, the thermonuclear blast of orgasm dying slowly, though he still had spots in front of his eyes.

Bits of him came back as he slowly regained consciousness and he became aware of parts of him that weren't his cock.

Nose, buried in her hair. It smelled faintly of fruit and spring and was thick and soft and warm against his face. Her breasts, crushed beneath his chest, feeling incredibly soft against him, rubbing lightly against him as she breathed. Silky legs along his side, hugging him.

And then back to the biggie—his dick. Oh God, he was never getting out of her little cunt, ever again. She held him tightly in a molten hot embrace.

Had she come? Who knew? He'd nearly passed out with the pleasure, barely inside his own skin, too blasted to wonder about her.

Maybe he should find out?

"You—" Only air came out. Jesus, he'd lost the power of speech. He cleared his throat, tried again. "You okay?"

She arched her back a little, sliding against him, and a blast of heat ran through him.

Against his thighs he could feel her wriggle her toes and she drummed her fingers against his back. "I think so," she breathed. "Extremities are working."

Okay. Step Two. "Did you—did you come?" Mac meant to make it sound like a normal question and tried to sound matter-of-fact. It came out a wounded growl.

In answer, her cunt clenched around him and his dick moved inside her, like a little dance.

"Mmm."

He was still hard as a rock inside her but a little bit of blood was returning to his body. He lifted his head enough to see her face. She was in profile, like some cameo. Eyes closed, long lashes against her high cheekbones. Pink and perfect, those pillowy lips were slightly upturned, thank you God. That was in anyone's books a smile. Or at least half a smile.

He drew in a deep breath and felt her breasts and belly slide against him. He closed his eyes, then opened them. "I think we should talk, but I don't think I can pull out. Just not an option."

His dick had a mind of its own and nodded enthusiastically inside her. It was rewarded with another small clench. That was a yes. They were talking with their sexes.

Fine by him.

"Okay," she breathed. "Let's talk."

"Wow." It came out in a rush. "I don't know what that was but I saw fucking *colors*. It was sex but it was more than sex. I felt like I was inside your head and I can tell you it blew my mind. Are you sure you didn't cast a spell? Did you inject me with something? I don't mind, I just want to know. And let me say very sincerely I hope it was as good for you as it was for me, but I have no idea if it was because I was too busy dying there to pay much attention. So can you tell me what just happened?"

Her eyes opened, cast a look his way. Man, silver eyes were the way to go. He couldn't even remember another eye color. "I have no idea what just happened," she whispered. "It was, um, completely new to me."

Oh Christ. Mac pulled out just a little—a teeny bit because his dick definitely did not want to face the cold, cruel world outside Catherine's body—then slid back in. Jesus. Tight. Very tight. Very very tight.

He swallowed. "You're not a virgin, are you?" he asked in horror. "Or were a virgin?"

That earned him a small smile. "No. Rest easy." A small hand came up, caressed the scarred side of his face, then dropped back to the mattress. "Whoa. I'm wiped."

Tell me about it.

"Did I hurt you?"

She huffed out a little breath, but maybe because he was lying on her with his full weight. If he were a gentleman, he'd lift his torso up off her and take his weight on his forearms. But no one had ever accused him of being a gentleman. And besides, he didn't think his arms would support the weight. Every muscle he had except the one buried deep inside her was lax and loose, as if all his tendons had been cut.

"Do I look like I'm hurting?"

"Tell me no," he insisted. It was suddenly really important to him to hear her say it. "Say the words. I need them. There wasn't much foreplay—any foreplay actually—and you were so tight."

Another upturning of full lips, more a smile this time. Her lips were red and swollen, giving her that sexy Angelina Jolie look. Watching them made him hard. Harder. He swelled inside her and her eyes opened wide in shock. "Wow. From a smile?"

"Just your breathing does it for me," he croaked. "Try it."

"Try what?"

"Breathing."

Those gorgeous eyes rolled. "Mac, I've been breathing all along."

"No, no." Man, this was fun. The teasing tone, the sense of closeness. Well, they *were* close, he was buried deeply inside her. But he'd never had this sense of togetherness, ever. "Do it. Take a deep breath. See what happens."

"Okay." A sigh and another roll of the eyes, indulging the nutcase. She drew in a deep breath, held it, let it out. And oh, fuck me if it didn't lift her breasts more tightly against his chest. He slid a little more deeply into her while his cock got another infusion of blood. Her eyes widened. "Whoa."

"Tell me about it." His hands cradled her head as he bent down to her, nose to nose. "I'm not too sure what to call this. Sex seems so . . . so banal."

A startled laugh came out of her. "Banal? Did you just say banal?"

"Yeah. I think we're going to have to come up with some other name for it, for what we just did. Like 'mex' or 'shex.' Shex would do it because it's a mix of *sex* and *hex*. Because you are not convincing me that was natural."

"I don't know." Her head moved and her small nose wrinkled. "It sure smells natural."

Yeah. He was sweating like a pig and she was drenched in his come. The smell of sex was so strong it almost overrode her natural scent. Something hot flashed in his mind—the image of his scent penetrating her, his cells sinking into hers, making him part of her forever.

"No, no, it was something else." Mac dropped his forehead onto hers. "We'll figure out a word. Can we do it again?"

This time the laugh was loud, coming from her belly, sleek and flat against him. Her entire body laughed and she was irresistible.

He stopped smiling, bent to kiss her, opening her mouth with his, stroking her tongue with his, and his cock swelled even more and he started moving in her. You couldn't have stopped him with a gun to his head.

"Ahh," she breathed into his mouth, and lifted to meet his strokes.

Mac's hands moved down her side to clutch her hips, grateful that some reason remained as he tried not to grip hard. He had strong hands and the last thing he wanted to do was hurt this woman.

They moved into a perfect rhythm, his hands holding her hips, her heels riding his back. Slow strokes at first, moving easily in her She was small but he'd pumped all the fluids in his body into her so there was lubrication.

Maybe some of it was hers? God, he hoped so.

Catherine dug her fingernails into his shoulders, lifting herself against him, and he speeded up, moving fast and hard now, his bed creaking heavily. It wasn't just the bed making sounds. Their mouths as he kissed her at every possible angle, both of them breathing heavily, his cock sliding in and out, faster and faster, harder and harder . . .

She stilled, her entire body going stiff, and dropped her head back, eyes closed, mouth in a small O. A faint rose underlay the paleness of her skin, darker over her cheekbones. She was the most beautiful woman he'd ever seen at that moment, an almost otherworldly beauty.

She gave a cry, her back arched, and she convulsed around him in sharp pulses that echoed his heartbeat and on one of those beats he came, just like that. No forewarning again, from one beat to the next his body simply going into overdrive.

"God you're beautiful," he breathed, the words coming out of him unbidden when he could speak again. Not a compliment but something so very true it had to be said, acknowledged.

"I think I'm going to turn your accusation around," she murmured. "I'm sure you drugged me, did something to me."

He'd done something to her, all right. A lot of it. She looked wiped. Her arms had fallen away limply, as if she no longer had the strength to hold him, where during sex she'd held on tightly.

He was still hard. Amazing. He had stamina but not like this. This felt like he'd plugged into some universal power source, because he could go on and on and on, forever. Or that's what it felt like. He was still inside her, ready for Round Three. And Four and Five. But she did look tired, and between his ever-ready dick and her well-being, Catherine's well-being won out, hands down.

He placed his hands flat on the bed, pushing his torso up. It was harder than he would have thought. It wasn't just that he'd used up a lot of his energy but it was also that his body didn't want to leave hers, not in any way. Not even separating his chest from her breasts. And farther below, his dick was screaming *Are you crazy? You want out of here? What's the matter with you?*

His better nature was warring with his animal side, which wanted nothing more than to settle back down on top of her with a sigh, nuzzle her neck and start fucking her again.

His phone pinged. He'd set his text messages to hologram and the bright letters appeared above it. The message was from Stella.

outside door

He smiled. His better nature had just had a friendly shove.

Pulling out of Catherine was not easy, though. It felt cold away from her skin, outside her body. Standing up was harder than he thought. Her body was like this huge magnet pulling him toward her. He had to move each muscle consciously to get out of bed. With a sigh he bent to retrieve his pants.

"What was that?" Her voice sounded sleepy.

"Something you might enjoy. Sit up in bed."

She shook her head, eyes still closed. "No way. Something or someone stole my spinal cord. I may never sit up again."

Well, he had a way to persuade her. He opened the door and sure enough the magic cart was outside. Bless Stella. He was in no shape to get dressed and go down in search of some food. He didn't want to see anyone or talk to anyone except Catherine. Stella made sure he didn't have to.

Right now, this room held everything he wanted.

He wheeled the cart in, leaning over and breathing deeply, luxuriating in the smells, like a foretaste of heaven. The smells reached the bed and Catherine's nose twitched, her lips moving in a ghost of a smile.

"Sit up, honey," he said. "But keep your eyes closed."

That earned him a full-blown smile. "If you think it's a surprise, I can smell it from here. Only I have no idea what time it is, and whether it's breakfast, lunch or dinner."

He lifted covers over dishes, peeked. Jesus. His mouth started watering. "Dinner. Now sit up."

"Can't," she sighed.

"Okay." He bent over, grasped her under her arms and easily lifted her until she was sitting against the headboard. "No peeking now."

Her head tilted to one side, eyes closed. "Okay. No peeking."

Her head slumped a little more to the side.

"No falling asleep, either." She smiled, eyes closed, and he couldn't resist her, bending to touch his mouth to hers.

His world exploded.

Christ. He did see colors. Bright shards of light moving through him as he felt her. *Felt* her. Felt her bone-deep contentment like smooth honey in his veins, felt how unusual sated contentment was to her, felt . . .

He swallowed heavily.

He could feel, so strongly he could almost touch it, her affection, a burst of emotions centered on him. Through her eyes he was handsome and strong and good. Though she wasn't touching him in any way, was indeed resting bonelessly against the headboard, eyes closed, hands limp, palms up on the bedspread, tendrils of her warm feelings reached out and grabbed him, hard. These . . . things snaked through his body, tangling through his system until he couldn't tell where he stopped and she began.

It was like being lost in a fragrant, sun-filled jungle, vines clutching at him, holding him down, and damned if he didn't want to be held.

He stood for a second, looking down at her, at this woman who had unexpectedly crawled inside him, right under his skin. Beautiful and smart and somehow wanting him.

Mac had never had this in his life before. The closest relationship he had ever had had been with the Captain, but that had been a bond of duty and admiration and obedience. Nick and Jon—they were his men and he was sworn to lead them and protect them, but before the Arka fiasco had gone down, he hadn't known them well. After Arka, they'd worked hard together to protect themselves and to protect their little community, but Mac felt more loyalty to them than affection.

Affection, love—these hadn't ever played any kind of role in his life. He'd built himself from the ground up, an orphan who'd nearly drowned in the sewers of the system. The navy had saved him, given him direction and purpose, and the Captain had given him pride and duty and responsibility, but none of that had ever touched his heart. He wasn't even sure he had one, though he was now.

Because it was beating for her.

Because this woman touched his heart. No, she didn't just touch it. She reached out past skin and bone and muscle and grabbed his heart directly, squeezing it hard, wrapping herself around it so tightly he didn't know where he ended and she began.

Dangerous, heady stuff and it made his head swim.

He straightened, scowling, wishing like hell he could put all these roiling emotions inside him down to some drug or fancy form of hypnosis or some crazy mind-control technique, but he knew it wasn't that. It was all real and it came from him, from the deepest part of him that responded to her like a key in a lock.

Dealing with a firefight was easier than this. This was mind-bending, life-altering stuff and knocked him straight out of his boots.

"So?" she asked softly. "Can I open my eyes?" She drew in a deep appreciative breath. "It smells glorious."

"Not yet."

He angled the cart close to the edge of the bed, wondering how this was going to work without plates, then realized there was stuff on a shelf below. God, he was going to get something special for Stella the next time he went out into the World because bless her, she'd thought of everything. On the lower shelf was a foldout tray, plates, glasses, napkins and silverware.

Mac started to fold the tray out over her lap when he stopped, frowning. She was naked, the sheet barely held over her breasts, tucked under her arms.

Though a naked Catherine was a very good thing and though he couldn't imagine anything finer than seeing and touching her breasts while he ate, a lot of the food was hot and the thought that she might be burned by hot food made him queasy. Mac knew firsthand the blinding pain of burns, soul-searing torment that went on forever. He couldn't bear to think of Catherine going through anything like that.

Not an option.

"Hold up your arms." He pulled out a clean folded tee from a drawer, shook it out, floated it over her head. "Here. You'll be more comfortable this way. And you can open your eyes now."

They opened immediately and met his and it was a punch to the stomach. No soft tendrils around his heart, no glowing heat flowing gently through his veins like honey. This was desire, hot and strong and hard as rock. Nothing gentle about it, just something vast and necessary. Strong as painless fire.

She knew it, she could feel it, he could almost see the lines going from him to her. Connection, deep and clear. Desire, like a blast furnace, fiercely strong, from him to her, strong and hot.

Her eyes widened and she instinctively flinched back against the headboard. God. She looked almost eerily delicate, his tee on her so huge the neck almost slipped off her shoulders. Her eyes were wide, fixed on his, confused swirls of emotion buzzing around her, darkening, and he realized with a sigh that she wasn't ready for Round Two. He frowned. Round Three.

At some deep level she wanted it but at an even deeper level she was frightened by it and it scared him that this made sense to him. That he could read her like that.

He brought her hand to his mouth and kissed her knuckles, one by one. He turned her hand over and kissed the palm. Her hand cupped his chin, one finger stroking his burn scars.

Normally, he hated that. He didn't like being touched, not even in the heat of sex. He often held a sex partner's hands above her head because he had heavy scars along his back, too. The deep, thick scars—shrapnel from an IED—were souvenirs of Fucked-upistan, well before he was fucked up at Arka, but the two together were like a roadmap of pain and violence. What he'd done with his life written on his skin.

He didn't need the light for a woman to be curious. Even in the dark, you could feel his scars and he hated the question—*what happened?*

What the fuck do you think happened? He'd had to bite that one back a lot.

This was completely different. Catherine ran her soft fingers over the entire scar, rippled, melted flesh on the left side of his face that went from the top of his forehead down to under his chin. He had a working left eye by a miracle.

The tone of her feelings changed, softened. No fear, something else.

"I can feel your pain," she whispered.

And she could. He could tell. Everything about her darkened and tightened, and Christ, he couldn't stand it, not for one second. He didn't want her to feel his pain. He didn't want her to feel any pain, ever.

"Don't," he whispered back, clasping his hand over hers. Her hand under his was warm and seemed to emit light. All of her was light. "Don't think of it."

She shook her head, eyes never leaving his. "How can I not think of it, when it's so close, right there under your skin? I can feel it. It never goes away. Not physical pain but the other kind." Her hand traced down, over his neck, chest, to rest over his heart. Her hand seemed to pulse in time with his heartbeat. Skin against skin, skin melding into skin. "The kind that's worse. I wish I could take it away for you."

He smiled, something he did rarely. The burn scar puckered and stretched when he smiled. It wasn't painful, just uncomfortable, and so he hardly ever smiled. There wasn't much to smile about anyway. There'd never been much to smile about.

"You are taking it away," he said in a low voice. It was true. Heat spread from her hand, filling his chest, curling inside him like smoke. The Captain's betrayal, he and his men, who had pledged their lives to their country, on the run like outlaws, accused of treason . . . it faded to background noise. The sharp pain of it was gone, dissipated like morning mist.

The spiky, ragged, almost painful desire he'd felt only a few minutes ago had subsided, replaced with a liquid glowing need for her, strong and steady and true. Sex, surely. Desire, yes. But something else, something deeper and more necessary than that. What he felt was passing through her hand into her.

He took in a deep breath, her hand rising and falling with his chest.

"I want you. Again." The words came out a gentle whisper, where moments before they would have come out painful and raw.

He leaned into her hand, knowing she could read everything about him through the skin of her hand, something flowing between them, hot and rapid and bright with the glow of passion laced with tenderness.

He didn't press against her, didn't try to convince her, just waited, feeling the ebb and flow and swirl of emotions in her. He watched her carefully, though he could read her better through the hand touching him than he could from the expression on her face.

But oh God, he couldn't take his eyes from her face. She was so beautiful. It was as if someone had reached deep into his head to pull out his own personal template for a beautiful woman and had created her entirely from what was in him. Everything about her was just so fine—the pale, porcelain-smooth skin, huge silver eyes, luscious mouth, long, slender neck. Though his tee covered her breasts, he didn't need to see them because burned in his memory was the feel of them in his hands, soft and firm, the way her nipples felt against his tongue . . .

A flash of heat. From her. He could *see* colors swirl around her breasts, faintly red and orange, while her skin turned rosy from her face to her shoulders. And there, between her thighs, under the blanket, a glow—unmistakably warm with desire.

Catherine let him pull his tee over her head and rose up onto her knees, kissing him gently, the hand over his heart smoothing its way up, over his shoulder, around his neck.

"Yes," she said.

Chapter Twelve

Millon Laboratories
Palo Alto

Lee loved the forbidden and secret fourth subterranean floor of the laboratory.

Level 4.

Millon management had no idea it was there.

With Flynn's money he'd bribed the construction company, who had brought in an entirely new crew for the floor and had sealed it off. It was more than state-of-the-art, it was years ahead of its time. There could be a magnitude 8 earthquake, a ten-ton atom bomb could be set off, a tsunami could roll into the Sierra Nevada and the lab would survive. It had its own generator, the power coming in over separate cables from hidden solar panels. Ferrite rods piercing the flooring into the earth were capable of sending very long-wave broadcasts directly through the earth to Beijing. Should anyone get through his net security he had a back-door method of communication.

Lee was king here. When he came to the Millon lab, he came

as head of research of the majority holding company, nothing more. Nobody at Millon had a clue he was directing research in a secret lab.

He loved slipping down to the fourth floor unobserved.

He had three assistants sworn to secrecy, thinking they were working under top secret conditions for the company itself and had been promised nonexistent stock options in a nonexistent roll-out of a drug that cured dementia. What was very real, however, was the money each lab rat had in an account in the former Maldives, now underwater and relocated to the coast of India.

The researchers and his personal security team were the only ones with access to the floor.

SL-59 was being tested. Behind a sliding steel door was the animal testing lab, where accelerated testing was carried out in ways which were illegal under the Animal Testing Bill. If they'd followed protocol they would still be on SL-8. Lee swiped his security card and walked through, feeling a slight wind at his back due to the negative pressure of the animal test lab.

The drug was delivered via a modified virus and care was taken to make sure nothing escaped. There was nothing contagious in this molecule, it was simply a precaution.

He strolled to the back of the huge room, ignoring the rows and rows of animals in cages in varying stages of death, knowing that federal officials would shut the lab down if they could see this. What they were doing contravened every single animal protection law on the books.

And yet the human experiments were perfectly legal, with the Informed Consent forms signed. Even though many of the consent forms had been signed five minutes before the patient had been declared incompetent.

It still baffled him how Americans almost seemed to care more for animals than for humans, though animals were absolutely necessary for testing drugs. Because here he was, very close to the formula of a drug that would enhance soldiers' abilities by a factor of ten, and it had only taken two years.

Yesterday, ten bonobos had been administered 5 cc's of SL-59. They would be thoroughly studied in the weeks to come, but Lee wanted to be the first to observe them, get a feel for the effects before analysis started.

The lab was huge, stretching four hundred feet toward the north gate, row after pristine row of animals in Plexiglas cages. Ordinarily, he'd check every cage, each row undergoing a specific test protocol. But he was angry at Flynn and pressed for time so he strode straight to the back, without looking left or right. The back row held the bonobos, infocubes of data accessible via a touchpad on the front of each cage. The gender and genetic history of each animal, a full medical workup, MRI and CAT scan data, results of intelligence tests, remote sensing of EEGs and EKGs, dosages of SL-59—all that and more was in the infocubes.

He went down the row, clear cage after clear cage, swiping his finger on the touchpad, screening for major anomalies. Two of the animals were dying, EEGs irregular, EKGs with unusual spikes he'd study later. The spikes would hold the key to their deaths, he was sure.

Four more seemed normal, with normal readings, but they were listless.

Number Eight, a largish male, on the other hand, was standing, eyes alert. Hmm. Lee swiped and scanned the data that appeared in light letters in the air. Perfectly normal values. The animal was watching him, seeming almost to take his measure, brown eyes deep and steady.

Interesting.

Bonobos were a placid species, not aggressive by nature, but their heart rate tended to increase slightly in the presence of an alien species. Number Eight's heart rate remained steady and regular. The animal stood straight and still and watched him calmly. Only his eyes moved, checking Lee's face, then his hands. Was he checking for weapons? That would be a sign of unusual intelligence.

Very interesting.

Lee stepped forward, and so quickly the EKG didn't have time to measure the acceleration of heartbeat, the bonobo flung himself straight at Lee, so hard and fast the animal's snout smashed against the Plexiglas at the front of the cage, inches from Lee's face, spattering blood out to the corners. The glass was so transparent Lee took a quick step back, flinching, before he stopped himself. The blood looked as if it were drops suspended in the air.

Undeterred, Number Eight smashed against the glass wall again and again in a frenzy of ferocity, trying to bite his way to Lee, striking his snout so hard against the unbreakable glass that bloody shards of teeth flew in all directions. He tried to claw his way to Lee, too, striking his paws so hard he broke first his left ulna and then his right humerus in compound fractures exiting bloodily from the hairy flesh of the arm. Number Eight struck again and again and again, even after he surely understood there was no breaking through the glass.

Bonobos reasoned, on a primitive level. Lee had watched them make rudimentary tools, obey a limited vocabulary of words. An ordinary primate would have learned that attacking the wall was utterly pointless, yet Number Eight kept battering himself wildly against the wall of the cage, which was no longer transparent but covered in blood and fur and spittle.

He attacked, over and over, mindlessly, eyes trained on Lee's.

He was beating himself to death, killing himself with his own ferocity.

With a swipe of a finger, Lee switched on the sound system. His eyes widened slightly at the noise level. Number Eight's snarls and howls were loud in the large room and made the other animals stir uneasily. The bonobo next to Number Eight, Number Nine, had been sitting listlessly with a straw in his mouth, but at the howls he stood up unsteadily, turned to Number Eight, the straw dropping, forgotten, to the bottom of the cage.

Lee watched, unmoving, as Number Eight battered himself to death against the blood-spattered wall, finishing himself off with one final blow to the head as he tried to ferociously butt his way through to Lee, breaking his own neck.

He dropped instantly to the ground, body nearly unrecognizable. So many bones were broken that the body looked like a hairy, shapeless sack filled with marbles.

The other bonobos turned, restless, some trying to scratch their way out of the Plexiglas cages but none with the ferocity of Number Eight. Nothing Lee had ever seen matched the ferocity of Number Eight. It was unprecedented, and artificial. Induced by SL-59.

The interesting thing was that Eight had managed to control himself for the first few minutes, even though his limbic system must have been screaming *attack*! He hadn't, not right away. Perhaps he'd tried to reason it out and had then been overwhelmed by the attack imperative infused in him by the drug.

But that time gap was interesting. So there was some kind of trip wire that had induced the out-of-control violence. Find the trip wire, modify it, and they would be well on their way.

Lee studied the battered body for another few minutes, then swiped a finger for the recording function.

"I want an autopsy with toxicology and hormone levels. I want the exact level of SL-59 in the blood-brain barrier. I want a brain dissection and analysis of neuronal connections. I want it all."

Another flick and the recording function switched off.

That had been interesting, he thought as he exited the lab.

And promising. Very promising.

* * *

Mount Blue

Yes.

She'd said yes, when she was hungry, when delicious-smelling food was right there, all she had to do was reach out her hand, when she'd already had more intense sex than she'd ever had in her entire life, when she was a little sore, feeling unused muscles stretch every time she moved in the bed.

She said yes when she thought she'd need at least a day to recover and feel desire again.

Oh, how wrong she'd been.

She'd said yes because she couldn't resist. There was nothing in her that could resist this man, standing half-naked in front of her, intensely aroused. She could tell not only by the steel rod prodding at the front of his jeans, but in the slight red tingeing the sallow skin over his high cheekbones, the flaring nostrils, the tense cords of the tendons of his neck.

And of course she could tell by his touch. His desire flowed straight into her, hot waves of his heat piercing her skin.

At just the touch of him, feeling Mac's heartbeat against her hand, feeling how much he wanted her, needed her, desire rose again like water rising to replenish an empty well. Coming from him? Coming from her? It was impossible to tell and it made no difference because now it was inside her. Part of her.

"Come to me," she whispered, or maybe she thought it in her head? No matter. He shucked his jeans and moved to her, over her, settling on her heavily, yet she welcomed his weight, welcomed him as another wave of burning desire swept over them.

"Make me go slow," he whispered in her ear, and she shivered as his breath washed over her. He took her lobe and gently bit. Goose bumps broke out all over.

She held on to his shoulders, something to cling to in this new world where desire rolled over her in hot waves. She was bobbing in this sea of desire and needed something stable. She clutched him, those extra wide shoulders.

If ever there was a man built for hanging on to, this was that man. Everything about him spoke of strength and stability. That he was the one making her feel unsettled, rushed away in a liquid sea of desire, was ironic.

"Slow," he insisted, even though his stiff penis was prodding her thigh, then her stomach as he settled more completely over her.

"Slow," he moaned, and kissed her.

It was slow, his mouth, his tongue moving slowly, the rest of him still. In the end she was the one who started moving. Her legs opened, lifted, settled against his back, and he was naturally there, the hard tip of his penis right at her opening.

It felt so huge and she had to remind herself that they'd done this twice before and he hadn't hurt her. He wasn't moving, though, wasn't shifting to enter her, and all of a sudden she felt *empty*. Her sex felt empty, an organ that wasn't filled with what nature intended. Like a stomach with no food, lungs with no air.

It was as vital as that. A yawning, searing *craving* for him to enter her, take her because that's what her vagina was for. It wasn't pleasure so much as need. Just feeling him there, not in her but against her, made her clench so hard even her thigh muscles pulled.

And still, he didn't move, just kissed her and kissed her and kissed her.

Catherine dug in her heels against the small of his back and lifted herself. He slid in a little and stayed there, unmoving.

"Mac," she sighed.

He certainly wasn't moving out of a lack of desire. He was hard as a club. He was sweating all over his back.

"Foreplay." He lifted his mouth just enough to talk. She opened her eyes and saw him, face pulled in lines of pain, nostrils thin and white with tension. "I can't keep doing this to you. To you, of all women. I want to take an hour just to kiss those pretty breasts. An hour kissing your feet and sucking your toes. You have gorgeous toes, did anyone ever tell you that?"

"Honestly?" She smiled. "No."

"That's because most men are idiots."

"True."

"And then I want to take an hour just to touch your hands. You have the most gorgeous hands I've ever seen."

She laughed. It wasn't a big laugh because he was lying on top of her, nearly squeezing the breath out of her, so it was more a huff of breath. It was okay. She loved his heavy weight bearing down on her.

Something magical was happening and his heavy, earthy presence kept her grounded, reminded her it was *real*. There was magic but there was also reality. That weight, the bite of his beard while he kissed her, the sweat that plastered her breasts to his chest, the heavy mat of hair on his chest rubbing against her, the hair on his legs abrading the skin on the inside of her thighs. The earthy smells of sex and sweaty man. His heavy heartbeat, slow and strong, the heart of an athlete, beating against her breasts, against the palms of her hands as she moved her hands down over his back . . .

That was all real.

Then there was the magic.

Feeling his heart beat against hers, as if they were two organs beating in the same body. Being under his skin, knowing what he felt, sometimes what he thought. They couldn't be more different. She had no idea what his background was like—that wasn't her gift. But she knew what *he* was like because that was.

Knowing his bravery, his essential goodness, his loyalty. Knowing there was violence in him, feeling his toughness, knowing this was a man who would never break.

What he felt for her was right there, right under his skin. The heat of sex, the warmth of affection, the iron grip of his desire to protect her, keep her safe.

"But the thing is"—Mac sighed, and slipped in her just a little farther, just enough to open the lips of her sex and make her writhe with desire—"the thing is I keep getting sidetracked, by *this*."

He slid into her, inch by slow inch, carefully, every muscle tense with effort. He stopped when he was fully inside her, panting a little. His heart had stepped up its rate, as if he were running.

She felt that heartbeat in his penis, pulsing gently inside her.

"Now, Mac," she groaned, shaking. "I don't need foreplay." Every touch of his was foreplay.

It was such overkill, holding that huge body in her arms. So utterly male, so utterly tough, so utterly hers.

Every touch told her he was hers. Every touch, every kiss was for her.

He started moving and it was a luscious dance, skin on skin, beating heart against beating heart. Hard to soft. Meltingly tender this time. Every inch of her was taken up by this man.

Her hands and legs followed that huge bowed back as he thrust in her so carefully, smoothly, movements controlled. It was like being on a sea, waves rocking her, and she lost herself in the rhythm, in the heat. Her senses blanked out, one by one. She closed her eyes and couldn't see. The beat of her heart and his filled her ears until she heard nothing. She couldn't feel her limbs anymore, all she felt was the center of her being, filled with him rocking into her, rocking, rocking . . .

She pulled into herself until there was only that small center of white-hot heat, incandescent as the sun, and it went nova.

Mac held himself still inside her as she writhed around him. It felt like that sun was bursting out of her body and she had to let it go in wild pulses of heat and light.

"God," he muttered as she slowly relaxed. Under him, and against her arms and legs, she felt him explode into action, hips pumping as he moved in and out of her, so fiercely it almost—but not quite—hurt. It would have if this had been any man other than Mac. With anyone else it would have felt like a battering invasion of her body but she was with him every step of the way.

It wasn't an invasion. His body was trying to get as close to hers as it could. If he could have, he would have crawled inside her, and if she could have, she would have let him.

This was the next best thing, this utter and complete claiming of her, making her completely his.

When he collapsed on her, face planted on the pillow next to hers, she felt as wrung out as he was.

The room was so quiet, the only sounds their heavy breathing. His heart was pounding as if he'd run a hundred miles. She felt it—both their hearts. His thudding in a heavy, rhythmic beat, hers lighter and faster. She lay under him, eyes closed, drinking in this moment of utter closeness and listened as their hearts synchronized, beating together.

Everything about them was coming together. She felt stronger and was aware that his energy was sapped. She was inside his body, feeling the currents of wonder and joy coursing through him. The same currents swirling in her.

Her arms had gone lax in the thousandth orgasm—well, maybe that was an exaggeration but they had been too numerous to count, tripping from one straight into another. Suddenly, her arms and legs tightened around him, wildly, as if she suddenly had to hold him to her, but that was crazy. Mac showed no signs of wanting to get away. If anything, he seemed settled on top of her as if he was never going to move again.

It was just that she wanted to hold on to this. It seemed such a rare, such a unique moment. Something wondrous, magical. By definition fleeting, over almost as soon as it began. This couldn't last. How could it? What good ever lasted in this world? It was—

Mac lifted his head and gave her a huge grin and she was startled right out of her thoughts. The grin was wide. He was smiling with his entire face and every line in his skin told her it was unusual. The lines in his face naturally went to gravity, to grimness and frowns. This stretched everything out of shape and looked like it actually hurt his scars.

He smiled down at her and she swallowed at what she saw. She saw—so clearly—what he felt for her. Saw how new it was for him. And felt—deep down where there was no possibility of hiding—felt that he would undoubtedly die for her.

Her gift, her curse, told her this, told her that for the first time in her life she was loved. She was loved deeply.

"Wow," he said. "That was—" He broke off, the smile wiped from his face. He scowled down at her, wiping a tear away from her face with his thumb. "What's the matter?"

All of a sudden he looked appalled, actually frightened. He lifted up off her, pulled out from her, leaving emptiness and coldness behind. "Did I hurt you?" he demanded. "Are you okay?"

"Yes, I'm fine." Catherine sniffed, ashamed of herself. She'd suddenly been swamped by her emotions, and his. And she'd scared him. "I'm so sorry. It's just that—"

Her stomach rumbled, loudly, and she laughed, wiping away another tear with the heel of her hand. Laughing, crying, hungry . . . she was a mess.

Mac was sitting up, a little calmer, eyeing her cautiously. He visibly relaxed when she smiled at him. "If you're crying because you're hungry, I have the answer right here." He nudged the cart with a big bare foot sticking out from under the covers. "It's all cold but I've got a microwave. How does that sound?"

Catherine sat up in bed, grateful for the mundane thought of food. Her stomach rumbled again and she giggled, feeling calmer. "Sounds wonderful. I think I could eat a horse." A second ago all her emotions had been churning but now she was calmer and, upon consultation with her stomach, starving. "Raw. I hope I won't have to."

"No, Stella doesn't do raw horsemeat."

"Carpaccio," Catherine said, smiling. She leaned against the headboard and watched with interest as a naked Mac rose and started ferrying dishes over to a huge microwave against the wall. The back view was astonishing. Wide, thickly muscled shoulders tapering down to a lean waist, hard dimpled buttocks, long, hard thighs, the individual muscles visible.

He threw her a startled glance over his shoulder. "Carpo what?"

Catherine laughed. "Carpaccio. Raw meat or fish, thinly sliced."

The microwave was the new kind that heated in a second. He was already coming back with the tray full of food, placing it back on the cart.

The front view was as enticing as the back one with the addition of a still semi-erect penis.

"Nothing raw that doesn't have to be," he said, pulling out legs from the tray and placing it on her lap. He leaned over and gave her a quick peck on the lips. "Now pay attention here because this is a surprise."

Catherine sat up straight, wondering what he meant. "There's hardly anything here that isn't a surprise."

"No, this one's really good. Voilà." Mac touched something and Catherine gasped.

It was magic.

Three walls, to the right, to the left and straight ahead . . . disappeared. Simply vanished. In their place was an amazing nighttime view of the mountain as if they were on a platform jutting out from the mountainside. Snowy slopes of white firs swooped down to the valley bathed in moonlight. Far far away down the mountainside, almost in the valley below, a few lights twinkled.

Had they been outside all this time and the windows blanked?

It was impossible to tell. Every silvery moonlit detail was sharp and clear.

Mac reached out gently and closed her jaw with a finger and only then did she realize she was staring slack-jawed.

"What—what is this? Are we outside?"

He piled food onto a plate and set it in front of her. "Eat. I think we've burned about a billion calories. You're going to kill me, Catherine."

"Ha!" She jabbed him in the side and nearly sprained her hand. Rocks were softer than his muscles. "Not likely. So what is this?"

"Holo. We have security cameras ringing the property and Jon set it up so we can project it in our rooms, give us a view. Because it is a view—just not right outside the window."

"That is really amazing but so's this. Wait a second." She held up a hand, closed her eyes, savored the big bite of pumpkin ravioli with chanterelle sauce. Oh God. Heaven. The wild sex, the God's-eye view that appeared in the blink of an eye, the stunning food. This was sensory overload. "Okay." Her eyes popped open. "Ready for the view again now."

She looked around the three walls. A rabbit crossed a small, snowy meadow and stopped, nose wrinkling, sniffing the air. Satisfied, it hopped away. Off . . . screen?

Mac was chomping on a pulled-pork baguette and smiled secretively. "Watch long enough and you'll see a deer. I saw a coyote the other day. That's not all we can do, though. Watch."

He touched something on the bedside table and all of a sudden the room was filled with sunlight, so blinding Catherine had to shield her eyes.

"Oh my God," she breathed. It was a slightly different view, but the shape of the mountain and the valley below were the same. A blindingly bright sun rose over a hill, making the landscape glow. The sky was the brightest blue in the history of blue skies and there were only small patches of snow on the ground.

"Sunrise, three days ago," Mac said, and picked up another sandwich.

She watched, amazed, as a hawk flew high in the sky, elegantly gliding on thermals. The sun crossed some invisible barrier and shot light down to the valley in glowing beams coming straight out of Hollywood. Except CGI could never make this stuff up.

"How can you afford all this fancy stuff?" Catherine asked. This was at least several million dollars' worth of technology, shining into Mac's bedroom. Then she realized what she said and clapped a hand over her mouth, appalled. "I'm sorry!" she gasped. "So sorry! It's none of my business and—"

Mac calmly reached over, pulled her hand away from her mouth, kissed her knuckles. "Don't be sorry about anything, honey, ever. This is your community now, your people. Ask anything you want. And the answer to how we can afford it all?" Those dark eyes gleamed. "We steal it."

Another bite of that glorious ravioli stopped on the way to her mouth. "You *steal* it?"

He nodded, popped a slider into his mouth. Chewed. Swallowed. "Yeah. Or rather, Jon does. He was on a six-month mission to the Calderón clan in Colombia, undercover as a California dealer. He came away with a lot of intel, enough to hack deep into their systems. When we need something he just creams it off their accounts. Last week, for example, we bought a ton of seeds and fertilizer for Manuel, a new forklift and a crash cart for the infirmary. We've got a shopping list a mile long. Jon delicately goes in, takes the money and transfers it to a bank account in San Francisco in the name of a shell company, and we all have black credit cards. So far several Calderón lieutenants have been accused of embezzling from the boss and have been hung out to dry. Literally, with meat hooks. They ran the child prostitution business for the cartel. Couldn't happen to nicer guys."

"You've got quite a setup here, Mac."

He stopped smiling, met her eyes. "Yes. We do. We've got a lot of people we want to protect. We want to keep this community safe."

She stopped smiling, too. "And you think trying to rescue Nine will put them at risk. I understand that."

"There's no 'try' involved," Mac said. "If we go in, we rescue him. But a lot of things can go wrong and there's the possibility he's not there, the possibility that you read him wrong. The possibility it's a trap." He took in a deep breath, that broad chest expanding. "No, don't say it." He put a finger across her lips. "I know—and Nick and Jon know—you would never deliberately lead us into a trap, but there's a lot we don't know about the situation."

She kissed his finger, pulled his hand down from her mouth and held it. Felt his determination, felt his warring instincts—a desire to rescue a hurt comrade versus a desire to keep his people safe—felt honor and pride and dread. He wouldn't be her Mac if he didn't feel all those things.

"Are you guys still planning how to do it?"

"Oh yeah. We're not rushing into anything without doing a full recon. Jon's got drones flying overhead and Nick's analyzing the results. Jon's checking their computer systems with the codes you gave him. We'll go down at the new moon and do a thorough check of the terrain, and when our plan is solid, we'll go."

She was going with them but it wasn't the time or the place to say that.

She reached up, kissed the side of that hard mouth. "My money's on you guys."

Chapter Thirteen

January 8

Tired and pissed, Mac entered his quarters the next afternoon, hoping but not expecting and ah . . . there she was.

It had been a long, hard, frustrating day. Two drones went belly-up, and since they were urgently needed for the Millon recon, Jon and Nick had slipped over into Nevada to steal two of them from Nellis. They had walked onto the base in full uniform with fake ID, caught the codes for two drones, remotely flew them out, and drove back out of the base, calm as could be.

But it had taken them, door to door, twelve hours.

In the meantime, Mac had been stuck here doing his mayor/king thing, okaying Dane's request for a hundred miles of micro-steel water pipeline, Pat and Salvatore's request for a robosurgeon for minor surgery, Manuel's request for an experimental square-mile hydroponics bed and listening to a two-hour lecture by Stella on How Not to Fuck Up with Catherine.

One goddamned thing after another, when all he wanted was to spend time with Catherine. Possibly fucking her, without fucking it up.

He'd glimpsed sightings of her from afar, like some unicorn. Coming out of the kitchens as he talked with Dane, she was in the infirmary almost all day and had just left when Pat and Salvatore called him in, somehow she was always just out of his reach.

She'd just finished lunch when he finally made it to the communal eating hall and hadn't had dinner yet. He'd just checked.

It was the third time he'd checked in an hour and finally Stella told him to just . . . go home.

So he did.

He was frustrated as hell as he walked into his quarters, ready to put out a BOLO on the fucking intercom when there she was, staring out his window.

Oh man.

He stopped on the threshold and rubbed his chest as he saw her, back to him, looking at the view. Home. He'd never had a home before, unless you counted Bachelor Officer Quarters home. But here it was, his home, because Catherine was in it, waiting for him.

She turned around and smiled at him, and just like that, his tiredness and frustration and ill temper dissipated like smoke. He noticed out of the corner of his eye that dinner had been set out on a table and he drew in a huge breath of relief as he walked fully into the room, releasing the infrared sensor that held the door open. It slid closed behind him and he realized that he was truly home. The cares of the day slipped from his shoulders and everything in him lifted.

"Hi," she said softly.

"Hi, honey," he replied. "I'm home."

Catherine laughed. God, it was good to hear her laugh. He smiled back and felt some muscles crack in his cheek. It actually hurt him to smile and he figured he'd better get used to it because seeing Catherine and not smiling . . . well, it was almost impossible.

"Couldn't get in touch with you all day," he growled.

"I heard," she sighed. "But I was busy. Do you want to hear about my day or do you want to kiss me?"

Well, if she was going to put it like that. A few strides and he caught her in his arms and everything frustrating about his day just slid right out of his head. Her mouth was warm and welcoming and tasted like honey. And maybe it was honey, because something smooth and thick and warm moved through his veins as she moved in his arms.

He was lucky he had that first moment of gentle warmth because then it ratcheted right up to raw smoking heat in the space of a heartbeat and he was holding her tightly, kissing her hard, trying to figure out how to get her naked right . . . now.

She had the same idea and was frantically tugging at his sweatshirt, trying to pull it up over his head. He was way too tall so he pulled away from her and ducked so she could get the damned thing over his head. It was easier for him. By the time she got his sweatshirt and tee off he'd pulled off her sweater, unhooked her bra and unzipped her jeans.

Now he could kiss her, too. Light, biting kisses.

"I thought"—she unzipped his jeans—"we could have a cup of tea."

He sproinged out of his jeans, cock red and swollen, already hopefully aimed at her like a divining rod that had found water. She grasped him, gave him a stroke with a tight fist and nearly brought him to his knees.

"Talk about our day," she gasped. "Watch the sunset. Eat dinner."

"Later," he growled, and finished the job of getting them naked.

One day he'd do this nice and slow, he would.

Just not today.

She was like hot silk in his arms, moving slowly against him, rubbing against him like a cat, filling his head with heat and light.

The light was intense, a bright yellow glow so vivid it lit up his eyes even behind his closed lids. He lifted his mouth an inch from hers and opened his eyes, looked over her head. His breath rushed into his lungs on a gasp.

Catherine turned around in his arms, her gasp echoing his.

Magic. Utter magic.

The sun was just setting behind a hill and bright yellow rays, the kind kids drew with rulers and yellow crayon, shafted through the trees, lighting up the landscape with a glorious glow. The view she'd chosen stretched down to the valley and all the colors were intense—the dark green firs and spruces, the deep gray granite boulders, the blinding white snow. It looked like a fairyland instead of the dangerous, treacherous world outside their realm.

"So beautiful," Catherine sighed, and fuck him if it wasn't.

He couldn't remember the last time he'd looked out, either through the piped in view or on his outings, and considered the stunning beauty surrounding him. All he ever considered was perimeter security, lines of fire, presence or absence of threats.

Seeing the beauty of it was absolutely new and all due to the naked woman in his arms.

Keeping his eyes on the "view," he bent to kiss her neck and discovered that if he bit her very lightly, right under her ear, she shivered. Actually, he knew that already. He'd discovered that last night but in the general overload, he hadn't marked it down as important, but it was. Because here he had a whole body to explore, every inch of it with its own enticements.

That little spot behind her ear, the way her breathing stepped up when he touched her breasts, the way her head tipped back when she came . . . oh yeah, there were lots of things to learn and memorize.

And it occurred to Mac that maybe this was his new life. Coming into his quarters in the evening and instantly shedding his cares because there Catherine would be, smiling at him. And they'd watch the sunset together, have dinner together, go to bed together, wake up together.

His quarters would become a home.

He had no idea what the future held but he was pretty sure they could stay holed up here pretty much forever. In a couple of days, they'd go down to the lab where Catherine worked, infiltrate and see if Patient Nine really was the Captain.

And for the very first time in a year, his heart didn't give a painful thump at the idea of Lucius Ward.

He had the woman in his arms to thank for that.

"You blasted my mind and rearranged all my neurons," he whispered in her ear, and felt her shiver.

"Yeah?" she gasped.

One hand covered her breast, the other smoothed its way down her flat little belly.

"Yeah. Because not only do I have this woo-woo thing going on, I can now see into the future."

"Oh!" He cupped her, feeling the soft cloud of hair against the palm of his hand, sliding farther down. The flesh there was warm, soft, wet.

"Oh yeah." Two fingers circled her slowly and she gasped again when he entered her with a finger.

"Yeah. I can see me coming home here every evening and you waiting for me and us doing . . . this." His finger entered her deeply and she clenched around him. Jesus. He spoke against her neck, biting his way up a tendon. "Actually, I think that in the interests of efficiency when you're in here you should just be naked. What's with all this time we have to waste with buttons and zippers? Just have you be naked. And I'll strip just as soon as I get in the door."

She was breathing heavily, getting wetter by the second. Mac opened his eyes and looked down at her breasts, nipples hard and cherry red.

It was a nice seduction but now he was trapped in it, too. The air had turned hot, hard to pull into his lungs. His legs felt weak. When her cunt clenched around his finger again it was too much.

"Put your hands against the window. Open your legs." His voice was low, guttural. He considered himself lucky he could speak at all. On a sigh, she placed her hands against the window, the rays of the sun turning her into an ivory-gold vision. Mac looked down at the slender, strong back, narrow waist.

He grasped her hips and stepped closer to her. She knew what he wanted. She could feel it, just as he could feel what she wanted. She wanted this. Almost as badly as he did.

Her legs had opened and she arched her back, offering herself.

Mac didn't have to use his hands. His cock did it all by itself, sliding into her honeyed heat until he was fully inside her. He bent over her back, holding her tightly, and put his mouth close to her ear.

"Hi, honey," he whispered. "I'm home."

January 9
Millon Laboratories
Palo Alto

The next evening, after carefully reviewing the data from Level 4, Lee decided to check on the official patients, up in the official facility. One in particular. He most particularly wanted to visit Patient Nine. Formerly known as Captain Lucius Ward.

Lee was still convinced that Ward—now forever Patient Nine—held the key to a breakthrough, or at least his brain did. It was time to see what was inside that brain.

Lee waited until the day staff had left the facility, with only a skeleton crew and security, none of whom were going to bother him. The security guards changed shifts at 10 P.M. and that was when he walked down the empty hallways. He entered Nine's room, quietly closed the door behind him.

Patient Nine was upright in a chair, bands holding his forehead to the back, bands holding his wrists to the arms of the chair, bands around his knees and ankles. The bonds had been tested and required two hundred pounds of shear pressure to break, something Patient Nine could never marshal in his current state. He was completely immobilized.

Tiny sensors all over his body were transmitting every single biological marker to a highly secure computer. The data was visualized in holo charts next to Nine's head.

Heart rate, brain waves, adrenaline level, all blood markers, even skin conductivity. Everything that made up Patient Nine, the very essence of Patient Nine, right there in white letters in the air.

His use was at an end. The military history of Patient Nine had made him a perfect guinea pig for the testing of the various iterations of SL, as was the case for the other three patients in Level 4. But they were recalcitrant, rebellious in the extreme, and had turned out to be almost more trouble than they were worth. Like Patient Nine.

Even nearly comatose, Patient Nine was rebellious, pitting his will against the chemical properties of the drug so strongly the effects were almost always vitiated.

Patient Nine's EEGs were now so skewed as to be almost worthless.

Lee wanted to discover the hidden trip wire he had sensed watching the bonobo, but it was almost impossible given the fact that Patient Nine still somehow had reserves of willpower he was able to bring to bear.

Amazing, all things considered. But terribly unhelpful.

Lee looked him straight in the eyes, knowing that somewhere inside there was an intelligence listening and understanding, though Nine's body was beyond his control.

Lee leaned forward, just barely, satisfied to see Nine's eyes widen slightly. What was about to be said was important and Nine understood that.

Lee held a tablet in his left hand, tapping quickly to input instructions with his right. The baxter sac moved slightly as the feed valve opened. A flood of 59 was heading toward Nine's system, enough to overwhelm him.

They were beyond scientific testing now. Nine was going to be sacrificed so there was no use proceeding by increments, following the protocol of the scientific method. What was about to happen was more in the nature of art. A forcing of the situation to give Lee a sense of the power of the drug.

The clear liquid of 59 was making its way down the tiny tube. It was viscous and would take its time. Which was fine. Lee watched Nine carefully. He could read the monitors without taking his eyes off Nine's. Heartbeat, slow. EKG, 64 beats a minute with some extrasystolic arrhythmia. EEG showing minimal cognitive function. Hormonal levels consonant with the lack of effect of advanced dementia. So far so good.

The liquid hit the subclavian vein, started moving through Nine's system. There would be heat, pain, soaring adrenaline levels. Soon it would be moving through the blood-brain barrier, right into the brain itself.

Ah. EEG spiking in ragged waves.

Patient Nine had given Lee endless trouble so he allowed a touch of pleasure in his words. It was useless calling Nine by his real name. Captain Ward. The good Captain had left his identity back with his cognitive functions a year ago. He was no longer Captain Ward of the U.S. military, he was a miserable and diminished *thing*, barely more than an animal, only a native but low-level endemic hostility keeping a few cognitive functions alive.

But Lee hoped Nine was getting the message. He hoped it fucking *hurt*.

For a second, for just the smallest possible space of time, the scientist in him dropped away and the naked human stood there. Raw and needy, desperate to fulfill his mission, desperate to make it back home to a country he'd last seen when he was seven years old. Desperate to come back a winner, a hero, the man who was going to single-handedly place China at the top of the heap for generations and generations.

And he was going to do it not by weaponry that drew blood, not by megatons of explosives, but by the force of the mind, honed and sharpened by decades of study until it was, in and of itself, the finest of weapons.

His goals were so clear he saw them daily, nightly. He saw the steps to get there, the necessary passages, the hurdles to be overcome not with violence but with knowledge.

And it seemed that what stood between him and his world-changing goal was sitting slumped and beaten in front of him. Lee had been so *certain* that a man like Lucius Ward would make the perfect test subject. A man who by training and nature was a perfect soldier would turn into *his* perfect soldier by the alchemy of modern biochemistry and yet, and yet . . .

Nine had blocked him every step of the way. Lee was a year behind schedule. Even that lump of obtuse protoplasm of Clancy was able to excoriate him, a man who to all intents and purposes was barely sentient in Lee's book.

Captain Ward. It was all his fault.

Well Captain Ward was over. Usefulness gone, he was now merely an obstacle to remove. But not before making him suffer. His last thoughts on this earth would be of pain and defeat.

"Your men are here," he hissed.

Ward—no, Nine!—blinked. The frontal cortex flickered. Nine's face was impassive—there wasn't enough cognitive function to fine-tune the facial muscles—but the message was getting through.

"Your men have been here all along. Six survived the fire that night at the Cambridge lab. I have them, everyone except McEnroe, Ross and Ryan. They're in hiding, on the run, accused of treason. I have no idea how they have evaded every single law enforcement agency in the country, but they can't last forever. The rest of your team, Romero, Lundquist, Pelton—they're *here*. Except they are Patients Twenty-Seven, Twenty-Eight, Twenty-Nine. They don't remember their own names. They've been here all along, right here, underground. And if you think we've put you through the wringer, you should see the shape they are in. Your men, the men you failed to protect."

If this had been an old-time cartoon, Lee reflected, smoke would be coming out of Nine's ears as his brain melted. The EEG looked like the tracing of an earthquake. It was very possible there was subdural bleeding.

"I'm going to kill you all tomorrow. Only we don't call it killing, we call it 'harvesting.' That's right. As if your brains were tomatoes. Or corn."

Every sensor showed spiking values. Heart rate 140, BP 190/130, the hypothalamus was sending massive amounts of CRH to the pituitary gland and the cortisol level rose to 1,000 nmol/L, high enough to cause instant Cushing's syndrome.

The drug was now fully in Nine's system and he fought wildly against the restraints, so wildly Lee straightened, a whisper of fear in his system.

Nonsense. No one could get through the restraints. Certainly not a man who'd lost half his body weight and was drugged to the gills.

Still . . .

The chair was bolted to the floor but it seemed to move a fraction of an inch. Nine was shaking wildly, writhing, every muscle standing out in full relief on his emaciated body, pulling, straining at his bonds.

The bonds held, though Nine's movements became powerful, controlled, pulling, straining, a low animal moan coming from deep in his throat. The bonds rattled but held. Nine was helplessly restrained.

All values were haywire, the man should have been unconscious minutes ago; clearly SL-59 was allowing him this extra effort. Lee was going to study the recordings of this carefully, was going to correlate every muscle twitch, every pull of his arms and legs, with brain activity and blood adrenaline and cortisol levels.

These moments were going to be richly harvested for data. But there was also revenge, hot and sweet, laced through with utter triumph.

"I'm going to be studying your men's brains under a microscope tomorrow morning," he hissed, knowing it was true, reveling in the knowledge. His eyes were fixed on Nine's face, strained in a rictus. The values were right next to Nine's face. Nine's brain readings were compatible with a massive stroke, and yet he still fought hard against his restraints.

There was an ominous rattling sound audible over the low moans coming from Nine's throat. The moans grew louder, the rattling louder, the chair was actually shaking a little. For a startled moment, Lee wondered whether it was an earthquake. The Big One, finally here.

But no, it was Nine, muscles somehow infused with extra power—that was definitely 59—straining so hard at his bonds blood was seeping under the leather straps holding down his wrists. He was moving so violently he was actually making the chair bolted to the floor shift a little.

It would hold. The bonds would hold.

Nine's strength would go out presently. It was artificial and would leave him limp and depleted when it ran out.

Lee knew a way to burn it out of him.

He placed his nose next to Nine's, his hands over Nine's. The skin over the hands was loose, crepe-like, the hands shaking violently inside the restraints.

Lee smiled into Nine's dull eyes. "I am a scientist and I am trained to observe dispassionately, emotionlessly. But it will give me great pleasure tomorrow to have your men put down like the dogs they are. I will watch their eyes as they die and I will exam their brains personally, slice by slice. You will be in the room with me, watching everything I do, and then it will be your turn and I will enjoy every minute of it."

The shaking was more powerful, Nine's bare feet drummed against the floor, fingers curling and uncurling. Every muscle, every sinew, was visible.

The rage and frustration rose in Lee. "Your men will die, Captain, and so will you. Die accused of being traitors!"

With a wild shriek coming from deep in his chest, Nine wrenched his right hand free from the restraint, blood drops flying, grabbing Lee's arm, smearing it with blood. He screamed hoarsely, and before Lee could react, Nine's hand dropped and his head lolled forward like a dead man's.

Frowning, Lee pulled back his eyelids, two fingers on the carotid artery, then raised his head, satisfied.

Unconscious, not dead.

Today was not Nine's day for dying.

Tomorrow was.

Mount Blue

Mac quietly entered his quarters late in the evening. *Their* quarters. Catherine was living there now and he couldn't imagine coming into his quarters without the hope of seeing her there.

And yes, there she was, sitting up in his bed, head slumped to the side, fast asleep.

He stopped right inside the door as it slid closed behind him, looking at her, absorbing the blow to the heart at seeing her in his bed. The walls were on "vista," Jon's name for the program. Ever since she discovered what the system could do, it was never switched off, always seemingly open to the elements. She'd elected to keep it attuned to the timeline, and it was deepest night outside, the moon turning the deep snow bright silver. She'd selected the camera that had the widest view down into the valley and, he had to admit, it was spectacular.

She was spectacular. She had fallen asleep with his eReader on her lap. The eReader was linked to an untraceable credit card and she'd loaded up though she hadn't had time for much reading. She'd spent the whole day in the infirmary going over supplies, setting a broken bone, and Pat and Salvatore now officially adored her.

Look at her, he thought as he crossed the room. She'd fallen asleep in an uncomfortable position, head tilting over on her shoulder, eReader in a lax hand. He gently took the reader away and managed to get her to lie down without waking her up. She'd tried to stay awake for him but he'd worked late in HQ, plotting out a scenario to infiltrate Millon Labs with Nick and Jon that wouldn't get them killed and wouldn't be a huge arrow pointing straight back at Haven.

They'd sent their brand-new drones over the lab, flying at ten thousand feet for hours. Two missions each. One by day. One by night.

They'd continue sending drones and in a few days Jon and Nick would go on a two-day recon.

Mac had mixed feelings. He believed whatever Catherine said. If she said the sky was made of cheese, he was willing to entertain the notion. He certainly believed she believed Lucius was in the lab. Whether he actually was, was another matter.

So. They were going in.

From what they'd seen, security was tight and the guards were armed. Ordinarily, Mac didn't care. He'd pit himself, Nick and Jon against any number of armed guards. But—and this was a constant for a soldier—shit happens.

He'd always been perfectly prepared to die. He was a hard man to kill but dangerous situations were unpredictable and he'd seen good men, well-trained men, die, because they were in the wrong place at the wrong time, stepping on that hidden mine, unable to dodge the bullet.

For the very first time in his life as a soldier, Mac didn't want to die. He had something—someone—to come home to. No one in Ghost Ops had anyone to come home to, by definition, but now he did.

He wanted, fiercely, to live. He wanted to live with Catherine for the rest of their natural lives. He wanted to build their community, protect it, watch it grow. He was on the run but he could even marry Catherine. Not legally, of course, but there was a man in Haven who'd been a pastor of a church that had been bulldozed by a developer and had made his way to Haven. He was a good pastor and a good man and they could have a ceremony. One of those New Age things he'd always laughed at but he'd do it. Commit to her before his community.

Stella would cater.

Oh yeah.

Mac stripped, slipped into bed beside Catherine, turned off the lights with a flick of his finger.

He was hard as a rock. Just touching her, feeling all that warm softness next to him, set him off. But he didn't really need to feel her or even see her. Just the thought of her was enough.

Slowly, slowly he eased her into his arms, settled her head on his shoulder and lay there, one hand behind his head, staring at the ceiling, wanting Catherine more than he wanted his next breath.

She was there, right there. He knew, beyond a shadow of a doubt, that if he woke her up, she'd welcome him. She'd open those long legs, open her arms, open that delightful cunt. He'd slide into her, like sliding into home, and they'd start moving together in perfect rhythm.

At some point, though, he was going to have to do more than slide on top of her, then into her. However welcoming she always was, women wanted—needed—foreplay. And by God, he'd give it to her if he wasn't always so fucking blasted from the heat in his head.

He did foreplay. He was even good at it. A man who looked like him had to know his way around a woman's body, and he did. He once got a woman off by sucking her toes. He knew what to do. And he wanted to do it with Catherine.

God, yes. He wanted to kiss those pretty breasts, over and over, until his mouth knew her shape instinctively. He wanted to suck them, kiss them all over until the nipples turned cherry red and hard. Then he'd kiss his way down over that flat belly, slowly, feeling her writhe, until he got to the main attraction.

Oh yeah. He didn't mind going down on women but he craved the thought with Catherine. Lifting her legs, opening them, settling down between them. God, he was sure he could stay there for hours. Puffy pink lips in that soft, dark cloud of hair, begging to be kissed. What he really wanted was for her to come while stroking her with his tongue, feeling the sharp contractions against his mouth, hearing her cries and moans while fucking her with his tongue . . .

Oh shit. He felt like whimpering. So good, it would be so good and why the fuck hadn't he done it before? Because his brain blasted, went nova, the instant he touched her. There wasn't anything else in his mind other than getting inside her with his cock. It was pure instinct, absolutely irresistible.

Maybe when he'd had her a few thousand times, maybe when they could settle into a routine like normal couples—though he had no fucking clue how normal couples behaved—maybe then he could indulge in some foreplay.

But now he had the burning images of his face buried between her thighs, of sucking her nipples with his hand inside her—and now that he thought about it, wow. Feeling her climax with his hand instead of his cock . . . except his cock, which had a mind of its own, was going to want to be inside her, too.

It was all too much for him, just the thought of the thousands of hours ahead of him with Catherine as his own personal playground. God.

His cock hurt. He could feel his heartbeat there and he felt like he would split open at every pulse. His balls were pulled up tight, ready to blow. The solution to his problem was right there, right in his arms. If he went down on her right now, he could make her wet enough to take him in no time. They could be fucking in a few minutes, no question, and he wouldn't hurt so much.

But . . .

But she'd looked so tired. There'd been blue bruises under those glorious silver eyes. Pat told him she'd worked all day with her and Salvatore in the infirmary, had patched up one of their engineering guys who'd broken an arm trying to wrestle a beam into a wall. She'd had nothing but surprises since setting out to find him, she'd nearly frozen to death, he'd nearly fucked her to death . . .

Couldn't do it. He couldn't do it. He would just lie here with his blue steeler and listen to her breathe and be happy she was getting some rest. There was always tomorrow and tomorrow and tomorrow. They'd have plenty of time together. Eventually, he'd get around to foreplay.

He closed his eyes and drifted . . .

He was drifting along a river, warm water lapping around him, soft and gentle. He floated on his back, the sun warm on his face, the cloudless sky a blue so perfect it hurt the eyes. Mac smiled, eyes closed.

Perfect. Everything was fucking perfect.

The water lapped around him softly, moving him gently. A

river? The ocean? If it was the ocean it sure as hell wasn't the Pacific around Coronado. That had always been cold as hell. This was somewhere else. Where? Who the fuck cared?

Wherever it was, it smelled really good. He drew in a deep breath. Most of the smells he could identify spelled trouble. Semtex, cordite, gun solvent. This wasn't like those smells at all, this was like heaven, like springtime, clear and clean and fresh. Maybe he actually was in heaven. That didn't make sense, though. Ghost Ops guys weren't going to heaven, unless maybe Catherine could get him in.

There was something on his arm, light and warm and soft, weighing it down. He should look and see what it was, but his eyes simply wouldn't open. Wouldn't do it. Everything felt so damned good he couldn't bring himself to exert himself in any way.

And besides, if this was heaven, who wanted to mess with heaven?

He drifted, content, on a sea of pleasure.

A cry of agony pierced the air, sharp with pain. Terrible, unending pain, raw and unbearable.

Mac shot up, grabbed his Glock from the bedside table. He was a soldier, he came out of sleep fast. In a nanosecond he was oriented. He was in bed and Catherine had been sleeping on his shoulder.

She wasn't asleep now, she was screaming her head off. It was a good thing all the rooms in Haven were soundproofed.

Mac snapped his fingers and the room lights came up, on dim. She was terrified, no sense in making her feel she was under a spotlight. He gave a swift look around the room just to make sure there weren't any hidden dangers, but the room was as empty as it had been when he fell asleep. There wasn't a man alive who could sneak into his room undetected. Not even Nick or Jon.

No external threat. He established that in a second. Now he could deal with Catherine. Placing the Glock back on the bedside table, he pulled her gently into his arms, holding her as tightly as he dared.

The screaming had stopped but she was making frightening noises in her throat, harsh cut-off sobs that were almost worse than the screaming, as if she didn't dare scream any longer, as if she were too scared to scream.

She was panting, shaking wildly, bone white down to her lips. Taking in air in great gulping sobs, muscles rigid as wood as he held her. He had a hand over her back and could feel her heart beating wildly like an animal facing down a predator. Like an animal facing death.

It hurt him somewhere deep inside, a place he'd never felt before. It hurt so badly, seeing, hearing, *feeling* her panic.

He hugged her more tightly, letting his body absorb her shudders, trying to offer the comfort of his body, like you'd comfort a terrified child or animal. She seemed beyond words but he tried anyway.

"Shhh." He rocked with her in his arms. "It was a dream, honey. A nightmare. A doozy by the look of it. But just a dream. Nothing can hurt you, you're safe now—"

Catherine pushed at his chest, hard, and he let go of her in surprise, instinctively. It was the push of a woman who was saying *no*. The instant his arms loosened she shot out of bed, rushing frantically to find her clothes, pulling on her jeans, shuffling sockless into her boots. All the while shaking and shivering as if just pulled out of freezing water.

"Honey," Mac said carefully. Everything he knew about her was that she was sane and stable. Her emotions were steady, tinged with a little sadness. But this had all the hallmarks of an emotional breakdown, a psychotic episode. "Tell me—"

"No time." Her teeth were chattering. "No time." She looked up, eyes wild, searching for her shirt and sweater, but only for a second, snatching up his huge tee and throwing it over her head.

It billowed and settled on her slender shoulders, making her look like a fragile teenager. "Where do you guys meet?"

Mac was already dressed. Whatever it was that had happened, whatever she needed, he wanted to help her and he couldn't do that with his naked ass hanging out.

That threw him. "What?"

She put her hands on her head and twirled around, as if unable to contain her agitation. "Where do you guys meet, do you have a meeting room with communications? Some kind of headquarters?"

"Of course. Do you want me to take you there?"

She was already at the door, standing in front of it, practically dancing in place, searching for the door release button, missing it in her anxiety. "Let's go, let's go," she chanted under her breath. "Get your men. Do you have anyone else besides Nick and Jon?"

He shook his head no and tapped on his ear, glad he'd automatically put in the comms.

"Yeah," he said when Nick answered. He'd been asleep but Nick woke in a second, fully operational. They all did. "HQ, two minutes. Tell Jon. Slingshot." Their code for an emergency.

He touched the right spot on the wall and the door slid open. Catherine shot out into the hall looking wildly right and left. A vein was pulsing visibly in her throat. "What direction?"

"Right. Elevator at the end of the corridor."

She took off, running. Mac easily kept pace. From ten feet out, he waved and the elevator doors opened. Without breaking her pace she ran inside. He followed her in, calmly punched in the floor and turned to her.

She was shaking, arms wrapped around herself as if to keep herself warm. It hurt him to see her like that. He stepped to her, wrapped his arms around her, rested his cheek against the top of her head.

"It's okay," he murmured, rocking her a little because she

needed movement to dissipate some of the anxious tension racking her. He knew the mechanism well. The body is screaming for action but you don't know what action to take, so the body just hums with tension. "It'll be okay."

"No," she whispered into his shoulder, though the shudders had subsided some. "I don't know if it will." Catherine pulled her head back to look him in the face and he winced at her expression. She was white-faced and hurting. Tears welled in her eyes, and as he watched, one slipped over and slid down her cheek, like a drop of water over marble. "We have to move so fast. It will be so hard."

Mac didn't make the mistake of smiling. Whatever had spooked her was terrifying her and was real, to her at least. He wiped the tear with the pad of his thumb and bent to kiss her cold mouth. "We can do hard, honey. We've been doing hard for a long time. We specialize in it."

A soft ping and the doors opened. Mac took Catherine's elbow and walked fast to their HQ, Catherine running to keep up. Two people across the great atrium looked at them, frowning at the speed, then looked away.

Nick and Jon crowded into HQ right behind them. Catherine looked around, noting the monitors and chairs. The vast amount of high-tech Jon and Nick had installed that allowed them to have eyes and ears almost anywhere in the world was visible. The servers were a mile away, in a secure air-conditioned bunker. They could fly to the moon with the computing power they had.

"Sit. Please." Catherine's voice was high, vibrating with tension. Nick and Jon looked at each other, shrugged and sat. She gestured at him so Mac sat, too. They settled in, comfortable with the situation. This was a briefing. They'd been briefed all their adult lives and Mac knew that they all had their minds open, ready to hear what Catherine was going to say.

It was still a blow.

"Patient Nine is Captain Lucius Ward, no question," she said baldly. Mac shifted slightly in his seat, shooting glances at Nick and Jon. She met his eyes then Nick's and Jon's, in turn. Mac had never seen a woman so beautiful, utterly concentrated on her task, a modern-day Joan of Arc. Her trembling started to subside as she spoke, intent on her mission.

"Now I understand he's been held essentially a prisoner at the Millon facility. What I thought was a form of advanced dementia was pharmacologically induced. I know this now. We must go get him."

Mac thought—*What's this "we" business?*

She looked regal, like a queen mustering the troops for battle. Not Joan of Arc. Boadicea. She should have a plumed pennant streaming in the wind, riding her chariot.

Where before she was vibrating with panic, now she thrummed with determination and purpose. *God, just look at her,* he thought. Straight and elegant, gray eyes flashing silver like a sword caught in the light. Shiny, dark hair sliding over her shoulders as she paced back and forth. His enormous black tee looked like some elegant warrior's cloak.

He knew every inch of the body beneath the clothes, every sleek muscle, every tender dip and hollow, knew the softness of her breasts, how hard her nipples could become . . . but now this was a new Catherine. Not the frightened, frozen woman who'd arrived—what was it? Only three days ago? Not the gentle doctor who'd helped a terrified woman bring a healthy baby into the world, not the passionate woman who'd cried out in his arms. This was another Catherine—strong and determined and just as irresistible as the others.

"He needs your help desperately. They are going to kill him tomorrow. We must go now."

Jon was leaning back in his chair, looking relaxed. Mac knew better. His blue eyes were glittering. "Darling, you know we like you. Everybody likes you and Mac more than likes you so you're okay in my book. But with all due respect to Mac, you don't know anything about this. Any kind of hostage rescue takes planning and time and we are not there yet."

When Jon was like that—when his eyes glowed and his body was coiled for a strike—people did a double-take because the danger that lived just beneath his tanned skin flashed bright, like a rapier suddenly catching the light.

But Catherine was unfazed. "I don't care how ready you are, we must go, right now. I gave you that striking hawk. It meant something to Mac though he tried to hide it. I don't know what but you"—she turned slowly—"all three of you know where it came from. It came from Lucius Ward. He was once one of you and he is in deadly danger *right now* and we are going to go get him."

"Prove it," Nick said suddenly. His dark eyes narrowed. "I like you, too, Catherine, but you're asking us to risk a lot for a man who left us to die. How do you know he didn't betray us? What real proof do you have? What are you going on? And how do you know that he's going to be killed tomorrow? We're not cowboys. We can't just ride to the rescue right now on your say-so."

Mac saw her hesitate. She shot Mac a glance but he opened his hands briefly. Empty hands. He couldn't help her. Nobody could help her. She had to convince Nick and Jon all on her own. And whatever she wanted, he couldn't do it without Nick and Jon.

She drew in a deep breath, blew it out. Stress reliever. "I imagine both of you were listening when Mac was interrogating me." Nick and Jon shifted in their chairs, not saying yes, not saying no. She nodded sharply. "Quite right. I would have done the same. You've got a community to protect and I was an intruder."

"Not now you're not," Mac growled, the words torn from his chest. Not for one second should she doubt she belonged here.

She smiled at him, the smile sad and brief. "Thanks," she said softly. Their eyes connected and held. Damn right she was one of them. "Patient Nine couldn't talk. I know"—she held her hand up—"I know how that sounds. He couldn't talk so how can I know what he wanted to say? He conveyed information to me nonetheless. Important information, and he was so determined I think he opened up an avenue of communication between us."

Jon and Nick shot glances at each other. Nick's jaw muscles jumped.

Catherine moved until she was close to Nick, her knees touching his. "The situation is desperate and we don't have much time. So I'm going to have to use a shortcut to convince you I communicated with your Lucius Ward."

Without warning, she reached for Nick's hand.

Mac tensed, ready to head off trouble. There was no way Catherine could know that Nick didn't like being touched, by anybody. He'd seen Nick slap a man's hand away from his shoulder so hard he broke the wrist. Mac watched Nick's hands. Teammate or not, fellow outcast or not, if Nick made a move against Catherine, he was a fucking dead man.

But Nick didn't move, didn't react at all. He simply sat still as Catherine took his hand. Nick's face never showed anything, but his jaw muscles tightened.

"Oh," Catherine said, surprised. "Oh my." Her eyes never left Nick's face. Her expression softened. "She thinks of you all the time, Nick. I think . . . she loves you. Desperately. Still. After all these years."

Mac glanced at Jon, who looked as surprised as he felt. Someone *loved* Nick? Cold, self-contained Nick? Christ, who knew? If she'd said that about Jon, who was a love-'em-and-leave-'em guy, okay. Jon had fucked his way across the country and over several continents. But no one had ever seen Nick with a woman. He was all cold hard mission. The job and nothing else. A lot like Mac.

Nick stirred. "I haven't seen her—"

"Since that time." Catherine nodded. "I know. But she still loves you, nonetheless."

Nick swallowed heavily. Mac could see his Adam's apple bob up and down. "Do you"—he licked his lips—"do you know where she is?"

Catherine shook her head, a sad expression on her face. "No, Nick. I'm sorry, but I don't. I have no idea. I'm only reading her through you, through the things you know but won't acknowledge. You don't know where she is so I don't, either."

Nick looked sad and vulnerable, an amazing sight. Nick had no known weaknesses. Except, apparently, for this woman who was lost to him.

"Is she . . . all right?" His voice was hoarse.

Catherine shook her head and shrugged. "I can't know that, either, Nick. But I can read from you that you are worried about her. She's not . . ." Catherine closed her eyes, frowned. "She's not home. At her home. You've checked and you keep checking. You don't know where she is. You worry that she might be sick or in trouble. That she might need you. It's eating you alive."

To Mac's astonishment, Nick simply bowed his head. Whatever it was, it *was* eating him alive. And for a second there—though he wouldn't swear to it—it seemed there was moisture in Nick's eyes. Nick *crying*? Mac would have sworn the world would come to an end before Nick could cry.

Nick lifted his head. "So you *can*—"

"Yes." Catherine nodded to him. "I can."

"Jesus," he whispered.

"I don't like doing it, but I can read you. Not your thoughts so much as your emotions. And I opened to you. You read me, too, didn't you? At least partly. Enough to know I'm telling the truth."

She let go of Nick's wrist and he lifted his head. Whatever moisture had been in his eyes had gone, but there was a slight softness there, where there had been none before.

"Fuck," he breathed. "Sorry. Nothing like that has ever happened to me before. It was like—"

"Like I was in you, right, Nick? Inside your head, feeling what you're feeling, thinking what you're thinking."

He nodded, lips clamped shut.

She put a hand on his shoulder. She was touching cloth so it wasn't any of the woo-woo stuff. It was simply a gesture of human connection.

"I know how off center you must be feeling. And believe me when I say I would never read you deliberately. This—this ability I have is incredibly draining. I feel like I could sleep for a week. But I had to do it, you had to know the truth. And you do, don't you?"

He nodded.

"What?" Jon exploded, bristling with hostility. Mac tensed. "What do you know? Goddammit, Catherine, did you just drug him? Because this is crap. It's crap, Nick. You know it. You know the Captain hung us out to dry and he's not in some lab, you know that, too. Why should he be? I like you, Catherine, but I think you were sent to lead us into a trap. Maybe unwittingly, but there's no way we're coming off the mountain to—"

Catherine reached over and grabbed his hand. Jon stopped suddenly, eyes wide open with shock, jaw dropping.

Catherine smiled gently. "You were betrayed once, Jon. Badly. Worse than what you think Lucius Ward did. It blighted your life. You've never let yourself trust anyone until you joined . . . the teams?" This last as a question, aimed at Mac.

He nodded.

"The teams. You found trust and acceptance there and then your leader betrayed you. But, Jon, he didn't. He couldn't. It isn't in him, just as betrayal isn't in you or Nick or Mac. He is just like you and he's hurting. He's in trouble and about to die and his last chance is the three of you." Her slender hand tightened on Jon's wrist, but Mac didn't worry that Jon was going to attack her. He looked wiped out, almost frightened, though Mac could have sworn fear wasn't in Jon's vocabulary. He'd seen Jon take outrageous risks without a thought to his own safety.

His attention focused tightly on Catherine when she gasped and swayed a little. He was about to leap to her side when the words she spoke froze him in place.

Her voice deepened, became low and rough, as male as her vocal cords allowed.

"Saddle up, boys, it's time to ride. You wanna live forever?"

It was the Captain's war cry at the beginning of every mission. Catherine even had a touch of the South in her voice, a faint echo of the Captain's deep Georgia accent.

The hairs on Mac's forearms rose and brushed against the sleeves of his sweatshirt and he felt the blood drain from his face. Nick and Jon looked pale, too. Jon actually looked sick, a drop of sweat dripping off his temple.

Catherine let go of his hand as if it burned her and opened her eyes. Her hand went to her throat and she looked frightened. "Mac . . ." Her voice was a mere thread. She coughed and tried again. "Mac. What just happened? I blacked out for a second."

It took him a moment to find his own voice. He couldn't stand to see that lost look on her face. He stood and pulled her into his arms. She was trembling as she put her arms around his waist, hiding her head against his shoulder. He held her tightly, looking over her head at Nick and Jon.

They both stood, as determined as he was.

"She was reading me and then I heard—" Jon shook his head sharply, as if he wanted to get rid of even the thought, but it stuck. "I heard the Captain. He was in her head and in mine. He's alive in Palo Alto, and he's in danger. Right now. We have to go get him."

"No question," Nick growled.

"Yeah." Much as he didn't want to, Mac let go of Catherine. Her trembling had subsided. He wanted to keep her in his arms but he was already switching into mission mode, half of him here with her, half of him planning an on-the-fly hostage rescue mission. They'd been working on it, but at a slow pace. Now they were going to go with what they had.

They could do it. They'd rescued a downed American pilot in the heart of Tehran. All they needed was more intel and Catherine would have that.

"Okay, men, we've got some mission planning to do. We've got about six hours of darkness still. Go get your gear and suit up and I'll start debriefing Catherine. I'll have the beginning of a plan by the time you get back. Double time."

"I'll need some gear, too," Catherine said, and they all three froze.

"What?" She looked each one of them in the face. "I'm coming with you, of course."

"No," Nick and Jon said together, horrified.

"*Fuck* no," Mac said.

Chapter Fourteen

Millon Laboratories
Palo Alto

His strength was ebbing, the cold fingers of death reaching deep into his heart and squeezing. The fingers had reached for him often, he was used to their icy touches, the feeling of falling, falling . . .

He'd resisted up until now even though he had almost lost all sense of himself. Who he was, what he was—a blank. Lost. He sometimes tried to recall something of who he'd been but everything always danced just out of his reach. There was no language left, only images, growing more and more faded.

Men. Hard-faced, dressed in black. One, taller than the rest, bearing the scars of burns. He'd seen those burns, seen him on fire. The men . . . they were somehow his. Somehow . . . him. He didn't know who they were or where they were. He had no names, just the faces floating in and out of memory, always just beyond reach.

Pain had blasted so much out of him. He had the faintest recollection of resisting when he'd started this new existence.

When he'd lost the man he'd been and became Patient Nine. He'd fought . . . hadn't he?

Images came. White-coated men with syringes and worse . . . liquid that burned his veins. Waking up over and over again with new stitches, with lost memories, ever weaker. They wanted something from him and he wouldn't—couldn't—give it. There had been anger, more needles, more surgeries.

Now they left him alone. It had been days since he had seen anyone except—except The Man. He had no name for the man, but if he concentrated hard, he could see him, as if in a fog. Tall, thin. Dark skin, thin nose, clever, slanted black eyes. The needles came from him.

The man disappeared and though he clutched at the image it was gone. It was all gone, everything.

It was the end. He accepted it, almost welcomed it.

He'd made one last effort, reaching out, touching . . . someone. Someone familiar. A . . . woman? Soft voice, long, dark hair, very pretty. Yes, a woman. She wasn't here but . . . she was. He'd heard her voice, in his head. When she came and touched him, warmth spread through him, the first warmth he'd felt in . . .

It was gone. Sometime in his life he'd known warmth, physical warmth, the sun on his skin. But he didn't know when, he didn't even know if the faint memory was true. Maybe he'd spent his entire life here, half-naked, with needles and probes and liquid fire in his veins.

No.

No, there had been a time . . . before. Again, hard-faced men appeared briefly in front of him, then disappeared.

He'd called out. He had. He'd called out so hard he had lost consciousness, with no idea whatsoever of how long.

He'd called because he was dying. Someone was going to make him die, soon. So he'd reached out and someone had been there. Softness and warmth. The woman.

But there was no woman, there was only an empty room filled with beeping machines and bright lights that never let him sleep.

Sleep . . . soon he would sleep. Soon he'd sleep forever.

Mount Blue

It wasn't a funny situation, but Catherine had to stifle the urge to laugh.

All three men looked horrified, and Mac looked both horrified and angry. An angry Mac was formidable. If she didn't know him so well, know him down to his bones, she'd be frightened.

His face was dark, the scarred parts pulled tight with tension, eyes narrowed. He seemed even huger, broad shoulders blocking the rest of the room from her sight, enormous hands opening and closing as if ready to do battle.

He was.

With himself.

Catherine looked him in the eyes, then at Nick and at Jon.

What a revelation the two men had been when she'd looked inside their souls. Nick, with his lost love, yearning for her, knowing he would never see her again, sick with worry that she might be in trouble. No one would ever know looking at that cold closed façade he faced the world with that he had all those emotions inside. That he had all that love inside.

And Jon—burning with rage at the treachery that had undermined his life. She hadn't understood who or what had betrayed him as a boy but it went beyond the betrayal as a man. No, this was something in the past and colored his every emotion. And again, who would have thought all that rage and pain swirled under the Surfer Dude exterior.

Three large, strong men, warriors, trained to kill, standing right in front of her and looking enraged and determined to block her from going with them into the lab to rescue their former leader.

"You can all stand down," she said quietly. "You know deep in your hearts that I have to come with you. If we have any hope of saving your leader, you need me. I know the laboratory inside out. I know their security system, I know the layout. Above all, you're going to need me when we find Nine. He is hooked up to machines and it will be a very delicate task to detach him from the machines without killing him. None of you have a hope of doing that. Only I can free him from the machinery he is tethered to, and only then can you rescue him."

There was utter silence in the room if you could ignore teeth grinding. Well, they were going to grind even harder.

"And I have something else to say. I am not trained as the three of you are. I promise that I will obey you absolutely. Tell me to duck and I duck. I will be your shadow and will follow your instructions. I know full well I am a potential liability, and trust me, I don't want to be, so count on me to do exactly as you say. But"—she held up her hand when Mac opened his mouth—"the instant we are inside the facility you obey me, all three of you. Instantly. Unless we are actually being fired upon, at which point your training trumps mine, you do exactly as I say. There can be no other way."

She looked at each one again. "So. You can all stop scowling now and man up. Nick, Jon, go get your gear like Mac said, get something for me, and we'll reconvene here in ten minutes. I'll prepare the briefing on the lab."

For such determined men, they looked strangely uncertain. She knew that having her along went against every instinct they had. Not only because she wasn't trained but mostly because each man, quietly and deeply, couldn't endanger a woman. All three of them had a furious protective streak in them that wouldn't allow them to contemplate putting her in danger.

Catherine made a show of checking her watch. "You've used up a full minute. A minute that might make the difference between life and death for your captain. Mac?"

She looked up at him, appreciating his struggle, knowing he hated this, knowing he understood how necessary it was. He stood immobilized by warring factions inside his heart and reason won out. By a hair.

"Get going," he said tightly, then pulled her into his arms the instant Nick and Jon left the room. "God," he said into her hair, "I hate this."

"I know." She did. She could feel his heartbeat against her cheek. In bed, it had been the steady beat of an athlete's heart but now it beat fast and furious and wild, as if he were running. He was, in a way. He was conducting a running battle inside himself, an internal war. Keep her here and have already slim changes whittled down to nothing, or take her along, worry dogging his every step.

No good choices.

Mac didn't worry when he was in mission mode. She'd read that in him. Anxiety wasn't part of his mental makeup. She understood that he prepared as hard as a man could—and she'd felt that most of his life was training—and then he just went ahead without any fear.

She also knew he was fully prepared to die at any time. That kind of thing simply could not be hidden.

But now fear all but oozed out of his pores. It wasn't fear for himself but for her.

"Mac." She kissed his chest over his heart and pulled away. His face was cold and hard but his nostrils were pinched white with stress. "It has to be this way. What I told Nick and Jon is true for us as well. Every second I spend trying to reassure you, give you strength, is a second lost and drains my energy."

His hands dropped with surprise. She'd done it deliberately, pretending she was infusing him with strength when the opposite was true. She gained strength and courage just from being near him. But the thought that he might be endangering her with his fear shocked him.

"Okay. Let me set up to brief them on the facility. I'll need to use one of your computers."

"Over there," he growled. "Tell me what I can do." Unexpectedly, he looked awkward, big hands held clumsily to his side, opening and closing futilely, when at all times he was the epitome of male grace.

"There's not much you can do until I get some information together," she said gently.

"Can I get you coffee at least?"

He needed to do something for her. She understood that. Her stomach was roiling and the last thing she needed was caffeine but . . . "Sure, that would be helpful."

He pressed a button and spoke quietly.

Millon had the blueprints of the facility, plus security regulations and lab safety rules, in a file given to all employees. She pulled it up, ran it through a program that created a hologram and enlarged it. She had just finished printing out the security and safety rules when Jon and Nick came back together with a Haven citizen rolling in a cart.

Stella again, bless her.

The cart had coffee and tea, bless her again. On the cart were plates piled high with mini panini, mini donuts and apple slices with a sprinkling of fresh cinnamon. Mac, Nick and Jon fell on the coffee and panini and donuts while she savored the tea and ate the apple slices. She felt energized by the instant injection of fructose.

"Okay, settle down, men." The three men exchanged glances but obeyed without grumbling. Catherine paced back and forth as she briefed them. A comforting, familiar feeling. She'd taught undergrad classes for several years in Boston, and though these three tough, fierce men were totally unlike the soft baby nerds she was used to, she couldn't complain about their attention. They were focused on her, taking in every single word.

"Let's go over this again. This is the main facility. There are ancillary structures but this is where the work is carried out and this is where the Captain is held." The holo was slightly tilted, giving an indication of its shape. Size in meters was given in white letters at the top. "It is an L-shaped facility, one long wing and one shorter wing. The shorter wing is only labs and the other wing has what some of my creepier colleagues calls 'meatware'—the human patients and test animals." She indicated both wings with a pen, touching air. Mac's computer system was top-of-the-line. The holo was so realistic it was like having a 3D copy to scale of the facility in front of her. When she tapped the air to indicate each wing, she kept having a tiny jolt of surprise that her pen met air and not steel and glass. "There are three aboveground levels and three belowground levels. The bottom level is given over to production of test batches. It is a production facility and has separate entrances. My security pass covers the six levels but that will of course have been canceled. Jon, do you think you could make me a duplicate in the name of a colleague I know is out of state?"

"No problem," Jon answered.

"Great. So, before I go through the building floor by floor, I need to brief you on what I know of security arrangements. Millon has to turn a family-friendly face to the world so it is not surrounded by a visible wall but an invisible one. There is a microwave beam circling the building, strong enough to cook anything mammalian, certainly including humans. The beams lose focus after about ten yards so these very expensive designer vases rimming the periphery are actually microwave emitters."

She zoomed in on the line of huge gray-and-tan ceramic vases, man-high, that circled the company, containing pencil-thin Italian cypresses imported at vast expense from Tuscany. There were more than three thousand of them. It was visually stunning and had featured in a number of design magazines.

"The system is turned off at four A.M. and an army of sweepers rushes in to sweep away the dead animals, insects and leaves burned to a crisp, and the microwaves are turned back on again at four-fifteen."

"Do you know where the C & C is?" Nick asked.

Catherine frowned, confused. She shook her head.

"Command and control," Mac said. "Where they give the orders and check that they're carried out."

"Oh. No, I'm sorry, I have no idea. There is a security module on the first floor in the lab part of the facility and in the wing where the patients are kept. But I have no idea whether the microwave fence is controlled from there. It could also be controlled from the security module in the entrance."

Mac nodded. "Okay, we need to know whether their security perimeter stretches out past that. I'd be surprised if it didn't. Jon?"

From his tablet, Jon projected another holo. A bird's-eye view of the Millon facility only with a much larger footprint, and at night. At a guess, Catherine would say that the footprint was a mile on a side. As she watched, lights flashed by almost faster than her eyes could perceive and the image changed from black to light gray, then back again. About ten red points moved back and forth in a short arc.

She looked over at Jon. "What am I seeing?"

His jaws bunched. "I went back in time. You're seeing about a week's worth of night shots from a Bright Eye satellite. It can see the balls on a mosquito so I enlarged the scope of it and created a bot that blanked out random events, otherwise the detail would overwhelm us."

"Wow," she breathed. She had a low-level government security clearance linked to her job at Millon but it didn't cover anything like this. The Bright Eye series of orbiting satellites were a rumor that often showed up in novels and tabloids, capable of amazing detail. Privacy activists often marched against them, though the government blandly denied Bright Eye existed. "Please don't tell me how you got that. I could probably go to jail for knowing this."

She got three hard, blank stares and suppressed a grin. She could probably go to jail for knowing *them*. "But if I have to go to jail, at least let me know what I'm looking at."

The holo kept flashing, black to gray and back again.

"What you're seeing is a recording from last light to first of that area. We're now going back to a month ago." With a swipe of his finger, Jon stopped the flicking images. "Here's what we need to know. Screening out random events—events that are not repeated at least three times in one month—we have vehicles patrolling this area on a regular round." His finger sketched a perimeter a mile out surrounding the facility. "They mainly use night lights but I used an algorithm and enhanced the light so we could see them. I'd estimate these are people carriers—roofless, all-terrain vehicles, carrying five soldiers plus one manning what looks like a .50 cal." The image zoomed and zoomed again until four shapes inside the vehicle were visible, plus one man sitting on a sort of raised platform on the back manning a long cylinder.

Catherine stared. This was far beyond the level of security that she was aware of.

Mac was tapping on a handheld. "I've got their routines and I'll get the security holes. Go on."

Jon pointed with a pen to the red lights moving back and forth quickly in short arcs farther in near the facility. "And that's patrols. There are ten of them covering an arc of about a mile, hourly patrol. They are backup to the wheeled patrols."

"Wait." Nick leaned forward, his hard dark face intent. "Run those through again."

The holo showed the series of vehicle and foot patrols, gray to black and back. He studied them, eyes tracking back and forth for several minutes. Mac and Jon gave him the time. Mac continued tapping into his handheld and Jon was using another computer, doing some complicated research. She could see screens flash by, too quickly for her to understand what it was he was looking for.

She could do nothing but wait. Once she'd given them the security protocol that had been in her initial briefing, she had nothing else to offer.

"Security is aimed inward," Nick said finally, sitting back.

Mac stopped tapping on his handheld and Jon's hands lifted from the keyboard.

"Look." Nick pointed at the red dots, freezing the faint images of the vehicles, tilting the Millon holo. "Every weapon is aimed inward. The path the patrols take, the direction of the .50 cal, it all makes sense if you are directing your security to keeping things in instead of out."

"Jesus," Mac breathed.

"Does that make sense?" Catherine asked. "I mean, surely Millon is guarding against intruders. This lab alone must have a billion dollars' worth of industrial secrets to steal. Surely they must be scared of someone coming along and stealing them?"

"Nick's right," Mac growled. "They have plenty of internal security. What you showed us is already top-of-the-line. These outer-perimeter trip wires—they are expensive and labor-intensive. They make sense if they are there in case someone from inside escapes and the alarm is sounded. That security is definitely aimed at keeping whatever is in there from getting out."

"Well," Catherine said, considering. "Maybe that makes our task that much easier. Maybe we can get in."

"Yeah." Mac sighed. "The trick will be getting back out alive."

Fifty minutes later, Mac tapped his ear. Or rather, tapped a spot on the lightweight helmet.

Catherine obediently tapped the same spot on her own helmet. It was the spot that connected her to the team leader, Mac. A spot an inch to the left hooked her comms system into the entire team's system.

"You okay, honey?" Mac's deep voice sounded in her ear. The sound was so good, so deep and calm, so all-enveloping it was as if he were talking inside her head. "You remember the drills?"

A huge amount of information had been fed into her earpiece from him as she was being dressed by Nick and Jon in an amazing lightweight, flexible suit she was assured would stop bullets. On top of the suit, though, she was the only one wearing another layer of protection, a light plate covering her chest and back which Mac said would stop a missile. Then Nick winked at her. Nick! Cold, remote Nick. Maybe she imagined it because when she looked at him again, his face was as frozen as ever.

Luckily, she was a fast study and could retain big chunks of technical data.

The combat suits were made of nanotube carbon technology. The material tightened under ballistic pressure and was much more resistant than the old-fashioned, heavy Kevlar protection some police officers still wore in poor cities.

What she was wearing also repelled infrared and instantly took on background coloring, making them almost invisible all along the visible spectrum.

"I remember the drills," she answered softly. He looked at her intently for a long minute in the dimness of the helicopter cabin, then nodded and turned away.

She knew he'd just paid her a huge compliment. She knew how protective he was. When he held her hand she could feel his terror for her, feel how badly fear sat on him and knew that it was exclusively fear for her, not for himself.

But right now, he trusted in the information he and Nick and Jon had given her and her ability to process that information. She understood what a struggle it was for him and the demons he'd had to overcome to trust her to keep safe.

Jon was piloting a helicopter the likes of which she had never seen. It was tiny. They sat tightly squeezed together. The men's gear and weaponry were loaded into two metal bladders affixed to the sides which Jon said were bulletproof.

The helicopter was a stealth one, invisible to radar, with a heat signature so dissipated it took highly sensitive instruments to track it or even show up on IR scans. Mac was counting on the fact that no one scanned the sky and the fact that they were off every flight path.

The helicopter was also completely silent. That was another thing that astonished her. Even inside, there was barely a sound—not louder than wind rustling in the trees. They were communicating via their inbuilt helmet comms because the men didn't want to have to stop to put them on and test them when they landed.

And when they landed, Jon had assured her that they would have to land right on top of a person for him to hear the "helo," as the men called it. And they weren't going to do that because the helo boasted every single imaging device known to man and some that were unknown even to her. Jon was getting readouts about every single data pertinent to the mission, complete pictures of the terrain they were flying over, a complete picture of the empty sky around them, info so complete all that was missing was the price of pizza in the fast food franchises they flew over.

The bird was practically flying itself, though Jon told her he could grab control back in a microsecond. She believed him. On a mission, he was no longer Surfer Dude, laid-back and detached. He was all fervent focus, like Mac and Nick.

The men were bent over a tablet showing a bird's-eye view of the Millon compound, sent from a drone that had preceded them. They had watched as the sentries changed over at 2 A.M., as per protocol.

It was 2:30 A.M. and they were scheduled to land just outside the furthermost security perimeter in fifteen minutes.

The men were discussing tactics in a low murmur inside her helmet, their deep calm voices sounding like a river rushing by . . .

She started as a large gloved hand shook her shoulder. "We're there, honey," Mac said in her ear. "ETA sixty seconds. You ready?"

Her heart was pounding and her mouth was dry. She willed her heart rate down, thankful for all the biofeedback exercises she'd taken in grad school, took a sip of water from a reservoir that was secreted somewhere on her back and nodded.

"Yes," she said, glad her voice sounded calm. "I am."

She saw his eyes narrow at her. "Remember the drill. You stay—"

"Inside the triangle you and Nick and Jon make at all times. I obey all hand signs—halt, forward and down—and I am to keep a low profile." She narrowed her eyes back at him. "I told you. I know the drill."

"Landing," Jon's voice sounded in their ears, and the little helicopter simply drifted down and landed with barely a bump.

"Go go go," Mac said, and the men simply ghosted out, making no noise whatsoever. Catherine tried to emulate them but wasn't as graceful as they were. Her boot brushed the helo skid with a little clang. She winced but they weren't paying attention as they unloaded their gear in total silence from the external bladders.

"Gear check," Mac said quietly, and they ran down the frighteningly long list of things they carried. At the end they jumped up and down silently, checking to see if anything jingled as they moved, but nothing did.

Mac gave the forward hand sign and they moved out, Catherine in the middle of a triangle of three very large and very brave men whose lives she held in her uncertain hands.

As they moved forward silently into the night, through a hole in the outer perimeter of security Mac had discovered, she sent her mind out tentatively, little tendrils of thought. Coming in on the helo, she thought she could detect faint echoes from Nine—

Lucius Ward. It was a new development, a talent she had never had before and she had no idea if she could trust it.

It might even have been her intense desire to save the man blinding her into thinking she was receiving signals. If so, they were in deepest shit. It was terrible to think she might be leading Mac, Nick and Jon into danger on the false premise that she could somehow communicate with Ward when actually what she was communicating with was her own mind, leading them straight into the heart of danger.

What if Ward was already dead?

When the men halted at Mac's raised fist, she stopped and closed her eyes, wiped her mind of all sense of self and sent herself out, as if dissolving into mist.

Where are you?

It came from her, though she had no memory of formulating the question. It was out there on its own.

Then the thought formed—*We're coming for you. Your men are coming for you. Where are you?*

A faint . . . what? Sense of something. A burst, like fireworks behind a hill.

Coming . . . as faint as the mist at dawn.

Yes, we're coming for you. Adrenaline spiked through her system. This was him! Unmistakable, though she had no idea how she knew that. But it was, like recognizing someone's voice or their face. Something in the quality of the whisper in her head.

. . . moving

Oh my God! She'd missed that, a sound at the very edge of her consciousness.

What?

"Go," Mac said in her ear, and she shot her closed fist up, their sign for halt. The three men stopped immediately and looked at her. She shook her head frantically, they couldn't bother her now. She had to concentrate, focus, because the voice in her head was becoming fainter. She held her fist up high, closing her eyes to concentrate better.

She could sense Mac's stillness and that of the other men, and then she banished them from her thoughts.

Tell me where you are.

Silence, but her head filled with pain. Wherever he was, he was hurting. She concentrated so hard she could feel an echo of his pain. Trying to keep all the avenues of communication open, she tried to analyze it. One part of her, the empathic part, linked to the man lying on a bed, perhaps dying, and the other part of her, the neuroscientist, observing and analyzing.

The pain—it was systemic. Most pain is organic and focused. This was diffuse but intense. Fiery. Another wave of pain, coming from . . .

Catherine bent her head, trying to slow her breathing, trying to take her mind out of herself, throwing it over the wall of cypresses, through concrete walls, down laboratory corridors, down to . . .

Him.

What was the pain? Burning, throughout his body, under the skin. When another wave came, she was able to pinpoint its source. Under the clavicle. Coming in through his open shunt. Some kind of drug they were using on him whose side effects were excruciating pain and a dulling of the senses.

Were they killing him?

She hunkered even deeper inside herself.

Where are you . . . Lucius?

A start of surprise.

You know . . . who I am?

Yes, and your men are coming for you. Right now, Lucius.

Lucius . . . A wave of sadness swept over her so profound it nearly knocked her to her knees. *I was Lucius, once. Was I?*

You still are. We're coming for you. But we have to know where you are.

Sadness, resignation. *It's too late. Will die, tomorrow.*

No! She sent herself out on a wave of energy that came from deep in her bones, a fierce blast she didn't know she had in her. *We're here! Minutes away! Where are you?*

Close? The voice so faint, lightly tinged with hope.

Very close.

Can you come . . . now?

Yes, now. Where are you?

Silence. But she was in his head now, tied there by the faintest of bonds. A whisper and the bonds would break. She could hear what he heard, see what he saw. The drugs in his system were strong, but he was stronger. His vision blurred, focused.

Where? She sent the message frantically. *Where are you?*

Going soon . . . to Level 4. The thought was sad, growing fainter. *To die.*

She lost him and swayed as if a strong wind had suddenly blown up.

Christ!

Mac shot out a hand and grabbed Catherine's elbow, then the other one as he felt her weakness. She was barely able to stand. What the fuck just happened?

He had on night vision so she looked pale green as he held her, possible scenarios running through his mind, each one more terrifying than the next.

Heart attack. Embolism. With all the mind stuff that was going on, an embolism made a lot of sense. Millon had some kind of trip wire system she had stumbled on . . . no. That one could be eliminated. She was in the middle of a safety perimeter they provided; if anyone was to activate a trip wire it would be the man on point. Him.

She was boneless, head tipped back over his arm, long white throat vulnerable and delicate. Her head came forward and she coughed. He could feel strength returning to her. He bowed his head for a second, a rush of something powerful moving through him so strong his entire body broke out in a sweat.

He'd thought she was dead. For one horrible, nausea-inducing second he thought Catherine Young had died trying to rescue his commanding officer. All that warmth and gentleness gone. Gone from the world, gone from his life.

He'd never have it again, of that he was certain. With Catherine gone, Mac's world would shrink to its usual grim contours, with himself at its cold center. His life would return to iron duty with nothing else. There was no question that he would ever have her warmth in his life, ever again. He hadn't found it—hadn't even suspected it existed—in his thirty-four years in this world, and he knew beyond the faintest shadow of a doubt that with her gone, it would disappear from his life forever. He would be condemned to live out the rest of his existence in the icy cold confines of his heart.

Mac shuddered and looked down at the beautiful face of the woman who had changed his life.

They'd had so little time. Three days. Nothing, really. They were three days that had turned his existence upside down. For the very first time, he looked forward to the future. He never had before. The future had been this endless . . . thing stretching out before him. The same as today only perhaps harder. No reason to want the future to arrive. When it did, it would be no different from today.

And yet, with Catherine, the future had looked—well, enticing. Better. Finer. Living with Catherine, sharing his life with her, maybe even forming a family . . .

He'd kicked the thought out of his head the instant it had formed but then it had returned and stuck, like a burr. Family. Families were for other people, not for him. What he knew of families was that they were violent places where people tore each other apart.

Except, maybe not the one he could found with Catherine.

It was crazy thinking, he knew that, but once there, the thought would not leave his mind. Not thought so much as images. A little dark-haired daughter with silvery eyes. That image stuck in his head, together with a crazy flutter in his chest. Creating a new human being, a small child, watching her grow up, protecting her . . . shit, talk about crazy thinking.

"What's the matter with her?" Jon asked in his ear, and he started.

"I don't know." His voice sounded hoarse in his own ears.

"Mac." On his other side, Nick placed a hand on his shoulder. It was only then that Mac realized he was shaking. "She's okay."

Behind her eyelids, Catherine's eyes moved back and forth, as if she was following something. Her gloved hand gripped his.

He tapped her cheek. If she'd been one of his men, he'd have slapped her, but the thought of slapping Catherine made his system break out into another sweat.

"Honey." Tap, tap. "Honey, wake up. Come on, honey, open up your eyes, you can do it."

Something in his voice must have been way off because Nick and Jon looked at each other, faces carefully blank. Mac didn't give a fuck because there she was, his Catherine, back from wherever it was she had gone.

"Mac?" Her voice was raw, as if she hadn't spoken in days. "What happened?"

"Fuck if I know." Relief coursed through him. "You fucking zoned out. Scared the shit out of me. Don't ever do anything like that again. Fuck."

She gave a faint smile, looking at him, then Jon and Nick. "Your vocabulary deteriorates when you're scared."

"Fuck yeah." But he was smiling, too. "So what the fuck happened?"

Catherine touched her head. "I hope you believe me when I say that I communicated with Lucius Ward. He's going to be taken down to Level 4 where he thinks they are going to kill him soon. There were rumors that there was another, secret level but I never really believed them. So apparently Level 4 really exists. They gave him a drug that is extremely painful but which I think increased . . . whatever it is in him that can talk to me." She looked at the three of them. "If he's taken to Level 4 before we get to him I don't know how to access it. He might be lost to us. We need to hurry."

"You can walk?" Mac wanted her to stay right where she was though he knew she wouldn't, not unless she couldn't physically walk. If he had to, he could carry her.

"Oh yes. I'm fine." She touched her head again, tilting it one way, then the other, as if testing it out. "If I zoned out it was because of the link with Lucius, not because of anything in me. We're going to have to hurry. We have to get to him as fast as we can."

"Roger that." Nick was readying something he called the Anthill, checking his handheld, making adjustments. "As soon as we're past the microwave barrier I'll unleash the Antz. If we get past the front door we should be able to get to the Captain undetected. I don't think there's more than ten men on duty inside the facility."

"Antz?"

"I'll explain later, honey. Let's get going." Again, Mac marveled at Catherine, at his woman. She simply nodded, readjusted her light backpack and started forward when they did. No questions, no fuss. She wasn't trained, but she was a teammate down to her bones.

A wave of love shot through him. If they survived this, he was going to marry her the instant they were back and never let her out of his sight again.

They moved forward smoothly, at an even pace. Catherine kept up, carefully staying exactly in the center of their security triangle. The outer perimeter of security was behind them and they were coming up on the microwave barrier.

Their night vision included IR and the area between the huge vases showed up faintly red. The tablets showed no guards within a hundred-meter radius. Nonetheless, Mac kept to hand signals. He signaled for Catherine to stay by his side.

At the barrier, Nick, Catherine and Jon were each behind a vase. Mac was behind Catherine. At his signal, they all climbed the six-foot-high vases, Nick and Jon flowing easily up and over. Mac gave Catherine a boost and Jon was on the other side, helping her down. Mac went over and they huddled in a crouch.

Mac pointed to the small cannon in Nick's hands and gave the order.

Nick lifted it to the sky, made some adjustments, then pulled the trigger. A bolus lifted in the air, disappeared from sight. They bent over Nick's handheld, watching the screen.

A thousand tiny drones, small as ants, colored white and nearly invisible, scrambled fast into the entrance of the main facility. A special program put together the jumbled transmissions so the screen showed a clear image of what was in front of them. There were a few blank spots on the screen but a filler program interpolated. What they were seeing on the screen was about 98 percent correct. More than enough. In the upper right hand was the blueprint of the facility showing the position of the drones.

Catherine smiled. "Antz," she said. "I get it. Mini drones. Smart."

Nick was calling the scene. "Two guards at the entrance. Armed with?" He glanced at Catherine.

She shrugged. "I don't know. I'm not familiar with weaponry. I know that some of the guards have weapons in their holsters with a particularly thick, heavy handle."

Mac's jaws clenched. "Stunners. Fuck. They can deliver anything from an incapacitating up to a fatal dose of electric energy. Can stop a man's heart at a hundred meters. Experimental."

"Not good," Jon murmured.

"Not good," Mac agreed.

"Direct them there." Catherine pointed to the end of a hallway on the short end of the L.

Nick made some adjustments and the image moved in a blur down corridors. At one point, a tech rounded a corner and the image tilted, turned upside down, the floor sliding by fast as a river in spate.

"They scrambled to the ceiling to avoid detection," Nick said.

They waited, following the grouping of tiny red dots as it made its way across to the corridor Catherine wanted.

"Can you split them up?"

"Sure," Nick said. "What do you want?"

"Check these four rooms." Her finger landed on four boxes.

The images became slightly less clear as the drones separated into the four rooms. Three empty. One with a figure lying on a white cot, tubes going in and out of him. His head lolled to one side, mouth slackly open, eyes closed.

"Fuck," Nick breathed. "The Captain. Is he dead?"

"Tilt the drones so I can see the monitors," Catherine ordered. "And get all the drones into this room."

The image tilted, became clearer. "No, he's not dead. But his heart rate is very low. EKG shows only baseline function. He's essentially in a coma. Nick, show me what's on his IV bag."

The image tilted again, focused on the clear bag hanging from the tree.

"They're pumping him full of SL-59!" Catherine sounded angry. "Damn them! That's a highly experimental drug. We haven't even completed animal testing yet. It's viscous and extremely painful. I felt his pain. I can't believe they are doing that. They're pumping him full of the drug and then they'll dissect the brain soon and see the effects."

"How can they do that?" Jon asked. "Isn't it illegal?"

"Of course it's illegal, it's murder." Catherine stood. "We're going in right now. I don't know how long his heart can stand up to this, and he was in a weakened state already. That drug is killing him. We can't wait any longer. Mac, get us in there now."

Her look was imperious. Mac's heart swelled with pride and foreboding. She had clearly forgotten any danger to herself. She was totally focused on one thing and one thing only. If she'd been alone he had no doubt she'd march right in and try to rescue the Captain.

She was brave and that scared the shit out of him. Brave, untrained people died often and badly.

"It's pointless going in through the main entrance." His finger moved to a point fifty meters from where the Captain was lying. "That's the closest door. Is it alarmed?"

"They are all alarmed," Catherine replied. "And they all require a swipe card. Let's hope what Jon cloned will work."

"Damned straight it'll work!" Jon answered indignantly. "I don't do failure."

"We need a way to mask the infrared, too. On most doors, the security system counts how many people come through an entrance, and if there is a discrepancy between numbers of entrances and number of swipes an alarm sounds."

"I'll take care of it," Jon said, and Catherine nodded.

"Then let's go." She was quivering with impatience. All three of them looked at him.

"Saddle up, boys," Mac whispered, and gave the go sign.

Lee leaned forward and tapped his driver on the shoulder. "Can't you go any faster?"

"No, sir. I'm not allowed to exceed the speed limit. Not for anyone, not even for you. I could lose my job." The driver answered in a monotone. He was a Millon employee with no special brief to cater to Lee's needs. Lee made a note to get himself a driver with explicit instructions to do what he was told.

Lee checked his watch. 3 A.M. He'd given the order to start the

IV infusion of SL-59 an hour ago. He'd harvest the brain at eight, together with the other three soldiers, who'd proven almost as useless as Nine himself. Six hours of perfusion should be enough to get an idea of the effects on the nervous system and on neurological tissue.

This could have waited until next week or even next month, of course, but something was eating at him. His usual calm was broken and a huge sense of urgency was riding him. It was ridiculous. He was in the middle of a twenty-year plan. Urgency wasn't necessary, thoroughness was. But though he was a scientist and though he believed in the rigors of reason, he had also learned to follow his gut.

It made him uneasy to be rushing to the laboratory in the dead of night to oversee something his secret team could easily take care of themselves, but it made him even more uneasy to stay at home.

Sleep was out of the question.

Perhaps it was like dreams. Though a scientist, Lee believed absolutely in the predictive power of dreams. Dreams were a manifestation of what the conscious mind had observed and extrapolated. He felt this biting drive to be there perhaps because it was important for him to observe firsthand the effects on Patient Nine. Maybe he would see something that eluded the vidcams or that the techs would fail to report.

If his subconscious told him to be there, it was for a reason.

Not to mention the fact that that idiot Flynn was threatening to cut off funding.

And then, of course, there was the sheer pleasure of watching Nine die. He'd been recalcitrant, a difficult patient. The most difficult patient Lee had ever had. It was going to be a real pleasure watching him die in a useful way.

He checked his watch again. Nine had received an infusion of 20 cc's.

At a guess, Lee imagined that the useful dosage for performance enhancement would be 2 cc's over a period of a week. Twenty was ten times the amount, delivered in the space of six hours. The autopsy was going to be very interesting.

On the whole, Lee was glad he'd decided to come along now. He'd observe the final effects firsthand. He tapped his ear. "Levinson, in half an hour take Patient Nine down to the autopsy suite in Level 4. I'm coming in."

"Yes, sir." Levinson was one of the three scientists who knew of the secret protocol.

"Driver, take me around to the side entrance. Entrance D. Drive directly to the loading area." From there it would be a short descent down to the autopsy suite. He'd have time to suit up and set up his private recording equipment.

"Yessir," the driver answered, and Lee tapped the button that lifted the privacy screen and sat back, pleased.

All in all, a good night's work.

At first, it was hard for Catherine to run. Her legs wobbled, her head felt light and far away, and she could barely concentrate. But minute by minute she came back into herself.

Mac was there beside her, every single step of the way. If she stumbled, his hand was there, on her back, steadying her, so surreptitiously that Nick and Jon never noticed.

It was the aftereffects of her connection with Lucius Ward. He had sapped her strength. Connecting with another mind, another heart, was as hard as lifting weights. She felt as if she'd been punched in the stomach while running a marathon.

But as they crossed the wide lawn, Mac having calculated sentry guards' rounds to the second, she came back into herself. Remembered what she was doing, and why.

She was saving a life.

They were at the side of the building. The three men watched as she swiped her colleague Frederick Benson's code through the system, hoping Jon knew what he was doing.

He did.

The door clicked open. Catherine pushed and the four of them walked through as if they were one. The recorder at the side would merely have registered a larger than usual mass. Not something that would trip an alarm, but definitely something that would target them when looked at tomorrow, with Patient Nine gone.

Catherine was well aware of the fact that she was not only illegally entering Millon Laboratories. She was also crossing over into a new life. She was now a member of Mac's team, an outlaw. Tied to the men by her side and tied to the community that had congregated around them with unbreakable bonds. Forever now cut off from her old life.

She'd spent four years with Millon and the parent company Arka in various laboratories. They would never give her references, and a scientist with a four-year gap in her résumé was unhireable. She would never work in science again.

It wasn't important, though.

She was with Mac, for as long as he'd have her.

Jon was consulting his handheld but she didn't need anything now. She knew where to go. "Come with me," she whispered, and they moved fast toward the patient wing. She stopped them at the corner before Hall B. They stacked up behind her.

"Clear?" She looked up at Jon.

"Clear."

"Hurry!" Catherine broke into a run and they followed her. She ran to Nine's room, ran to the still man on the bed. The first thing she did was cut off the clavicle catheter. Whatever amount of SL-59 Ward had absorbed, she could only hope it wasn't going to prove a fatal dose. She gently pulled the long needle from the permanent shunt and started disengaging him from the EEG, EKG, the catheter, the pads on his chest measuring muscle electricity, the tube down his throat giving extra oxygen, the parenteral feed tube.

Somewhere an alarm was sounding as the machines went dead but she couldn't think about that as she moved as quickly as she could to disengage him.

Finally, he was cut off from the machinery, a tall, once well-built man, now a husk of a man, a pathetic creature who'd been tortured nearly to death. Something about the quality of the air made her look up and she froze at the expression on Mac's face. Nick and Jon looked stunned, sick.

"What?"

Mac swallowed. "What did they do to him?"

She looked down at the patient. She'd never seen him in his prime. She'd only ever seen him as he was now—helpless, weak, a shadow of a man. She touched his wrist and suddenly there he was in her mind. The man he'd been. Ramrod-straight in a starched uniform, a black beret on his shaved head, fierce and strong and formidable.

That was the man he'd been. That was the man Mac remembered.

The man on the bed was emaciated, skull criscrossed with scars, skin hanging off his bones. Pale, sunken in, barely alive.

Anger filled her. He didn't deserve this. The man she'd touched and who had touched her was hard but fair. Unswerving in his duty to his country, unswerving in his loyalty to his men.

The man she'd touched had been fully prepared to die in battle, prepared to die an honorable death. This wasn't an honorable death. It was a lab rat's death.

Anger, white and hot, shot through her.

"They nearly killed him. They robbed him of his life, of his honor, Mac. We're going to rescue him." She shot Mac a glance and saw he understood her. Understood her anger and her own sense of betrayal.

Everything she'd done in life had been with one goal. To understand the human brain, to make things better. To make people better. She'd dedicated her life to science and now someone had taken *her* science and twisted it to dark ends. Twisted it until it had become a source of horror and pain.

She'd been betrayed, too, just as much as Mac.

"Can you carry him?"

"Yeah. No problem." Mac bent and, with a gentleness she'd only seen reserved for her, picked Ward up in his arms as if he were a child. He looked down at the unconscious body of his former commander and there was such pity in his face Catherine nearly cried.

"Captain," Mac said softly, and the man stirred, as if troubled.

Catherine was still touching his wrist and she suddenly stiffened. "Wait!"

Jon tapped on his screen, frowning. "Catherine, we've got guards coming. We don't have time to waste."

Darkness, pain, despair.

Bodies on beds like moths pinned to felt.

Brave men, reduced to animals.

Her heart pounding, Catherine looked up at Mac. "Were there other men with you?"

He frowned. "When?"

"When"—she pointed at the scar on the side of his face—"when that happened."

The frown deepened. "Yeah. They're all dead. Why?"

Awareness burst inside her together with dread and sorrow. "Because they are here," she whispered. "Three of them."

Nick grabbed her arm. "Who? Who's here?"

She met their eyes, certainty blazing through her. "They're here," she said clearly. "The men who were with you that night. They didn't die. They were captured. They are being used as guinea pigs. As lab rats. Tortured. They are here and we must go to them. Captain Ward doesn't want to be rescued if he has to leave his men behind. He would rather die."

She could feel their shock. It came off them in waves.

"Romero, Lundquist, Pelton?" Jon whispered. "Alive?"

With each name she felt a shock of recognition. "Yes. Alive. And here. And we must rescue them."

"Where are they?" Mac asked.

She listened inside herself, felt for the answer. *Oh God.* "Level 4," she said, shocked.

"How do we get there?" Mac asked urgently.

"I don't know. But I know who does." She looked at the man lying limply in Mac's strong arms. He looked close to death. Perhaps a less strong man would already be dead. But there was something in this man, and it was the same thing that was in Mac. And Nick and Jon. A core strength that would carry them beyond what other men could do. This man had commanded them. He would be as strong as they were. Maybe stronger. She had to count on that.

"I'm going to try something. I don't know if it will work." She put her hand on Mac's arm. She didn't need her psychic powers to draw strength from him. The steely arm under hers belonged to a man whose will was as strong as his muscles. "You're going to have to trust me. Can you do that?"

She looked up at him. He was tense with the effort of standing still. She imagined every instinct in him was screaming at him to escape. They had their man, now they had to go. Yet he stood unmoving, waiting for her word.

It was at that moment that she realized how much she loved Mac. Loved everything about him. Loved his strength and his loyalty. Loved the fact that he was willing to risk his life on her say-so. He'd come here at enormous risk, believing in her implicitly, the first human being who'd ever done so. She loved him, and because she did, she knew he could never live with himself if he abandoned the other men here. This had to be done.

They needed to get to Level 4, fast. Level 4 had been a rumor, almost a joke. There was no way she could get down there unless . . .

"I think I'm going to hurt him," she murmured, watching Mac. "I have to."

He nodded.

She looked at Nick and Jon. "Can you two buy us some time?"

At Mac's nod, Nick said, "Sure. I'll send the Antz out, they'll give us an early warning sign."

They left the room, two utterly tough and competent warriors. Catherine knew they'd provide her with a window.

Both Catherine's hands hovered over Ward. "I hate to do this," she whispered. "But I have to."

"Do it," Mac ordered.

She pulled down the neck of the hospital johnny, placed her hands over Ward's heart and closed her eyes. For the first time, she tried to push her thoughts into someone else's head, tried to control instead of read. Though the skin of her palms lay lightly against the man's emaciated chest, she felt as if she were pushing through his skin, down past bone and muscle, to reach into his chest cavity and seize his heart.

She squeezed, hard.

A rattling gasp of air and the man arched in Mac's arms as if given an electrical shock.

"Jesus!" Mac tightened his grip on him as if on a slippery fish as he bowed and twisted.

Catherine went deeper, pushing herself into Ward's psyche, as if going spelunking. Deep, deeper, plunging down until . . . ah.

Your men need you. Help us.

I . . . can't.

He was awake! Aware, on some level of his being.

Yes. They will die without you. How do we get to Level 4?

He twisted wildly, arms flailing.

Help us help your men. They need you, Captain.

Silence in her head.

He writhed wildly, seeming to want to reach back to the bed, clawed hands reaching for the sheets.

Was this the dying throes of a man who wanted nothing more than to die in bed?

She pushed him harder, feeling his heart beat wildly, muscles twitching, wondering if she was killing him.

Dull moans came from him, then grunts, as his feeble muscles tried to claw his way to the bed.

"What's going on?" Mac demanded. "I don't want to hurt him but he's out of control! What the fuck does he want?"

To die in bed, she thought. *That's what he wants.*

But—but that didn't make sense. Everything in that ravaged, emaciated face spoke of discipline and duty. There was nothing in that face that spoke of a man whose greatest wish was to die in bed.

He was like Mac.

What would Mac do? Whatever Mac would want to do, Catherine would want to help him do it. "I don't know why, but he wants to get to the bed."

Under her hands she could feel Ward's withered muscles straining. Under that, iron will straining . . . Bed . . .

The clawed hands fell, grasping . . .

Bed.

Something in the bed.

Catherine leaped.

"What?" Mac grunted as he tried to calm Ward without hurting him. "What are you doing, honey?"

She was scrabbling madly in the sheets. The bed, the bed . . . echoes of what she'd heard as if a faraway scream sounded in her mind.

The bed.

She stripped the sheets off, shook them out.

The bed . . . *under* the bed.

She fell to her knees so hard she hurt herself and scrabbled wildly in the darkness under the bed. Nothing.

It had to be here, whatever it was.

Think, Catherine!

His hands, flailing, reaching . . .

She lifted the side of the mattress and there it was, on the orthopedic support. With a cry, Catherine lifted it up, and like a button had been pushed, Ward stilled in Mac's arms.

She studied the bloodstained card, studied the 3D hologram of the face. The face of the enemy. "This is Lee's own pass. The head of research at Arka. I can't believe it. He stole Lee's card. This definitely has clearance to Level 4, if it exists. We can get in and get out now."

"Boss, Catherine." Nick's quiet voice was grim in her earpiece. "Company. Coming fast."

"How many?" Mac asked. The shit storm was almost upon them. They'd got this far, they'd already been lucky. There was only so much luck to be had on any mission and they'd just used up all of theirs.

They were going hot now, and Mac wanted Catherine out of here. She'd done a fabulous job of getting them here. Smart and beautiful and kind. And now brave. He wasn't going to lose her. Not now, not after just finding her.

He had to get her out of here, fast.

The Captain was still in his arms, after having what felt like a seizure. His eyes were closed, ravaged face slack. He weighed less than some of the backpacks Mac had carried into battle.

Mac could carry him anywhere. He could carry him down to Level 4. He could do anything as long as he knew Catherine was safe.

"Listen," he said urgently. "We've got the pass. We'll get down to Level 4, get the men out. Take the Antz, they'll help you navigate your way out. Can you make it back to the helo and wait for us? You remember how to get over the microwave screen? You—"

She was already walking to the door. "No way, Mac. No way am I leaving you. You need eyes and ears that aren't the Antz, eyes and ears that know their way around. And you're definitely going to be needing me to detach those men from their machines, if they are still alive. Make sure you close the door behind me." She opened the door and signaled Nick at the end of the corridor, looked back at him. "Come *on*! Close the door."

There was no time to argue and he recognized that it would be useless anyway. Every cell in his body told him to get Catherine out of there but his head told him she was right. They needed her.

Never before in his life had he gone on a mission with a split goal. He was always narrowly focused on getting in, getting the job done, getting out. He went in with men who trained as hard as he did and who were perfectly capable of taking care of themselves. He'd never gone in worried about a teammate like he was now with Catherine, and he hated the hell out of it.

But what could he do?

He followed her out, the Captain in his arms, closing the door. She was already running down the corridor, Nick and Jon following her. He caught up with Nick. "How many?" he asked.

"Three." He was watching Catherine as she hurried down the corridor. "They'll be at the corner any second now and they'll see us."

"You and Jon be ready to take a knee."

"Yeah." Jon and Nick had their weapons out. Mac shifted the Captain to a fireman's lift and drew his own.

Nick had shifted the screen image to holo. "Boss? They're just around the—"

"Here!" Catherine had stopped at a door, opened it and ushered them in. Mac, Nick and Jon turned, came in at a dead run.

She shut the door quietly just as Nick's holo showed three guards rounding the corner. There was a quiet sound as they all exhaled. None of them wanted a firefight with a wounded comrade to carry and a noncombatant to protect.

Mac looked around. They were in a large room full of equipment. It wasn't a sickroom, though. There were no beds, only inert machines stacked all around the walls. The only light came from the holo by Nick's side. They watched it.

The three guards were walking slowly, completely alert, hands on weapons. These weren't rent-a-cops filling time.

"Will they check the rooms?" Jon whispered.

"Yes. The Captain's machinery is dead, there will be a red light flashing above the door. When they see the body missing they will sound the alarm. We have to get down to Level 4 fast. Follow me."

Catherine didn't wait for them to acknowledge her, but rushed to the end of the room. There was a door there Mac hadn't noticed, hidden behind what looked like a huge old-fashioned MRI, completely different from the new handheld ones.

They filed out, into a large, dimly lit corridor.

"That room is essentially a storehouse for equipment that needs recycling or repair or discarding. No one enters except tech guys on a schedule. We're now in a part of the facility used for maintenance. It's off the security camera web system. We should be okay until we get to Level 4. And pray there is one." She was panting as she spoke. Mac let her lead. He had the layout of the Millon facility memorized but they were off the blueprints.

Once again, she was saving their asses.

The corridor ran over three hundred meters and at the end there was an elevator—a freight elevator from the size. They ran to it and Catherine swiped Lee's card. They filed in and she swiped the card again. There were only three buttons, but when she swiped the card, a big 4 pulsed on the screen. She pressed the screen and they dropped.

Nick had managed to herd a troop of Antz into the elevator and they clung to the ceiling. Mac looked at the handheld and saw the five of them in a bird's-eye view.

The doors opened onto a huge, gleaming hallway.

An alarm sounded, a big foghorn sound, wailing every two seconds.

Shit.

Catherine looked up at Nick. "I'm sorry. I don't know what to do now. Nick, can we use the Antz to check the rooms?"

He was already deploying and the nearly invisible creatures were scattering, scrambling along the walls, looking into every room. They watched the screen showing room after empty room.

Catherine put her hand on his arm as she watched and Mac felt warmth and hope and fear in equal measure enter his system. With the Captain in his arms he couldn't cover her hand with his so he bent down and kissed the top of her head.

"Wait! Have them back up." She still had her hand on his arm and he could feel a jolt of excitement in his system and had no way to tell whether it was hers or his. "There!" She pointed. A dimly lit room with three beds. Three bodies hooked up to machinery.

Outside the door was a brightly lit corridor. As they watched, two people, a man and a woman, both wearing lab coats, came out of a room. Two guards ran around a corner.

Jon was already pulling a flashbang from his backpack.

"Turn your back, close your eyes, open your mouth," Mac said urgently to Catherine. Nick and Jon had already fitted their tiny ear protectors, handed two to Catherine. Mac gently eased the Captain over his shoulder in a fireman's carry and fitted his own in. He gave Jon a nod.

"Fire in the hole," Jon whispered, peered around the corner and lobbed the canister down the corridor.

Light bloomed around the corner accompanied by a sonic boom

that was nearly painful in its intensity even through the muffler buds.

The jagged image the few Antz who'd followed them showed the two techs falling to the ground, curling up in a fetal position, hands clutching ears. Two sentries ran around the corridor. Nick checked the handheld, stepped out and took them down, one shot each. The screen showed them down, dead.

"Go go go!" Mac chanted, and they rushed the corridor.

Catherine ran to the room, looked in, then looked over at him.

Mac stiffened. Her look was sorrowful, solemn.

It was bad.

They rushed to the room and stopped on the threshold.

It was very bad.

Romero, Lundquist and Pelton were in three beds. If Mac hadn't seen the jagged, moving colored lines of the machines next to each bed and heard the soft beeps, he would have been convinced they were dead.

They looked worse than the Captain. Thinner, more messed up. The surgeries had been more extensive, probably the drugs they'd been subjected to stronger.

They were very strong, resistant young men. The kind of men sick fucks loved to mess around with. They were comatose, sunken faces already looking like death masks. Dark blue patches showed where IV injections had been used for prolonged periods of time.

Each man was naked, without even the dignity of a hospital gown, spread-eagled out as if a human sacrifice, which was true since they were sacrifices. To someone's greed.

All three men, young and strong and brave—the best in the world—looked like POWs in a particularly savage prison camp. And yet they were here—in Silicon Valley in the good old US of A.

Mac never went into battle enraged. Rage, anger, revenge—they were all emotions he couldn't afford. You don't go into combat with emotions because they blinded you. They were handicaps and they were dangerous. So he made sure he fucking well washed away all emotion before suiting up for an op, and when he went operational he was all cold, clear reasoning and hard calculation.

That was all swept away right now as pity for his men swamped him. Pity that they'd been brought to this. Clearly tortured, tormented, treated as less than animals by their own countrymen.

The rage washed over him, a huge uncontrollable wave he was helpless to resist. He knew he was engendering them all, endangering Catherine and the Captain, and there was nothing he could do.

He stood still for a breath, two. Nick and Jon stood still as statues, too. For all the combat they'd seen, for all the deaths in battle they'd watched, there was something so inherently evil in this scene they were shocked. As if touched by the Devil's hand.

Catherine was the first to move. Her hands were swift and sure as she gently, quickly started unhooking the men from the machinery. She was whispering under her breath, and after a moment Mac realized she was running down a checklist, much as he and his men checked gear just before going into battle.

Finally the men were unhooked, lying there unmoving, like meat on a butcher's marble slab, barely breathing. Catherine looked at them in pity.

"Wrap them in sheets, Nick, Jon. I'm going to do something."

They nodded, and started wrapping the sheets around their fallen comrades' naked torsos. They had barely finished and were hoisting them up when another alarm sounded, high-pitched, even more urgent than the other one.

Catherine ran back into the room.

"What's that alarm?" Mac asked.

"I pulled the fire alarm, and that's the evacuation signal. All external doors are now open. Let's go."

Lee got out of the limo, thinking he might stop by the recreation room. At this time of night, it would be empty.

Millon treated its employees well. There was a Nespresso machine which made divine coffee, there were trays of loose-leaf Chinese teas, a large selection of herbal infusions.

The chairs were comfortable and the staff kept the place very neat and clean. All in all, Lee thought, he deserved a nice cup of tea. Review his notes while he was at it, and perhaps even meditate. He was early.

He was looking forward to this, in every sense. Patient Nine and his confreres had proven to be most meddlesome. All in all, it was going to be a pleasure harvesting Nine and the others. Though he was a scientist and didn't believe in something as arbitrary as luck, he did feel that the program would regain its natural rhythm once these men were out of the way and he could test on more ordinary patients.

Nine and his men were outliers, in every sense of the word.

He got out of the car and signaled the driver to pull away, watching the red backlights disappear from view.

Lee knew the grounds were patrolled by security agents, but for the moment it was as if he were alone in the entire facility. In the state of California, even.

They were close. Lee could feel it. Once his outliers were gone, he was certain he could start bringing the program to a successful conclusion. Another six months of testing—or rather having that moron Flynn test the program—and he'd be ready.

Why, this time next year he could be in Beijing, undersecretary to the Minister of Science. Or perhaps to the Minister of Defense. An honored member of the high councils of his country, a man who had been instrumental in shaping his country's future. A man who had been true to his country through a long, lonely and bitter exile.

Ah, but the taste of triumph would be all the sweeter for having waited. He was a young man still, not even forty yet. He'd handed over the cancer vaccine. Members of the Politburo were given the finest medical care the world could offer.

He could live to be a vigorous eighty-year-old, even ninety-year-old. Another forty, fifty years of power at the pinnacle of the world's most powerful country to look forward to.

He drew in a deep breath and glanced west. He was inland, of course. But thirty miles would take him to the Pacific. He could almost feel his homeland calling to him across the wide body of water. The greatest civilization mankind had ever known, triumphant once more.

Thanks to him, Charles Lee.

He smiled and reached for his security pass, frowning. Odd, it wasn't in his front pants pocket, as it usually was. It wasn't in any pocket at all, he found as he rummaged. Nor in his briefcase.

The stress was getting to him and he was very glad the major source of his stress—besides that moron Flynn—was going to be eliminated tonight. He had never forgotten an important document in his life and here he'd forgotten or misplaced his security pass.

Well, there was a go-around.

The security staff had prepared for just such a contingency. He and ten others also had a special code assigned them in case they didn't have their pass or the pass was chipped and had to be replaced. He entered in the code.

In his head, he was already in the recreation room, calmly preparing his tea, settling his troubled spirit, so at first he didn't understand what was happening.

The door didn't open. Lee punched in the code again and the fire siren sounded from the outside loudspeakers, signaling evacuation, and the door opened. He knew why the door hadn't opened at first, why the alarm was sounding and who had pulled it. The system had already clocked him in and it hadn't clocked him out. He was being read as an intruder. Someone else had clocked in using his security pass. And he had a good idea who.

The same person who called in the fire alarm.

Catherine Young.

She was here.

Christ! Four nearly dead men and three men to carry them. Nick and Jon were already stripping a bed to fashion a travois to be carried by two men, each also carrying a man. It was going to be hard and they were going to be sitting ducks, but there was no question of leaving their teammates behind. They weren't going to die like rats in a lab.

Catherine stood for a second with a frown on her face, clearly puzzling something out, and Mac nearly dropped to his knees in a burst of love for her. Any other woman in the world would be screaming in panic or rushing around using up her energy in useless things but not his woman. No, she was thinking.

"Mac," she said urgently, "we need to get these men to an exit point. Can the three of you carry these men about five hundred yards?"

"Sure. Tell us where the exit point is and we'll make it. Get out fast. We went over the sentry positions in our drills. If you go out the east side you should be okay. We'll rendezvous at the helo. If we don't make it, there's a kit with survival equipment next to the pilot's seat. It has ten thousand dollars in cash, take it and go—"

She was shocked, mouth open, eyes wide. Then she looked angry as her eyes narrowed. "What's *wrong* with you? We went over this before and you still want me to *leave* you? I can't believe you said that. Back home you're paying for that comment, Thomas McEnroe. Nick, Jon, since neither of you appear to be boneheads, follow me."

They headed out as fast as they could, Mac carrying the Captain over his shoulder and holding on to one side of the blanket with Lundquist in it while Jon held on to the other, Romero over on his shoulder. Nick had Pelton over his shoulder and was checking his screen.

They were following Catherine blindly. After her outburst she hadn't looked at him. Even her back, beautiful as it was, looked mad.

"Rule Number One, meathead," Jon muttered out of the side of his mouth. "Don't piss off your ladylove."

"How the fuck would you know about ladyloves," Mac answered. "Your record is four nights in a row."

He'd make it up to her, if they survived. They weren't able to go at a dead run and carrying the men meant they couldn't reduce their profile. The men they were rescuing didn't have camouflage body armor. They'd be big fat targets out there. And the helo was rated for five people, not eight. She might not lift off.

They were not making good time. Mac estimated they were a good fifteen minutes out from the helo, not counting the fact that they would have to blast their way through the microwave barrier.

A lot of shit could happen in fifteen minutes plus. A lot of fatal shit.

Mac tried to go to that cold place inside himself that was his fortress in battle. He was used to taking himself right out of the equation, as if he were a Cylon, a robot. A mass of flesh and bones, yes, but a compendium of battle strategies, lines of fire, the deadly ballet of battle.

He couldn't find that place, however frantically he looked for it. He was team leader, and now not only Nick and Jon depended on his cold-blooded ability to strategize, but also the Captain, Lundquist, Romero and Pelton. Not to mention Catherine. If they were going to get out of this alive, he had to become a soldier, not a man.

But someone who reminded him every step of the way that he was a man, with a man's weaknesses, was running ahead of him. Catherine.

She was messing with his head. She was messing with his ability to distance himself from the situation and think coldly and clearly.

On a mission, in a fight, Mac did everything he could to protect his men but, always, the mission came first. They were all soldiers, they all knew the price to pay and they all accepted it. Some of them might not make it to home base, but as long as the mission was successful, it was acceptable.

Losing Catherine was not acceptable. Not an option.

Fear for her fried his circuits, made him slow. He was operating under a pressure so intense it almost made him crack wide open. Loving Catherine made him a better man but a worse soldier, and she needed the soldier now, not the man.

"Up ahead!" Catherine turned, gasping, and Mac saw the fear on her face and another huge pulse of love ran through him. She was terrified but she was working through it. Not slowing them down, not at all. Helping them with every fiber of her being, notwithstanding the fear.

This woman deserved his best. He was going to see her through this because she was the most important mission of his life.

"What, honey?"

They were almost at an intersection. Catherine had stopped, small fist raised, and they all stopped, too. She was winded, narrow chest billowing in and out, but she ignored that, turning to Nick. "Anyone in the corridor to the right?" she gasped.

The ceiling rippled. Nick was turning what was left of his Antz to the right.

"Not getting a completely clear picture," he murmured. "But the corridor is empty. Except for a piece of machinery."

She grabbed the screen, smiled, and gave a little panting whoop, reached up and kissed Mac on the mouth. Mac smiled back, because he simply couldn't not smile at Catherine and because he was forgiven.

"You can't see that from here but it's an electric cart. If you're sure the coast is clear, we can load Ward and the other men on it, and if we time things right, we can make a run to the helo on it."

Nick gave a whoop, completely un-Nick-like, leaned over and kissed Catherine. A big, loud smack on the mouth.

"Hey!" Mac frowned.

"Just thanking the boss lady, boss." Nick concentrated on his screen. The image was fuzzy, with sections of static. "We're good to . . . go!"

They ran around the corner, down the hallway to the cart. It was used to transport equipment but it could transport people, too. They lay the men down on the back, stacked like firewood. Mac pulled out a small ball of material, opened it up, pulled it fast over the Captain and his teammates. A refractive blanket. It wasn't perfect but it should shield them from IR imaging.

"Jon, take the wheel, Nick face the rear," Mac ordered, and they took up a defensive perimeter. Nick and Mac were back-to-back. Mac faced front, behind Jon and Catherine.

Jon started the cart up and they rolled down the corridor.

The alarm changed in pitch again, much higher and more strident. "Second evacuation signal," Catherine said.

That was good news. More confusion, legitimate people running around. Security guards would hesitate before firing. Mac and his men wouldn't. After seeing the Captain and the rest of his teammates, anyone in this facility was fair game and would be shot on sight.

Another intersection. Catherine leaned to Jon and murmured something. Jon never slowed but turned to the left. In the distance was a long ramp, at the top a set of huge metal double doors.

"Jon!" Mac called. "Can you make this piece of shit go faster?"

"Only one way to find out," Jon said grimly, increasing the speed fractionally. As the cart made the transition from the horizontal corridor to the beginning of the ramp, the doors started to open. They saw the night sky, velvety smooth.

"Night vision, men," Mac said, as he switched his on. The enemy would have night vision, too. Didn't matter. Mac felt his spirits rise as they rode up and out into the night. Trapped in a building they weren't familiar with, he'd felt cornered, but now they were on equal ground, and however many guards Millon employed and were able to deploy, they were no match for him and his men.

They could face down a hundred. And with Catherine to defend? A fucking thousand.

"Nick," he said quietly. Nick rolled off and began running. Mac turned sideways, covering a 180-degree field of fire, then turned back. Jon was driving with one hand, weapon in the other.

"Mac?" Catherine turned her face up to his. He didn't dare look straight at her but he had good peripheral vision and could see her beautiful pale face, looking worried.

"Don't worry, honey. Nick's going to give us a diversion on the other side of the building. He'll catch up."

"Okay." Her face cleared and she turned back to face the front.

She trusted him. She trusted them.

He wasn't going to let her down.

Lights were on all over the facility, bright spotlights lighting parts of the grounds like day, leaving cones of darkness. The lights had been designed by architects, however, for beauty and not for security. If Mac had designed the lighting system he would have made sure the entire place was lit up like a fucking Christmas tree in an emergency.

He and Jon were ready, but Catherine flinched at the sound of the huge explosion. They couldn't see the fire and destruction, they only saw the smoke billowing over the rooftops, but from the sound and size of the cloud, Nick had done a good job.

Jon was driving them at the cart's maximum power. Not fast but faster than they could have run weighed down with the deadweight of the wounded men. They powered over a hump, landing with a thud. The Captain stirred, eyes flickering open, then closing.

The night vision showed everything a flat green field but Mac knew the distances, knew the microwave barrier was a hundred meters out. He could see Nick running flat out fifty meters to their right, heading straight for the microwave barrier.

Men were running in the distance, but running toward the explosion, paying them no attention. Somewhere, a guard was seeing them in his IR field, but so far the intel hadn't filtered down.

Mac tapped his earpiece. "Grenade," he said. "Catherine, cover your head." She bent forward, arms over her head.

"Yeah." Nick didn't sound winded. They all kept up with conditioning in exile. If anything, they'd stepped up their daily training. Having the entire U.S. government and military hunting you kept you on your toes. "Now."

Nick's arm came up and out, lobbing a grenade precisely where the cart was headed. It detonated on impact, taking out six of the vases, interrupting the transmission of microwave beams.

Clods of dirt rose up and fell onto the cart, together with shards of the hard ceramic. It all bounced off their suits and the refractive blanket harmlessly.

Jon drove straight through the center of what had once been a deadly microwave fence, the cart bouncing hard off the uneven terrain. The camouflage blanket came loose, lifted up, blew away.

Shit! They were visible now to guards with scans.

A shout, and five men veered off and started running toward them.

"Busted!" Jon shouted, looking in the rearview mirror to the side of the open-topped cart. "Hang on tight!"

He began a series of evasive maneuvers as more clods of earth sprang up from the bullets. It was a numbers game now. Number of minutes times number of shooters. Nick was behind them, now pacing them . . . he hopped aboard, walking over the sick men to his sentry position. In a second, he had his rifle to his shoulder and they were back-to-back again, covering 360 degrees.

"Drone!" Mac barked. "Outer perimeter?"

Nick had his screen set to holo, he positioned it to the side so they could both see. There were three red points running forward, the outer perimeter guards. Fuck, this was exactly what the guards were trained for. Preventing an outbreak.

Nick sent a copy of the holo to the front of the cart so Jon and Catherine could watch it. They were four minutes out.

IR showed dots converging on them, a hundred meters away.

"They can't see the helo, they're coming for us!" Jon shouted.

They needed to get to the helo fast and get out of Dodge. Once they were in the air, they could breathe easy. Until then, they were targets and outnumbered. And Catherine was with them.

She was quiet, hanging hard on to the bar in front of her, beautiful face set, saying nothing. Not wanting to distract them.

Three minutes out.

The dots were running fast toward them, weapons up, seventy meters away. They shouldered their rifles at a dead run. Mac shouldered his own rifle, took aim, feet naturally counteracting the bouncing vehicle, waiting . . . there it was! A moment of steadiness. He breathed out, and halfway through the breath squeezed the trigger. One down. Another steady moment and the other went down. He swiveled and the third went down.

Two minutes out.

The three guards would have given their coordinates. Now the entire compound would know a Millon cart full of armed men was making a break for it. Nick shouldered his rifle and a man speaking into a shoulder mike behind them went down.

One minute out.

They were near the helo, though they couldn't see it. It was going to be tight. Red dots were converging on them from all points of the compass.

Mac tapped his ear, to the entire team. "Catherine, pull the camouflage tarp off the helo. Nick and I will provide security. Jon, load the Captain and the men. We'll have a window of about a minute and a half to take off."

Unspoken was the idea—*if we can take off.* The helo was rated for speed and invisibility, she wasn't a workhorse. She was a sleek piece of technology but she had her limits and carrying seven people was definitely it. The only thing that could save them was that the sick men were so emaciated. Together, the four men weighed as much as two men.

The helo would simply have to be up to it.

Mac quickly ran alternate scenarios through his head if they crash-landed somewhere between here and Haven. They could steal a van, make it up the mountain . . .

Here they were! The cart stopped, rocking a little. Catherine raced out and quickly, efficiently started pulling the tarp off. Jon was loading the Captain and the men. Catherine had finished and had hopped up and was helping to position the unconscious men and restrain them for takeoff.

Four men were running toward them, shooting. Mac felt a sharp pain in his side and ignored it. The ballistic vest would take care of it. He might have a bruised rib but that was all. He took the fucker down and the man next to him. Nick took care of the other two.

Jon was in the cockpit, powering up the engine. *"Go go go!"* he shouted.

Mac grabbed hold of the strut, pulled himself up with a wince. Man, his side hurt like a bitch. The helo started lifting, slowly at first. Nick had put on his harness and was hanging outside the open door, laying down suppressive fire. Another bright light, and another man went down.

Something crackled and danced.

Fuck! That was a stunner! Put on high, it would have dropped them like cattle.

A bullet pinged harmlessly off a skid. They would be barely visible to the men on the ground now and invisible on scan.

Nose down, the helo rose in the air, now beyond the reach of bullets and stunners. Mac looked down at the pale green faces, guns pointing in every direction as the guards lost them, unable to track them by sound and radar and IR. The helo veered north, gaining speed with every passing second. They were headed home.

Mac heaved a sigh of relief. Nick was disengaging himself from the harness, looking back into the small bay. His eyes widened.

Mac whirled, weapon to shoulder, ready to take down anyone who'd jumped aboard at the last second but there was nobody.

Except . . . a pale figure slumped over the bodies of his teammates.

Catherine.

Dead.

Lee strode down the corridors, listening to the guards sounding off. There'd been a break-in, an equipment cart had made it out of the compound and had been abandoned close to the outer perimeter.

No one had any idea who had been in it.

Lee knew, or he suspected. The two men at the entrance, who kept an eye on the vidcams, swore that nothing amiss had happened, but Lee knew that someone had come for Patient Nine.

Patient Nine was the key. Someone knew that and someone had stolen a year of work from him and perhaps his future with it.

He stepped into the room, alerted by the red light flashing above the door.

Nine was gone. Disconnected from the machinery, not ripped from it. He'd been disconnected by someone who knew what she was doing.

Oh yes. Catherine Young.

He keyed in the code for the entrance security. "Who entered the premises this evening besides those who were scheduled?"

A pause, then one of the guards answered. "Ah, Dr. Benson, sir. He entered at 3:17 A.M."

"His emergency contact number is listed. Call and tell me where he is."

"Ah, sir, isn't he—"

"Now!"

"Yessir." The line was kept open and Lee listened as the guard called Benson and asked where he was. He didn't hear Benson's answer but he knew where he wasn't. At Millon. "Sir." The guard sounded confused. "Dr. Benson isn't here. He's in Boston, visiting his sick mother."

Lee closed his eyes, then opened them. The guard was squawking in his ear but he paid no attention.

"Tell security to stand down from the cart and send a team of techs to gather forensic evidence. If there is a molecule of DNA or extraneous material, I want it."

"Yessir."

Through the bedlam of the sirens, Lee slowly made his way down to Level 4. The building was deserted, the evacuation protocol having been followed to the letter.

At the entrance to Level 4, the sirens suddenly disengaged. Security would be doing a sweep up in the upper levels, gathering evidence, interrogating the night shift workers. They wouldn't be coming down here; Level 4's secrets were safe.

Lee walked to the entrance of the door where Patients Twenty-Seven, Twenty-Eight and Twenty-Nine had been kept. They'd been comatose, now they were gone/missing. No one person could have carried four men away.

So this was an organized raid. Could Catherine Young have organized it?

Nothing he knew about her suggested that she could have done so. She was a brilliant researcher, a fine scientist, but not a leader. Her personality was quiet and withdrawn. But the fact was, she was missing, and his lab had been raided.

If she had anything to do with this, he would hound her to the ends of the earth.

In the meantime, he wouldn't let this stop him. In fact, he'd found something very interesting in Young's brain scan. Something he could use, build upon.

This was a setback, nothing more.

Nine and the other patients were close to death anyway. He'd been deprived of their brain tissue, that was all.

But he was getting closer to his goal.

No one could stop him.

"No!" Mac screamed, pure panic prickling through his system. Panic and blinding, crippling fear.

He knelt, gathering Catherine to him. She was utterly slack with the boneless look of the dead.

No!

"Medic bag!" he screamed just as Nick thrust it into his hands. As he scrambled to find the defibrillator patches, fit them into the tiny battery, disengaging the Securloc of Catherine's ballistic vest, tearing open the shirt underneath and fitting the patches to her white white skin, he totally ignored the fact that touching her was like touching something inert . . . dead.

No!

Every time he'd touched Catherine her skin sang to him. Life pulsed in her, touching her was like touching life itself. Warmth and energy traveled through him at the slightest contact. He could feel her heart beating, the swirl of emotions that was Catherine, the gentleness and light that was uniquely her.

Touching her had been sheer magic, always, a touch that brought him to life, too.

Not like now, where there was nothing beneath his fingers but a cold blank void.

He turned on the switch with sweaty fingers. Her back arched and for a second he thought—*She's come back to me!* But it was nothing. It was the electrical current running through her muscles, artificially contracting them.

He pressed the current again and her back arched again, high, slumping back down lifelessly.

There was a loud noise in the cabin and it took him a moment to realize it was him, screaming at her to *live, goddammit live!*

Another pulse, she arched and fell back. Mac laid his hand on her chest, something he'd done a hundred times these past days and every time it was as if her skin kissed his. Warmth and welcome slid into him in honeyed pulses and he'd grown addicted to the feeling. Always, always . . . except now.

Now there was nothing under his hand but emptiness.

No!

He had no idea if he screamed it aloud or only in his head. Didn't matter. He tore the patches off and began manual stimulation of her heart, the skin lifeless under his hands but he didn't care because he was going to bring her back to life himself, she was going to live through his hands, as he lived through hers.

Left hand on her chest, the heel of the right hand over the back of the left, compression at least 5 centimeters deep, 100 compressions per minute.

Training kicked in and he pumped her chest hard, rhythmically, unceasingly, counting the compressions like a chant, over and over again. Sweat dripped from him onto her chest and his hands were white with the pressure and he couldn't give up, wouldn't give up . . .

"Boss." Nick's hand on his shoulder. "She's gone. I'm so sorry. I saw the stunner, it was green, set to kill. She caught killer current. I'm so sorry, boss."

Mac wasn't listening, could barely hear him. There was noise in his ears, the static of panic as he tunnel-visioned and there was only his hands over Catherine's heart and Catherine's heart silent under them, and nothing else in the entire world.

He chanted the numbers, loud, so he wouldn't have to listen to Nick. He didn't want to hear him, he didn't want to hear anyone, he didn't want anyone or anything, all he wanted was to feel her heart beat under his hands and he was going to stay here for a hundred years if he had to, just like this, willing her back to life.

Pumping his own life into her because he couldn't exist without her. Everything he was, all his thoughts and dreams and fears, it was all there in his hands, his hands were beating her heart for her. He'd do that. He'd do that forever, his heart would beat for hers, he'd do anything, anything at all . . .

Tears were mixing with the sweat and dripping onto Catherine's chest. His eyes stung but it never even occurred to him to wipe his eyes, his brow, because Catherine needed his hands, needed him for her heart to beat.

"Boss . . ." Nick spoke again, a note of pity in his voice.

Mac shrugged away the hand. He'd slap it away if he could but he couldn't leave Catherine, not for one instant because he was her. His hands were reaching deep inside her now, beneath the skin, through bone and muscle, reaching for her heart, pumping heat into her . . .

His hands grabbed her heart, squeezed it directly somehow, though he was still compressing her chest, 100 beats a minute, steady steady . . . and below, he was touching her heart, touching it with everything in him, and if he could have he would have given her his own life but he couldn't, he could only work his hands on her chest, 100 compressions a minute.

He chanted and worked and sweated, frenzied and terrified.

"ETA fifteen minutes," Jon announced, but Mac didn't hear. Didn't want to hear. He wanted to stay here forever, heels of his hands over his love's heart, because as long as they were here he didn't have to let her go, didn't have to say goodbye . . .

"Mac . . ." Nick said low. It was the first time Nick had ever called him by his name. Mac chanced a look up and saw tears in Nick's eyes. He didn't know Nick could cry. "She's gone," he whispered.

No!

No, he wouldn't let her be . . . gone. His mind shied away from even thinking the word *dead*. Because Catherine couldn't be dead. Nothing would make any sense at all in the world if she were dead. She was life itself and joy and that heart of hers, that magical heart of hers . . .

Was beating.

Was he hallucinating? He couldn't feel anything under the heels of his hands but that other sense, the one that allowed him to feel, touch her heart with his phantom hand, it felt a pulse, a sharp electric jerk.

Catherine's back arched again as if under the patches but she wasn't wearing patches. She arched, coughed, her head turned.

"Jesus fucking Christ!" Nick yelled, backing away, hands up.

"What?" Jon yelled from the cockpit.

Nick was white. "She's . . . Catherine's . . ."

"Alive!" Mac screamed. He pulled her up and into his arms, held her tightly and cried, great gulping raw sobs, crying so hard he couldn't breathe but he didn't need air, all he needed was Catherine, alive once again in his arms.

Something brushed against his scar. Her hand. It stroked him once, then fell weakly. "Mac," she whispered, the sound barely audible above the raw sounds coming from his chest. "I love you."

"Oh God!" His throat was so tight he couldn't speak, couldn't get the words out. *I love you, too,* he screamed in his mind, but she couldn't hear him.

She slumped in his arms in a faint.

They rode into Haven like that, Catherine held tightly in his arms, his hand over her back, feeling her heart beat. Her precious precious heart.

Beating.

Two weeks later
Mount Blue

"Did you eat?" Mac asked anxiously, closing the door behind him. He walked across the room and sat down across the table from her.

She should be asking him if he'd eaten. He'd lost tons of weight these past days. At least that was what it seemed like to Catherine. She'd been in a coma for ten days and had woken up only four days ago. Pat and Salvatore had kept her hydrated and she'd been on a parenteral feed course and a glucose drip, so when her eyes opened, she felt . . . refreshed. As if she'd slept for a very very long time and was now awake.

Mac had looked like a human wreck. He'd been sitting by her bedside when her eyes opened and later Stella told her he'd left her side only to go to the bathroom the entire ten days.

He hadn't shaved and he had barely eaten and he certainly hadn't washed in those ten days.

When she opened her eyes and saw his face, with a beard beginning to grow mountain-man bushy, red-rimmed eyes, new hollows under his cheeks and new permanent lines, she'd smiled, then frowned at the big, fat tears running down the sides of his face. He'd ignored them totally and simply smiled at her and said, "You're back," in an unused voice that cracked.

That had cracked her heart wide open and it hadn't closed since.

She'd gotten her strength back quickly, no thanks to Mac, who was against her doing anything more strenuous than lifting a fork to her mouth.

She was in her room and had finished off some of Stella's food which had been arriving in industrial quantities. Mac had been called away because in the ten days he'd been offline a lot of things had happened. At first, Catherine had had to pry him away from her with bolt cutters and a crane, but slowly he was persuaded that she wasn't going to die on him if he disappeared for an hour or two.

The thing was, she felt great.

She knew, intellectually, that she'd received a lethal shock and that her heart had stopped. But she couldn't remember anything about it. The last thing she remembered, they'd been racing to the helo with four very sick men in back, then they were in the helo and then nothing until she woke up in the Haven infirmary.

But it was theoretical knowledge, not knowledge she kept in her heart or even in her body. She felt a little weak and a little light-headed but that was all.

Actually, she felt something else. It was too soon to tell and there were no pregnancy tests here on Haven but there was an unmistakable glow inside her. A hidden bubble of light and joy and the faintest tendrils of life. It made her hum with delight.

Mac narrowed his eyes at her. "Was the food that good?"

"Fabulous." She pushed her plate across to him. "Try it yourself. You need to put on weight. You look awful."

He winced. "I've never been handsome, honey. If that's what you want, you're with the wrong guy. However, if you do find that guy I will bust his pretty face to a pulp so you might as well stick with me."

She grinned. "Eat."

He did. The first time she'd seen him eat with appetite since she woke up. It felt good. He felt good, she knew. She could *feel* him feeling good.

"How's the Captain? How are the men?"

"They're . . . stable. Pat and Salvatore say they should recover eventually, but it will take a long while and a lot of rehab. Stella's taking extra care of the Captain. At some point we'll be able to debrief them and we'll decide what to do about it."

That sobered her up. "You're going to want to clear up your names. You were framed. You could come out in the open once the Captain testifies."

His grin stopped. "Yeah. We'll clear up our names eventually. With the Captain and the rest of the men here, somehow it seems less of a priority. We got five new people in Haven last week. We need to upgrade the water system and Jon has plans for a community center. We think—" He drew in a deep breath, looked her in the eyes. "We think our place is here. But I can't make decisions for you. You're a scientist, with a billion degrees. I don't think I can ask you to give up your research career to stay with some outlaws in a high-tech outlaw camp. So you say the word and we'll start petitioning the U.S. government for a reversal of our conviction in absentia."

Catherine was appalled. "Oh no!" Her hand reached out to his and his curled up around hers immediately. That instant connection, warmth and love, their two hands melding together. Her talent—her *gift*—was growing stronger as if her time here in Haven had shifted her into a new gear. But there was nothing like what she shared with Mac with anyone else. Their bond was strong and deep and . . . three-way? "I don't want you doing anything of the sort. We're building something here. Something important. I can't tell you why, but I believe that down to my bones. That something is happening here that mustn't be disturbed or broken. Can't you feel it, too?"

The corner of Mac's mouth lifted. "I don't feel much beyond tiredness these days, but yeah." He blew out a breath. "I want us to stay here and continue building—whatever it is we're building. And I want us to do that together."

"I know something else I want us to be doing." Catherine slid out of her seat, rounded the table and sat on Mac's lap. His eyes widened in surprise but his arms closed around her carefully.

He'd been very very careful around her since she'd awakened. Treating her like a porcelain doll, something that would shatter if he held it too hard. He'd barely kissed her since she'd come back from the dead. If she hadn't known better, she'd have thought he'd lost interest in her. But he hadn't. He hovered over her constantly, fed her, walked with her wherever she went and would have washed her if she hadn't put her foot down.

One thing he hadn't done was make love to her and she felt that absence like a shard of glass cutting through an artery.

He was holding her loosely. Not like a lover, but like someone waiting to catch a fall.

She put her nose against the skin of his neck and inhaled. Her Mac. She missed him so. "Make love to me," she whispered, and bit his ear lightly.

He jumped. She pulled back to look at his face. He looked alarmed.

"Do you think—what did Pat say?"

"I don't need Pat's permission to make love to you." She inhaled again, rubbed her breasts against his chest. "And to answer your question, yes I think I can and yes I think we should."

"Oh God." Mac shuddered, closed his eyes, leaned his forehead against hers. "I think I'm still in a state of shock. When I thought you'd died . . ." He gave another shudder.

"Well, I didn't die." Catherine nipped the skin of his jaw, kissing her way to his chin. She knew he felt the wash of her breath over his mouth. So close . . .

"Man. Sex." Mac shook his head. "I don't even know if I can. I think I'm impotent. I think all my hormones were knocked out of my body. I didn't think of it at the time, but I'd have taken a vow of chastity just to make your heart start again."

"But you didn't." A light taste of his mouth. "Nick and Jon would have told me. And anyway, vows like that under duress don't count. And for the record?" She slid her hand down over his chest, over his hard belly, into his sweatpants, and ah yes. He was already hard. "For the record, I don't think you became impotent at all."

At her words, his penis swelled and moved in her hand and Mac laughed.

"You're outvoted, Tom McEnroe. Me and him against you. Two to one." She kissed the edge of his mouth and he kissed her back, lightly. "And since you make such a big deal about Haven being a democracy and all, I think you should just go with the majority vote."

"Mm."

She smiled against his mouth. When he lost words, he was all hers.

"Up."

She stood and he pulled down her pajama bottoms and panties. He lifted slightly and pulled down his sweatpants. He went mainly commando as most Special Forces soldiers did. She remembered her surprise when he told her that. *Saves us from crotch rot,* he'd said, whatever that meant.

But now she was just grateful because he sprang free, fully erect, lying against her belly.

Ah, this. She'd craved it so. This heat, this closeness, the sheer soaring pleasure of it. He was kissing her deeply now, one hand holding her head to his, the other against her bottom, holding her tightly against him.

Then he was touching her between her thighs. He was trying to see if she was ready for him because he had gone from zero to a thousand in a few seconds. He felt as hot and heavy as a club against her stomach. His fingers were telling him she was ready. She'd gone from zero to a thousand, too, all of her focused tightly on where he was touching her, oh so carefully.

She didn't want careful.

She hadn't died. Against all the odds, she hadn't died. Nick told her a few days after she woke up that Mac had simply refused to let her die and here she was. Young and healthy and in love.

Alive.

A big finger entered her and she gasped with delight. Her vaginal muscles contracted around it, as if wanting to keep him inside her. His hand was shaking slightly, all of him was fairly thrumming with control because he didn't want to hurt her.

She could feel so clearly how he didn't want to hurt her, how much he cared. It was in every touch, every kiss. And more, it was there, beneath his skin where only she could touch him, reach him.

She lifted her head from his kiss and looked down at him, at that beloved face. At some level she knew he wasn't handsome. He was scarred, his skin was pockmarked with old acne scars. His nose had been broken several times and was flat against his face.

But she didn't see that, she saw *him,* what he was, beneath the skin. In that place only she could see.

And he was so beautiful.

"Now, Mac," she whispered.

"Now," he repeated, watching her eyes as he held her up, positioned her and let her slide slowly down on him. Deep. Deeper. Until he reached so deeply inside her she couldn't fathom how they could ever be separated.

Ah, he felt so good. Her eyes fluttered closed, then opened suddenly when he shook her a little.

"No," he commanded. "Keep your eyes open."

So she did. He held her slightly above him and he moved his hips up and into her, so she was over him, her hair creating a little dark waterfall around them, sealing them off from the world in their own little private paradise.

His hips moved up strongly, pulled down, then up. She gasped, but he knew it wasn't pain because he was touching her and he *knew* her. This was what she wanted. This closeness, this feeling of being one in two bodies.

Her hair swayed as she swayed with his thrusts. He was holding her so tightly she couldn't move, but she didn't need to, Mac was doing everything and he was doing it perfectly. He went slowly at first, getting her used to him again, but he felt, he knew, when he could speed up.

The thrusts became harder, faster, and heat was spreading from her groin up through her whole body. She wanted to close her eyes but she couldn't. She couldn't look away from him as his features tightened, became strained.

He was pumping heavily now, the chair rocking, joints squealing, and the heat rose and rose and rose . . .

Catherine's whole body tightened and released as she rose slightly on her knees, head thrown back, convulsing in hot waves that rode the edge of pain.

It pushed Mac over the edge, too, as he gave one last hard thrust that shook her body and came in endless hot liquid spurts, pouring into her body with a harsh cry.

She slumped against him, damp and flushed and happy. Together.

They sat in silence, her head nestled against his shoulder, in his arms, him still half-hard inside her.

It was the happiest moment of Catherine's life. She felt as if they had climbed a mountain together and stood looking at the promised land.

She turned her head lazily and kissed his ear. "You know what?"

She felt rather than saw him smile. "What?"

"I think we made a baby."

His entire body jolted and she felt a rush of joy flood through her and she couldn't tell whether it was his or hers. Or both.

* * *

San Francisco
Arka Laboratories

The local police force has carried out extensive forensics on the scene of the break-in at the Millon facility. The weapons are military-issue but are not found in any military database. No fingerprints or DNA were found. The video cameras were disengaged and steps to ensure that never occurs again have been taken. The security company has been fired and a new one, a very reputable company run by a former general, Clancy Flynn, has been hired.

An exhaustive inventory has been taken but it appears nothing has been stolen from the laboratory. The computer system is intact. It is my considered opinion that the break-in was unsuccessful and has proven to be nothing more than a spur to increase security.

Lee finished the report and sent it off to the Arka board where the old men who sat on it would have their office managers read it to them and would sign it unread.

Lee had a new, interesting avenue of research. Arka had developed a miniature, handheld fMRI that could scan brains without the patient knowing. It could be used in the field and already his assistants were taking surreptitious scans of people in movie theaters, in libraries, on athletic fields.

Interesting things were showing up.

But what was most interesting was a paper no one had read because Lee had read it before it could be published and the researcher had had an accident.

Lee had given the researcher, who worked at a psychiatric institute, a prototype of the fMRI to use on the clinically insane. But there were several patients the researcher considered sane, but with unusual talents. He'd written extensive dossiers on the patients, so extensive Lee was convinced they could do what the researcher said they could do.

One could foretell the future.

The other could astrally project.

The third had telekinesis.

Lee had their scans up on his screen, side by side by side. Each had a tiny point of light in the parahippocampal gyrus, a part of the brain normally considered inert. With a slide of his fingers the three scans superimposed and the same point of light existed in the exact same spot.

He had a fourth scan. Of Catherine Young, taken without her knowledge a few weeks before she disappeared. He slid that in on top of the other three, and though the morphology of the skulls was different, that point of light was there, in exactly the same place.

There was something in Catherine Young's brain Lee wanted, very badly.

And he was going to get it.

Lisa Marie Rice is eternally thirty years old and will never age. She is tall and willowy and beautiful. Men drop at her feet like ripe pears. She has won every major book prize in the world. She is a black belt with advanced degrees in archaeology, nuclear physics, and Tibetan literature. She is a concert pianist. Did I mention her Nobel Prize? Of course, Lisa Marie Rice is a virtual woman and exists only at the keyboard when writing erotic romance. She disappears when the monitor winks off.

Sensual Books
by LISA MARIE RICE

HEART OF DANGER: *A Ghost Ops Novel*

ISBN 978-0-06-212179-0 (paperback)

They are Ghosts. Their birth certificates have been destroyed, all traces of their civilian and military pasts wiped out. They wear no uniforms or insignia, save a tiny steel pin of a striking hawk forged from the rifle that killed Osama Bin Laden. Lisa Marie Rice delivers a sizzling, heart-stopping new series as only she can tell it.

DANGEROUS LOVER

ISBN 978-0-06-120859-1 (paperback)

Caroline, in desperate financial straits, welcomes a tall stranger who wishes to rent a room in her mansion. Overwhelmed by the desire he sparks in her, she aches to experience his touch . . . and wonders who this mysterious man really is.

DANGEROUS PASSION

ISBN 978-0-06-120861-4 (paperback)

Head of a billion-dollar empire, Drake has survived numerous attempts on his life at the hands of greedy men everywhere. And when a gentle beauty turns his life upside down, he will stop at nothing to protect her and his newfound love.

DANGEROUS SECRETS

ISBN 978-0-06-120860-7 (paperback)

Charity never thought she'd fall in love with a man like Nicholas Ireland. Rich, witty, and sexy as hell, he takes her to new sensual heights. When he asks her to marry him, it's like a dream come true. And then the nightmare begins . . .

INTO THE CROSSFIRE
A Protectors Novel: Navy Seal

ISBN 978-0-06-180826-5 (paperback)

Struggling with a new company and a sick father, Nicole simply can't deal with the dangerous-looking stranger next door. But when evil men come after her, she must turn to the cold-eyed man who makes her heart pound—with fear and excitement.

HOTTER THAN WILDFIRE
A Protectors Novel: Delta Force

ISBN 978-0-06-180827-2 (paperback)

Harry owns a security company whose mission is to help abused women escape violence. When a damaged beauty shows up on his doorstep with an army of thugs after her, Harry realizes that this is the woman of his dreams.

NIGHTFIRE
A Protectors Novel: Marine Force Recon

ISBN 978-0-06-180828-9 (paperback)

After spending her childhood in and out of hospitals, Chloe is finally able to reunite with her long-lost brother Harry. But when she steps into the path of the Russian Mafia, it's Harry's colleague Mike who risks everything to protect her, despite his own painful past.

Visit www.HarperCollins.com/LisaMarieRice for more information.